The Burden of the Crown

Book three in the Sword Masters' Universe

Book one *Sword Masters*
Book two *Jabone's Sword*

Selina Rosen

YARD DOG PRESS

The Burden of the Crown
Selina Rosen
Copyright © Selina Rosen, 2015

Published by Yard Dog Press

ISBN 978-1-937105-71-6
First Print Edition Copyright © Selina Rosen, 2015
First EEdition by Yard Dog Press 2015

Yard Dog Press
710 W. Redbud Lane
Alma, AR 72921-7247

http://www.yarddogpress.com

Edited by Sherri Dean
Copy Editor Robert Ryburn
Technical Editor Lynn Stranathan
Cover art by John Kaufmann

First Print Edition date October 1, 2015
Printed in the United States of America
0 9 8 7 6 5 4 3 2 1

Dedication

For Sherri Dean...
My best friend
and
Queen of the Monkeys

Chapter One

"Are you sure, Jestia?" Tarius asked looking from her to the boat and back again. "Are you really sure this is what you want?"

"Tarius... You know I don't have to tell you what this means. If I go back to the castle now, that will be it. I will be a slave to the crown, but we all know I can't be and I won't be. I'm not going to give up Ufalla or the life I want to live to serve the kingdom. Look at me and answer truthfully. Do you ever want me to rule the Kartik?"

"Seriously, I'd love to see you take the throne. I think you'd do a much better job than even your mother has much less one of your stupid kin. But only the Jestia that stands before me now would make a good leader. The person they would insist you be in order to wear the crown, someone that bitter and unhappy with your power? No I don't want that person to rule the Kartik." Tarius looked from Jestia to her goddaughter. "And you, little sister, what do you want?"

"I don't care where I am or what I do as long as I'm with her. You know that," Ufalla said. Jestia took strength from Ufalla's hand on her shoulder. "I will go where she goes. I will miss you and my family and this place, but it's no secret that I also love the sea. Besides, this ship is crewed by our pack so we will not be alone. Perhaps a time will come when we can come back and start the life we really want here. In the meantime this will serve us just fine."

Jestia knew what Ufalla wasn't saying because she felt the same way. Ufalla didn't want to be Jestia's secret lover and stand by and watch as she was married to some noble and made royal babies for the kingdom. Ufalla didn't want to be a side note in Jestia's life any more than Jestia wanted her to be.

Above all else Jestia had no desire to rule—none at all—as was obvious by the fact that she was even considering getting back on a boat just seconds after landing in her homeland—and it was a fishing boat no less.

"Why not tell my parents that I was killed in the battle, Tarius?" Jestia suggested seeing a way out of her obligation without fleeing the Kartik.

"There are two reasons I will not do that. First your mother is my friend and she trusts me. She has lost one of her children; I would not lie and tell her she has lost the other as well. That would be beyond cruel. Second, we have been in port less than two hours and already stories are being told of the battle. How you fought with us. Of your power and how you gave us the day. All of those stories end with them riding home with you and your mate. It would only be a matter of time till she knew I had lied. I would not shatter the trust between us like that."

"And she's always been a crappy liar anyway," Harris said at Tarius's shoulder.

Tarius looked at him like he was an imbecile. "What?"

"Fadra, she hid as a man in the Jethrik army for years. It is only the most celebrated lie ever told," Ufalla reminded.

Harris laughed at himself, nodded, then handed his daughter a large sack. "Your mother has packed... Well most of what you own and a bunch of jerky... elk your favorite."

"Where is she?" Ufalla asked looking around anxiously.

"Your mother has come completely undone. She is at home hugging your younger siblings and crying. Frankly I think she's scaring them a little." He smiled at her. "She doesn't want you to go, and she doesn't want you to see her cry because she knows that you must go. Your place..." He cleared his throat. "Your place isn't with us anymore; you belong to Jestia and she to you. We know that even if the queen doesn't."

Ufalla hugged him and her tears started to fall. "Tell Madra we will be back."

Harris nodded held her tighter and then let her go wiping his own tears from his eyes. Her brother Tarius—not Tarius the Black, but a younger, lighter-colored hero—hugged Jestia and then hugged his sister.

"You'd better come back and often," he ordered.

Ufalla nodded silent.

Sorak, the Katabull captain of the Marching Night's fishing vessel walked up the plank making a face. "Enough of this now, you act like we will be gone forever and we will be back in port in five months rich from huge catches. We sail with the tide." He pointed up the gang plank.

Jestia looked at Tarius the Black. "What will you tell my mother?"

"The truth. That you don't wish to rule and have taken your lover and headed for the coast of the Territories."

"Hestia will just crap," Harris said.

Tarius nodded in agreement.

Jestia watched with longing as she saw the last of the Kartik disappear into the waves. She sighed. They'd been able to stand on dry land for only a few hours. It didn't matter. She couldn't stay, not now, and she had to be gone before her mother knew that she had left. She sighed again.

"It's alright, Jestia, We will go back soon and someday we will be able to do all we planned."

"It won't make me feel better for you to say things we both know aren't true. I appreciate the effort, but my brother is dead and I'm next in line for the throne. That being the case, they will never leave me alone now. My brother is dead. My... brother... is... dead. Why when I think it, why when I say it, do I feel nothing but anger at having all our plans ruined?"

"Because brothers are annoying?" Ufalla said with a smile, hoping to lighten Jestia's mood.

"Your brother is one of the most annoying people I have ever known, yet I saw you dive into an icy swollen river, nearly drown yourself, and then blow your air into him to save him. That's how much you love him, how much he loves you. My brother is dead, yet I feel nothing but put out. What sort of person am I?"

"An honest one." Ufalla wrapped her arms around her and brought her close. "You didn't know him and he didn't know you. You never did anything together. You were bound by blood and nothing else. The only thing you have really lost is your right to live your life as you please and that is what you grieve because it's really all you lost. If something— by The Nameless One never let it be so—were to happen to my brother although he annoys us both to no end, you would be deeply grieved because you love him and you love him because he loves you. You share a bond forged in friendship and in battle. You had neither of those things with your own brother. There is nothing at all wrong with you. You were just raised weird like Kasiria." Ufalla made a face that had nothing to do with Kasiria or how Jestia had been raised. "I am not good with words like my brother, but you know what I mean."

Jestia nodded and rested her head on Ufalla's shoulder. "I am sorry that because of me you have to leave your kin behind. And Jabone, I know he is your best friend and you didn't even get to say good bye to him."

"Jestia I love Jabone, but you are my best friend. You

always have been and always will be. He and Kasiria were half way to the lake before we even learned your brother was dead. He will understand that I left without saying goodbye because he understands exactly how I feel. I meant what I said to Tarius; I don't care where I am as long as I'm with you. I think you forget how long I have loved you. How long I loved you while you felt only friendship for me. You have had all of my heart since I knew what love was. We have walked in the bowels of the earth with demons and walked away only because we were together. Together is where we belong and to hell with Hestia and the kingdom or anyone else who wants to pull us apart. If the sea is the only place we can be together we will live on the sea, and it will be amazing."

"You do know I hate to fish, right?"

They were three days out when they started to cast nets— only a half day out from the Kartik-held territories of the Amalite. They would fish the whole day and then head for the port of Kosick to sell their catch. The Amalite ports had mostly been sacked during the Great War and had only really gotten up and running about a decade ago. The territories were still short on ships, so the Katabull often went to the Amalite shore to fish and make money selling to the people of the territories.

Their ship was huge with three masts that towered above them, but even a huge ship shrank every day you were on it when there was nowhere else to go. Jestia knew they were lucky to have their own cabin but in truth the closet in her room was bigger.

Captain Sorak approached Jestia and Ufalla where they stood on the deck. Ufalla was helping put the nets into the water; Jestia was just watching.

"Jestia..." He cleared his throat. "Could you cast something to make our nets come in full?"

She nodded, cast something, and kept right on talking to Ufalla. "And really it's one thing to be stuck on a fishing boat and quite another to be expected to fish and..."

Sorak cleared his throat again.

"What?" Jestia asked out of patience with... Well everything.

"Might you cast a spell to help with our fishing?"

"I already did," she said, looking at him as if he had a cat crawling out of his ear.

"She's really good," Ufalla said with a smile, lifting the

huge nets over board into the water.

Jestia continued talking to Ufalla as if the Captain weren't there. "We are members of the Marching Night. I am next in line to the throne..."

"Which is why we are here, dear. As long as we are here I would rather help than sit and do nothing, and need I remind you that we are all Marching Night?" Ufalla said. She looked at the Captain who was still standing there. "She really has cast the spell already."

He looked troubled and Jestia looked at him and smiled. "Don't worry; I'm mostly harmless."

He laughed then and started to walk away. "You're about as harmless as I am," the departing Katabull said over his shoulder.

"Cheeky bastard," Jestia mumbled to Ufalla.

"He's right though." Ufalla smiled. As she threw the last of the net over a large wave smacked the boat making it lurch. Ufalla stumbled and almost went over with it. Jestia grabbed her arm and steadied her. Jestia started shaking like a leaf, and Ufalla helped her to walk over and sit on a crate against the ship's cabin. "Jestia what's with you? You're white as a sheet. I just tripped even if I had fallen in..."

"I'm still battle ready, Ufalla. I can't help it. Less than two weeks ago we were in the earth with those things. We were bathed in blood and nearly died countless times and everything gets my heart pounding and..."

A teapot appeared in the air followed by a cup and then the pot was pouring into the cup.

Ufalla grinned. "Have a cup of tea. You know it always helps settle your nerves."

"It's not funny, Ufalla," she said. But she took the cup out of the air and took a long sip. They all thought the teapot and cup was funny. They didn't understand how unsettling it was because it appeared without her casting it. It appeared without her even knowing that she wanted a cup of tea, and sometimes it appeared when she certainly didn't want one. When Ufalla had tripped and she'd grabbed her... She didn't have the physical strength to stop her going over; she had cast something for strength that again she wasn't aware of casting. She didn't know whether this was some blessing or some curse. She had hoped to go to their home—the one they'd never been allowed to live in—and be able to relax and continue her studies with the witch Jazel. Jestia was very powerful, but though she put up a completely different front she knew that her power exceeded her knowledge—which wasn't a proper balance. There was more she didn't know about her craft than she did know. She wasn't comfortable at all with this uncontrolled magic that seemed to leak from her.

Now because her stupid brother had to go and die she was the heir apparent and she'd probably never be able to do any of the things she wanted to do. She caught Ufalla's eyes and knew she was worried about her. "You giant hypocrite, my casting without being aware I'm doing it scares you as much as it does me."

"Your power doesn't scare me because you would never use it to hurt anyone who didn't deserve it. I trust you even if you don't trust yourself. The truth is I'm not as calm and cool as I'd like you and everyone else to think I am. I too was in that battle. I know it can't be, and yet I just keep tasting blood. In the battle I got blood in my mouth more than once. I had blood everywhere. So did you. We washed it off but it leaves a stain that goes to your very soul."

Jestia nodded and offered her cup to Ufalla who took it and drank. She smiled. "It is really good tea."

"You do know that I can't just make stuff like this from nothing. It has to be coming from somewhere." She sighed. "Somewhere there is someone who never gets to drink their tea."

Chapter Two

Jena looked at Tarius where she was sitting on the Katabull throne holding their new son talking to him in a way that Jena was sure no one but their immediate family would believe. It was so not the image anyone had of the Great Warlord. It was, however, precisely the way she had talked to their grown son Jabone when he was a baby.

"Who's a good baby then? Oh yes you are you are. Such a good boy yes..."

"Tarius stop shaking him so hard or you're going to make him throw up everything he just ate," Jena said. Darian wasn't a healthy baby, not like Jabone had been, and none of them were as young as they had been although she had to admit that lately she did feel stronger and had more energy than she'd had in years. She thought maybe just having a new baby to love and care for was the reason but also suspected it might have something to do with the tonic Jestia had given her to start Jena's milk so she could feed him. Since she was the one feeding him, and her nipples were still mostly raw from the effort, she didn't want him puking.

Jena loved her new son, but it wasn't the same love she had for Jabone and she admitted it probably never would be. Tarius had given birth to Jabone. She carried him to term and handed him to Jena when he was still wet. Jabone was a product of the love Tarius had for her, and Jena extended the love she had for Tarius to encompass Jabone. She loved Darian, but it was different.

Of course as rough as Tarius was with the boy she seemed to be the only one who could get him to sleep. Still she quit shaking him quite as hard.

"He's not a Katabull like our other son, Tarius. He's just a normal human."

"Normal human, ha!" Tarius said loudly in the baby's face, so obviously she wasn't trying to put him to sleep. The fact that the baby didn't start and scream showed that he was the same infant that Tarius had carried in the crook of her arm through a battle till they were both drenched in blood.

He just acted like he knew from the moment she lifted him from the floor of the cave that she would never let anything happen to him. "No son of ours will ever be normal.

For he is born to the most brave and noble of fighters. Oh, yes he is he is."

"You haven't forgotten that I didn't really give birth to him have you?" Jena said in a whisper.

"I have, and so should you. He is our baby; that is all that he will ever know," Tarius said firmly. Then she continued making an ass of herself talking baby talk to him. "Isn't that right, Darian? Oh yes it is it is and..."

Arvon walked in then and shook his head. He ran his fingers through his shaggy but short hair now nearly as gray as it was blond. "I'd like to say poor little guy, but it's all of us who will have to hear her talking to him like this for the next year. Tarius you sound like a great fool, and I will tell you what I told you with our other son. If you don't make him talk like an imbecile it will be a miracle."

"And Jabone is just fine, so... Shut up."

Arvon looked at her hard.

"And I have already told Jena and now I will tell you. I will go to see Hestia when and if I feel like it."

Arvon sighed. "And I will tell you again that I do not think that it is at all cute the way you just always seem to know what I'm about to say."

"We think it's funny don't we? Oh yes we do."

"Tarius, she has summoned you three times in as many weeks," Arvon said with a sigh. He was Katabull, but he was also half Jethrik and he'd been trained in the Sword Masters' Academy. He now considered himself a follower of the Nameless God, but he was probably never going to get used to how cavlier the Katabull were when it came to royalty, and Tarius was worse than the rest. Arvon couldn't quite lose the training that said when a royal bellowed you jumped and bowed. "She wants to see you."

"And she still doesn't understand that you cannot summon the Katabull. She will especially not summon me as that is an insult to the entire nation. She may *ask* me to do something and I may do it or not, but she will not *tell* me what to do."

And this was just exactly what Tarius had just told Jena. Tarius had a point; Jena knew better than to tell the Katabull to do anything, this wasn't even Jena's country though she'd now lived with the Katabull over half her life. Hestia, Queen of the Kartik, had lived around the Katabull her entire life; she knew them. Better than that she knew Tarius, so she should have known better than to have ever "summoned"

Tarius.

"Perhaps her grief over the loss of her son..."

"Hestia is my friend and ally but don't think for even a moment that she has the attachment to her children that we have to ours. Katan is dead, and I'm sure it grieves her on some level, but mostly it is an inconvenience. She summoned Jestia and by now she knows full well that Jestia has fled from her position and that I helped her do so. Hestia is pissed off at me, so instead of asking nicely she orders me. She orders me to the castle because she believes that I can make Jestia do her bidding. You and I both know I couldn't even if I wanted to."

Frankly Jena thought Jestia would do anything Tarius asked her to do but this was Tarius's rant so she didn't interrupt with fact.

"Jestia is far too powerful and willful to be forced to do anything she doesn't want to do. Besides, those girls, like you and I, are joined in their very souls. You couldn't pull them apart with a crow bar, nor should anyone try. Hestia is acting like a child. She wants to have her way and like a child throwing a fit she is demanding things from people instead of asking. I will not go to the castle now. We just got back from a brutal campaign. You have only recently given birth and can't be expected to take such a journey with an infant in tow..."

Jena smiled. "Arvon and Dustan and I are perfectly capable of taking care of an infant, Tarius."

"Speak for yourself, Jena," Arvon said, pouring a drink of water from a pitcher. He took a long drink. "Our new son screams every time I so much as touch him, and Tarius alone can get him to sleep."

"See? I'm not going. I'm needed here. With me family comes first always." She looked at Jena. "You come first always."

"Again," Jena whispered with a smile. "I feel I should remind you that I didn't actually give birth and I don't really need to be coddled."

"You did and you will be," Tarius demanded.

"Well now who's telling people to do things without asking?" Arvon mumbled in Jena's ear. Because of course Tarius—who was and always had been a follower of the One Who Has No Name and who truly believed no person was better or worse than anyone else, that all was one and one was all and a bunch of other things Jena still didn't really understand even after all these years—had been Great Leader so long that she was used to people doing what she wanted and often expected them to just add a "Could you please?" to whatever she said.

The truth was Jena didn't want Tarius to go anywhere without her. They hadn't been further than the length of the compound away from each other since the day they had been reunited in the tavern all those many years ago. Part of her thought Tarius should do what the queen asked of her. The part of her that knew it wouldn't be good for their somewhat sickly baby to make the ride, which meant she would have to stay home with him alone, thought Hestia could just handle her own problems herself.

As if on cue there was a knock on her door. "Come in," Tarius said. The door opened and it was Rimmy. "What is it, Rimmy?"

Rimmy sighed and gestured over his shoulder with his thumb. "It is one of Queen Hestia's heralds again."

Tarius nodded and Rimmy moved aside. The herald entered looking like he'd rather chew glass. "A missive from my good Queen Hestia, Daughter of the Moon…"

"Just get to it, boy," Tarius growled. "Can you not see that I'm trying to put my baby to sleep?"

"Queen Hestia summons to the throne Tarius the Gre…"

"Just get to it!" Then added, "Please."

The herald looked at the parchment in his hand. "She orders Tarius to come to the palace at once and give her the details of the battle and tell her exactly where Princess Jestia is."

Tarius looked at Jena and laughed then looked back at the herald. "Then tell her in two days' time to expect Tarius."

The herald looked confused but relieved and backed out. Forgetting himself he bowed, and Rimmy hit him with the back of his hand so hard he landed in a heap in the dust outside their hut. Rimmy walked out closing the door after him and they could hear him say, "How dare you disgrace the Great Leader in such a way."

Jena looked at Tarius feeling a sudden panic at the thought of being separated from her or having to travel with Darian—either one.

Tarius smiled reading her mind. "Don't worry, I'm not going anywhere."

"What then?" Arvon asked confused.

"I said she should expect Tarius. I didn't say I was going

anywhere."

"What's this then?" Hestia asked. Her tone made it clear just how put out she was as she looked at Tarius and his retinue. "I summoned Tarius the Black..."

The youth interrupted her as easily as he might a serving girl in a tavern, proving that he was a follower of the Nameless God and not just Tarius the Black's namesake but her own godson.

"She has sent me. She has much to attend to, and I know everything you need to know."

The cheeky boy was abrupt, almost rude, no doubt because she had dared to order the Great Leader to do anything. She wanted to scream, stomp around, and just throw a fit which would rival anything her daughter might throw, but she had handled this poorly and was paying for it with a Katabull game of wits.

She took a deep breath and asked calmly, "And just what is so important that she couldn't travel here and attend to this herself?"

"Jena gave birth just before the battle and their baby isn't strong enough to travel yet."

"Jena gave birth! What?"

"The Great Leader and her family have a new baby," he answered.

Hestia was more than a little taken aback; Jena was after all her age. It didn't surprise her at all that Tarius wouldn't come without Jena. In all the time Hestia had known them she'd rarely seen them more than an arm's length away from each other.

If she'd had a great love like that maybe things would have been different between herself and her children, but she had Dirk, so not love but a contract signed by their parents bound them. They had been friends and had cared for each other at one time, but now even that was gone. Tarius would not travel without Jena so maybe she wasn't just being stubborn. "Where is Jestia?"

"I have no idea," Tarius said with a shrug.

"Does Tarius the Black know where my daughter is?"

"No, I'm sure she doesn't. Jestia has become a very powerful witch."

"What did Jestia say when she heard her brother is dead?" Her voice caught in her throat. Her own son, the son she'd given birth to was dead and the tears she felt welling up weren't so much for the loss she felt as the fact that she now had a throne with no heir to leave it to. "What did she say?"

"That she doesn't have any desire to be heir apparent, so she took my sister and left. I don't know where they went."

He was lying. He knew exactly where they were, and so did Tarius the Black.

"So she didn't even shed a tear for her brother. Had no thought at all for me or her father or the kingdom?"

He said nothing, but she could read the boy's features. He didn't think she deserved her own daughter's consideration because Hestia wasn't any sort of mother in his eyes. He was Jestia's lover's brother. No doubt he took Hestia's rejection of Ufalla as a suitable partner for her daughter as a slap in his own face, and this was who Tarius the Black sent to her.

Tarius thought she was clever sending her namesake. She was eluding Hestia no doubt because she felt the same way as this young man did. "Where has she gone?" Hestia demanded.

As if it answered all her questions young Tarius looked at her now with an expression that was unreadable and said, "Jestia is now part of the Marching Night."

Hestia took in a deep breath and held it. Jestia loved a woman, didn't give a damn about crown or country, and was a very powerful witch still seemed doable. *Jestia is part of the Marching Night* made the whole thing impossible. She looked around the room at them their black armor glistening in the sunlight that was streaming in the windows, their skull-shaped knee cops and pauldrons polished and shining. Each one of them seemed bigger than the one before, and most she knew were Katabull. Now Jestia was one of them. She was part of the Marching Night which meant they were no longer just dealing with a willful, magic-wielding child. They were now dealing directly with Tarius the Black, the Marching Night, and possibly the whole of the Katabull Nation.

She took in a deep, shuddering breath and then let it out slowly. So... That was it. She had no heir. It made everything she'd gone through till now seem so pointless. She supposed she could do like Jena and have a child in her old age, but as she thought of Dirk she just didn't think she could part her legs for him even one more time—not knowing where he even now was. And there was something else. Let's face it I'm a crappy mother. I gave my children nothing of myself and then expected them to love me and be loyal to me and only me. Poor Katan he so wanted my love and attention that he just always did exactly what I asked of him. He never had any will of his own. How sad that even at his death I can't say that I truly loved him the way a mother should and now I realize that's all he ever really wanted, my love. Running down the hall towards me that night just trying to get my attention calling out for me and I didn't even turn around because I was just so tired of his constant neediness. I just wanted to go to my room and be left alone. I didn't turn until he tripped and he was falling and then... Now it's always going to be too late.

She looked at young Tarius. He was a small man, and not attractive by any ruler she could measure him by. His father was a tall, handsome man, his mother was attractive, and his sister was absolutely stunning. He had grown up surrounded by some of the largest, strongest and most beautiful people in her kingdom. By all rights he should feel like a toad among gods, and yet it was clear by the way he held himself and the pride in his step that he did not. *They made him this way. They loved him, didn't judge his appearance or his size, and they made him into a strong, good man. He has no fear of anything or anyone. He trusts himself because he has always had unconditional love. My own son was so cowed and unsure of himself, a beautiful kind man with no self-confidence, and I never even really saw him. Dirk was no better. He never had time for either of our children because he was always way too busy with whichever whore he'd recently fallen in love with. His whole world always revolved around his rather unextraordinary cock.*

I'm bitter because I hate my life yet I want to order Jestia to have the same life I've had. When I took the throne I was sixteen. Dirk had already been chosen for me, so I never had a chance to have anything resembling a life of my own.

It's not too late for Jestia. I will choose a successor from one of my kin and have them trained as Katan was being trained. I'm the queen; I can do that. I can do what Tarius told me to do. I can show Jestia that I love her by letting her follow her heart.

She took a deep breath, let it out slowly, and then looked at young Tarius. "So, Tarius, tell us all of what took place in the territories." She smiled then, at least for the moment feeling as if a weight had been lifted from her shoulders. "Start with this new baby of the Great Leader's." She watched with a bit of humor as the whole of the boy's retinue seemed to physically relax. It only strengthened her resolve to let

Jestia go; these people were always battle ready. She doubted the whole of the Kartik army could stand against them—if she could get them to fight them at all. Too many Kartik soldiers had stood shoulder to shoulder in battle with the Marching Night. They knew what they were capable of. But beyond that she was sure the Kartik army was more loyal to Tarius the Black than to her. After all Tarius had been kingdom war lord for decades.

As had so often been the case in her life she found her decision was much easier to digest when she knew she really had no choice.

Tarius launched into his telling of the story being sure to tell the baby part exactly the way Tarius the Black did. After all, she had promised to split anyone who said Darian wasn't their own flesh and blood baby. The more he told the story the more even he believed it.

Then he was talking about the battle with the Amalites in the cave and realized how many times he had to give credit to Jestia only when he saw how many times he had to speak her name. He had reached the part of the story that made his blood run cold. "And then the Amalite's blade was coming for Jena and Tarius felt it and turned but knew she wouldn't make it in time and it was clear that Jena was about to breathe her last…"

"Jena fought in the cave with you less than an hour after she gave birth? How did she do that?" Hestia asked.

Tarius didn't like being interrupted especially not in his favorite part of the story and especially not when she pointed out an obvious hole he hadn't thought of but it was easily fixed. "Jestia did a spell. Anyway we were sure that Jena was about to breathe her last and even Tarius felt it." The queen had totally ruined his flow. "Then just when it looked like all was lost Kasiria turned and ran her sword through Jena's attacker. Jena didn't even know how close she'd come to death. Later Kasiria told us that she didn't kill the Amalite that it was her sword. For you see Kasiria's sword used to belong to none other than Jabone the Breaker, and the sword wanted to be bathed in the blood of the Amalites. It knew Tarius—who was Jabone's child—would not live a day without Jena…" He finished telling the whole story and when he was done Hestia, all of her people, and his as well clapped loudly.

"Young Tarius I believe you are as fine a bard as your namesake. Now let us go to the Great Hall for I have had a feast prepared for you and your retinue."

Tarius found himself sitting next to Hestia, his wife Eric sitting to the right of him. He had smiled up at Eric as he went to sit down and she had smiled back. She was easily twice as big as he was, but she didn't care so neither did he.

He had to admit he was a little nervous to be in charge but knowing Eric was with him made him feel like he could do just about anything. He loved Eric mostly because she was just like Jabone—except she was a pretty girl—so she reminded him a lot of his mother, too.

No one really spoke during the meal but now that the food was mostly forgotten everyone having eaten their fill Hestia turned to him. He swallowed hard and decided he didn't really like being in charge as much as he had thought he would.

It was easy to see where Jestia got her good looks. Hestia's long, black hair went to the middle of her back. Her skin was a wonderful bronze, and her eyes a warm, dark brown. In her youth she would have been every bit as stunning as her daughter, though Jestia was slightly shorter and had more curves while her mother had a classic Kartik build: tall, slender, regal. Yep, for an older woman she was incredibly hot. Of course thinking such things when he was supposed to be in charge wasn't helping him... Well, be in charge.

"Congratulations on your... Do you call it a marriage, Tarius?"

"You can and thanks." Hestia already knew Eric so he saw no reason to introduce them again even though he was pretty sure that Hestia didn't remember meeting Eric at all.

"About Jestia..."

"I will not hear even a single unkind word about my non-blood kin," Tarius interrupted. "Nor will I tell her that you order her to do anything. She can be really mean."

"Yet you don't know where she is," Hestia said with a smile. Tarius actually didn't know exactly where they were, but he knew they'd be coming back. He must have looked as nervous as he was because then she said, "It's alright. I have a message for Tarius..."

"I certainly will NOT tell the Great Leader that you summon her to the presence. I don't think you have any idea how mad that makes her—or all of us for that matter."

"Well then I guess for starters you can take my apology to her." She took a breath and let it out. "Please tell her to tell Jestia that I remove her from her duties as Heir Apparent.

She may have the life she chooses, and I will never order her to take my crown from me or to study to do so." She looked to where Dirk was chatting up a young woman. Everyone in the kingdom knew that theirs was an open marriage. "I never had what your sister and my daughter have, but I always longed for it. Come a little closer." She leaned in conspiratorially and so did he. "I never wanted to be queen. The truth is I was more like Jestia than I'd like to admit. I let myself be bullied into the crown."

"You've been a very good queen," Tarius said with real admiration.

"Thank you. I've always done what I thought was best for the kingdom; I wish I could say the same for my children or myself. The only time I was ever happy was during my time on the front during the Great War. What does that really say about me or my life that I was happiest while my comrades died all around me and I was slaying Amalites as fast as they could run onto my blade? When I was so drenched in blood I could taste it in my mouth. All of this..." She waved a hand around elaborately, and in that moment he could clearly see Jestia in her mother's face. "It has never made me happy for even a second. I won't, I can't do to Jestia what was done to me. I lost one child without ever giving him what he wanted, and I won't do it to the other."

She sat back and so did he.

Tarius smiled at her and said, "You know she's going to want that in writing don't you."

"Tarius?"

"You know Tarius would take your word for it; I was talking about Jestia."

Chapter Three

Jestia watched as they hauled in the nets, all of them acting surprised that they were completely filled with fish. She sighed and mumbled to herself, "Did I not cast fish in nets as I have done for five long months? Yet every time they act surprised that their nets are full." Jestia was bored. You could just look at so much pretty water before it all looked the same. She knew she'd been at sea too long when she met the occasional whale, dolphin or shark sighting with the same excitement she normally reserved for sex.

Mostly Jestia just felt kind of useless. The spells they asked her to do were simple. Most of the day while Ufalla helped the crew put out nets and then pull them in Jestia had nothing to do but sit and watch them. While she loved to watch Ufalla, she really wanted something to do that was a challenge.

A few short months ago she had been in the bowels of the earth fighting the Amalites, casting one magnificent spell after another and frankly saving everyone's asses. She came home and every Katabull who could get close to her touched her, knowing that she had killed many of their enemies. Now it was, "Jestia sing a pretty song, help us get more fish, turn that tiny cloud, put more or less wind in our sails." During battle it had been, "You're the only one who can save us Jestia!" and now it was, "Jestia cast something to make the fish less smelly."

Alright so no one had actually said, "You're the only one who can save us." But it was certainly implied. And without her there was just no way they could have won that battle. She had been super important. Now... well she was the fish-in-nets girl.

Days of fishing and eating fish were broken every few days when they were allowed a few hours to run around Kosick which was far from the hub of civilization. It was in fact a grubby little place with more Amalites than Kartiks living in it. The Amalites had a nasty habit of throwing their slop buckets and crap into the streets. Apparently the Kartiks living there hadn't been able to break them of doing it or they simply weren't trying hard enough. Either way the Kartik-held territories were not at all like the Kartik itself. The place reeked of human waste and the stench of Amalites mixed with the heady odor of fish in all its out-of-water forms.

After facing Amalites in battle Jestia found when they did make it to the one pub in town she couldn't relax and just have a couple of drinks. There were blond heads everywhere she looked in Kosick and while her logical mind kept telling her they weren't her enemies the part of her that had fought them wasn't there yet.

Most of the crew were Katabull and they had an ancient hatred of the Amalite's religion which they still couldn't scrape off the Amalites themselves. Sorak didn't let the Katabull on his crew drink at all for fear they might cost him valuable fishing time. Sorak was all about catching and selling fish. He didn't really have to make a rule about drinking though, Jestia doubted the Katabull were any more comfortable drinking in a bar full of Amalites than she and Ufalla were.

Fishing was the main trade of the Katabull Nation. It was just one of many ways the Marching Night paid for the things they couldn't trade for or produce themselves in the compound. Jestia was starting to realize with admiration that the Marching Night were proficient at far more than just killing. Though they did all practice fighting nearly every day.

When Tarius, Radkin, Rimmy, Arvon and Harris—just to name a few—were beating the crap out of her and all her friends on a daily basis "training" them to go to the Jethrik territories, she had been sure she would never want to practice again. That seemed like a lifetime ago, and now she looked forward to the time they spent in practice bouts on the ship because at least it was something different.

Of course half the time she wound up casting something which made her fight better which had most of the crew refusing to fight with her and calling her a cheater. She had tried to explain she didn't cast the spell on purpose, but they still had no desire to fight with her. Ufalla always would, but she felt bad when the magic kicked in and she wound up smacking her lover upside the head.

Wagons met them every time they pulled into port, and most of the fish was taken directly to a huge smokehouse in Kosick where they would be cleaned, processed, smoked and then taken inland and sold. She, Ufalla and most of the crew would get off the boat, walk around trying to find something to do, give up and get back on the boat way before they were due to leave port.

To make matters worse the entire time they'd been at

sea it had grown progressively colder. Every day saw them wearing more clothing than they had the day before, and the only time she'd been warm enough was when she'd been cuddled up in bed with Ufalla. In fact, the only real plus to their whole fishing boat adventure was that with so little to do and it being so cold she and Ufalla spent huge chunks of each day in their room alone together coupling.

The nets were all hauled in, and the whole crew was busy now securing the catch and preparing to sail to Kosick. She wished they could at least put in at another port but no this was the one with the big smokehouse.

I am so tired of the smell of shit, Amalites and smoked fish.

Captain Sorak walked up to her and smiled. "Thanks for all your help; fishing has never been easier."

She smiled back and said, "You know you aren't really helping my mood right?"

He laughed, no doubt because he didn't really know what she meant, and walked away.

Ufalla started to run past her, but stopped and kissed her on the cheek. "Bored?" she asked even though Jestia knew she knew the answer. Jestia just nodded.

"Sorak said when we dump this load of fish and get our pay we will be going home."

Jestia smiled. Ufalla always knew what to say. "What if she's waiting for me?"

"At the Katabull seaport on this side of the Great Wall where she'd have to come through the Katabull compound right in front of the Great Leader's huts? I don't think that's going to happen."

"We won't be able to stay," Jestia said.

"Maybe next time we will ship out with a trade ship going to some exotic port of call," Ufalla said. Jestia nodded. Ufalla kissed her on the cheek again and then ran off to do whatever she'd been going to do in the first place.

That might not be too bad. No fish would be good. Of course when you're on a ship you always have to eat fish, but at least their slimy dead bodies wouldn't be washing back and forth across the deck. It might be nice to go someplace we've never been before see things we've never seen before.

She looked up and saw Ufalla walking back down the deck towards her, a sway in her hips and a smile on her face. Jestia's heart suddenly felt like it was going to beat out of her ribs. Ufalla was beautiful in every way. She was six feet tall, which was four inches taller than Jestia, and though

Ufalla's father was of the Jethrik she was as dark as any Kartik and built more like them than Jestia was. *My gods look at her! She is amazing, and I forget... I forget how much she loves me. She really doesn't care where we are or what we do. She doesn't just say those things because they're pretty; she means them. She loves me. She's only here now instead of with her family and friends because of me, and I'm whining about being bored. I... I don't deserve her. Of course I'm never giving her up because she's mine, all mine.* As if on cue Ufalla started whistling some sea shanty. Jestia found herself driven off the crate she'd been sitting on and she ran to Ufalla grabbed hold of her hand and started dragging her in the direction of their room.

Ufalla just laughed and followed her. "So I'm guessing you need me to help you warm up and combat boredom once again. Well if I must I must."

The crew started to whistle and tease them. Jestia didn't care; in fact, she felt like telling them that she was the luckiest girl in the world, but that would have taken time she'd rather spend naked. As soon as the door to the tiny cabin closed she shoved Ufalla against the door and undid Ufalla's pants. Before the weight of the dagger Ufalla wore in her belt sent her pants crashing to the floor Jestia was already touching her.

"Gods Jestia what was that for?" Ufalla asked as she held her.

"I'm a dumbass," Jestia answered. She was lying with her head on Ufalla's chest which was probably her favorite place to be.

"No you're not a dumbass. Now—not that I'm complaining—but what was all that about?"

"How could I ever be bored when you are near me? When I love you so much it consumes me how could anything else matter to me?"

Ufalla laughed. "You're allowed to want other things besides me you know... though you aren't allowed to want anything *more* than me."

"I never could."

"Jestia... don't be so serious. I worry when you're serious because usually it means something horrid is going to happen and..."

"Nothing is wrong." She pushed her face hard into the center of Ufalla's chest. She'd done it so many times she didn't even have to explain herself.

Ufalla just held her tighter then whispered, her lips touching Jestia's ear, "You know sometimes I can't get close enough either."

Suddenly there was a loud knock on the door. Jestia was instantly pissed off. "What?"

"Princess, please come quickly. Something is wrong," Sorak said.

The urgency in his voice had Jestia untangling herself from Ufalla, and well she wasn't aware of casting the spell, but before she had a chance to pick her clothes up off the floor she was dressed. And then her sword was on her side. She didn't stop to worry about it; she unlocked the door and stepped outside. She didn't have to ask what the problem was; there was a dark black cloud heading their way.

Wordlessly she walked to the stern of the ship and looked hard at the storm. Ufalla appeared at her shoulder pulling her shirt into place. "What is that?"

"That's no normal storm," she said, taking a deep breath and wishing it was possible to kick her own ass. How dare she sit and be bored and want a challenge? Did she call that into being? But as soon as she thought it she knew she hadn't, it reeked of another witch's magic. "Get below deck," she ordered. Ufalla just looked at her, smiled and shook her head no. "Please."

"I'm not the Katabull my love; I just won't go. I will stand with you even if all I might be able to do is catch you if you fall."

Jestia took a deep breath and yelled out. "Away from me, away!" She spoke to the storm not Ufalla. She even slung her hands around. The storm seemed to slow down, but it didn't stop. "Sorak, how far are we from port?"

"Maybe an hour."

Jestia looked at the sails. "Wind in sails!" Then she looked at the secured nets, and the catch was thrown back into the sea. Sorak didn't even seem bothered, which meant he knew the circumstances were dire. "That is a magic storm created by some other witch. I may be able to slow it, but I don't think I can stop it. We need to outrun it if we can."

Jestia was putting everything she had into pushing the storm back. Ufalla had lashed Jestia to the rail and she'd lashed herself right beside her because though they were trying to outrun the storm it just didn't look like they were going to make it. Sorak was at the helm and only those needed to trim the sails if they had to were left on deck. Everyone else had gone below. Everyone who was Katabull had catted out, and this reminded Ufalla of something. "Jestia, magic can't work against the Katabull," she said, thinking she was giving them a reprieve.

"You can't put a spell on a Katabull. The spell isn't on the Katabull; it's on the storm. The cloud has been loaded with magic; the storm is what will attack us," Jestia explained. Her brow was creased with concentration and worry which certainly didn't put Ufalla at ease. They were drenched already and the air was frigid. Ufalla was a sword woman; give her something she could fight and she wouldn't be afraid. Give her a fight where she could protect her mate not one where her mate was the only one who could fight. One where Ufalla was out in front and Jestia was safely behind her. Ufalla hated this. She didn't know what to do; Jestia was the real hero not her. Jestia could do something about this and Ufalla was just there. She couldn't even protect Jestia from this thing; she was just there pretending. Jestia didn't really need her.

Ufalla started to panic for a plethora of reasons, and then Jestia without turning said, "Yes I do."

"What?" Ufalla screamed over the sound of the storm which was already too close.

"I do need you. You ground me. You help me pull power from all around me. I wouldn't be as strong as I am without you." Jestia turned, looked at her briefly and smiled. "And no, I can't read your mind, but I do know what you're feeling most of the time. We will be fine because you are my anchor. Right now I need you to tell the crew to take the unnecessary sails down and get below deck. This is going to get a whole lot worse before it gets better." And then all her attention was on the storm again.

"Captain, prepare the ship! The storm is over taking us," Ufalla shouted. Sorak started giving orders. That was the nice thing about being on a ship with a Marching Night crew. You didn't have to repeat yourself; they listened to you. You never had to explain yourself, either, because they knew what to do. In minutes only the storm sails were still up. All the others had been lowered and lashed tight, and most of the crew was below deck.

For the next hour Sorak did his best to keep them from running onto rocks as Ufalla kept hold of the rail in one hand

and Jestia in the other. Jestia cast spell after spell. Ufalla knew this because holding Jestia Ufalla could actually feel the energy running over and through her. Every time Jestia cast it felt like a thousand points of sunlight were running across her skin. Jestia's face was a mass of concentration as she worked to save them from the wrath of the storm.

It was still daytime, but in the heart of that storm you couldn't tell. It wasn't just going away and leaving them alone, either; it was moving with them. Jestia didn't have to tell her the storm was meant for them. Ufalla could tell. But as far as she knew the only person who might be this mad at them that had a witch in her employ would be Hestia, and she wouldn't want them dead or driven into the coast of the Kartik-held territories of the Amalite. In fact that was directly counter to what Hestia wanted. She wanted Jestia to go to the palace without Ufalla and start getting ready to be queen. She wanted Jestia to marry a man and have heirs to the throne. She couldn't do that if she was dead

Ufalla had been wondering why Jestia would prefer to run off with her. She had to admit that she still hadn't trusted that Jestia really loved her. Wasn't sure that she wasn't with Ufalla just to piss off her mother or almost worse just because Jestia knew Ufalla loved her. But in that moment as she felt Jestia's power surging over her she knew that they had the same life. She knew that Jestia's love for her was true. She didn't know how she knew; she just did.

Which is a good thing because we're probably going to die here in this storm. This isn't the way I wanted to go. I wanted to die in my old age yelling, "Oh my gods that's the best sex I've ever had." Not like this... young and running from the queen in a stinking storm. Because when we all die there will be no one to tell the story of how brilliant Jestia was and that what killed us was no ordinary storm. They'll all think it was just bad luck.

"Hang on. We're about to hit!" Jestia yelled over her shoulder. Ufalla did, but it didn't matter. They struck with such force that she lost her grip on the rail. At some point the lashings had come undone, so she and Jestia both went crashing to the deck, Jestia landing on top of her. Ufalla's head hit something—she had no idea what—and then there was nothing.

Jestia was feeling the effects of all the energy she'd been channeling through her, though nothing she did seemed to do more than temper the storm. Then she felt more than saw the land behind them and knew they were about to be driven into the shoreline. There was a loud crunching noise and then Ufalla lost her grip on the rail but not on her and they were both falling. Then the ship was dead still. She felt Ufalla's arm as it let go of her and knew what that meant even before she crawled off her.

"No!"

Above them the clouds broke up and the storm left telling her what she already knew. The spell wasn't meant to kill them; it was meant to strand them. Now that the sun could hit them again she could see Ufalla's still form. To Jestia's horror blood was pooling around the back of Ufalla's head. Jestia knelt beside Ufalla picking her up and looking at the gash in the back of her head. She called a towel into her hand and stuck it against the wound hard. Yri, one of the Katabull, ran over with a medic bag. Without being told what to do he got ready to stitch Ufalla's head back together. When his needle was threaded he pulled Jestia's hand and the towel away and started stitching Ufalla up. "Come on little sister," he said to Ufalla, "this isn't the worst wound you'll ever get." Some Katabull thing that was supposed to be comforting Jestia supposed. For the life of her she couldn't think why.

Sorak walked up to them as the medic was working. "Is she alright?" He was asking Jestia not the medic. A medic could take care of a wound but when someone was out he had no idea whether they'd live or die—a witch was a different story.

"Her life force is strong. She's been knocked out, but I can't reach her," Jestia said. It was a nasty wound. All the casting had left Jestia feeling weak and her vision was a little blurred. She started crying. "I have no idea how bad she's hurt. It's a head injury, and there's nothing I can do. I'm a witch not a healer. She's hurt and it's all my fault."

Sorak patted her back in that way that left your teeth rattling, and Yri gave him a glare because Jestia was holding Ufalla so he could work on her and all the jerking around was making his job nearly impossible. Sorak stopped patting her looked at the medic and shrugged, then said to Jestia, "A witch put a spell on a cloud to chase us. How is that your fault?"

"Because they had to be after me. In fact, I know they were."

"I still don't see what makes it your fault, little one," Sorak said. "If an archer puts an arrow in your leg and you have done nothing to him your pain is his fault not yours. It is on the one who cast the spell not you. I have to check on my crew and the ship's condition. You just worry about Ufalla and I'll hear no more of this being your fault."

The ship had run aground. The navigator was working overtime trying to figure out just where they might be. Sorak found major damage to the hull which Jestia could probably fix with a spell after she got some power back, but they had been driven way up on the beach and she was pretty sure she couldn't move an entire boat from the shore to the ocean even if she had all her strength. The ship was at an angle but Jestia had done a spell to make the bed lie flat and now she was just standing beside the bed washing Ufalla's face and willing her to open her eyes.

A pot of tea appeared and poured her a cup. She didn't even think about it just plucked the cup from the air and started to drink it. She didn't care what Sorak said it felt like it was all her fault. Ufalla stirred but didn't open her eyes. Jestia set her tea aside stood up and took Ufalla's hand.

"Please open your eyes. Please be alright."

Ufalla opened her eyes, looked right at Jestia, blinked looked confused and said, "Who the hell are you?"

"You told her what?" Tarius asked her godson with a smile.

"I said Jestia did a spell, which since the story is full of those worked just fine," young Tarius told his mentor.

"Except that Jestia is a witch. She can make healing potions which aren't magic at all and she can't do a healing spell except the one we know nearly kills her to cast," Jena said, moving her baby from one breast to the other. Darian was getting stronger. He was starting to sleep nearly through the night, but mostly he'd started smiling and when he did his whole face lit up. She found that while she still didn't love him as much as Jabone, she did love him more every day. "I don't think this secret is one we can keep and..."

"There is no secret!" Tarius boomed. "He is our son; you gave birth to him. How many times do I have to tell you that?"

Young Tarius laughed and the Great Leader cut him a look that would curdle milk. He stopped laughing and looked at his feet to hide the grin he couldn't wipe off his face.

"I don't know! How I can forget such a thing?" Jena said with a smile and looked at Darian as he ate greedily. When she looked at him he let go for a second and smiled at her then went right back to eating. Jena smiled back and stroked her finger down his forehead to the top of his nose. "He's my baby," she said happily.

"She probably did a strength spell," her mate said thoughtfully, and Jena could nearly see Tarius's thoughts as she rewrote the story in her head to include this information.

"My sister and the witch should be home soon. I'll be sure to tell Jestia," young Tarius said.

"I'm sure she'll be happier to see this," Tarius said, holding up the proclamation from the queen. She folded it and stuffed it into her pants pocket unceremoniously. Jena made a mental note to retrieve it from Tarius's pocket that evening before it wound up in their wash. If she did the wash she always checked the pockets first, but Tarius *never* did. No, Tarius just threw everything in the caldron together, stirred it around a bit then took it out, wrung it out, hung it up till it was dry then took it down, wadded it all into one ball and called it clean.

Jena usually did their wash just to save their clothes.

"Who would have thought that I'd ever miss my little sister who has always been a giant pain in my ass?" young Tarius said. "Do you need anything else from me, Tarius? It was a long, hot ride and Eric waits for me at the lake."

"Better hurry along boy, you can't keep a Jethrik girl waiting."

The boy laughed and took off.

"Now what's that supposed to mean?" Jena said.

"Only..." Tarius sighed and looked at her. "...you know how you Jethrik girls are always using your mates unmercifully for your pleasure."

Jena laughed. "Oh it's *my* pleasure then."

"I'm not complaining of course."

"Oh, of course not."

The baby, having eaten his fill, pushed away turned to look at Tarius and smiled the most brilliant smile. Tarius smiled back in a way that told Jena that she literally felt no different about this baby than she had the one who had issued from her own womb. It made Jena feel all the worse that he still didn't have that warm spot in her heart that Jabone had.

"Who's a bright, good boy?" She took him from Jena and put him on her shoulder and patted him—way too hard—till he let out a huge burp. Like their grown son, if he had any trouble with how rough Tarius was with him it never showed in his face or his actions. Tarius walked over and sat on her throne and Jena got up and joined her, sitting beside her and running her hand over the baby's head of white curls. He certainly looked like he could be her child. Tarius was so dark the child's color was a drastic contrast to hers. The way it must have looked when she took care of Jabone, and yet it had never dawned on her till this moment watching Tarius hold Darian close that people must have looked at Jena with Jabone and thought, "That can't be her child." But he was and so was Darian; it was just different.

Where was it written that mothers had to love their children the same? Elise had no trouble at all telling Jena that Ufalla was her favorite child. Elise made sure her children didn't know, but she didn't have guilt because she had a favorite.

Of course Elise was a little different. Perhaps the funniest story Elise had ever told her was why she and Harris had four children instead of the two they planned. It seemed that their third child had been an "accident." The Kartiks had ways to keep from getting pregnant that most of the world still didn't know about, but they didn't always work. Apparently their "birth control" failed and their third child Terrance was born. Elise had told her, "Our first two children fought constantly with each other and without that I don't think tiny Tarius would have ever gotten as strong as he did. You see he had to get strong just to keep Ufalla from running over him. The first two were so much older than Terrance that they just loved and coddled him so we had Hera on purpose so that Terence would have someone to fight with."

It was a beautiful day and the throne sat outside their huts as it usually did. They loved to be outside, Tarius was Katabull and all the Katabull preferred to be outdoors if they had a choice. Jena had always preferred the outdoors; it was just one of the many reasons they were so perfect for each other.

Jena laid her head on Tarius's shoulder and sighed.

"What?" Tarius asked.

"Very happy, but still missing Jabone. I have to admit the baby is helping to fill that hole, but it's still hard to walk by his room and he's not there. To think of him grown and married and gone and neither of us expected Jabone to just stay gone so long with no real contact from him. We only know he's alright at all because Riglid and Laz saw him when they went to Montero to get their sister."

"That girl." Tarius shook her head. "As if Radkin doesn't have enough on her plate, that girl would drive a wizard crazy."

Jena nodded. Word came back to the compound that Rea had been on a drunken toot in Montero and several pubs were complaining about property damage. Rimmy and Radkin sent their two oldest boys to go pick up their wayward sister. They had run into Jabone while looking for her said hello briefly and that was absolutely the only thing approaching contact they'd had with their son in months.

Jabone had taken Kasiria and they had gone to Montero a day after the boat docked. They wanted some time away from everything to be together and relax, to forget the battle and just enjoy each other. Jena understood this. It was what she and Tarius had done when they found one another after having so completely lost each other. A couple needed time away from family and friends to just wallow in each other's company especially when love was new.

The part of Jena that was completely attached to her mate in every way understood this. But as Jabone's mother she was having a little trouble with him not coming home.

"I don't know why they stay so long gone," Tarius said with a frown, then pushed it away and grinned. "He'll come home, Mama... but as I said you Jethrik girls..." Jena slapped her in the shoulder hard and Tarius laughed. Jena caught Tarius's eyes as she looked at Darian and suddenly she knew exactly why Tarius had grabbed him up and kept him.

Jabone had left them to go have his own life and had left a gaping hole in theirs. Men—no matter how sensitive they might be—never had the bond to a child that a mother did. And Arvon and Dustan, though they'd lived there as long as she had, at the end of the day they were Jethrik men with Jethrik sensibilities. In spite of their best efforts they still felt child rearing was best left to women. In fact they were nearly as active in Darian's life as they had been in Jabone's which meant occasionally they bathed him, or rocked him or talked to him but basically she and Tarius had taken care of Jabone just like they were now taking care of Darian while the men were off doing whatever it was Jethrik men did when they didn't want to get stuck taking care of a crying infant.

Katabull men were normally very hands on with their young even more so than Kartik men, but though Arvon was Katabull because he'd been raised in the Jethrik by humans he had less to do with the children than Dustan did.

Arvon and Dustan missed their son but they didn't worry

and fret and want him the way Tarius and Jena did. As his mothers they had put everything else aside to care for him; he became the center of their universe. Children turned into adults and then they wanted to have a life separate from yours and they never really knew how much that hurt. And all they'd gone through to have him, he just didn't know and now he loved them but their importance in his life was all but gone. He didn't need them.

As much as they loved each other and as much as Tarius normally talked to her about everything, while Jena had said exactly how she felt about Jabone being gone daily, Tarius hadn't. Jena realized only now that Tarius had been every bit as lonely for him and felt every inch of the emptiness that she had.

Tarius took the baby and kept him because she needed him, and it could only help that he needed them even more than they needed him.

Jena moved and kissed Tarius on the cheek. "Have I told you recently how amazing you are and how much I love you?"

"Not recently enough," Tarius said. She turned her head and kissed Jena on the lips. "I love you and thank you."

"For what?"

"For indulging me with this baby," Tarius said softly.

Darian was asleep on her other shoulder occasionally sucking the air and making happy baby noises.

"You know by the time this one is grown the other will have given us grandchildren, and by the time they're nearly grown Darian will be giving us grandkids and we'll never have to have that horrid feeling that we have no children to care for again," Jena said in a whisper.

"Well that was the plan."

Chapter Four

"Seriously Ufalla, is this some twisted joke? Because if it is it isn't very funny," Jestia said.

"Who is Ufalla?"

"You. You are Ufalla, dumbass."

"What an odd name Ufalla Dumbass."

"Your name isn't dumbass; you're acting like a dumb ass. Please tell me you're just having me on Ufalla that you know who you are—more importantly that you know who I am." Jestia looked into Ufalla's eyes and saw not the least sign of recognition. "This can't be happening."

"My head hurts," Ufalla said, putting her hand to her head.

"Do you remember anything?"

Ufalla returned a blank stare as if she didn't even understand the question.

"Yri!" Jestia yelled. She walked to the door and yelled even louder. "Yri I need you!"

Yri had worked on Ufalla earlier, so he came running. When he entered the room Ufalla let out a shriek like a little girl then said, "What by all the gods is *that*?"

Yri was of course in his Katabull form which meant he was all muscle and bulk, hair claws and teeth, with cat-like eyes. Yri, knowing that Ufalla not only knew him well but had grown up in the Katabull compound turned to Jestia and asked, "She doesn't remember herself?"

"Worse than that, she doesn't remember me," Jestia cried.

Ufalla was now whimpering and had sat up and pulled the covers around her neck as she watched Yri carefully.

Yri motioned for Jestia to follow him out of the room which she did. "Do you know what's wrong with her?" he asked.

She knew why. He asked because she should know but of course she didn't because when she was supposed to be learning such things her mind had been occupied by nonsense. Now that she really wanted to learn all she could about medicine and potions she couldn't because her mother wanted her to be queen instead of a witch.

"The day Jazel was trying to teach me about maladies of the brain and what potions to create for them I was mostly wondering how I could sneak away and go to a tavern, so now I have failed Ufalla twice. Can you tell me what's wrong with her Yri, and is there anything we can do?"

"She is suffering from amnesia. You gave her a potion for swelling?"

Jestia nodded.

"That's about all we can do for her. The good news is that the effects usually only last a short time," Yri said.

"Usually?"

Yri avoided her question. "The important thing is not to feed her too much information at one time. She needs to remember on her own. Give her too much information at once and you may cause her to go into a state of shock."

"But she doesn't remember me, Yri. Who could possibly be more important in her life than I am?"

"No one I'm sure," Yri said, shaking his head. "I'll tell the crew we need to cat down around Ufalla so we don't upset her." He looked through the door at where Ufalla was still sitting with the covers pulled around her looking petrified. He looked back at Jestia and laughed. "It will be great fun to tease her about this when she is well."

Jestia wasn't seeing the humor. "She will get better then?"

"Oh I'm sure she will. I can't imagine you would allow anything else, princess." Yri patted her hard on the shoulder nearly bowling her over and then took off to do whatever the Katabull were doing. She walked back into the room and went to stand at the foot of the bed. How much could she say? How much was too much information?

"What was that thing?" Ufalla demanded. She didn't even sound like herself.

Well she'd already seen him and since they were surrounded by them she supposed she'd better explain him. "He is the Katabull. They are shape shifters. This is a Katabull ship." There was no sign that she recognized even the word Katabull. "You were born and raised in the Katabull compound."

"I'm one of them!" She started running her hands over her own face.

"We should both be so lucky. No, you're a human." Well at least it appeared that Ufalla understood what a human was. It then became apparent what the Katabull were doing because the ship was suddenly not at such a tilt. They had pushed the ship up and propped it so that they were level from side to side. They still weren't level from bow to stern, but this was certainly better. She adjusted the bed accordingly as Ufalla screamed like a child.

"What just happened?"

Jestia sighed. "They have straightened the ship a bit is all. Calm down."

"What happened to me?"

"Do you not remember anything? I swear to all the gods, Ufalla, if I find out you are just doing this for fun I'll split you," Jestia said.

"Split you. Split you," Ufalla said slowly. She looked at Jestia. "I have heard that before."

For the first time since Ufalla woke up Jestia had hope that she really would come back. "Yes Ufalla your godmother Tarius the Black says it all the time."

Ufalla giggled in a very un-Ufalla way. "Tarius the Black, what a funny name."

Jestia sighed and then felt sick to her stomach. *My gods, she is just like one of those imbecile ladies-in-waiting. What am I going to do if she is like this forever? It will be like she died. I can't think that. I must not. She's going to be fine. She's going to come back. My Ufalla would never leave me alone.*

"What happened to me?" Ufalla asked again.

Jestia told her the truth. "There was a storm, our ship ran aground, you fell and hit your head and turned into a huge ninny."

Tarius stood on the dock with Darian on her hip looking out to sea. Jena was mostly holding Darian's head up. In Jena's opinion he really wasn't big enough for being on his madra's hip, but that didn't stop Tarius bouncing him around, his head just popping back and forth, Jena running along beside them propping his head up. She didn't think Tarius really understood that a human baby wasn't as resilient as a Katabull baby. When she tried to explain this Tarius just told her to look at how happy the baby was. And he was, too. He didn't seem to mind his head popping back and forth. When Jena grabbed his head and held it he just grinned like it was all just some great game. Tarius pulled an eyeglass from her pocket, now more propping than holding the baby and Jena'd had enough. She grabbed Darian.

"Give me our baby before you break his neck."

Tarius reluctantly let her have him, and Jena held him, resting his head on her shoulder. So of course he picked his head up and looked at her like she'd gone mad. "Don't you get smart with me mister." She said and he lay his head down and cuddled into her neck which meant he was sleepy and now he would actually go to sleep for her which was nice.

Tarius worked the eye glass looking out at sea. "The ship should be back by now," she said, and it was clear that Tarius was worried.

"When should it have come into port?" Jena asked.

"Three days ago," Tarius said.

"They had Jestia with them. Perhaps the fishing was just too good for Sorak. You know Sorak and catching fish."

"He had Jestia with him which is precisely why he would not have stayed longer than was intended," Tarius said. Then she called out, "Rimmy!"

Rimmy appeared—as he always did—in seconds no matter where he was or what he was doing. "Great Leader," he said. After all these years she'd stopped even trying to make them stop calling her by her title.

"Rimmy, tell the captain of that ship that he is to hold off leaving and prepare to do a rescue mission. Captain Sorak's ship is late in returning and since Jestia is on it we can take no chances. Send someone to Montero to retrieve the witch Jazel. When she is here she will be able to tell us whether or not—one way or the other—we are wasting our time going after them. Gather the Marching Night in the Great Hall and I will send a contingent of our pack in the ship. That is all."

Rimmy nodded and took off at a run.

Jena was worried mostly because Tarius was. "Do you think the girls are in trouble, Tarius?"

"I think it would be difficult for them to find trouble Jestia could not get them out of, and that is not just any crew; they are Marching Night. However something isn't right and I don't want to take any chances," Tarius said.

News traveled quickly through the Katabull compound. For all their wonderful qualities there was one thing that drove Jena nuts about the Katabull there really was no such thing as "private." If one of them knew something in minutes they all did. Unless you specifically said, "Don't repeat this," they did as quickly as they could. And the concept of personal space completely eluded *all* the Kartiks not just the Katabull though they were by far the worst offenders. They would sit right up against you or come inches from your face to speak and walk in no matter what you might be doing. Jena wasn't surprised at all when within minutes Harris came racing down to the docks.

"Tarius, they said the girls' ship..."

"My dear friend, Harris, I am only being cautious. You have seen Ufalla and Jestia in battle and the crew are some of the best of our pack. I'm sure they are fine. I just see no sense in taking chances."

Harris looked at Tarius suspiciously. "You would say anything to put my mind at ease."

"True, but I'd also tell you if I was sure some tragedy had befallen them. I would not lie to you where one of your children was concerned," Tarius said.

"But you are worried about them or you wouldn't be sending for the witch Jazel and sending part of the Marching Night to go look for them."

"I am," Tarius said. "It is not like Sorak to put in to port late."

"Are you going?"

"I am not," Tarius said. This seemed to put Harris right at ease and Jena knew why. If Tarius thought the girls were in any real danger she'd lead the mission herself.

"I will take command," Harris said. "Elise and I will go. Tarius and Eric can watch our little ones."

"Sounds a great plan, my brother. Jazel will be with you and should you run into trouble all you have to do is call for me and I will bring the entire Katabull fleet."

That first night on the beach had been rough for a number of reasons not the least of which was the cold. The crew was fine; the only one injured had been Ufalla. But even after propping the ship on one side and putting in timbers to steady it on the other it was still tilted at an uncomfortable angle from front to back. It made it hard for them to work on and to stay on. No one really knew what they were going to do or where they were.

But the worst thing about that first day was when, exhausted from the casting she'd done, further drained by being worried sick about Ufalla, and cold as a toad she tried to get into bed.

"What... what are you doing?" Ufalla demanded.

"Getting into bed. I'm cold and exhausted."

"Isn't there another bed?"

"This is our bed."

Yri in his human form appeared in the door coughed and nodded his head that she should join him.

"What!" she'd demanded when she did.

"I don't know how much is going to be too much."

"What do you mean?"

"I don't know if you should tell her that she's your mate, and you certainly shouldn't tell her that you're a witch."

She glared at him. "Are you just trying to make this as hard for me as possible? You know Yri that I am way too selfish for all this crap," Jestia said. "Didn't I hear that if you smack someone in the head again...?"

Yri interrupted her shaking his head no. "That doesn't work. You'd most likely just make her worse."

Defeated she had wound up sleeping in a hammock she hung in the corner of the tiny room.

Five days had passed and Ufalla wasn't any closer to being... well Ufalla. They had figured out where they were, but it wasn't much help because they were at least fifty miles from the nearest port. Sorak didn't seem to have a plan other than to keep catching fish for them all to eat, keep a big fire going on the beach, and wait for Tarius to send a rescue party which he seemed more sure was going to happen than she was.

Jestia still felt spent. Ufalla looked like herself but she wasn't, and the connection they had wasn't there. She felt alone. Alone hundreds of miles from home and... The land was crying out to her, and she needed Ufalla.

"Yri said you should get up, get dressed, and come outside for some fresh air," Jestia said.

Ufalla nodded and got out of bed acting like it was a great effort. "It's very cold." She had been wearing one of her own shirts and underwear as bed clothes. "My clothes?"

"Right there, your highness," Jestia muttered, pointing at where Ufalla's pants and belt were sitting on top of her sword and dagger on a chair.

Ufalla picked up the pants with two fingers as if she were picking up some rotten, dead thing. "Surely I don't wear these." She looked at the weapons that lifting the pants had revealed. "What sort of woman am I?"

"You're my woman, dammit, and frankly I'm tired of all this shit."

"What does that mean I'm your woman?"

Jestia was about to tell Ufalla just what an imbecile she was being when Yri came to the door of their cabin he waved her over. "Any improvement?"

"Only if getting stupider by the minute can be considered an improvement," Jestia bellowed.

Yri smiled. "Is she really getting dimmer or are you just

getting irritated that she isn't instantly well?"

"Probably that. I can't do this, Yri. I need her. I look at her and she's my woman then she opens her mouth and... How can I be so in love with Ufalla yet want to pinch her head off and tell the gods she died just because she doesn't act the way I want her to? And this whole not telling her anything is not working. Are you sure it's the only way?"

"Actually no. I've never dealt with the illness before, only learned about it from books and teachers."

Jestia frowned, instantly angry. "Then you could be wrong."

He shrugged. "And I might not be. It's what I was taught. Get her up and get her outside. Maybe something mundane will stir her memories. Maybe the fresh air will get her thinking. Either way I will need the light to remove the stitches from her head."

Jestia nodded, feeling defeated, and went back to Ufalla. "Put your clothes on please." She said through gritted teeth. Ufalla just looked at the pants in disgust. As she did the land called out to Jestia for help and she just couldn't take it anymore. "Ufalla I swear by all the gods if you don't snap out of it and go back to being yourself I think I'll go mad. Dammit, Ufalla, I need you. I love you. You're in there somewhere you have to be because I can't live without you, and I sure can't live with you like this."

Yri came running in—damn the Katabull and their fantastic hearing. "Jestia, don't do this." Yri looked from her to the look of utter confusion on Ufalla's face and back again.

Jestia rushed past him out of the room, and she didn't stop walking till she was off the ship and on the beach. Let him handle Ufalla then. Jestia couldn't stand to see her like that. Of course being on the beach she could better hear the land crying out, and that accompanied by the bitter cold made her head hurt. She sat down on a rock and started to cry. Sorak walked up to her and started patting her back.

"Are you alright?"

"I wouldn't be crying if I was alright you giant dumbass. My lover is someone I don't know and who doesn't know me, and I still can't get my own strength back and the land is crying out to me."

"What do you mean the land is crying out to you?"

"What do you think I mean? You're a Katabull; can't you feel that something is wrong here?"

"I am the Katabull and all I smell is Amalites on the wind.

I have fought them shoulder to shoulder with you in the cave, but I also fought them in the Great War, and when I smell them it is all I can do to keep from going to attack them. But we are in the Kartik-held territories of the Amalite and this is their land. We have eradicated their religion and the people I long to kill are probably nothing but farmers. I can feel that something is wrong, but that is all. What do you suppose it is?"

Jestia sighed miserably. "I don't know, and I should care but the only reason I care at all is because I can hear it, feel it, and it adds to my own misery. All I really care about—all I've ever cared about—is Ufalla, but she's gone and I just feel this growing hole where my heart should be."

"She'll come back, Jestia. I've known Ufalla all her life and I've never known her to run from a fight."

"Ufalla no, but what about that thing in there? Does that seem like Ufalla to you at all?"

Sorak was silent which told her all she needed to know.

"When, *when* will she come back? I need her *now*. We're lost at sea, tossed on some foreign shore, and the land is crying and I need her *now*."

"Is there nothing you can do?"

"Give her potions to reduce the swelling. Cry a lot. I haven't noticed that's helping anything. I have all this power, but all of it is useless. She's gone. I can't explain it, but that thing that looks like Ufalla is just empty."

"What did Yri say?"

"He says I must let her remember things on her own."

"You know Jestia…" He stopped.

"What?"

"Healers don't know everything about medicine, any more than sailors know everything about the sea, or swordsmen know everything about war, or witches know all about spells."

"Damn the Katabull and your riddles. Why can you never just say what you mean and mean what you say?"

Sorak smiled and patted her some more. "Ah, little sister, you are indeed not yourself any more than Ufalla is herself. You've never had any trouble understanding us before. Yri was there the day Tarius the Black breathed her own life into a dead baby and brought him to life, and that was Tarius the Black—a warrior of renown and the Great Leader—but not a person of books or hidden knowledge as you are. Ufalla is your woman, Jestia, and maybe you know better than Yri how to bring her back. What do *you* think *you* should do?"

"I think..." She didn't finish. She jumped up, turned on her heel, and started back for the ship. She found Ufalla back in bed with the covers pulled around her just glaring at where Yri was standing holding her pants up. Jestia took the pants from Yri and said. "Go away and close the door as you leave." Then remembering she was talking to the Katabull added, "Please."

"Jestia, I do not think..."

"Then don't, Yri. If I ruin her further it will be on my head not yours and none will blame you."

Yri nodded and left closing the door.

Jestia threw the pants on the floor and walked to the foot of the bed. "I have had it with you and all this crap."

"You... you left me to be dressed by a man."

"Normally I have trouble keeping clothes on you! You could hold all your modesty in a thimble."

"What sort of woman am I?" She shrieked, making Jestia's ears hurt.

"The sort of woman who makes love all night and fights all day. You are the bravest, most loving, most courageous, funnest person I have ever known. You love me with your whole heart and soul not because of my title or my power. You love me and I love you as I have never loved anyone or anything..."

"I'm queer."

"Yes you're queer, of course you're queer. You made me queer but *you* have always been a great lover of women. Too many women for my liking actually, in fact, if I have to see even one more woman look across a room or a table at you in that all-knowing way, I just might scream. You and I were going to get married but my mother decided I had to come home, and since she's the queen of the Kartik..."

"You're a princess?"

"Well you don't have to sound so surprised. I'm not just the princess; my brother died and now I'm the heir apparent."

"What does that mean?"

"It means I'm supposed to succeed my mother to the throne."

"Oh. Then what are we doing here?"

"I don't want to be queen. I can't marry your stupid ass if I'm queen."

Ufalla giggled. "I really like girls?"

"Gods and spiders, Ufalla. Yri said telling you too much might make you crazy, but I swear I'd rather have crazy than the simpering, stupid, titty-sucking mama's baby you have become. Has it even dawned on you to wonder why your bed is level when the whole of the rest of the ship is off kilter?" Ufalla shook her head. "Because I'm a great and powerful witch that's why. I'm a witch and those creatures you are so afraid of, the Katabull, you were raised with them. For the love of the One Who Has No Name your own godmother is their ruler. This ship is entirely crewed by the Marching Night."

"Marching Night, Marching Night that sounds familiar."

"I swear, Ufalla, I might strangle you myself. *Split you*, you remember and *Marching Night* sounds familiar, and yet you have not a glimmer of recognition for me." She shrugged. "We fought the Amalites together in the caves. You protected me and I saved you. We have known each other and been best friends since we were children. You have always loved me, Ufalla, and I can't stand that you don't now..." Ufalla was just staring at her. And of course the teapot and cup picked that moment to appear. It poured a cup and Ufalla's whole face lit up.

"I remember that! Oh the tea is very good. Can I have a cup?"

"Knock yourself out," Jestia said with a sigh and watched as Ufalla plucked the cup from the air and took a drink. *Maybe that's what Yri was really wrong about. Maybe I should just hit her in the head. All this time I really thought if I could just tell her who she is she'd remember. A lifetime of memories made her who she was and without those she's just a vapid girl that frankly I can't stand.* She watched as Ufalla sipped at the tea. "How could you ever forget me? I could never forget you."

"I'm sorry."

Jestia wasn't aware of how mad she was till she snapped her fingers and the teapot and cup were gone and she thundered, "Don't be sorry; just be you! I need you to be Ufalla. I can't do this, any of it by myself; I'm not brave like you. You are my courage and my warmth. Without you... well I'm rather like you are right now. I don't like me without you and..." Ufalla was just looking at her with no understanding or recognition at all.

She was all out of ideas. Knowing everything hadn't made Ufalla any worse, but it certainly hadn't fixed her. "I don't care if you remember anything else couldn't you at least remember me?" Ufalla didn't say anything, no doubt because saying she was sorry had sent Jestia off on a tirade. "I am exhausted in every way, Ufalla, and heart sick and..." She started taking her clothes off.

"What, what are you doing?"

"I need some rest. I need to be close to you even if you aren't you. I'm tired of trying to sleep in that hammock and tired of sleeping alone which I'm not really doing—sleeping that is. I need some rest and as long as you're wearing my lover's body you're just going to have to put up with me in your bed. So don't even worry about getting up and putting on clothes you don't like or getting the stitches taken out of your head. Just scoot over."

Ufalla nodded and moved over. When Jestia looked up Ufalla had averted her eyes so as not to see Jestia's naked body. "For the love of The Nameless One, Ufalla, you and I have made love hundreds of times. Neither of us sleeps in clothes unless we are in danger. The crew is mostly Katabull and we are miles from anyone, so we're safe." Of course now she was naked she was cold so she wondered how smart it was to take off all her clothes. She crawled under the covers and scooted over to Ufalla who stiffened. Jestia didn't care; she ignored the pain in her heart and wrapped her arms around Ufalla.

"Hundreds of times?" Ufalla asked.

"Yes, hundreds." Jestia relaxed. Just holding Ufalla made her feel better. "I love you; I need you. Please come back to me."

Ufalla looked at the naked woman wrapped all around her, sound asleep. She lifted the covers and took a good look. The witch was gorgeous no doubt but if she was a great lover of women why was she not more aroused? Was Jestia lying to her about who and what she was? She put the cover back down and looked at her hands. They were calloused and covered with a dozen scars, but above all that her right pinky finger was missing, so she must be a sword woman. Then a flash of memory ran through her brain so strong that it couldn't be denied and she looked at where her sword lay neglected on a chair only a few feet from her and *knew* that was where her missing finger was. She looked again at the sleeping woman lying wrapped all around her and she touched her back experimentally. It felt good; it felt familiar, so she started to stroke her hand down the other woman's back.

Jestia started awake and looked at Ufalla. For answer Ufalla said, "My finger is in my sword and you... This feels right." She continued stroking Jestia's shoulder. The next thing she knew the very naked woman had crawled up her body and was kissing her hard on the mouth. She automatically kissed her back which meant she must be used to it. She could feel the other woman's love wash over her like a wave, and then her memories were flooding her mind till it was almost overwhelming.

Jestia pushed away from her and smiled. "So you decided to come back to me."

"Jestia." She kissed Jestia's forehead. "Why does it feel like it has been a hundred years since I held you?"

"Oh my dear love, you have no idea how much I have missed you or what a huge pain in the ass you've been."

Jestia kissed her again and all the cobwebs were gone. She just had a burning need to be with Jestia completely and as always Jestia did not disappoint.

Ufalla didn't remember the five plus days she had amnesia at all, but it didn't matter because Jestia and the crew did and they were only too happy to tell her every embarrassing thing she had done or said.

It seemed that without her memories she had been some overtly feminine, whining woman child. It wasn't flattering, and she wondered how long it was going to take them to stop riding her high about it. And of course Jestia was pissed off no end because Ufalla hadn't even remembered her. Apparently it was looking at her sword that had opened the gates to her memory and how could anything be more important to Ufalla than Jestia? No matter how many times Ufalla explained that nothing was and nothing ever could be Jestia would just point to the hilt of Ufalla's sword where her missing finger was.

Ufalla had even explained. "It wasn't till I was holding you, not till you kissed me that I really started to remember."

"Whatever." Jestia fired back. Then her anger subsided. "You know I don't really care what brought you back my great love. Just that you're back. After all there is a reason your pack does that with your swords; there is magic in your blade."

"My blade?" Ufalla asked. She had done it just because it was a tradition in her pack because Tarius the Black, her son Jabone, and Ufalla's older brother had done it and she wanted to be like them. Why the practice put magic into a

Katabull's blade she understood, the Katabull were magical creatures. She had been raised with the Katabull and was part of the pack of the Marching Night but she wasn't Katabull. "Jestia how could there be magic in my blade?"

"You are not untouched by magic, my life."

And that was another thing. Jestia had been overly sentimental ever since Ufalla had come back to herself. It was starting to wear on her last nerve, and she hoped it ended soon. Although she supposed if she'd thought Jestia was gone from her for even a minute and got her back she'd be acting just as silly.

"You grew up with the Katabull and you're my world. As you know I am a very powerful witch and I'm nothing without you. You are my sun and my moons and..."

And Ufalla wondered how long it was going to be before Jestia stopped talking to her like she was writing a love poem.

Chapter Five

Jazel pointed towards the shore and clicked her tongue.

"What?" Elise demanded, "Is Ufalla safe?" She could see the ship sitting on the shore, but nothing else.

"Your child is safe as are all the others, but their ship was beached by magic."

Harris took out an eyeglass and looked at the coast. Jazel didn't have to ask why. He wanted to see his daughter. Foolish humans. "I told you days ago that I could feel that Jestia was alive and as long as Jestia is alive so is your daughter." And now that they were close enough to see the ship she could feel the Katabull and they were all accounted for, too. She wondered what witch or wizard had cast the spell. What was their reason to go after Jestia? Jazel had no doubt that's what the caster was about—not because she could see the caster's intent in the vapors the spell left that only a witch could see, but because it was the only thing that made any sense. There would be no reason at all for anyone to go after a fishing vessel; therefore, they had to be after the heir apparent. What evil did they plan that they would target the royal throne in such a way?

The caster was obviously reckless because when you picked a cloud, cast a storm into it, and told it to go somewhere or chase someone, you had little if any control over what that storm would do. It rather depended on the intention of the cloud you cast the storm into, and you could never know what that was. If the cloud was going to be nothing more than a tiny rain burst you wouldn't get much more than a minor storm. However if that cloud was destined to become a major storm then casting on it would do something... well like cast a boatful of seasoned Katabull sailors with a powerful witch on board onto the shore and strand them.

Then something hit her like a bolt. The land was crying. She could tell now looking around at the Katabull that they could sense it, too.

"What's wrong?" Harris asked at her shoulder. He'd been Tarius's-right hand man so long he could read people nearly as keenly as she could.

"All our people are fine, but there is something wrong

with the land." How did a witch explain such things to people who couldn't feel the energy of the universe course through their veins? She couldn't explain what she and the Katabull felt. Normal humans didn't have a connection to that which couldn't be seen or felt or tasted.

Harris didn't question her just nodded and set his chin, more than ready to put into shore so that he could see his child for himself.

The closer they got to the shore the louder the noise got until Jazel had to block it out, and even then she could still hear it. Something was badly wrong with the very earth of the Kartik territories.

Ufalla saw the ship first and started throwing the green leaves onto the fire to make smoke just in case they hadn't been seen. It was really a wasted effort because she could clearly see the Katabull flags and sails and knew it was a rescue ship. Since it was they would have been searching the shore for them and weren't likely to miss a huge ship washed up on a white sand beach.

Jestia walked up to her and handed her an eyeglass, then she wrapped her arms around Ufalla's waist and rested her head on her back. "Jazel is with them."

"You could see her?" Ufalla looked through the glass and could just make out people on deck but not who they were.

"I can feel her."

Ufalla watched as she saw three row boats lowered and people getting into them a few minutes later. As they started rowing towards them Ufalla smiled. "My madra and fadra are with them."

"He would have insisted, and Ufalla you have to know that Tarius would do nearly anything your father asked of her."

Ufalla did know that. Her memories still weren't a hundred percent, but when someone told her something the memory instantly came back. Then she knew something else. She could feel it in the way Jestia clung to her.

"What's wrong?"

"I just want to go home." Jestia sighed. "Even if we can only stay a little while. I certainly don't want to have to go back into battle. I almost lost you, and I just don't ever want to do anything remotely dangerous again."

"Being who we are dear that isn't very likely." Then she realized what Jestia had said. "What battle, Jestia?"

"I told you, you huge dumbass." For a second Ufalla thought maybe Jestia was finally done punctuating every sentence by telling her how much she loved her, but she wasn't. "I love you more than life itself, but I told you the earth is crying, and now Jazel is here and a huge slice of the Marching Night as well. There will be no reason, none at all, to not go and see what the problem is."

Ufalla nodded knowing she was right. In between Jestia's words of undying devotion she had been talking about the earth crying. Apparently the Katabull could feel it because they were all talking about it, too. Ufalla felt this niggling pull at the corner of her brain, but she couldn't be sure that wasn't just her head injury since she still had occasionally bouts of dizziness and nausea. Neither Jestia nor the Katabull had any idea why the earth was crying, only that it was bad.

"Whatever it is we can handle it," Ufalla said.

"Eternal light of my life, you are just now getting over a serious head injury. You should not be going into battle— any battle—and..."

Ufalla removed the eyeglass from her eye, disentangled Jestia and turned to face her. "No matter what I acted like when I was out of my head, I am back now and fully capable of taking care of myself and you. Even though I know you don't really need my protection."

"Yes I do," Jestia said with that bit of fire in her eyes that always made Ufalla's blood run hot. "Don't you ever say such a stupid thing again. Without you I am nothing. Ask anyone here and they will tell you how worthless I was. Then when you are finally coming back, do you say, 'Jestia how could I ever for even a moment forget you for you are my very breath?' No, you say, 'My finger is in my sword.' How romantic is that? My finger is my sword!"

Ufalla kissed Jestia gently on the lips then pulled back from her. "Jestia, how could I ever for even a moment forget you for you are my very breath..."

Jestia popped her in the chest with her hand but then smiled at her and wrapped her arms around her neck. "You know it doesn't count if you just repeat what I say, right?"

"I know that is how we will tell the story, and then it is how everyone else will tell the story, and though you have never heard me it was only you holding me, me touching you that brought me back."

"Get to your room," Sorak said from somewhere behind them. Then he added in a falsetto that sent the whole crew into near hysterics. The fact that they were about to be rescued only made them a bit louder than they had been before. "I'm not queer; I'm a dainty flower. Give me my pink dress."

Ufalla sighed and rested her forehead on the top of Jestia's head. "I don't know what's worse: you constantly having the need to tell me—in some new way—how much you love me or them ribbing me about things I don't even remember doing."

"It wasn't funny then, but it sort of is now. You were really silly."

"As you and everyone else has told me. I doubt seriously I will be able to change that part of the story, and it will no doubt follow me to my grave," Ufalla said with a sigh. "I'm sure it will bring my big brother great joy when he tells of how I shrieked at the sight of the Katabull and wouldn't look at you naked." She picked her head up and looked at Jestia. "I don't suppose you could put a spell on them so they would forget?"

"I could but I won't. Seeing what it was like when you forgot I don't know that I will ever be able to cast that spell in good conscience again. I surely don't ever want to forget how it felt to almost lose you."

"Why would you want to remember that?"

"Because as long as I remember that aching hole in my heart and the deep grief—how I could barely function—then I'm never going to take you for granted or forget to tell you just how very much I love you."

"About that, honey..."

Jestia put up a hand. "I will stop when I feel like stopping."

Tarius was in the Great Hall sitting on her throne with Jena by her side. Darian was lying on her knees looking up at them as Tarius was settling the last of the disagreements between her people. A bird flew in the open door and landed on Darian's head. He laughed and tried to grab the bird, but Jena grabbed the baby's hand.

Jena didn't wonder why the bird acted this way; she knew it was enchanted, sent by the witch Jazel. Tarius took the bird from her son's head and unwrapped the note from its leg. She then let the bird go, breaking the spell. It panicked for only a second and then flew out the open door. Darian looked put out and Tarius said to him, "Maybe we will get you your own bird someday. Or maybe even a monkey. You'd like a monkey, oh yes you would…"

"Great Leader, about my garden…"

Tarius looked not at him but at the other man standing in the hall.

"Your goats got out and ate his garden. Give him two of your billy-goats for him to eat, and you shall be even. In future, both of you build better fences, and you watch your goats. Now you can go back to your own work." She looked at the note in her hand. "Can you not see that this is important? Do you think birds just fly around me all day leaving me messages?"

"No Great Leader," they said in unison and left as always satisfied with the verdict.

Katabull rarely had a dispute that was any worse than that one, and in the over twenty years Tarius had been on the throne Jena had never seen one of them show even a hint of anger at Tarius's ruling. They'd never even disputed her—which they had the right to do. The reason was obvious if you knew the way the Katabull mind worked, and after all this time she mostly did—until she very clearly didn't. One of them was wrong and the other one was right; they hadn't already made up their minds which was which before they got there. If they had, the dispute never would have reached Tarius, so they were mostly waiting for someone else to tell them what they should do because they didn't really know.

Most simple disputes were settled by wrestling which was just one of the things Jena still didn't fully understand.

Tarius handed the note to Jena. Tarius could read, but it was a chore for her.

Jena read the note out loud. "Tarius, all are fine here. The ship was beached by a storm and I don't know if Jestia and I together can put it back out to sea. The land here is crying. Some great wrong is being committed against the earth itself. We will be camping here a few days and then move in to see what the problem is. I will make reports daily to tell you of our progress. Then it's signed by Jazel's hand."

"What do you suppose that means—the land is crying?"

"Don't ask me; it sounded like something a Katabull might say. I figured you'd know."

Tarius adjusted Darian and then stood up. She started for the door. "What's that supposed to mean? Something a Katabull might say?"

"You know, cryptic and not terribly helpful." Jena got up and followed her and two men picked up the throne and carried it after them. After all these years she hardly even noticed this tradition which had caused Tarius the most annoyance when she had first taken the position of Great Leader. It went everywhere they went. To this day any Katabull who saw Tarius sit anywhere else got greatly annoyed, not that Tarius paid much attention. She sat on the throne if it was handy and she felt like doing so, if not she sat wherever she pleased and dared anyone to tell her otherwise. "Talking around and over things—that's what a Katabull does."

"Woman, you cut me to the quick," Tarius said. She shrugged. "I'm sure this crying land is nothing Harris, two witches, and a huge chunk of the Marching Night can't handle."

Jena walked behind Tarius having never been able to keep up with her without running. Besides, she was enjoying the view. She couldn't explain it, but thought it probably had a lot to do with nursing the baby or the potion that made her capable of doing so. Jena felt better than she had in years, and her libido was right back where it had been in her twenties. As she followed Tarius—who was wearing nothing but a loin's cloth and a sleeveless blue shirt (you had to love a Kartik winter) that tied in the front and her sword—Jena could easily watch the sway of her hips and found that she was getting more aroused by the moment. She ran to catch up to Tarius. "Give me that baby. It's time for his nap." She took Darian and started for their huts at a near run.

"He's not on that tight a schedule," Tarius said with a laugh.

Jena turned to look at her and Tarius read her expression. "Ohhh, a nap."

"Yes a nap. And I expect you to be naked and on our bed when I get there."

Harris and Elise had hugged their daughter and then they had hugged Jestia. Jestia warmed inside from the affection they showed her. Soon the whole of their crew were filling in all that had come to shore about everything that had happened and mostly just how silly Ufalla had acted. It was obvious that Ufalla was greatly embarrassed to have her parents told all she had done.

Jazel walked up to Jestia and they embraced.

"And how are you little sister?" Jazel asked.

"Fine, grateful that she didn't stay an imbecile, happy

that she's back. I'm starting to understand what it means to be part of the Marching Night. And, yes, I'm well aware that the land is crying and that we will have to do something about that. I'm already tired of risking me and mine to save... well, anything at all. I now fully understand why Jabone did not want to come back here to fight the Amalites in the hive. I almost lost her, and at the end of the day I don't really care about anything except her."

"You know that storm was meant for you?"

"I do, though I can't imagine who would have sent it. Surely it wasn't Mother..."

"No it wasn't your mother; in fact, in all the commotion we had all forgotten. Harris!" He walked over. "Do you have that letter for Jestia?"

Harris handed the letter to Jestia. "It's from..."

"My mother." She could clearly see the kingdom seal pressed into the wax. When she'd been at Pearson Garrison everyone had gotten mail from home except her. Now she had mail from home and she found she was afraid to open it. She looked at Ufalla, who was trying to explain for the umpteenth time why she shouldn't be held responsible for the stupid things she said or did while she had a head injury.

Jestia looked at the note in her hand. Maybe she should go back and accept her role as heir apparent. Maybe that would be better, safer for her and Ufalla. And maybe safer was better and, *I don't want to be queen and I want to marry Ufalla not have her for a mistress. She's the love of my life not some dirty secret.*

"Open the letter, Jestia, I think you'll be pleasantly surprised," Jazel said, nudging her shoulder with her hand.

Jestia popped the wax seal off noticing that her hands were shaking. She opened the letter, she read it and then she read it again.

My dearest Jestia,

> *I hope this missive finds you well and happy.*

> *After much thought and soul searching I have come to the conclusion that I cannot in good conscience ask you to take a crown you do not want. Add to that the fact that you are a powerful witch and a member of the pack of the Marching Night, and I would be foolish to try.*

> *I give you, my brave girl, the greatest gift I can bestow. I remove you from your duties to the crown and give you your freedom.*

She wasn't aware that she was crying until Ufalla ran over to her, "Jestia, what's wrong?"

"Nothing's wrong, you giant oaf." Jestia laughed and handed the note to Ufalla then dried her eyes on the sleeve of her blouse.

Ufalla looked at her all smiles. "We can go home."

"We can all go home as soon as we fix whatever is wrong here," Jazel said.

Chapter Six

Tarius looked at the two notes sitting in front of her on the small table in their bedroom. One was a request for her presence at the castle. The other was a note from Jazel saying all was well and that they were starting to send out scouting expeditions in the direction she and Jestia felt the land was crying. Further Jazel said she didn't feel there was an impending battle. Which basically left Tarius with no excuse not to go to the castle. Darian was strong and healthy now, so she couldn't even use him as a reason.

But Tarius hated going to the castle. She hated the whole idea of people being put in charge simply because of their blood line, and she was sure she knew exactly why the queen was calling for her counsel.

Of course Jena rather enjoyed going because it gave her an excuse to wear beautiful dresses. Tarius had to admit she didn't mind at all seeing Jena all dressed up making every other woman look like an emaciated girl. Jena was of the Jethrik, a woman of curves and sensuality. She looked to where Jena was sitting on the edge of their bed combing her long, blond hair. She looked at Tarius and smiled reading her mind.

"So are we going or not?"

"We will go, but only for a few days. We still don't know what threat this crying land might be. We will take the rest of the Marching Night that can go with us." Because of course there were children to care for, gardens to tend, and animals to feed and milk. They were no longer just mercenaries. The Marching Night now had other responsibilities and while so many of them were off in the Kartik territories those responsibilities were spread thinner and thinner. "I wish we'd gone with them out to sea now."

"Just so you wouldn't have to clean your armor and get dressed up?"

"Well yeah." Tarius pushed the papers aside and turned to give Jena her full attention. She was beautiful always had been. Tarius wondered how long it was going to be before Jena figured out what she had done and how mad she was going to be when she found out. But if she hadn't figured it out yet maybe she never would. Tarius didn't care either way because she wouldn't undo it even if she could. "I love you. Every time I think I couldn't possibly love you any more than I already do, I do." She walked to the bed, took the brush from Jena's hand and started brushing her hair for her.

Jena lay wrapped in Tarius's arms. This was the Tarius only she knew. Tarius was never this openly gentle or loving with anyone else. Even Jabone as he grew older saw his madra as the Great Warrior. He felt her warmth but didn't really understand the depth of her love for him. Darian was wrapped up in it now just as Jabone had been. Tarius's love warmed and sustained them. Jabone had forgotten his madra's true nature.

As Jabone grew he heard the stories and knew all that his madra was and he forgot that Tarius's love flowed truer than her sword. He clung more to Jena because Jena wore her feelings on her sleeve while Tarius rarely showed her belly to anyone.

No, this part of Tarius was and always had been all hers. She understood Tarius in a way no one else really did.

"Tarius, will we go through Montero and get Jabone?" Jena asked.

"It is on the way; of course we will stop and get him and Kasiria." Tarius held her closer in that not-quite-uncomfortable-but-close way she had that somehow always made Jena feel like no one could ever hurt her.

The scouts had come back with nothing. Jestia and Jazel had decided they didn't know what to look for, so they were all going to look for whatever was making the land cry. Ufalla had no idea at all what they were talking about, but something didn't feel right. Since she now didn't feel like she was either going to fall over or puke, she didn't think it had anything to do with her head injury.

They hadn't brought any horses which meant they were on foot, and for the first time in her whole life Ufalla realized that her father really did have a rather serious deformity. The club foot didn't just look different, it *was* different, and walking for miles through the woods she could see was taking its toll on him though he didn't say a word.

"Jestia." Ufalla whispered in her ear. "Can you do something to help my father walk?"

"A strength spell," Jestia said, then cast it. Ufalla knew

she had because her father turned, caught Jestia's eyes, and smiled. Jestia smiled back.

"Thanks," Ufalla said.

"I owe him. This is the second time he has ridden in to save us. He and your mother have welcomed me into your family with open arms. If it wasn't for them I wouldn't have you, my one true love."

Ufalla groaned. Who would have ever in a million years thought she could get tired of Jestia professing her love for her?

They came to a river and Harris called a break before they crossed. Thirsty and wanting to save the water in their canteens, most of the troop started to go drink from the river.

"Stop! Don't drink it," Jestia ordered. She ran up to the stream. There was a hint of ice at the edges, but that wasn't why she told them not to drink it. Ufalla followed Jestia, and Jazel who was stationed in another part of their formation moved up to join them. Ufalla saw the dead fish before Jestia pointed them out, and there was a strange odor that had nothing to do with decomposing fish.

"The water is poisoned!" Jazel shouted back to Harris.

Harris and Elise walked up to join them. Harris looked from the dead fish to Jestia. "Why would anyone poison the river?"

"I'm sure I don't know, but the water isn't safe to drink."

"We don't need to cross the river," Jazel said to Jestia.

Jestia nodded. "It's flowing down. Whatever they are doing to the land is flowing down with the river."

Harris nodded. "We follow the river up then." He turned and cupping his mouth yelled, "Don't drink from the stream! The water is bad!"

When they started moving again the stench got worse. There were more dead fish and now other animals as well: wolves, rabbits, birds, and they even saw a bear—all dead. Everywhere they looked there were animal carcasses. A little further on and the water in the creek was actually discolored an ugly, reddish tint with an oil-slick rainbow effect towards the edges where the water was still. Ufalla had no doubt this was why the earth was crying. That this was what Jestia and Jazel were talking about. The land was literally bleeding.

Suddenly her father called a halt. He pointed in front of them, and through the trees they could tell that there was some vast clearing. He motioned for her to come up, and she did with Jestia nearly hanging onto her. "Ufalla, go ahead and scout..."

"No, I don't think so," Jestia said shaking her head.

"I'll go." Elise offered.

Ufalla shook her head. "I'll go. I'll not have my mother go in my stead because it upsets Jestia."

"Jestia, go with Ufalla," Harris said with a sigh.

"Jestia, you giant pain in the ass," Ufalla said. She started off knowing Jestia was right behind her and that it didn't hurt to be stealthy but that Jestia would be casting any number of different spells that would mean Ufalla would have to do something pretty stupid to get caught by anything or anyone. "You know he sent me because I'm a good scout, right? I don't really need a baby sitter."

"I'm not your baby sitter; I'm your partner, and I won't be left behind."

Ufalla was suddenly over her mad. She reached back and took hold of Jestia's hand and led her behind her to what she thought was a fairly covered spot. Then she pointed. An area as big as the capital city had been clear cut of trees. There was a giant pit in the ground, and everywhere they looked there were tailing ponds—all of which were leaking into the river. On the opposite side of the clearing from their position was a tent city. Between them and the tent city, Amalites with wheel barrows and buckets were hauling loads up the sides of the big pit and pouring the contents on a belt that was run not by horses but men. Then she saw something that made her blood run cold: Kartik men—all with whips and sword on their sides—yelling commands that the Amalites probably only half understood.

"They're mining for gold and they are using the Amalites for slave labor," Jestia said what Ufalla was already thinking. "What evil is this? To do this much damage, this must have been going on for decades. Our own people tearing a hole in the world, poisoning the water, enslaving other people—this is not what I expected."

"It explains why the earth was crying."

"Aye, but I was hoping to have some Amalites to kill not our own people."

On the outskirts of Montero Tarius called a halt and told the Marching Night to do whatever they pleased and to meet them on the other side of town at first light the next day. Then she and Jena—and the wagon holding the Katabull throne—rode on into Montero and right to Jazel's spa. But

Helen told them what Jazel had not—Jabone and Kasiria had moved to a small house on the outskirts of town.

Montero was only half a day's ride from the Katabull compound, but they had a new baby and they were trying to give their son and his new wife some space. Maybe they had given them too much space. Tarius was silent as they followed the directions Helen had given them.

The house was small but made of stone and well built. The yard was big, the obviously new sign over the gate said "sword lessons," and from the look of the earth in the yard many had already been given. Jena thought it was cute, but Tarius just frowned as she got off her horse holding their son cradled in one arm. She walked over and helped Jena off her horse with her free hand, not that Jena needed it just that Tarius always did it.

Tarius motioned for the two men on the wagon to stay put. Her face was set in harsh lines a child could have read.

"What's wrong?" Jena asked.

"Our son has not come home in months, and now it is obvious he has no intention of moving back home," Tarius said, pointing at the sign.

Now Jena wasn't happy either. "He wouldn't make this kind of decision without even telling us. Would he?"

"I'm pretty sure he has," Tarius said.

Jena watched as the door opened and Jabone walked out. He looked beautiful and more than a little shocked. "Madra, Mother, how good it is to see you."

"Is it then?" Tarius asked, looking with meaning at the sign.

Jabone opened the gate and walked out, hugging her first and then his madra. He moved to kiss Darian on the head.

"He has grown like a bad weed."

"That's what happens when you stay so long gone," Tarius said.

"Where are my fathers?" Jabone asked, and Jena realized, *he's not shocked to see us. He feels guilty.*

"Home. You know your fadra does not travel well these days. I'm sure he expects that his son will come home eventually."

And every word she is saying is to make him feel worse. To make him feel as if he has betrayed us because she can't stand it any more than I can that he just doesn't need or seem to even want us in his life anymore. But she'll never tell him it hurts;

she'll just let him go right on thinking she's just angry.

"Are you staying long?" he asked. It was hard to read whether he wanted them to stay at all or not.

"We are on our way to the palace to placate the queen over my recent bout of unrelenting I-don't-give-a-shitness-over-what-she-wants. So what's all this then?" Tarius pointed at the sign.

"Kasiria and I have started a sword training school here. We like it here. She likes it... It's more comfortable, closer to what she's used to. I like it..."

"Say no more. You've the right to live your own life."

The way she said it made Jabone look as if his madra had pulled out her sword and cut off his good arm. He looked at Jena, expecting her to say something to bend Tarius to his will, but how could she when she was just so hurt and mad herself? She looked at her grown son, then Tarius, and then finally at their baby, and all she could think was that Darian was going to grow up and leave them, too. Before she could stop herself she was just speaking from her heart.

"I knew the minute I saw that girl that I would lose my son. That Persius would finally have his twisted revenge, where he does something to us and then wants us to pay for it. She has poisoned you against us." The shocked look on Tarius's and Jabone's faces might have been funny if Jena wasn't so upset. "I told your madra that girl couldn't be with you, but she insisted I shouldn't and couldn't be the one to stand in the way of your love. Now you are gone to us and..." She looked at Tarius and accused, "This is all your fault."

Jabone looked at Jena in disbelief no doubt because in his whole life she'd never shown she was the least displeased with him and certainly she'd never yelled at Tarius in his presence. "It is no one's fault, Mother. I love Kasiria; she loves me. We made the decision together to stay here. We are a half day's ride away."

"Yet you have not been home even once in nearly six months," Tarius said.

Jabone gave Jena a wounded look. "I didn't know you hated Kasiria." He looked close to tears, and since Jena was already crying and because she knew how bad this hurt Tarius she didn't care and she was silent.

"Your mother doesn't hate your mate; she hates your mate's father," Tarius explained. "And like me she isn't pleased that you have chosen to leave the Katabull compound."

Not pleased! Our son has turned his back on us. He's left us and we didn't do anything wrong. Why does he have no loyalty to us? Because his loyalty belongs to her now. You lose your child when they find love. When they find someone to share their life with they are no longer part of yours. And it hurts, but it's not their fault. We have to let him do what he wants and maybe someday we'll matter to him again.

Darian started crying. Jena didn't even think just turned and held out her arms for Tarius to hand him to her. She needed to hold him, to comfort him, to be needed by him. She needed him to make her feel better.

Kasiria returned from town with a bucket full of food she'd purchased to find the Katabull throne stuffed into their tiny living room and the female part of her in-laws there with their baby. Tarius and Jena both sat on the throne, and from the silence in the room and the way everyone was just sort of not looking at each other, she knew they weren't happy with Jabone's plans to live in Montero.

They greeted her stiffly and without getting up much less hugging her the way they normally did. She knew this had nothing to do with being weary from their day's travel. No, it had everything to do with them blaming her because their son wasn't coming home. She glared at Jabone who shrugged as if he couldn't guess why. She was pretty sure that he knew she was ticked off because he was letting them think this was her idea. The truth was it was *his* idea not hers. She'd tried to get him to go home a half dozen times just to talk to them, but he wouldn't go because he didn't want to tell his madra what he wanted to do. And looking at the set of the warlord's chin she really couldn't blame him. Who in their right mind wanted to upset Tarius the Black? It was like poking some avenging god with a sharp stick knowing they wanted nothing more than to bite off your head and chew it up.

"Darian has really grown," Kasiria said.

"Yes," Tarius said stiffly.

"I can't believe you are this mad over where we choose to live," Jabone said to Tarius.

Tarius said nothing. Kasiria was surprised when it was Jena who broke the silence although she realized she shouldn't have been. All the stories told about them represented Jena as a woman who wasn't afraid to speak her mind and who knew how to get what she wanted. It was only Jabone that talked of her as if she were all sweetness and light and fragile beyond description.

"She's not mad; she's hurt. And she's not the one who yelled at you about it; I am. So if you have something to say, say it to me."

When Kasiria looked at Jabone he looked like he was on the verge of crying which was something you didn't expect from such a huge sword-wielding man.

"I'll just go make dinner," Kasiria said. She was glad that the kitchen was on the back porch out of the house and away from all of them. She realized it might be cowardly, but they were his parents not hers and she didn't see why she should have to be part of their argument. After all wasn't that supposed to be the big plus of having her own family on the other side of an ocean? Besides the truth was she sort of hoped he lost this argument and they had to move back to the Katabull compound.

She loved him and she loved the Kartik and she didn't really care where they lived, but she really wanted to train with Tarius, Harris, Jena, and Arvon. It had been a dream from her childhood, one she'd never thought could be fulfilled. Jabone was the one who had the need to separate himself from his famous family, not her.

She liked their little house and they were starting to get enough students that it felt like a real school, but it wasn't her dream to train fighters. Her dream was to *be* a fighter. It was pretty obvious from the looks on those two women's faces that having their son decide to live apart from them was breaking Jena's heart and was just unacceptable to Tarius.

"Can I hold him?" Jabone asked. Jena nodded and he walked over and took Darian from her. He looked at his Madre and started, "I know what you think..."

"Oh I don't think you do," Jena interrupted. "Your madra didn't want you to go to the territories in the first place and I talked her into letting you go so." She looked at Tarius. "I'm sorry for what I said earlier because as I thought about it I realized that it's all *my* fault." Then her attention was back on him, and Jabone found that he'd much rather deal with his madra's cool, angry scowl than his mother's obvious disapproval and hurt. "You want us to be there when you need us and then go away when you don't, and it's very hurtful, Jabone."

"That's not true! I don't want you to go away," Jabone

said. The thundering of his voice made his baby brother cry, so he rocked him and lowered his voice. "Can't it just be that I like it here? Ufalla and Jestia plan to live here; their parents didn't throw a fit."

Jena looked at him like he'd grown another head. "Really, son? Hestia forbade their union. Forget where they want to live; it's why they're at sea. As for Harris and Ellis, they have four children between two people. We only have the one between four."

"Until you had Darian," Tarius reminded.

"Yes until I had Darian." Jena looked at Tarius. "Don't you have anything to say to our son?"

"I think you've got it about covered. Ungrateful child breaking his parent's hearts, yadda, yadda, yadda." Jabone saw the hint of a smile playing at the corner of his madra's lips and felt he might actually live through this.

"I'm sorry I didn't come to visit and talk to you about this I just didn't ..."

"You didn't want our input. You want us to be happy with any stupid-assed thing you want to do as if it doesn't concern us at all. You want us to applaud and say, 'Oh what a wonderful choice.' Well we aren't happy with this, Jabone, and you can't make us be any more than we can order you to come back home and live with us."

In his whole life he'd never seen his mother this worked up about anything. He had been told by Harris and by his other parents that his mother was a hot-headed and passionate woman, but he'd never seen that. She'd always been infinitely patient with him. Then he realized something as he stared into her face. "Mother... You look much younger." His madra shot him a heated look, and then his mother laid into him again.

"Jabone, do you think flattery will make me change the subject?"

"I was just saying..."

"That you think I'm so frivolous that a compliment will make me forget that I'm hurt and angry."

"I never wanted to hurt or make anyone angry least of all you, Mother."

"That's another thing, Jabone. You shouldn't be like everyone else and think your madra has no feelings. Just because she doesn't cry and carry on at the drop of a hat doesn't mean she doesn't feel things just as deeply if not more so than the rest of us."

He just couldn't believe how mad she was. He looked at his madra, and she said in that *I am the Great Leader and wisdom spills forth from my mouth every time I open it,* tone she had, "She hasn't seen you for months. She's had all that time to think about things to say. She had to work at liking Kasiria in the first place, and now she feels like she's stolen you away from us. I don't think you have any idea how hard it is for us that what we want is no longer even considered in what you do."

Jabone nodded, though hearing her talk to him that way only made him more certain that he had made the right choice in moving to Montero. He loved her but he didn't want to be under her very-powerful thumb. "What if we visit regularly?"

"That would be a good start," Tarius said.

His mother looked at him and ordered, "You hug your madra right now."

He walked over and hugged Tarius with his free arm and then without being told he hugged his mother.

"I'm sorry, Mother."

Dinner had been a time of barely-edible food—as a cook, their daughter-in-law was a fine swordswoman—and clumsy conversation. Then they had said their good byes and gone to Jazel's spa. Helen fed them a wonderful meal that since they were still hungry they had no trouble at all eating.

Darian was now fast asleep in the nest Tarius had made him on the Katabull throne.

Kasiria had made a point of telling Jena how much younger she looked, and she thought it was just more flattery, but now she was looking in a full-length mirror in their room and she swore she looked like she was in her twenties again. There were no mirrors in their huts and few in all of the Katabull compound—not because the Katabull cast no reflection as was the rumor in the Jethrik where she had grown up—no, they had few mirrors because any time they looked at themselves they were really only seeing half of what they were.

She looked at herself more closely. Surely this much change couldn't be just because she was suckling an infant. Perhaps Jestia had heard her talking about how foolish she felt having a baby at her age and had put some glamour on her. But she didn't just look younger, she felt younger, and wouldn't she herself be able to see through any glamour?

"Why do you suppose he lets her destroy food when he

can cook and she cannot?" Tarius asked.

"She probably wants to cook for him, to take care of him. It's what we're taught in the Jethrik. Women do the cooking and cleaning."

"She's a royal, the servants..."

"Which is no doubt why she can't cook, but she still would have been taught 'women's roles' and 'men's roles'. Remember how I used to take care of you all those years ago when you were 'the man of the house'?" She looked at her reflection again. *So much has happened since then and yet I look the same, how?*

"Who would have thought that our son's leaving us would wound me deeper than the worst blow I have ever taken," Tarius said as she was undressing beside the bed.

Jena turned to look at Tarius, forgetting her own thoughts. Tarius's body was a testament to the great many battles she had fought. There were dozens of small scars on her arms and legs. Then there were the three big ones. When Tarius was only a child her throat had been cut and the scar had never faded. There was a scar that ran down the length of her face from a sword blow, the smaller one on her chin was part of the same blow, and the horrid scar where Persius's arrow had pierced her that still gave Jena nightmares. So considering all that Tarius's body had been through what she said had a great deal of weight.

"I would have thought it," Jena said softly. She walked over and wrapped herself around Tarius. She rested her head on Tarius's chest relishing her warmth. "I knew. And he's not really doing anything to us my love. He just wants to live his own life, and I just want to strangle him and that girl because of it."

"It's not you, Jena, that he wants to be free of, nor is it the compound. It's me. Only me. He wants to have his own life. He as much as told me he could never be his own man as long as he was beside me."

"After the battle in the territories he said..."

"Jena, you are the veteran of dozens of battles. You know as well as I do that after a battle emotions run deep. We often speak things we will forget later. In the heat of battle he was happy to be my son and fight by my side. Back home away from the fight he doesn't want to be constantly compared to me. He hates it when people say he is just like me."

"That is his fault not yours, and he's not doing this to hurt us; he's just young." She moved her head to look up at

Tarius. "Remember when we were young? The stupid things we did and thought and felt? We learned from our mistakes and did better, and he's got to do that, too. We can't shelter him from life, Tarius."

Tarius nodded. "That doesn't make it hurt any less."

"No it does not."

As they watched the mine it became more and more apparent that the Amalites weren't working because they wanted to. The Kartiks watching them work were whipping them, chunking rocks at them, and spitting curses at them. It wouldn't have been hard to get Kartiks to treat Amalites as if they were something less than human. After all, it was the way the Amalites had treated every race they had encountered when they'd been in power. Kartiks had a powerful hate of Amalites.

But these people were never in power. They weren't allowed to practice their hateful religion, and most of these were young enough they had no connection at all to the old Amalite rites and rituals. There was no excuse for what these Kartik men were doing. It was a very odd place for Harris to find himself—watching a situation trying to figure out how to stop the Kartiks and save the Amalites. He knew it must be even worse for the rest of the Marching Night. After all, he at least looked very much like an Amalite with his blond hair, blue eyes and light skin.

The Kartiks were dark-haired, brown-eyed and had a naturally dark skin color like rich honey. Most of the Marching Night were Katabull now, and the Katabull were even darker than the Kartiks, taller and thicker and with more reason to hate the Amalites. After all, the followers of the old Amalite religion just wanted to convert everyone else, but they actually wanted to kill every Katabull and had nearly succeeded more than once.

He didn't like it, and that only made him madder at the situation. He said as much to Elise. She nodded in agreement and handed him an open canteen. He took a swig and went back to watching.

Gold. The Katabull didn't understand the value put on gold at all. After all, it couldn't be worked into tools or weapons, nor could it be eaten. Money was only as good as the things you needed to buy with it. No one needed anything more than what they needed. Having more than you needed was a waste. Certainly they couldn't imagine anything was worth so much that you would destroy the land, the water, and the trees to get it. Since Harris had now lived amongst the Katabull most of his life he didn't feel the damage like they did, but it angered him just as much.

Gold was a foolish thing to spoil land over. Having never been rich, he didn't understand what people gained from having more than they could spend. Harris could conceive of no wealth that would be worth the carnage or the brutality he was seeing. He was a follower of the One Who Had No Name, had been almost from the moment Tarius had explained to him what she believed—or didn't believe was closer to it. These Amalites were not their enemy. Their old religion was a problem, but without it they were no different than him. They, like him, were part of all, and all was part of them.

They were only a few hours walk from the shore, and they had seen all they needed to see. "Let's go back to the ship and strategize. With a little planning this should be a quick and easy mission."

His orders were whispered through the ranks and they headed back the way they had come. He was second-in-command only to Tarius herself, so no one ever questioned him.

Chapter Seven

Tarius entered the Kartik throne room and was met with more than the usual pomp and circumstance. When she walked in with Jena by her side, her son on her hip, and the Marching Night behind her, she looked around the room and it was clear to see why. The room was loaded to the brim with royals. It was as she had thought; the queen wished her council in choosing a new heir.

None of them will rule as well as Hestia has, all are greedy and selfish. Jestia would make a much better queen than any of this lot, but only if they would let her be true to herself. Which they wouldn't because they are stupid and short sighted: rules within rules on top of stupid rules. Why will people insist on making rules that try to force everyone to fit into a mold that no one could fit into?

When they were all inside Hestia smiled. "I see you've brought your new son."

"Aye, we call him Darian," Tarius said and held him up for Hestia to have a better look.

"He is a fine-looking boy. Congratulations to you both and to the men of your household as well."

"Thank you," Tarius said as she lowered Darian back to her side. "Have you decided on a new heir yet?"

"I have not. As you can see there are many to consider. I would not choose without first speaking to the Great Leader of the Katabull people, the Queen's most treasured subjects."

And Tarius scanned the room doing just that—considering each one, noting which ones actually squirmed and which ones looked nervous. None of them could look her in the eye and hold it which didn't bode well for any of them being a suitable monarch. They all wanted to lead which meant that in Tarius's eyes none of them were fit to rule. But that was a Katabull belief not a Kartik one.

Tarius mentally dismissed them. Turning her attention once more to Hestia she smiled. "You do know that we Katabull have trouble being considered subjects."

"I had forgotten. Please accept my apology," Hestia said.

Ignoring all the other royals in the room she looked right at Hestia. "I tire of this show; I need to talk to you alone at once." There was a stirring and muttering amongst the other royals. Tarius growled and gave each one in turn a look that seared through them. They were quiet.

"Come then." Hestia rose and started for a door on the western wall. Dirk followed her as did Tarius and Jena. As Dirk was about to go in the door Tarius put a hand on his arm, stopping him.

"I need to talk to Hestia alone," she whispered.

"Of all the bloody cheek, Tarius..."

"Dirk, we have been friends for many years. We fought shoulder to shoulder in the Great War and I know your heart. It is not you I do not trust." She moved her mouth till it nearly touched his ear. "It is no secret, my friend, that you drink too much and keep a great many women. Drink loosens the tongue and makes us do things we wouldn't do sober. Lovers tend to tell each other things without thinking, and while I know you sober, no one truly knows a drunk man, and I do not know your whores at all."

Dirk knew better than to start an argument with her. He nodded and backed away.

They went into the room and Tarius herself closed the door.

"Really, Tarius, Jena is with us but Dirk is not?"

"Let us not mince words. We both know there is a world of difference between mine and Jena's relationship and yours and Dirk's. There is no easy way to say this, Hestia; there is a plot against the Kartik throne."

"But surely you don't think Dirk... He can't take the throne unless a hundred people die, and..."

Hestia knew all about Dirk's other women, so Tarius said, "I told him and now I'm telling you. It's not him I don't trust except that we all know he can't really hold his tongue; he drinks too much and is always whoring around. It would be far too easy for someone to get information from him."

Hestia nodded walked behind her desk and sat down. She motioned to the two chairs in front of her desk and Tarius and Jena sat. "I take it then that this plot against the throne is real."

"Jestia and Ufalla took off on a fishing boat to work the shores of the Kartik territories."

"I had figured it was something like that." Hestia smiled in spite of the grim nature of their conversation.

"I'm afraid it was an all-too-obvious plan," Tarius said. "Before the rest of the royals knew Jestia had been removed as a candidate for the throne a magic storm was cast to drive their ship onto the shore and strand them."

"Is Jestia alright?"

"Yes, but as you can see one or more of your candidates for the Kartik throne is trying to stack the deck in his favor. Since you are still young and will most likely live to a ripe old age the next question must be if they will drive Jestia into the shore of the territories to become heir apparent, what else might they be planning?"

They had counted fifty Kartiks who were guarding and working what looked to be about five hundred Amalite slaves—some of whom were children not much older than ten. They were using poison to separate the gold from the rock and letting it spill into the river. The Katabull had heard the Kartik men talking about how rich they were going to be. The Katabul also heard the land crying and they were more than ready to attack.

These people cared nothing for the land. All they cared about was the piling up of coin. It was a way of thinking so foreign to the Katabull that they couldn't begin to grasp why anyone would do such a thing.

Harris listened to the Marching Night talking and cursing and knew he wouldn't be able to contain them long, but he was waiting—waiting for word from Tarius. He would act without her go ahead if he had to but he preferred to have it and told the Marching Night as much.

He saw the bird flying towards them, Jazel lifted her arm and the bird landed on it. She took the note from the bird's leg and released the bird. She opened the note then handed it to Harris.

Harris read it quickly. "We attack at dawn. The Great Leader needs one of the guards left alive to be questioned."

There was a great roar of satisfaction from the Katabull.

Elise looked at him and smiled.

"What?" Harris asked.

"I just love it when the Katabull are happy."

"Well I'll take it over pissed-off Katabull any day," Jazel said. She quickly wrote a reply. Then reached into a small cage full of little blue birds she'd been carrying around. She drew one out attached the note and then let it go. "Fly high, fly fast, till you find the Great Leader at last."

Elise was sitting close to the fire on a chair that had been brought from the ship. Harris was sitting on a log close by. Ufalla and Jestia walked over to join them, and from their rumpled appearance he didn't have to ask where they had been or what they had been doing. Ufalla, all six-foot of her, walked right over and sat in her mother's lap, putting her arms around Elise's neck and resting her head on her shoulder. Her mother smiled and held her, wrapping her cloak around her daughter.

Harris laughed and shook his head. "Huge child, get off your poor mother."

"It's alright, father," Elise said, and held Ufalla tighter.

Harris just nodded and smiled. Twice now he had to gone to save his children and twice they had been alright. Yet he knew there would never be a night that he went to bed without worrying about one of them. And tomorrow he would take his wife and his child into battle and he would be more concerned with where they were and what they were doing than he would be with himself. As a warrior he knew that was a mistake; as a husband and a father he couldn't help himself.

Ufalla got off her mother's lap and moved to sit on the sand in front of her. He saw Jestia standing towards the back of the group watching Ufalla and Elise talk. She grinned as she watched them, but there was a hungry look in her eyes that had nothing to do with Ufalla.

Ufalla is mad in love with the girl, but Ufalla is literally Jestia's whole world. Harris stood up from the chunk of log he'd been sitting on and walked over to Jestia. He put his arm around her and pulled her tight to his side. "Thank you."

"What for? She was nearly killed because of me," Jestia said.

"She wasn't killed, none of them were, because of you. I have four children, Jestia. It's a great worry. But that one..." He pointed at Ufalla. "That one I never have to worry about because Tarius was right. As long as you're with her she's safe. More importantly she's happy. She loves you with all her heart and all her soul, and I never have to wonder if you feel the same."

"She's all I have."

He squeezed her shoulders. "She's not you know. You have us. In fact I'm sure Elise would let you sit on her lap." Jestia laughed and laid her head on his shoulder.

"You're the best father I've ever had," she said. "How are we all going to get back? One ship won't really hold us."

He hadn't even considered that might be a problem. He had assumed that with two witches around you could do just about anything. "Can you and Jazel not fix the ship and put it back in the water?"

"Fix the hull, yes, there is wood everywhere. It's a simple weaving spell; either of us could do it. It wouldn't take both of us. Pick the ship up and put it back in the ocean far enough away from the shore for it to float? Impossible. Nor can a witch change the tides. If we brought up a wind it would just as likely finish trashing the ship as push it back into the water."

He nodded. It was easy to forget that magic had limits when you saw and felt what Jestia could do. But it was like whatever she had done to him on the hike. It had helped him for several hours and then it was gone. Now he had aches and pains from the whole day's walking. The spell didn't stop his body from knowing it had been on a ten-mile forced march through the woods.

"With tomorrow's message I'll have Tarius send another ship. Part of us will stay here and the rest will go home."

"The whole of the Marching Night must return at once." It was Jazel who said it; Jestia just nodded.

He really hated it when witches or wizards said such things because what it meant was they had seen something that said the whole of the Marching Night would be needed in the Kartik, and that couldn't be good.

"We can't all go on one ship," Harris said. Even if they stripped the ship of all but the basics there wouldn't be enough room.

They all seemed to ponder the dilemma for a few minutes, and then Ufalla stood up and looked at all of them like they were the worst sort of idiots. "There are a hundred Katabull here."

"Exactly, and they are denser and bigger than humans," Harris said to his daughter, not understanding.

"There... are... a *hundred*... Katabull... here," Ufalla said more slowly as if to match their wit.

"Ufalla my love, we know how to count." Jestia said.

Ufalla sighed giving up on them. "A hundred Katabull have the strength of a thousand men. They can shove the ship back into the ocean if you can fix it. We can use trees for rollers, and they can roll it out as far as they can at low tide, and then at high tide..."

Harris hit himself in the head with the palm of his hand. "... it will float! Of course! In that case, Jestia, will you please fix the ship?"

"The spell has already been cast."

He watched as small trees and twigs started floating through the air towards the breached hull. It was fascinating to watch as the twigs attached to the wood of the ship, and then it was weaving and weaving thicker and thicker layer after layer.

"It will take hours," Jestia said. "But it's the only way to fix it right."

Harris sent a team of Katabull into the woods with axes to get several large logs to use as rollers. The rest of the Katabull spent the next few hours playing a game, ducking in and around the twigs as they flew through the air to the ship.

Ufalla had played with them for a while then she and Jestia had gone off somewhere. Harris wouldn't think about what they were doing because in his mind Ufalla was still his little girl and he didn't want to think about... well whatever they were doing all the time. He was sitting on a piece of driftwood looking out at the ocean as the sun was setting. Elise sat beside him and pressed a bowl of hot soup into his hands. She took good care of him, always had.

"I grew up with this kind of cold, but I'm no longer used to it," Harris said.

"It's miserable cold. No wonder not many Kartiks want to homestead the territories." Elise nodded and pulled her cloak around her tighter.

"Did you hear what Jazel said?" he asked.

"About the whole of the Marching Night must go home? Yes I did."

"What do you suppose she meant, Elise?"

"I don't know, but Jestia agreed with her. Ufalla told me that witches can't repeat a dream or it will come true. So they always know more than they can say. Which isn't terribly comforting when what they aren't saying is clearly more than what they are saying."

Harris nodded. That made sense. "It's why they talk in riddles." He smiled broadly. "I wonder why the Katabull do."

"I'm sure I don't know." Elise grinned back. "Ufalla is everything I hoped she would grow up to be, and I cannot lie, Harris I just love Jestia. She is so funny and just seems like she belongs in our family."

"But."

She put her lips almost on his ear and he smiled. The Kartiks really didn't have any concept of personal space.

"Ufalla doesn't need us anymore. They didn't need rescuing and even this mission they could carry out by themselves. We are just extra."

Harris nodded. It wasn't anything he hadn't already thought of. "It means we have done our job and raised a strong, independent young woman who has chosen her mate well. She still wants us, though, and maybe that's better."

Chapter Eight

Tarius picked at the food in front of her and only half heard Hestia as she filled her ear with the qualities both good and bad of the possible heirs to the Kartik throne. Tarius knew she should be paying attention but no matter how many times she tried to tell herself it wasn't so, she still felt like Jabone had turned his back on her. She looked at Jena where she was trying to talk their fussy baby into sucking on a piece of fruit. He wasn't having any part of it. Her food forgotten, she reached out and put her hand on Jena's arm.

Jena looked at her and said, "He's not interested in fruit yet, and he's hungry."

"Then feed him," Tarius said, not understanding the problem.

Jena shook her head. "Not in a room full of people."

"You flop your tit out in front of the entire Katabull Nation but here..."

"Exactly. *Here* I'd like a little privacy."

"Give him to me and I will see if I can calm him down while you eat your dinner."

Jena handed Darian to her and for the moment he was calm. She stood him on her knee and started cooing at him.

"Have you heard a word I've said, Tarius?" Hestia asked.

"Some," Tarius said. She kissed the baby's forehead which made him laugh. "Yes, such a good baby. Tell your madra say, I'm Tarius the Black's son. Don't give me some piece of fruit, put a tit in my mouth..."

Jena slapped Tarius's on the arm. "And that's enough of your mouth, Tarius."

"You do realize that you sound like a huge fool when you baby talk," Hestia said to Tarius.

"Thank you," Jena said, and started eating her dinner. She looked at Tarius's plate. "You need to eat."

"I've told you talking politics gives me indigestion."

"I think it is closer to the truth to say that our oldest son's decisions have given you indigestion."

"What is happening with Jabone?" Hestia asked.

"He has decided to live in Montero instead of with us in the compound." Jena said.

And the tone in her voice let Tarius know that Jena was

only slightly less bothered about this than she was. Hestia obviously didn't understand the problem. Having never felt a natural bond with her own children she couldn't know the pain of separation. One of hers had died and life went on. Frankly Tarius didn't know what would become of her if she lost one of her children. She refused to think it or she would live in constant fear. But she had Jena and as long as she had Jena she was sure she could survive anything. Hestia had no one to turn to. Even now as they sat feasting Dirk was chatting up some woman who sat to the left of him. He was ignoring Hestia and all matters of state. Tarius had sent a written message to Hestia sending she and Jena's and the whole of the Katabull Nation's condolences over Katan's death, but she couldn't bring herself to speak the words.

She has one child who ran from her and one in the ground and no one to love who loves her. I could never live like that. I don't know if that means she is blessed or cursed.

She moved Darian to lie in the crook of her left arm, and he turned his cheek towards her breast. He buried his face in the gambeson she was wearing as a shirt and searched with mounting frustration for something that wasn't there.

Hestia laughed and Tarius smiled and picked him back up to stand on her knee before he started screaming. He looked at her and frowned, scrunching his whole face up and she laughed at him. "In a minute, little man, let your poor Madra eat."

"So Tarius what made you two decide to do that?" Hestia pointed at Darian.

"Jazel said Jena might be healed from her miscarriage and that if she was going to have a child it would have to be soon." It worked because after all Jena had told Hestia all about her miscarriage years ago.

"And is Arvon..."

"No, Dustan is his father. Jazel didn't think it would be good for Jena to have a huge Katabull child," Tarius said. "Jabone had decided to go to the territories, we were about to be childless, it seemed like as good time to try as any and here he is."

"He's beautiful, Jena," Hestia said.

"And he's hungry." Jena pushed away from the table and stood up. She took the baby from Tarius and kissed her on the cheek. "We'll be back in a minute. I'm going to go find someplace private to feed him."

Tarius nodded and Jena adjusted her dress and her baby

and started out of the room. "I swear your mother lies as easily as she tells the truth," she whispered to Darian. He was not happy, but he wasn't crying. Recently he had started to make this noise that sounded a whole lot more like griping than crying, and he was griping at her now. She knew where she was going; the palace had a beautiful garden in its very heart not far from the feasting hall.

As she walked in she closed the door behind her and all the noise of the feast hall was completely drowned out by the calm in the garden. There was a natural waterfall about ten feet tall that was placed towards the back of the garden. A small creek ran from the waterfall and through the length of the garden, disappearing under the castle wall on the other side. The castle completely encircled this garden, but it was open to the sky and the plants were lush and in full bloom. The smell was wonderful and her hungry baby stopped griping and started to coo.

She kissed his head then found a bench close to the falls and sat down. The sound of running water was certainly preferable to a room full of people all talking at once. She felt a little guilty then because she'd used a hungry baby as a means of escape. Tarius was still trapped inside listening or at least half listening to Hestia go on and on about this royal and that royal. The Katabull in general and Tarius in particular hated the entire idea of royalty.

It took Jena a second to get her dress pulled down into a position so that she could feed the baby. When she did instead of having to put him to her breast he nearly pounced on her. He hadn't liked all the strange noises and people, but he'd been a trooper about it till he got hungry. She sang to him as she fed him the way she usually did and the way she had sung to his brother.

Jabone, no longer her child. A grown man and so changed by love and battle she hardly knew him. Where had the time gone?

She really wanted to blame Kasiria for the way their son was acting, but they had stopped by his home on the way out of town to try to get them to come with them, and it was clear it was Jabone not Kasiria who didn't want to join them. They hadn't parted badly, but they certainly hadn't parted well. Tarius had been mostly silent which Jena was sure told Jabone more than he wanted to know about how she was feeling, but Jena found that once again she could not stay her tongue. Her parting words to him were, "You owe her better than you are giving."

She realized only now why she was so infuriated with him. He was hurting Tarius and didn't seem to care at all. He was hurting her feelings, Jena could take. She could even understand why he wanted to do what he wanted to do. But the fact that he wasn't even trying to find the words to put his madra at ease, that he instead made it obvious he was only seconds from lashing out at her was unacceptable. Still Jena wished she'd said nothing at all. She didn't like being at odds with Jabone. It felt foreign.

Darian went to sleep still eating. It was a lot for a baby, different places and different things and most of two days on horse-back and then at a great feast. It was a lot for her, too. She just wanted to go home and she had wanted to come, so she could imagine how Tarius must be feeling. She decided to tell Tarius as soon as she got back that they should leave first thing in the morning and let Hestia take care of her heir problems herself.

Darian had finally quit sucking and was fast asleep. She wiped his mouth and pulled her dress into place. She had no intention of going back to the feast. She stood up and started to carry Darian around the garden still singing to him. They'd never traveled further than Montero when Jabone was this little. There had never been any need. He had grown up in a time of peace and as such they had just stayed home. He was a toddler when he first came to the castle. He'd always liked to come, had always enjoyed it. He had run around this garden just soaking it all up, and as he got older he and his friends would swim in the creek and play in the falls.

She was afraid Darian was not destined to grow up in a time of peace. Certainly he hadn't come to them in peace.

Tarius ran her hand down her face. "Are there any of them that don't have something that doesn't make them unacceptable to you? Are there any of them that you trust?"

Hestia was thoughtful for a moment then answered, "No and no."

"And why am I here?" Tarius asked.

"Well it would seem with what you told me there are a couple of reasons. But I asked you here because you are the wisest of the Katabull and I have never known anyone who knew the nature of people better than you do."

"Do not flatter me, Hestia," Tarius said with a sigh.

"I wouldn't. I am telling you the truth. You asked why I

called you here and that is why. You were right about Jestia, and..."

"My own son detests my name, Hestia. I'm not sure I am right about anything anymore."

Her stomach was rumbling yet she just couldn't even think about eating. She picked up the glass of juice and swallowed it in one gulp. She could feel the Night as it started to course through her body. She looked at Hestia in a panic. It had tasted like juice but it wasn't at all, which meant it was magic.

"I have drunk wine," Tarius said.

"That's alright."

"No it isn't; there is a plot afoot, Hestia." She looked around quickly. Jena wasn't back. "Radkin, Rimmy go and find Jena." She couldn't stop the change or the drunkenness; it was coming quickly. She looked at Hestia even as she could feel herself changing. "Jadon, Rea come get me. Hestia, they need to stick me in the strongest cell in the castle."

"Tarius, what the hell..."

"I will be the beast, and I will be drunk, and if anything has happened to Jena or my child no one in this castle will be safe."

Jena heard something and turned. There were five of them, and it was obvious they were about to attack her. She kicked one and dropped him.

"Tarius!" She didn't have her sword and she was holding her baby. Or at least she was till one of the men jerked him from her arms. She kicked him in the leg and as he fell to his knees she tried to grab Darian back but felt a blade against the back of her neck. She stopped short.

She looked at her son in the man's arms, and he looked back at her, his face a mask of fear and trust. Suddenly he was exactly the same to her as Jabone had ever been.

Radkin and Rimmy ran in the door, fully catted out and swords in hand, but they stopped cold when they saw the situation.

"That's right!" One of the Kartik men yelled towards them. "You'd best stand your ground unless you want to take your Great Leader her wife and child on a sword. Drop your swords and leave."

Radkin and Rimmy looked at her, and she nodded. They dropped their swords and backed out the door.

They tied Jena's hands behind her back and put a bag

over her head. Then she was thrown over someone's shoulder and her baby was screaming.

"I swear for every tear my baby cries I will shed a drop of your blood!" Jena yelled at her captors. "You had best let us go. Tarius will hunt you down..."

"The Great Leader isn't herself, and by the time she sobers up you will be so far away she will never find you."

Hestia led the way herself, and it was all Jadon and Rea in full Katabull form could do to shove Tarius into the cell and lock the door. Rimmy came running into the room, and before he could speak anything that was left of Tarius disappeared in a fit of Katabull rage. She started slinging herself against the bars, and Hestia wondered if even the cell could hold her.

"No! No!" Tarius screamed. "Rimmy?"

He obviously didn't want to tell Tarius.

"Rimmy!" Tarius demanded.

"Five Kartik men took Jena and the baby."

Tarius started roaring. Hestia had heard the Katabull roar in battle before but nothing like this. It made the hair stand up on the back of her arms and neck and broke her heart at the same time.

"Tarius, they wouldn't dare to hurt her, and nothing of the kingdom shall be held back to return them to you," Hestia said.

But the thing in the cage was drunk and more frightened and madder than even Tarius the Black had ever been, and there was no calming her.

Hestia knew watching Tarius that before this was over any way it went the streets would run with the blood of her people.

Chapter Nine

The ship had finished mending during the night and now Harris could not distinguish the patch from the rest of the hull. They had laid the logs out all the way to the water, the witches were using their magic to hold the ship upright, and now a hundred Katabull put their backs into it and were easily rolling it into the ocean, moving the logs from the back to the front over and over again as they cleared. Finally the ship was as far in the water as they could get it and with high tide only a few hours away it would soon be floating free. They armored up and headed towards the mine.

With Jazel casting speed from their rear and Jestia casting stealth in front of them they moved at a quick, silent pace that would have been more than a little unnerving if Ufalla wasn't getting used to having magic all around her. She thought it odd that in their Katabull form you couldn't use magic against a Katabull, but you could apparently use it *for* them all day long. She made a note to ask Jestia about it later.

They so badly outnumbered and outclassed their combatants that Ufalla would have felt sorry for them if it wasn't for the fact they had torn a huge scar in the land and poisoned a whole river. She even tried to feel bad for the Amalites, but she found she couldn't. She didn't think people should use other people for slaves, but it was too soon after having fought the Amalites in the hive for her to have real compassion for them. When the Katabull boiled onto the open land around the mine and the Amalites threw down their tools and ran off screaming into the woods she felt justified. Here the Katabull were risking their lives to save them from their tormentors, and they were still so prejudice that they thought the Katabull were there to kill them and eat their babies.

Stupid Amalites. There were only fifty Kartiks there, and they also saw the Marching Night and started running.

They should have known better.

Jestia looked to where they were running and said, "That one." One of the men went floating into the air. The rest weren't that lucky. They killed them all, stripped their armor and weapons, and then threw them in their own filthy hole in the earth.

Jestia and Jazel started casting. Jazel was doing one incantation after another, but Jestia was silent and still. Ufalla watched in amazement as the sludge from the containment ponds moved to the hole to splash on top of the dead and then the poison in the river lifted up out of the rest of the water and started flowing uphill into the pit till the water flowed clean. Then all of the equipment was flying into the hole. Then dirt and rock was being pushed back into it.

Sorak jumped over a huge rock sliding towards the hole. He held four bags he had taken from a shed that now lay in the bottom of the pit. "Hard to believe anyone would do all that for this." He handed one of the sacks to her father, and he nearly fell over from the weight of it.

"This isn't the worst of what they have done for it," Jestia said. "This is clean enough." She turned unceremoniously and started walking in the direction of the ships.

"A few more hours and we could have this mostly back the way it was," Jazel said, obviously not understanding.

Jestia turned and looked at Ufalla, and it was clear Jestia was distressed. Jestia then turned to Jazel. "Can you not hear it?"

"Hear what, Jestia?" Jazel asked.

Jestia ignored her, instead looking at the Marching Night. "Tarius is roaring."

No one questioned her. Ufalla certainly didn't as she nearly out ran even the Katabull getting back to the shore. Now she knew why Jestia had insisted that the whole of the Marching night must return. If Tarius was in trouble then it would take all of them.

They had stuck her in a wagon. She knew Darian was with them and alive only because he kept screaming. They were moving fast. She tried to keep track of how far and how many turns in an attempt to maybe find out where they were taking her, but she couldn't concentrate because her baby was screaming and she could hear Tarius roaring. Jena had only ever heard her do it a couple of times in battle, and it had never been like this, but she knew it was her. There was a man beside her holding her arm tight enough it was going to leave a bruise.

"I don't know who you are working for or what they are paying you, but do you hear that? That is my mate and she will not rest till she has tasted your blood. If you let me go and do no harm to our baby there may still be hope for you."

"Shut up, Jethrikian whore!" he spat back, but she could hear the fear in his voice.

"I have been a lot of things but never a whore," Jena said. Tarius roared again. "Do you hear her?" He was silent. "That is the sound of your doom if you do not release me."

"I said shut up!" He shook her hard.

Darian was still screaming. "Hush, son. It's alright. Your mother will kill all these men."

"Speak once more and we will throw your screaming baby from this wagon."

Jena fell silent deciding she would kill this dog first... and not cleanly. They rode till she could no longer hear Tarius. It was a long ride, several hours. She was shoved off the wagon then hauled to her feet and pulled along. Darian was somewhere right behind her. They walked for what seemed like an eternity but was probably only a couple of minutes then she was shoved into a cell. They untied her, took the hood off her head, and handed her Darian who stopped crying, started to whimper, and then lay his head on her shoulder as the door to the cell was closed.

"There, there my baby," she whispered to him. "I won't let anything happen to you." The cell had metal bars for a front and stone walls on three sides. In the back wall there was a small window that also had metal bars on it and openned to the outside. There were some filthy blankets on the floor but no bed and no place to do one's business. "We'll be fine."

Two of the thugs who had grabbed them were standing guard across the hall watching her. One of them she knew was the one who threatened to chunk her baby into the street, and she gave him a look that would make a frog's blood run cold. "I am going to kill you myself," she said with conviction.

He laughed at her. "Do I need to point out that I'm out here and you are in there?"

A tall, thin man wearing the clothes of a royal walked into the hall then. He looked her up and down. "I hope my men weren't too rough with you." She recognized him from the feast. He was one of the many people who hoped to become heir to the Kartik throne. He was older than the others, which would have meant he wouldn't have been in the running. "My, you are a pretty thing but then you always have been the Great Leader's very stunning, exotic out-country lover. When I saw you tonight I thought the stories really do not do you justice."

"What did you do to Tarius?"

"What makes you think I did anything to the Great Leader?" he asked innocently.

"Because I am here and you are still alive."

"I'm afraid she is in her cups."

"She doesn't drink," Jena said.

"Well I'm sure that Hestia is getting a big dose of why she shouldn't drink right about now," he said to his fellows. Then all three started to laugh.

This mess—none of it was Tarius's fault—but Tarius would never see it that way. Jena found herself more worried about her mate than she was herself and her baby.

"I told these idiots and now I'm telling you. You had better let me and my baby go or..."

A man in brightly-colored red robes came rushing into the hall and she didn't have to ask if he was a wizard because it was obvious by what he wore and the way he carried himself. He was Kartik but shorter than most, plumper, and he was homely. His dark green eyes glared at the royal turd.

"What in the name of all the gods have you done, Rorik?!"

"Secured a future of wealth for this country and the crown for myself," Rorik said. "And you are not supposed to be in this part of the keep. You should have kept to your tower."

"How could I do that when I saw your thugs dragging that woman and her child across the yards? Do you know who they are, Rorik?"

"Of course I do," Rorik said. His tone said he wasn't used to anyone having the balls to stand up to him. "This is the Great Leader's woman and child."

"No, you moron. The Great Leader is wise and reasonable, cool headed. That is Tarius the Black's woman and child, and Tarius the Black is a vengeful demon. You have brought death upon your head."

Rorik smiled then. "Only my head, cousin? Why would I have you cast a spell to make wine taste like juice? What did you think I was going to do with it?"

"I... I don't know. I didn't think which is totally my fault. But I never thought you'd do something like this. Not something so brutal and cowardly as grabbing a woman and her infant. Not something as suicidal as taking Tarius the Black's mate. Don't you know, can't you look at her and see? This woman is your age, does she look it? She does not because the Katabull has split the length of her own days with her. If you injure her in any way, Tarius the Black will feel it, and she will be at your door in minutes with the whole of the Marching Night."

"We all know of the war lord's undying love for her mate. My whole plan has been built around that. As long as I have Tarius's woman I own her. She will have to do anything I say. The brat is just a nice little extra. If she doesn't do what I say I will kill her child first and then its mother."

Jena started to make a retort, but she didn't have to; the wizard said it much better than she ever could. "Rorik, if you touch so much as a hair on that infant's head much less his mother's Tarius the Black will not stop killing till there is no one in your house left alive and there is no one to bury your bones."

"See here wizard, watch your tongue!"

"I am speaking the truth, Rorik. Let this woman go so that we might all live. Perhaps it isn't too late to turn the hand of fate."

"Oh it is way too late my friend. I will take the throne and discredit the Great Leader in the bargain, and when the whole of the Kartik army is turned against her and the Katabull I will feed Tarius's child to my dogs and lay with her woman."

"If you think the Kartik army can stand against the whole of the Katabull Nation, then you are mad. If you think the army *would* stand with you against Tarius, you are not only mad but an idiot as well. I will have no further part in your schemes. No amount of money and no position are worth having your guts torn out by a righteously angry Katabull."

"I didn't think you would." He nodded his head.

The next thing Jena knew Rorik's thugs grabbed the wizard, opened the cell door, and threw him in. The cell door closed with a clang behind him and then the lock was shut.

"You know, my dear cousin Eerin, I have always said your problem is that you lack ambition. Now I think it is more that you lack vision and the stomach to do what needs to be done. I don't think we'll be needing your services for a while. You know until some time in a cell makes you a little more pliable." Rorik turned on his heel and left.

Jena reached a hand down.

The wizard looked at her. "You'd help me?" She nodded silently and he took her hand. "Were it not for me he could not have captured you."

"I'm not so sure. I'm sure when Tarius realized what was happening she immediately sent Radkin and Rimmy. They didn't make it in time, and Rimmy is the fastest Katabull I know." Jena shrugged helping him out of the floor. He wasn't any taller than she was. Hardly the picture she had of a Kartik royal much less a wizard.

The fight, the rough ride and the terror of the whole thing had left her feeling spent. She started to sit on the floor and heard the magician intone, "My, she's had a really rough day. Make a chair. Do what I say."

A chair appeared behind her and she sat down. "Thanks, but how about a good ole get us the hell out of here spell?"

"You see now that's the problem with dealing with people like you who have only ever had contact with the most powerful of witches and wizards. Your expectations are unreasonable. I am not a very powerful wizard. I've had minimal training and most normal wizards have weaknesses of some kind. I'm afraid I have many, and one of them is cold iron like the bars this cell is made of. I can neither cast anything outside this cell while I'm in it nor do anything to it."

"Then where did the chair come from?" She knew things just couldn't appear they had to come from somewhere.

"I made it from the blankets." Seeing the face she made he added, "Most things seem to come clean in a transformation."

Their two guards seemed more preoccupied with some game they had started playing with dice on the floor than they were with watching them. Still she turned the chair before she started to nurse her baby. He was still just sobbing, and she knew it would help restore his faith in the universe to be held close and have warm milk in his belly. It wouldn't hurt her faith, either.

He started drinking and by playing with his toes she was even able to coax a smile out of him. "Feed my baby to the dogs," she muttered. "We'll see who feeds who to the dogs."

"I swear to you on all the gods that I didn't know that Rorik meant to target the Great Leader," the wizard said at her back.

Jena wondered how long her dreams and days would be haunted by the sound of Tarius roaring in pain. She thought of something. "Are you the one that set the storm on Jestia?"

"You know about that then?"

"Yes, we sent part of the Marching Night and Jazel to rescue them…" Jena stopped and her blood ran cold. "He knew she would. He knew we would be low in numbers and witchless. Did you know, wizard?"

"I had the storm drive Jestia's boat into the coast. Rorik didn't know that she was no longer the heir apparent. I didn't know, how could I know, that Tarius would send the Marching Night to rescue them?"

"By using what little brain you have. He knew." Jena realized then just exactly who Rorik was and why he looked so familiar. Tonight was not the first time she'd seen him. Rorik was Hestia's own brother. He had taken the throne briefly while Hestia had gone with them to fight in the Great War. He thought he knew how Tarius would react. He was clever even if he wasn't very bright because if he understood Tarius at all he would know that the wizard was right and kidnapping Jena and one of Tarius's children was like signing his own death sentence.

When they first attacked her and then when they were threatening her baby she had been terrified. But now she remembered who she was and their threats meant next to nothing. Tarius would not stay drunk for long and the minute she was sober she would figure out exactly where they were. When she did she would come and save them. And there was something else that she knew that moron Rorik couldn't know.

The Marching Night would soon be on their way home with *both* of their witches.

Chapter Ten

Tarius's breath came in quick, sharp blasts; no doubt because she knew her nightmare was real. This was driven home when, fully awake, she realized her face was pressed against a cold, bloody stone floor. There was only one other time in her life when she had felt so utterly helpless and completely alone.

Jena was gone, her baby was gone, and it was her fault because she'd been so preoccupied brooding about Jabone that she'd let Jena take the baby and go off by herself. Tarius had known one or more of the royals were up to no good but never in a million years would she have thought one of them would go so far as to dare to touch her beloved. She couldn't imagine that anyone could be so blinded by greed for money or the crown that they would stare death in the face. Anyone in the known world had to know that if they so much as touched Jena or looked wrong at her baby she was going to kill them.

It was clear to her that whoever had done this thought he could outwit her. He thought himself clever. He thought he could do this to her and walk away. He was the greatest of fools.

Her head was pounding and her body ached. She rolled onto her back and stared blankly at the ceiling.

"Great Leader," Rimmy spoke softly. "They took them alive."

"If I didn't know that, I would not have had your children put me in this cage. I would have ripped this kingdom apart and cared not at all who I killed or when I died. Jena is worth nothing to me dead, and so she is worth nothing to them dead." As she said it her heartache and pain were more tangible than her rage, and she could feel her rage clawing at her insides. "They mean to hold her for ransom, but not for money. So what price will they ask for my greatest treasure? Being morons what will they do if I do not comply?"

Rimmy unlocked and opened the cell door. It was only then that she realized she was naked and that her armor and clothes lay in useless, torn shreds all around her. She looked quickly for her sword and found it stuck in a timber that hung above the doorway to the dungeon.

Rimmy smiled and looked from the sword to her. "It very nearly hit me."

"I'm sorry. So what were you doing to incur my Katabull wrath?"

"I asked you to calm down. Thinking about it now it was a rather idiotic request."

"Indeed." Tarius got to her feet. She ran her hands across her face and through her hair. When she looked at her hands they were covered in her own blood. She walked out of the cell, and Rimmy handed her a pair of pants and a shirt. She quickly threw them on.

"Do we have any idea who took Jena?"

"No."

"Do we know where they took her?"

"No, but Radkin followed her."

"Radkin would not have let the trail run cold." She was the best of the Marching Night's trackers.

"But she will not return to tell us where Jena is," Rimmy said.

Tarius didn't have to ask why. She knew, and it gave her some comfort. "If I had been the Katabull this never would have happened."

"Is that why you are keeping this form?"

"Yes. Why would I go back to a form that would let this happen to them, to me?" Tarius hissed. "Why, why did I let her go alone?"

"We have always been safe here, Tarius," Rimmy reminded.

"But *they* were here—those people who think they are better than others just because they have the right blood. I knew at least one of them was up to no good and I forgot what people will do for the love of money."

"But to take Jena and the baby? No one—not you or I or anyone else—would have thought anyone would so pray for death as to do that."

"Is Hestia safe?" Because he was right, and going after Hestia wasn't nearly as mad as taking Jena and Darian.

"Yes. She ordered all the royals and their retinue removed from the castle. I actually tried to fight her on that because I thought we'd want to question them when you were yourself again, but her argument was sound. She said you were here and out of your mind and she was here, and if one or more of them was so crazed at to take Jena they wouldn't be above assassinating one or both of you. Further she said if some outside force was attempting to take down the royal house she didn't want the entire royal family in one place. Hestia is in her private quarters under double guard, and I have left Rea and Jadon with her as well."

"What do I do? Rimmy, for the first time since I was a youth I have no idea what to do."

Rimmy was silent. Finally he took in a deep breath and spoke. "I know you remember the last battle of the Great War, but maybe you have forgotten how I reacted when Tweed died. Radkin grabbed me and made me go with you and for a long time I hated her for that. But because she was able to stay my rage and pull me back I found new love. I was able to raise my children and enjoy my life. All the life I've had from that moment to this is only because I listened to Radkin when she spoke and I let her pull me along behind her.

"I am sure that the look on my face that day was the very same look that is on yours today. But my dear friend I don't think anyone can contain *your* Katabull rage. Maybe Jena could, but I don't think anyone else would have even the chance of making you see reason. Your loved ones are not dead, Tarius. I think if you want to make sure they stay alive you'd better slip on the form your soul is most able to control, and that isn't the one you wear now." He reached in a pocket of his pants took out a vile of blood and handed it to her. "Here."

She took it reluctantly and looked at it for a long time. He was right. The Katabull was more linked to the hind brain than the front, and though she'd never admit it aloud he was also right that she had less control over her Katabull form than most did. All it wanted right now was to see the streets flowing with blood. It had been hurt and humiliated and it wanted revenge almost as much as it wanted her loved ones back. She didn't feel like changing back; she was going to have to work at it. People thought a Katabull drank blood and immediately changed back, but that wasn't the case. If it were they'd never make it through a battle without being human again. Without blood they couldn't change, but even with it she had to have the desire to change back. She felt like letting the rage course through her being reckless and just killing any and everybody she thought might have something to do with taking Jena and Darian.

Rimmy knew her. He knew she couldn't really think like this. At least for the moment it was her head that would serve her best. Later on she would release the Katabull.

She drank the blood and concentrated on taking her human form, but it still took her several minutes to change. Rimmy took one look at her human face and winced.

"So I do look as bad as I feel," Tarius said.

"Oh aye."

"Come on."

He followed her. At the doorway she reached up and pulled her sword out only with an effort. She went to sheath it but remembered her sheath was among the rest of the stuff she'd torn up last night.

"Your other armor and sheath wait in your room."

Because of course she always carried a spare with her since you never knew when something was going to blow out.

Tarius nodded. "Go get them and bring them to Hestia's throne room. I must speak to her at once."

Radkin had grabbed Jena's sword and her own horse, and when the wagon drove away from the castle fast, she had followed. She'd had to stay far enough back to be undetected but close enough not to lose the trail. It was no trouble for her; tracking was her forte and she could clearly hear Darian screaming. But then a man stumbled out of a tavern drunk and spooked her horse. By the time she got the horse back under control the wagon was nowhere in sight. She could barely hear the baby and couldn't be sure which direction the sound came from. But she was sure she knew which direction it was going, so she ran the horse to catch up. When she didn't catch up to the wagon she knew she'd taken the wrong road, so she had doubled back and gone the other way as fast as the horse could run.

It was an unforgivable mistake, and she'd not seen the wagon again. She could tell that she was on the right road, though, because she could smell Jena. But then it started to rain and there was another fork in the road. She dismounted and sniffed around. Guessing more than deciding the right fork was the way they had gone, she jumped back on and started riding again.

I'm no good to anyone, she thought. *My pack is counting on me and I have let them down.*

Her children were grown and no longer needed her. Rimmy had joined with Hared ten years after the Great War had taken Tweed. When the last of the children were grown Hared and Rimmy had moved into their own hut. Then it was just she and Irvana and they planned to live a long, happy life together enjoying the freedom of having finished raising their children and looking forward to someday playing with their grandchildren.

It was not to be. Irvana got a wasting sickness that Yri had no medicine for and that Jazel had been unable to cure with potions. Not even the springs helped.

Radkin had cared for her day and night as she watched the light fade from Irvana's eyes. Irvana died in stages over the course of a year, and Radkin had mourned her in stages as Irvana lost this function and that function, so that as she at last died Radkin's first emotion was relief that at least Irvana wasn't in pain anymore. Relief was quickly pushed aside by crushing guilt, and then there was just despair and emptiness followed by praying for death for most of the last two years.

It just didn't make any sense. Radkin was the fighter; she was the one who took chances. In fact she was wild and reckless on good days. She'd lived through dozens of battles with barely a scratch. Irvana could defend herself but she'd never had either the desire or the skill to go into battle. She had stayed close to home, gardened, taken care of their goats, their chickens, and their cubs. Tweed had died first and then Irvana and so two of their children were without birth mother or father. That Tweed had died was no surprise. That they all hadn't died in that battle that day was a small miracle. But Irvana was never in any danger and now she was as dead as Tweed. Why then was Radkin yet still alive?

When Tarius announced there were Amalites in the ground in the territories, Radkin thought that this was the reason she was alive—to fight that battle. Rimmy was going so were two of their children. And when in Katabull form her sword and face were once again bathed in the blood of her enemies she felt alive again. When she saw the spear she could not stop rushing for her face she thought that she would die in glorious battle, but then that idiot Jethrik daughter-in-law of Tarius's, that crazy Kasiria, jumped over the shield wall and killed her attacker. She had to thank her but felt like cursing her instead. Once again Radkin found herself going home without a scratch, and her love was just as dead, and she just didn't know why she was still alive.

When she ran into that garden with Rimmy by her side and saw the men grab Jena and the baby she thought, "This is why I am still yet alive to save Jena and Darian." But now she wasn't sure she'd gone the right way and if she lost Jena, if she couldn't find her, no one would ever forgive her. In that case was she only alive to cause other people as much pain as she felt?

Oh Nameless One Who Knows All, please let it be the will of All that is that I find Jena. It would be better that I had died a hundred times over, better that I had never been born, than I should let down all whom I love and who love me in our hour of need. Please One Who Has No Name, if I have earned any favor help me find Jena.

She got off her horse and sniffed the air and now the scent was strong. She was not only on the right trail, Jena was close.

Darian started playing with the front of her dress, and she woke with a start remembering instantly where they were and how inappropriately dressed she was for an abduction. The wizard had turned the uncomfortable chair he'd made from filthy blankets into an uncomfortable mattress. He slept behind her with his back against hers. She looked and their guards were asleep as well. Darian had a huge smile on his face, and he was looking up towards the barred window at the back of the cell.

When Jena looked up to see what he was looking at, Radkin in her Katabull form was looking back at her. It was only then that she realized the bars at the back of the cell were at ground level to the outside. Jena got up carefully and walked to the window. "Am I ever glad to see you. Can you get me out of here?"

Radkin shook her head. "You are in some sort of huge keep and it looks like there are at least five hundred fighters here, maybe more. It's odd, though, I have not seen a single female fighter. Now I think about it I haven't seen a single woman. Of course I haven't actually been inside. I've already tried to pull the bars free and they will not budge."

"You will not believe the horrid things these thugs have said they would do to my baby. Let's see if Darian will fit through the bars." He wouldn't, and the more they tried the more perturbed he got till it looked like he might start crying. They certainly didn't want that because the last thing they needed was for the guards to wake up and see Radkin. Jena held him close and rocked him to calm him down. "Go get Tarius."

Radkin shook her head.

"Radkin, you have to go get Tarius."

"No, the Great Leader will find us. I will not leave your side, Jena. I will protect you and the baby. That is what Tarius would tell me to do, and... here... I have a plan."

Two guards forced the woman to her knees at Roric's feet. "We caught her sneaking around the grounds."

Rorik looked at her armor and the many earrings she wore and knew she was one of Tarius's people, part of the Marching Night and high ranking, too. But if she were Katabull she would be Katabull, and these men never would have laid hand on her. Still he was worried.

"Are there any more of you here?"

She didn't answer just stayed on her knees looking at the floor.

One of the guards grabbed her by the hair of the head and held her face up. Obviously the woman had put up a fight.

"I asked you a question."

"Did they find anyone else?" Radkin asked flippantly.

"I ask the questions here, girl."

"You may ask all the questions you like. I will tell you nothing."

They started to hit her, but Rorik raised his hand. "Don't waste your energy. She'd sooner you killed her outright than tell us anything. Take her and throw her in the cell with the others. Who knows but that she might prove to be useful. We may need to send the Great Leader a body part to make a point, and it would be a shame to mess up my pretty new Jethrik wife before I even got to use her." He glared at the woman but spoke to his men. "When we are chopping off her fingers one at a time we will see if she has anything of interest to tell us."

The woman before him glared at him. She wasn't afraid; she was mad, killing mad.

He turned to his aide who was standing beside him. "Go to the captain of the guards and tell him to sound the alarm. Check the grounds inside and out. If Tarius finds out who I am or where we have her woman and brat, losing our bargaining tools will be the least of our worries."

Tarius—even human Tarius—didn't like to wait; she was a person of action. Give her something to fight, some way to strategize, and she would be fine. They knew Jena and Darian had been taken in a wagon the tracks of which would be impossible to distinguish from any other wagon tracks, but the Marching Night cast the bottom of their horseshoes with a skull pattern. The distinctive pattern it left made it easy for them to track each other if they were separated. So Tarius and the Marching Night were looking for Radkin's trail. Unfortunately the rain during the night had washed nearly all the tracks away, and they couldn't find it.

Still they kept looking mostly because there was nothing else to do. There were just so many roads into and out of the capital city and only so many places to go. Eventually they had to find Jena, but Tarius was afraid she didn't have that much time.

There was nothing for Tarius to actually do but stand around and worry. She was talking to the queen's witch who in Tarius's opinion was worthless or at least she was pretending to be. At this point Tarius didn't really trust anyone not to have ulterior motives. "Can you not do some finding spell?" Tarius thundered.

"I would need something to go on."

"What about something of Jena's or my son's?" Tarius asked.

"I'd need something from her captors."

Tarius sighed, frustrated and angry. "Jadon, take this useless witch to the garden and see if you can find anything she can use."

They left. Hestia looked at her from her throne and said, "I know you have heard the expression you can get more bees with honey than you can with shit," Hestia said.

"Yes I have, but shit is all I have right now." Tarius ran her hands over her face and through her hair again. "You can't trust any of these people, Hestia. Does she really have no decent finding spell or does she hope not to piss off whoever is behind this plot so that if they take the throne they will be indebted to her? Or worse yet is she part of it?"

"I trust my people, Tarius, as you trust yours."

"Then you are a fool, Hestia. My people have stood shoulder to shoulder with me in battle. We live together, we have the same lives, and I know them. I know who is partnered with who and all their children and grandchildren by name. Who is sick, who is dying, and who has buried their loved ones. You don't know these people Hestia, not any of them. They live *around* you not *with* you. One of your people that you trust took Jena and my baby, and why do you think they did that Hestia, why? What do you think they will ask me for?"

"I have no idea," Hestia said.

"Well I do. You are not safe, and you are wrong to trust any of them. Two of the Marching Night will continue to guard you."

Hestia seemed to be ready to tell her no, but the words died on her lips and she nodded. Tarius saw the bird flapping at the window and ran over and opened it. The bird landed on her arm and she took the note from its leg, but when she released the bird out the window it flew right back to her. She read the note quickly.

"Rimmy, write this." She waited for him to find a qwill and paper. She leaned next to him and whispered into his ear and he wrote.

"So what's this Tarius, now you don't even trust me?" Hestia said.

"I do not trust them, Hestia, any of them!" Tarius roared. "Be happy I don't send for the whole of the Katabull Nation to fall on the throats of your kin. You have never known love. Do not pretend for even a moment that you know what I'm feeling or what I might do if anything at all happens to Jena or my baby. If something happens to them you had better hope that you didn't stand in my way of doing what I thought was right. If something goes wrong you'd better hope that I'm the only one to blame and not you." She turned her attention back to Rimmy and he handed her the note. Tarius fixed it to the bird's leg and held it up towards the window. "Find Jestia," she said, and the bird took off in the direction of the Katabull compound, so she was sure she had done it right.

"What did the letter say?" Hestia asked.

"I would tell you if you really needed to know."

"Now see here, Tarius," Dirk started. "How dare you talk to the queen in that way?"

Tarius closed the gap between them in three huge strides, picked Dirk up in one hand by the front of his shirt and held him in the air in spite of his efforts to hit and kick her. When he saw the look in her eyes he stopped trying to get free and was still.

"You have no regard for her at all. You only yell at me because you take it as a personal affront to you when I do not bow down to her. How dare you talk to me as if I believe that any person is better than another simply by the fate of their birth when you know that is only the crap you believe and not at all what I believe. We are all the same, you and me and her. One of *yours*, not one of *mine* has committed a great crime against *me* and not *you*. I trust Hestia, but I'm not so sure you aren't part of this plot, so I suggest till my family is whole again that you stay out of my face."

He nodded silently, and she set him back down. She walked over to Hestia and whispered in her ear. "Jestia and the rest of the Marching Night will soon make port." Hestia nodded silently being more interested in Tarius's reply to them.

Tarius took hold of Rimmy's arm and left bringing him with her though he would have followed without any incentive. She showed him the note and he nodded. Finally there was something she could really do.

Chapter Eleven

The man they had let live hadn't been much help. Jestia put a truth spell on him. He knew a Kartik royal was behind the open-pit mine operation but had no idea which one. He did know the name of the man who had hired them all, who had brought them the equipment and poisons to run the mine, and who took the gold back to the Kartik.

The Kartiks working the slaves had all been living in the territories. He said there weren't enough jobs and the land was hard to work. The task masters were paid a high wage as well as a percentage of the take. Apparently they'd had no problem getting Kartiks to take the jobs which was more than a little distressing, but they were all just hired bullies, so none of them knew anything about the real operation or where all the gold was going.

As far as any of them knew the man who hired them had gone back to the island a month ago and wasn't due to return for several weeks. By which time they would have twice as many bags of gold as they had now. The mine was apparently very rich.

After they had gotten all they could from him Jestia had lifted him from the spell.

"What should we do with him now?" Sorak asked.

Harris had looked towards the shore. "We can still see the beach; let the water decide his fate."

Sorak grabbed the man and lifted him from the deck of the ship.

"I... I can't swim."

"Well then I suggest you learn," Harris said, and Sorak tossed the screaming man into the ocean where he shrieked and cried until either they were too far away to hear him, he had started swimming, or he had drowned.

"Imagine, a Kartik who can't swim," Elise said, clicking her tongue.

Jestia had written the note and sent the bird, but it had been nearly two days and she was starting to worry. Jazel was on the other ship casting spells to speed their passage and she was on this one doing the same, but magic could only ever take you so far. They would turn a three days' journey into two days, but they could do no better.

Why wasn't the bird back yet? Had she screwed up the spell? Had a cat eaten the bird?

"What's wrong?" Ufalla asked at her shoulder as she looked off the bow into the horizon.

"Still no sight of land, and if the spell I did on the bird was going to allow Tarius to send the bird back to us... It should have been here by now."

Ufalla nodded. "What do you think is wrong there?"

"Something unimaginable," Jestia said. A cold chill ran down her spine. As if talking about it had brought it, she finally saw the bird. She put out her arm and seconds later it landed. She grabbed it and removed the note, read it, and her face went white.

"What?" Ufalla asked. For answer Jestia handed the note to her. Ufalla read it then ran with it down the length of the ship to her father. She handed the note to him and even from where Jestia was she could see Harris's face turn red with rage. Harris and Jena had grown up together; they were like siblings.

"Listen up!" Harris shouted and every eye was on him. "Jena and the baby have been kidnapped. Tarius orders the whole of the Marching Night to the capital city. As soon as we land we will saddle up and move out."

Muttering was at a near roar, and almost immediately Jestia could feel their outrage and fear for their loved ones. Yet it paled in comparison to the despair she knew radiated from Tarius the Black. Why did Tarius's pain feel like it was her own?

Ufalla brought the note back to Jestia. She took it, put a spell on it, wadded it into a ball and tossed it at the other ship. She saw Jazel catch it effortlessly then heard the other witch's voice in her head mind speaking to her. *I was afraid it was something like this.*

Jestia was just glad they weren't dead. She hadn't been sure till she'd read the note. She mind spoke as much to Jazel.

Harris walked up to them then and asked her, "What do we do?"

Jestia was a little shocked that he was asking her. "We are doing all we can do now. We will do what we have been told. We will gather the whole of the Marching Night and go to the capital post haste."

"Why would they take Jena?" Harris asked.

Jestia didn't even have to think about it; she knew. "Because they think it's the only way to control Tarius." What they didn't know and couldn't possibly understand was that no one could control Tarius the Black.

Tarius hadn't gone far from the palace when a beggar approached her. It was well known that she often gave coin to beggars, but today she was on a mission and in no mood.

"Great Leader."

"Go away," she growled.

"But a man paid me to give this to you." He handed her a note and she took it with a trembling hand. She read it then stuck it quickly into her pocket. She glared at the beggar and he cringed.

"Who gave this to you?"

"A man."

Tarius took the beggar by the front of his shirt with both hands and shook him till his teeth rattled. "Don't play me for a fool, man. I'd as soon bite your throat out as look at you. Which man gave it to you?"

"Just a man. I didn't see his face. He wore a hood." He whimpered.

"From where did he come and where did he go?" Rimmy demanded.

"I was at the Temple of the Morbidius Obesitus." Reading the lack of recognition on their faces, the beggar said, "He is the god of feasting. They give away food there. I didn't see from where the man came, but he gave me a bunch of money and said to wait here till you might come out and then give the note to you. I've waited a long time. From the temple the man walked towards the east."

"And where is this temple?"

The man pointed.

Tarius sighed. If he went east from there he would be going towards the palace, which wasn't going to help them find Jena.

"If you are lying to me, I will hunt you down and none will find your bones!" Tarius bellowed and she let him go. He took off running. Tarius started mindlessly moving in the direction she'd already been going with Rimmy right behind her.

"What did the note say, Tarius?"

"Nothing I wasn't expecting."

"Which was?"

"They have Jena and Darian and will release them only if I kill the queen."

"That's what you were expecting?" Rimmy said in disbelief.

"Really what else could it be?"

They had brought them some horrid swill for breakfast, but had left them a bucket of water and a dipper which was good because Radkin was a mess. Jena had torn off a piece of her dress and soaked it with water. She cleaned the cuts on Radkin's face and hands.

"Why did you let them beat you to a pulp?" she whispered.

Radkin smiled. "I gave as good as I got, and I had to make it look real, didn't I?" She looked over at the wizard where he was having some sort of heated exchange with one of the guards. "Is he alright?"

"Yes. I think he's just a dumbass which seems an odd combination with wizard."

"Yeah, crazy is more what we're used to," Radkin said. She was sitting on the mattress and Darian was asleep on it beside her. Radkin reached out, touched his foot and petted it. "I'd say I can't imagine what Tarius might be going through right now..." She winced as Jena hit a particularly sore spot.

"Sorry," Jena said.

"It's alright. I was moving, and I've been through this enough to know to be still. Anyway I know what Tarius is going through because I know what it's like to have the one you love most be attacked by something and not be able to just go kill it. To feel like you can protect everyone but the one you cherish most. But Tarius will have her day." She was suddenly far away.

Jena kissed her on the forehead. "We all love you, Radkin, but I understand that it isn't the same." She finished cleaning Radkin's wounds.

"She wouldn't live a day without you, Jena," Radkin said.

"She tells me that all the time. I don't know why you all think that is comforting in any way. Besides we all know it's not true, Radkin. We never speak of it because she won't allow it, but I'm human and she is the Katabull. She will live decades after I am nothing but dust."

Radkin looked at the sleeping baby then as if he had all her attention, and Jena suddenly remembered something curious the wizard had said the night before. Jena stood up and looked to where he was still talking crap to the guard.

"You, wizard, quit wasting your time with that dunderhead and come here please." He looked at the guard, threw up his hands and walked over to her.

"None of them will listen to reason. They are about to die in the most horrific way and yet none of them will even so much as upset Rorik."

In that moment Jena could not care less. "You said something last night that confuses me. What did you mean when you said Tarius had split the length of her days with me?"

Radkin didn't even look up. She just continued looking at the sleeping baby, so Jena was pretty sure that whatever it was Radkin already knew.

The wizard smiled. "You mean you really don't know?"

Jena shook her head no.

"The Katabull are magical creatures with a nearly three-hundred year life span. Whatever life your mate had left she split with you. It would have taken a very powerful spell caster."

"Hellibolt." Jena hissed. Tarius had gone off with him after the battle in the cave. It wasn't unusual for Tarius to have covert meetings with witches and wizards so Jena hadn't thought a thing of it. She looked accusingly at the back of Radkin's head. "And you knew."

"In hours you lost over twenty-five years. I suspected..."

"No you knew."

Radkin looked up at her. "I asked what she had done and she told me. If you had asked she would have told you. She almost lost you that day. If it hadn't been for Kasiria and her cursed blade you would have been dead. And I know why Tarius did it because I would have done it for Irvana in a heartbeat. Half my years not to be alone? What a great gift." Seeing the look on Jena's face she added. "She doesn't want to live without you; I don't see why that's anything to get mad about."

"It isn't the first time she's done something that directly affected me that she did without asking my permission." Jena wanted to be mad, but she didn't really have time for it because then the wizard, no doubt in an effort to prove he wasn't the dumbass she thought he was said, pointing at Radkin, "She's no human woman." Then pointing at Darian, "And he is neither your son nor your mate's." So all he really did was prove that he was a huge dumbass who didn't know when to keep his big mouth shut.

Jena turned and growled at him. Though she wasn't Katabull she had learned a pretty mean growl. "He *is* my baby. Tarius has promised to split anyone who says otherwise."

The wizard nodded. "He does have your eyes."

Tarius looked at the bloody, mangled corpse. They had spent most of the day finding this man and when they did he was lying over the end of his own bed cut to ribbons and several days dead. "I'll give the bastard this, he's good at covering his tracks," Tarius said. Rimmy walked out of the room and she followed glad to be away from the stench and the flies.

"How many days did he give you?" Rimmy asked.

"Three," Tarius said. "I don't know if it will be enough time for the Marching Night to get here, and if we don't know who our enemy is much less where he's holding them it won't matter anyway. I mostly need Jestia. May The Nameless One help me, who'd have ever thought so much would rest on that girl's head?"

The boat docked and then they were assembling every member of the Marching Night. The Katabull who were not of their pack would be taking care of the children and the chores of the pack of the Marching Night. When Tarius said ALL of the Marching Night she meant *all* of them, and when they heard Jena and the baby had been kidnapped some of them were armored up, on their horses and on the road before Harris could finish talking.

Ufalla was getting her and Jestia's horses ready and packing their gear. She looked up and saw Dustan and Arvon walk out of their hut with gear. They were obviously arguing about something, and it was clear by the scowl on his face that Dustan had lost. Arvon set his chin, limped over and got up on his horse, and then Dustan got on his and they spurred their horses into a gallop and were gone, rushing to catch up with Ufalla's mother and father.

She looked to where her family huts sat not a stone's throw from Tarius and her family's. The anger in her boiled up and she wished for the thousandth time since she was born that she were the Katabull. Tarius and Jena were her god parents. She had grown up with Jabone. In her mind there was no separation; they were one family. They had taken Jena, so they might as well have taken her own mother.

She could guess why Arvon and Dustan had fought because she knew them that well. Arvon wasn't aging like a Katabull. He was half human and he was aging like a human. He was ten years older than the Great Leader and his leg from the looks of it probably should have been taken off at some point. Even with powders and potions he was in pain most of the time, and they all knew that he used too much of the powders. It was hard for him to ride and worse for him to walk, but perhaps hardest on those that loved him was the fact that all the powders he ingested made him quick to anger. He took ever more of them in an effort to feel more like his old self and didn't seem to realize that all they did was draw him ever further and further from who he was.

Dustan was in his armor and had his horse ready so obviously there was no question he was going. He loved Arvon, knew he wouldn't have much more time with him, and he wanted every minute he could have. He wanted Arvon to stay home. Arvon was enraged because he knew what Dustan no doubt wasn't saying—that Arvon was not fit enough for a fight. Dustan should have known that Arvon couldn't stay. Tarius and Jena were his family, too.

Arvon was going which meant as they rode out he was second in command only to her father. Ufalla had the misfortune of understanding exactly how both men felt. Arvon didn't want to be left behind. Dustan wanted to protect Arvon, yet Dustan didn't have the nerve to tell Arvon he took too many powders. Ufalla found herself once again wondering about the stupid shit people chose to either fight over or to ignore. Dustan tried to make Arvon stay behind which no one should have expected him to do, not when Jena and his child were in danger. Yet he said nothing about Arvon abusing the powders even though he had to live with the effects of that every day.

Jazel had cast a speed spell on her horse and headed for Montero only minutes after they had docked. She needed to get herbs and potions she might need for the mission. She would pack quickly and join with them as they rode through Montero. There would be no stopping. They would ride through the day and night and hopefully reach the Capital by first light. Jazel was not part of the Marching Night, but this wasn't the first time she had agreed to fight with them.

"Hurry, Jestia! Everyone is leaving," Ufalla urged.

Jestia was basically ransacking Yri's apothecary. At least that was what Yri kept yelling. Jestia called out to her from inside the hut. "Mixing potions and powders isn't something I can just rush through, Ufalla. I'm going as fast as I can. I could use a nice pot of tea... and have you noticed I haven't accidently made a teapot in days?"

"Yes, I rather miss it," Ufalla said thoughtfully.

"Me, too." Jestia sighed. She showed up in the doorway a few minutes later with saddle bags filled nearly to the point of busting and put them on her horse. Yri walked out with saddle bags nearly as full and glared at Jestia.

"You might at the very least put things back the way you found them," Yri grumbled.

"Alright," Jestia said.

The Katabull medic must have felt the magic at his back because he turned, looked inside then turned to Ufalla and said, "That's a little unnerving."

Ufalla nodded her understanding. She often found it hard for her mind to balance Jestia the powerful witch with Jestia the woman she loved. It had been far easier to embrace Jestia's power when all she could do was throw a few minor spells and have a prophetic dream every once in awhile. It was harder when Jestia was throwing spells that fought storms and threw balls of lightning without even speaking.

Jestia got on her horse and looked down at Ufalla. "Well hurry up let's go."

Jena glared at the guard as he pushed three bowls of slop through a narrow slot between the bottom of the cell door and the stone floor, but it was the wizard who spoke his displeasure.

"Could you not bring us food that smells a little better than horse shit?" Eerin groaned.

"Change it into something better," the guard said with a laugh and walked back to his spot against the wall.

"Yes, wizard, change it into something better," Radkin said from where she was pacing the cell, rocking Darian. He had been fussy but of course the minute Radkin took him and basically started treating him more like a sack of feed than a baby he seemed perfectly happy. Of course he was used to a Katabull woman tossing him around like a sack of feed. As she thought it Jena's chest literally hurt. She was worried about herself and her baby, but she was more worried about Tarius. "Jestia would be able to make a six-course feast from that," Radkin added.

"Again I say you people are jaded where spell casters are

concerned. I can't make food. Well I can, but I have to actually make it... and well I'm not really a very good cook. I make a fine pot of tea... of course I don't always get to drink it."

"Why's that wizard?" Jena picked up one of the bowls of slop and saw what might be a piece of carrot floating in it. She didn't think about it just drank it down. She couldn't afford not to eat because she had a baby to feed.

"Often when I steep a pot of tea I turn around and it's gone. Vanished. It will come back and be mostly empty. Once it came back in a pile of shards."

Jena and Radkin looked at each other and said at once, "Jestia's teapot."

Jena smiled. "Well, she said it had to come from someplace."

"The princess has been drinking my tea?"

"Aye," Radkin said. "Many of us have drunk your tea. You do steep a good pot."

"Thanks," he said and sighed. "It seems my tea has had more adventures than I have."

"Eerin why would you help Rorik?" Jena asked.

"Greed mostly, and an overwhelming fear of being beaten to a pulp by men three times my size who delight in nothing so much as causing other people pain," he said. "And, well... he is my cousin and he has employed me for two years while I did mostly nothing. Rorik said there was much gold in the territories just ripe for the taking. He said Hestia was short sighted and would keep the kingdom poor but that he would bring about a golden age of prosperity. Mostly he promised to make me rich. I'm not good at much, but I'm a decent weather wizard. He said if we pushed Jestia's ship into the shore of the territories and stranded her there until the queen could choose another suitable heir then all he had to do was kill the queen and he would be king. That is kingdom law; I looked it up."

"His plan was to kill Hestia and you helped him?" Radkin hissed. She stopped and turned to Jena. "Here hold this baby. I'm going to kill him."

"No you hold the baby. No one's killing anyone." Then Jena turned to glare at the wizard. "You were alright with a plot that included killing Hestia?"

"Yes."

"Why?"

"She has always been very rude to me. When I was a child she used to call me Eerin the earwig."

"Now will you hold the baby so I can kill him?" Radkin demanded.

Jena smiled at the bigger woman and then said to her in a whisper, "If Tarius knows the kidnapper wants Hestia dead, she will figure out who has the most to gain and she will find us."

Radkin nodded. Then she glared at the wizard. "You stranded part of my pack in the territories, you got my leader drunk so your boss could kidnap Jena and Darian, and now I find you were alright with his plans to kill the queen. I don't like you, and if you so much as burp wrong I will split you."

The wizard nodded his understanding then said, "No offense meant, but what is the origin of this 'split you' thing? What does it really mean?"

Radkin looked at Jena, and it was obvious Radkin didn't know. Tarius said it and so most of the Marching Night used the expression. Jena knew where it came from. Surprisingly more Jethriks than Kartiks did. "In the battle of Riksdale in the Jethrik, they say that Jabone the Breaker killed five hundred men. That's probably an over estimate, but what is well documented is that at one point he hit a man so hard that he split him from the top of his head right down through his nut sack. From that day on if anyone angered him he told them he'd split them. Tarius learned the saying from him, and we all learned it from her."

The wizard made a face and Radkin looked at him and smiled. "Cross me and I'll *split* you."

Chapter Twelve

Jabone heard them coming. He pushed away from the table where he'd been suffering through his dinner and stood up.

"What's wrong?" Kasiria asked.

"Listen," he ordered and she did.

"What is that? It sounds like an army on horseback."

"That's not just any army, that's the Marching Night." Jabone quickly walked out of the house Kasiria by his side and looked down the road. He could just make them out. "The only time I have seen them, heard them in this number, was when we went to fight the hive in the territories. Only my madra could have called the whole of the Marching Night and what could have happened in the capital that she would call them..."

"We must prepare to go with them," Kasiria said.

"Aye. You get our gear. I'll get our horses ready."

They were already in their armor and on their horses waiting when the first of the Marching Night rode past.

"What is going on?" Jabone yelled at them. But they were going faster than normal horses could move, and he could feel the energy of the spell.

When he saw his fathers and Harris and Elise, he spurred his horse up beside his fadra and wasn't too surprised when his own horse started moving as quickly as all the others. Kasiria rode in right behind him.

"Gods and spiders!" She cursed as her horse started unexpectedly running.

"Fadra, what is going on?" Jabone yelled over the sound of the horses. Arvon cut him a look but said nothing. Jabone knew he couldn't have spoken to his mothers already, so he didn't understand why he was angry with him. "Fadra, what's wrong?"

"Someone has taken your mother and your brother. Tarius has called for the whole of the Marching Night. Perhaps you and your woman should stay here."

Jabone almost fell off his horse. "My mother? They took my mother."

"And your brother," Dustan said, and it was clear from the look on his face that he wasn't happy with Jabone, either. "Your fadra is right. You and Kasiria should stay here."

"It's my mother that has been taken. My own mother. I will not stay here. Madra said all of the Marching Night; are we not part of the Marching Night?"

Arvon didn't look at him but kept his eyes straight ahead. "I don't know, son. Are you? You have abandoned us. I know Tarius's intention was to take you and Kasiria with them and yet here you are. Perhaps if you had been with them all of this might not have happened. But you didn't have their backs. And for what reason? Do you think it is some great secret you despise our legend? That you wish we weren't your parents?"

"That is not true," Jabone insisted. "I just... in the compound I will never be more than just her son."

Arvon turned an angry face to him. "You will always be her son. You think moving to another town changes that? Do you think the people of Montero don't look at you and say that is Tarius the Black's son? You should be proud of who you are and where you came from." He turned away from him looking straight ahead again. "I am very disappointed in you."

Jabone hung onto his reins in one hand and ran his other hand down his face. He slowed his horse to let his Fadra get ahead of him and Kasiria rode up beside him.

"Are you alright, Jabone?"

"Someone has kidnapped my mother and my little brother, and my fadra blames me. What do you think?" he snapped. He took in a deep breath and let it out. "I'm sorry. My mother was displeased with me when she left us, Kasiria. We did not part badly, but we didn't part well. They wanted us to go with them, and I didn't want to go. If we'd been there maybe we could have stopped them. And why didn't I want to go Kasiria, why?"

Kasiria didn't bother to say because he knew she knew; he had told her.

"Because at the palace everyone knows I'm Tarius's son. To them no matter what I accomplish no matter what I do I will always and forever be just her son. My mothers were right to be angry with me and my fathers also have every right to be mad. I have left my family's belly open to our enemies only to serve my ego."

Jena looked at Radkin and snapped her fingers making everyone including the guards jump. "We both speak Jethrik," she whispered.

"Yes, and speaking a different language is always a useful skill when one is being held captive." Radkin rolled her eyes.

In Jethrik Jena said, "It is if our captors don't speak it."

Radkin popped herself in the forehead with her palm and answered in the language of the Jethrik, "Of course. What a giant dunderhead I am."

"Do you think the wizard knows it?" Jena asked.

Radkin looked covertly to where he sat on the mattress, a confused look on his face. She smiled back at Jena and said, "If he knows what we're saying he's a lot smarter than I'd give him credit for. Still to be on the safe side I think we should just kill him."

"I think he might be useful," Jena said, continuing their conversation in her native tongue.

"Well he does make pretty good tea." Radkin smiled.

"I'm sure he must have some spells that might be useful in escaping. If he looks like he might tell them anything we don't want them to know, just reach over and snap his neck." Because of course all members of the Marching Night were experts at Simbala, the Kartik martial arts, and Radkin was Katabull so the maneuver was just as simple for her as Jena made it sound.

Radkin nodded. "It will be my pleasure." She looked down at the sleeping infant cradled in her left arm. She could lay him down but she didn't want to. If their speaking in a foreign tongue was bothering the guards at all they weren't showing it. They were bent over a small stool playing some card game. "I'm pretty sure I could break that lock as the Katabull. Killing those two would be no problem for us."

"But could we get out of here, Radkin, just the two of us with Darian on one horse?"

"That rather depends if we can trust that wizard and if he really *can* do anything more helpful than brew a nice cup of tea. You're supposed to be the level-headed one, Jena."

Jena laughed. "Really, since when?"

"Unless it looks like we're in imminent danger I think our best bet is to wait for Tarius and the Marching Night. But I think we need a plan for when they get here as well as one for if they don't."

"You know what would be helpful for starters? If I wasn't wearing this fancy gown; if I had more practical clothes." Jena turned to the wizard and in Kartik asked, "Wizard could you make this worthless gown I'm wearing into britches and a shirt?"

He looked her up and down and nodded. "The pretty dress just gets in her way. Pants and a shirt the soldier's way."

In seconds Jena was standing there in a simple britches and tunic. "Thanks." She turned back to Radkin and they started to strategize.

Jabone was worried and brooding. It wasn't that Kasiria didn't understand how dire the situation was or that she didn't feel for him, she did, but the truth was that being in armor again and going to a fight was feeding the warrior inside her. Life in Montero was pleasant and beautiful and she loved Jabone, she really did. But all her life she'd ached for battle and now that she'd literally tasted the blood of her enemies she was all the more ready for another fight.

She had trained for two years at the Sword Masters' Academy and that had just seemed like waiting and waiting to do something real. And then she had been given command of the Kartiks at Pearson Garrison and there was more waiting. Finally they had gone out and fought, got their asses handed to them, and had to be saved by Tarius the Black and the Marching Night. She had nearly been killed, but Jestia's spell had not only kept her alive it had kept her from really feeling the impact of her near-death experience. When she had ridden in as part of the Marching Night with Jabone the Breaker's sword in her hand it had been glorious.

Training people to fight—mostly kids—was alright, but it wasn't the life she wanted. *This* was what she wanted: to be in her armor with her sword on her back, riding with the Marching Night on their way to do battle.

She worked at keeping the grin off her face because it wasn't appropriate. She did this by remembering that Jena and the baby were in danger because that was the only part of this whole thing she didn't like.

She noticed Ufalla had ridden up on Jabone's other side, and she was glad. Maybe Ufalla could make him feel better. The truth was he had always been more comfortable talking to Ufalla than he was her. Kasiria sometimes thought this should bother her but it really didn't. Mostly she admitted because Ufalla's beauty was only eclipsed by how very queer she was and how much she loved Jestia.

As if thinking about her had called the witch to her, Jestia rode up beside her. Kasiria was not afraid of Jestia as any sane person really should be, but she didn't want her company because Jestia seemed to delight in nothing quite as much as making Kasiria squirm.

"And why are we picking you up in Montero?" Jestia asked.

"Not that it's any of your business..."

"Oh that's good. You should start with that when you see Tarius. So you have been living in Montero." Kasiria wondered why the witch bothered to ask questions she already knew the answers to. "It was my dream to live there but no I'm off fishing for months and then doing battle while you live my dream." Jestia smiled that all-knowing smile of hers that just made Kasiria want to slap it right off her face. "But it's not your dream is it, Kasiria?"

"Jabone wants to live in Montero."

"Oh that's right. You Jethrik girls just do whatever a man tells you to do in between cleaning his dirty laundry and cooking his dinner."

"Now see here, Jestia..."

"And why did you not go with Tarius and Jena? They had to ride right past you. They wouldn't have done so and not stopped to see their beloved son."

"Jabone didn't want to go."

"Because war changes a person for the better or the worse. It has changed Jabone for the worse."

"There is nothing at all wrong with Jabone."

"Really?" Jestia gave her a look that said she felt Kasiria was a waste of her time and her breath and then moved up to ride beside Harris. Ufalla and Jabone were talking and Kasiria was alone with her thoughts.

That witch gets on my last nerve. If she hadn't saved my life... Well I'd be dead. But I'd strangle her. What does she mean the war changed him for the worse? Jabone is the same. The only thing that has changed is where he wants to live. But when she thought about it she knew it wasn't true. Jabone *had* changed.

When they'd first gone to Montero they were just supposed to be there a couple of weeks and then go back and make their own home in the compound. They enjoyed each other's company and made house plans and got rid of them and made new ones. By the third week Jabone changed the direction of the conversation to the beauty and peace of Montero and how it was really close to the compound. Kasiria was so in love with him she really didn't care what they did or where they were as long as they were together.

By the time he had her walking up and down the streets looking at houses he had more or less convinced her the whole living in Montero thing was her idea.

It wasn't till they had the house and were living more like humans than Katabull and more like merchants than sword masters that she even started to really think that it was more what he wanted than what she did.

While she hated to admit it the witch was at least half right. She had gone along with what Jabone wanted because she had grown up in the Jethrik. She had been raised to believe that a woman did what her husband wanted. As much as she had worked to break every mold they tried to pour her into, when push came to shove she had let her husband decide where and how they would live.

She didn't hate their life in Montero, but she hadn't realized how much she missed being part of a fighting unit until they were riding with the Marching Night again.

Jabone had changed and she hadn't even noticed because their lives had become routine—even dull. They had rehashed the battles they had fought a hundred times and only now did she realize that she was happy when they were talking about them, and he had looked distant and removed. When she thought about it he spoke more like he had watched it happen than been part of it.

And how many times had he told her… "Everyone thinks I'm just like my madra and I'm not like her at all because she can jump from a horse and pluck an arrow from the air in her human form. Yet even as the Katabull and standing on the ground with that arrow about to kill you, I failed."

The battle has changed him because now he doubts himself and he never did before. He had managed to hit her a couple of times in practice and thought he was as good if not better than she was until he'd actually seen her in battle. Till he was fighting beside her and she was killing three for every one he was killing they were all just pretty stories. She was the hero of his favorite adventures and none of it was ever quite real. But when he saw Tarius in battle, saw how she moved, how she fought, how she strategized, and how she lead he knew all of those stories were true. Now it's all real for him and he knows she is exactly the person in all those tales. He thinks he wants to do something completely different away from her so that he will be seen as his own man.

The truth is worse. He doesn't want to be around her because every time he looks at her he judges himself and finds himself wanting because he can't do the things that she does. What he doesn't understand is that no one expects him to be able to do the impossible and the impossible comes as easily to Tarius the Black as breathing. My own father must have told me that a hundred times.

"I thought I might as well tell you myself before everyone else did," Ufalla said, happy to see her friend smile at last even if it was at her expense.

"Jestia must have been beside herself."

"I have been told she was, and I don't think she's ever going to forgive me because I apparently came out of my daze saying 'My finger is in my sword.' You know instead of speaking words of undying devotion to her. Of course ever since she has been a huge pain in my ass for an entirely different reason, this is the furthest we've been apart since it happened and well here she comes and... You'll see."

Jestia had been talking to Harris, but she had slowed down and fallen in on the other side of Ufalla. She glared at Jabone, so apparently she blamed him, too. He wasn't blaming himself any more because he wasn't a prophet. His mothers had never before gotten into any spot his madra couldn't get them out of. If he had known his mother was in danger he would have gone. He'd had no vision, no dream.

But why didn't he? Before he'd needed them his mother had a dream that had his madra packing the Marching Night on ships. They got there just in time to rescue him and Kasiria and his friends. Why did he not have a dream? Why didn't he get that feeling that they needed to go with them? Would it have mattered? They didn't really know how it had happened. He and Kasiria being there probably wouldn't have made a difference at all in which case why were they all mad at him?

Well at least Ufalla wasn't mad at him.

"He's more moody than ever," Jestia said, speaking to Ufalla as if he weren't there at all but loud enough that he could hear her over the thunder of hundreds of hoof beats. "Other half of my soul, if we had been in Montero all these months just soaking in each other's love nothing would be able to put such a scowl on our faces, would it?"

"No dear because you wouldn't allow it," Ufalla said, proving that Jestia was right when Ufalla just grinned at her in that way that told Jabone that no matter what Ufalla might say she still thought every stupid thing Jestia did was cute.

"Jestia, must I remind you that my own mother and

brother have been taken hostage?" Jabone hissed in her direction.

And then much to his displeasure she looked directly at him and said, "Your madra has made sure your mother can take care of herself. If I were you I'd be more worried about Tarius." Then she turned to Ufalla "My one true love, I must go speak with Jazel."

"Be careful, Jestia. You are not immortal, and you've had little to eat and less sleep. You are keeping too many balls in the air," Ufalla said frowning.

"Quit making that face, my life, or you'll look just like your sad friend." Jestia rode away in a blur and Jabone blinked as the spell had caused her and her horse to all but vanish.

"And there is another spell. She's running at least three others at the same time just to keep us moving at this speed without running into each other. And apparently the one spell—the one that allows us to go faster or slower even at this pace—actually takes the weight off the horses' hooves. Jazel told me she herself can't cast that spell. I know Jestia draws energy from everything but I also know if she doesn't slow down she is going to wear herself out and be useless when we need her most."

"Does she ever listen to you, sister?"

"Oh aye, whenever I say exactly what she wants to hear."

"What's with the..."

"Never-ending stream of devotion that issues from her mouth whenever she speaks to me?" Jabone nodded. "She's been doing that ever since I came back to my senses. She tells me she will stop when she feels like it which I hope is soon," Ufalla said with a sigh.

"I have missed you," he said.

"And I you, but I have to tell you we have had the most grand adventure. You know except for me getting hit on the head acting like a huge idiot and being the brunt of every one's joke for the rest of my natural life." She told him all about finding the mine and the fight. "And until then Jestia was tired of the whole fishing boat thing and with the cold way before the storm ran us aground, but I have to tell you I really wasn't. As long as there was nothing else to do Jestia and I were making love all the time. "

"You do that all the time anyway," Jabone said, rolling his eyes.

"No, Jabone, I mean ALL the time. Like once we didn't

get out of bed except to eat and take a pee for a whole day."

"Jestia grows more beautiful every day," Jabone said with real admiration.

"That she does and I don't think it's a spell. Though it could be."

He shook his head then said, "What did she mean about my madra?" Ufalla was silent. "Ufalla, what did she mean?"

"I'm not going to pretend like I always know what Jestia means, but when we were in the territories—even there—Jestia could hear your madra roaring."

"How..."

"Jestia has this connection to Tarius that I don't fully understand, and Jestia is very powerful, Jabone, even more than she was when you last saw her."

As if to prove it Jestia was back and she and her horse were between him and Ufalla where there had been no room for a gnat only moments before. She looked right at him and said, "I have figured you out. All children—though they will never admit it—want to do better than their parents, even more so royal children who grow up with all eyes on them. Kasiria bested Persius the minute she decided to be the first woman to legitimately join the sword master's academy. And I shone brighter than Hestia the day I issued from her womb. But you, Jabone, will never outshine your madra. But ask yourself this, would you want to go through all she has been through? Because it is only the horrors she has endured that have made her who she is."

Then Jestia was gone in a blur again. Ufalla shrugged looked at him and smiled. "She must not have been finished talking to Jazel when she decided she knew just what to say to you."

Jabone thought only a second about what the witch had said. "She's actually very wise, isn't she?"

"It was a shock to me as well."

"No it wasn't. I won't pretend to know how, but you have always known her soul."

"Jestia has a very old, very full soul."

"She's right. I do resent that I know I will never be the great legend that my madra is. But I had never thought to realize all my madra has gone through that made her Tarius the Black. When I think of the stories, what I know, *all* that I know... I almost lost Kasiria and I nearly went mad. I wouldn't want to go through any of the things she's been through. Jestia was right about everything."

Ufalla laughed. "Don't worry; I will never tell her you said that."

"Hestia, think," Tarius said through clenched teeth. "Who has the most to gain by killing you?"

They were in Hestia's office in her private quarters as Tarius thought it was safer than other areas of the castle because it had been built to be so. Hestia looked at the papers and books in front of her then looked up at the Katabull leader on the other side of her desk, threw up her hands and said, "I don't know, and going through all these books and scrolls looking for answers is making my brain numb."

"Tell me again who asked your permission to mine the territories."

"Sedrik, Joran and Finias."

"We could start there, Great Leader," Rimmy said.

"We are running out of time." Tarius ran her hands across her face and through her hair again. It usually helped her concentrate, focus. It wasn't working and hadn't been.

There was some grumbling outside the door and Tarius jumped turning towards the door her sword in hand. Dirk poked his head in, "Tarius I know you have said..."

Tarius sheathed her sword. "Dirk, I am working on my last nerve." She waved him in. He walked just in the door and closed it behind him. "I am sorry for what I did and what I said," Tarius said.

"I understand completely." He looked from her to Hestia and back, so Tarius nodded and walked over to join him. She could smell the liquor on his breath.

"What is it?"

He whispered to her. "You know how you said I couldn't be trusted because I'm a whoremonger and a drunk..."

"I said I am sorry, Dirk, I'm not myself. I know you would never purposely do anything to hurt me or the kingdom."

"Not purposely I wouldn't, but..." Dirk smiled. "It's true that I am a whore monger and a drunk. You know how you said men talk to whores?"

Tarius nodded.

"Well, I was with a woman this afternoon. She had a client a few weeks ago who was bragging he was going to kill Hestia, defame you, and take the crown for himself and..."

From across the room Hestia interrupted—no doubt because she didn't like being the one left out. "Since there is no heir apparent my brother would take the throne. But Rorik is my own brother and he's never had any interest in being king."

"Until they learned the territories were full of gold," Dirk said aloud.

"Rorik? Are you sure?" Tarius asked.

"It makes sense and that's what the whore said," Dirk said returning to a whisper.

Tarius kissed him on the mouth. Then she turned to Hestia and said, "Send to have all your heirs attend the castle at once."

"What will that do?"

"Keep Rorik from killing Jena. He can't be in two places at one time."

"But Tarius if he wants to kill me... if he's not alone."

"By the time the royals get here the bulk of the Marching Night will be here with orders to protect you at all cost. Rimmy and Hared, come with me. The rest of you stay here and guard the queen till the rest of our pack arrives."

Chapter Thirteen

Radkin woke up wrapped all around Jena and she didn't let go. She looked over Jena's shoulder at the baby sleeping in her arms and remembered for a moment what it felt like to hold her own woman and look at her own cubs in Irvana's arms. She had never and would never look at the Great Leader's woman with lust, but Jena was a beauty.

Jena was her dear friend nothing more, but holding her made Radkin think that maybe she could find someone else. That if it wasn't her fate to die, then maybe it was time to at least look for someone to help fill that void. It just felt so good to hold a woman again.

Then as she felt the man's back pressed against hers fighting for his piece of the tiny mattress, she came fully awake and realized all that was riding on her.

As if sensing her thoughts Jena whispered in Jethrik, "I need you to put aside your death wish, Radkin. I need you to fight for your life as well as mine because if you fall so will I."

Radkin took a deep breath and let it out. Jena was right. There was nothing as unsafe as a fighter who wanted to die. She remembered that day so long ago when Tweed had died and Rimmy went into a Katabull rage. He had almost gotten them both killed. And what did he keep telling her over and over again? *That he has loved the life he's had since and that he wouldn't have that without me. But men don't love the way women do and it isn't so easy for me to just find someone else. Still for Jena and Darian's sake she is right I can't afford to have a death wish.*

"When the time comes, Jena, I will make sure you are safe."

Jena sighed. "Radkin my life and Tarius's would be diminished without you as would your childrens', Rimmy's and the pack's."

"Am I always then to think of others, Jena? I am broken and hollowed out inside. How you feel right now being separated from her not knowing whether you will ever see her again—could you go through that every day, Jena? Could you feel like you feel right now day in and day out?"

"I could not."

"And neither could she which is why she gave you half her years. Yet you both expect me to go on living feeling the nothing I feel."

Jena was silent.

"I will make sure you and Darian are safe. After that I make no promises."

It was closing in on the night when Jabone saw them. He didn't know if he was the first one to see them, but he was the first one to break ranks and spur his horse on to meet them. His madra had dismounted before he reached her and he dismounted when she did. She ran to him, threw her arms around his neck, and then she just started sobbing, her body shaking with the strength of her sorrow. His own tears fell freely as he held her tight and patted her back. "I am sorry, Madra so sorry for everything." She said nothing; she was beyond words. All she could do was cry, and he'd never seen her shed more than a few tears in her whole life. "My mother..." He couldn't finish his sentence but he didn't have to.

"As far as we know she and your brother are alive," Rimmy said.

"I don't have time for this," Tarius mumbled and pushed away from him. She looked up at him but she was still crying. "How could I have let this happen to us?"

And suddenly she was just his madra. No bigger-than-life creature in the way of him ever making any name for himself. She was just a woman who loved her mate and her children, who loved him in a way that he had forgotten. He wasn't a footnote in her great story; he was her beloved son.

"We will get them back, Madra," he said.

She looked at him, took in a deep shuddering breath and let it out. She ran her hands across her face and through her hair and when she looked back at him Tarius the Black was back and ready to do battle.

The whole of the Marching Night were now stopped awaiting their orders. "I need Jabone, Kasiria, Jestia, Ufalla, Harris, Elise, Rimmy, Hared, Yri, Riglid and Laz."

Arvon protested from horse back. "Dammit, Tarius, they are my family too I can..."

"Arvon, selfishly I need you and Dustan to lead our people and Jazel on to the capital. There is a great plot against the whole of the kingdom."

From the set of his chin it was obvious that his fadre

knew why she wasn't taking him with her, and he was having trouble not speaking his mind. But he didn't argue with Tarius because as much as he might want to help them save Jena, he also knew he'd likely as not just get in their way. His fadra had told Jabone himself he wasn't fit to fight. Jabone's mother and brother were already in danger; he wanted his fadra to be safe.

On hearing their names called, Riglid and Laz had made it to the front of the group as had all the others Tarius had called by name. Jazel had also joined them. Riglid looked from Tarius to Rimmy.

"Where is our mother?" Riglid asked. There was a hint of panic in his voice. Jabone didn't have to ask why; Radkin had always ridden with Tarius.

"She is with Jena," Rimmy said, but there was an uncertainty in his voice.

"She was captured with her?" Laz asked. After all this was his mother, too.

"No she followed them," Tarius said. From the looks on Laz and Riglid's faces they knew what that meant. No one knew what had really happened to their mother; they were guessing.

Except of course Jestia. "She is fine." Jestia looked at Tarius. "So are Jena and Darian. So let's hear the plan."

It was a little scary how calm his madra seemed to get the minute she saw the young witch, and Jabone knew it went deeper than the words Jestia had spoken. *She trusts her completely.*

Tarius laid it all out as the bulk of the Marching Night started to set camp. Jazel was to go with Arvon, Dustan and the others. As soon as his madra was sure they all knew exactly what to do, she and those she had chosen started riding through the woods traveling as the crow would fly at Jestia's direction. They would ride till they were only a few hours from Rorik's keep and there they would camp for the night. They all wanted to ride straight through and attack but also knew their best bet for success was to have some rest.

Kasiria rode up beside him. "How are you holding up?" she asked carefully. He looked over and found a smile just for her. They were riding in the dark now, but they were Katabull and Jestia had cast Katabull eyes on the humans so they could all see. Jabone could clearly see the worry on Kasiria's face. She wasn't afraid of battle. In a lot of ways he worried that Kasiria loved the sword as much as his madra did—certainly she loved it more than he did.

No, Kasiria was worried about him.

"I will feel better when my mother and brother are safe. For now your love warms me and keeps me going. I find that my madra's tears have shaken me to the core."

Kasiria nodded. "I cannot imagine what she is going through, nor do I want to think about it."

"I do know because I almost lost you. I know how she feels, but she comforted me then and I can't comfort her."

"Jabone I..." She fell silent.

"What?"

"I was talking to Eric and Tarius, and they have been practicing sword every day with the Marching Night."

"The Marching Night always practice sword every day," Jabone said, obviously not understanding where she was steering their conversation.

"We don't practice every day. Teaching kids is not real practice. Eric says your madra has taught her more than she ever knew before and... Eric was almost equal in skill to me before and I'm sure she could beat me now. I know you want to live in Montero, but I don't. I want this... well not exactly *this*, but you know what I mean. I want to live in the compound with our people. I don't want to train people who will never be as good as we are. I want to practice with people I can learn from, with Tarius and Jena and Harris, Radkin and Rimmy. I want to learn from them not teach others."

Jabone was taken aback. "But I thought you loved Montero."

"I do love Montero, but mostly I just love you and I wanted to make you happy. I love it there but I don't want to live there. If I wanted a life like that I never would have gone to the Sword Master's Academy. I want the life we first talked about, Jabone."

Jabone nodded. "Then that's what you shall have, Kasiria."

Chapter Fourteen

It was false dawn when Radkin woke to a familiar sound. She quickly woke up fully and shook Jena. "Listen," she whispered.

Jena listened.

Radkin heard it again. "Did you hear it?" Because of course being Katabull Radkin's hearing was much better than her human friends and she couldn't be sure Jena could hear it.

Jena nodded.

They both knew what it was. The Marching Night used a series of bird calls to tell each other what was going on without detection. This call clearly said that help was on the way.

The night before Rorik had appeared giddy with excitement and announced, "All the royals of the kingdom have been called to the castle without an excuse. That could mean only one thing. The Great Leader has killed my sister in order to save you. When I expose Tarius's evil plot the whole of the Kartik army will fall on her, the Marching Knight, and then the Katabull compound. And you will be mine," he said to Jena with a lecherous leer.

"You do know that Jena has already killed one man who tried to have her against her will, don't you?" Radkin told him.

"Grab the child and we will bring it to the Great Leader on a spit, as thanks for a job well done," Rorik said. Before the guards could open the door or Radkin and Jena could prepare for battle the wizard jumped between them and the door.

"Rorik, are you really that stupid? This child is not *her* child. This child is *Tarius's* own flesh and blood. Just like she would feel the death of her mate she would feel this child's death, and nothing would stop her killing you and all that you love. You don't know what might be facing you at the palace, so you'd best not show your hand so quickly. Besides, if you show up with that baby everyone will know of your treachery."

Rorik seemed to size the wizard up for a minute. "Eerin, if I find that you have lied to me your death shall be slow and painful."

When he left Radkin leaned into the wizard and whispered in his ear. "Now I will not kill you."

The wizard looked at her and whispered back. "That is only a small comfort."

As she and Jena listened they heard the call again. This time it was closer. She looked at where both guards were sound asleep. Then Jena got up and picked up the sleeping baby. Radkin got up slowly. She shook the wizard awake and then helped him to his feet.

"Tarius is coming," she whispered to him. He nodded, though it was clear from the expression on his face he expected he would die shortly. Jena handed him the baby and as Darian woke up he smiled at the wizard.

"Quiet, baby, don't make a peep. Let the guards sleep and sleep and sleep," the wizard whispered.

Darian must have thought this was funny because he laughed, but they heard no sound.

Jena reached under the mattress and pulled out her sword.

Radkin called on the night. When the change was complete she grabbed her own sword from under the mattress and brought it down hard on the cell door, cleaving the lock in two and waking the guards up. They came running and she kicked the door into them sending them both flying and then Jena ran through.

"Throw my baby in the street!" she bellowed. She hit the guard so hard she split his head in half.

Radkin killed the other one easily and made a mental note not to piss Jena off.

Several guards were coming down the stairs at them and she and Jena were easily dispatching them. Their attackers had no skill with the sword and apparently didn't know even rudimentary Simbala. They were of good size and all young, but it was clear they had little knowledge of the weapons they were wielding.

The cell wall at their back suddenly blew into many pieces, and moments later Tarius, Jabone and Kasiria had joined them. The men coming down the stairs towards them turned to run the other way and Tarius ran past Jena and started cutting a path through the enemy three at a time, giving none of the rest of them a chance to kill anything. Tarius always had been selfish like that.

Soon Tarius ran back down the stairs and took Darian from the wizard. She settled him in the crook of her arm and ordered, "Back the way we came."

A hand came down to help Radkin up—not that she needed it. When she took it and crawled over the rubble to the outside she was looking at her own son, Riglid. He smiled at her then embraced her, but there wasn't really time for sentimentalities because whatever Jestia had done to destroy the cell wall had made a loud noise and now the whole garrison was coming at them. Radkin looked at where Tarius was with Jena. The baby and Jena were no longer her responsibility. She kissed her son on the cheek and pushed him to arm's length. "Be safe my son." And then she left the rest of them behind and ran to meet the wall of fighters coming at them.

They had made a quick camp and eaten a half-assed meal. Jabone didn't know if any of them had slept any better or longer than he did. They woke before dawn, broke camp and took off in the dark. They rode as far as it was safe to ride without being spotted by anyone in the towers, and then they left the horses with Yri and the rest of them moved in on foot.

Jestia cast a spell to find Jena. When they found the cell window she threw the same ball lightning at it that she had thrown at the cave ceiling. Then he, his madra and Kasiria were jumping through the hole and he was more than a little surprised to see that his mother and Radkin had already broken out of the cell. His mothers didn't speak a word to each other, but they exchanged a look that lasted only a second yet which he was sure he wouldn't forget for the whole of his life. They didn't have to speak; they truly knew each other's hearts.

Jabone badly wanted to kill something just because he was so angry that anyone would dare to touch his mother, but his madra didn't leave him anyone to kill. But once they crawled out of that hole that was no longer the case.

He saw Radkin break rank and run into the fray, and he saw Laz chase after her. Then to his horror Kasiria was right behind Laz and he found himself once again wishing his madra had never given Kasiria his grandfather's sword. The fact that she was still in her human form told him she wasn't even scared. Kasiria still couldn't force a change; she still only changed when she felt she was in imminent danger... or while they were having sex.

Jabone couldn't follow her because he had to stay with his mothers. Ufalla fell in beside him, Jestia by her side. Somewhere on the other side of his mother were Rimmy and Hared, Harris and Elise. Then they were engaged, and he had plenty of people to kill. He had to just trust that Kasiria would be alright.

Tarius held her son tightly to her as she mowed down the men who ran at her. This was not like any battle she'd ever fought. These looked like their people. These should have been their people, yet they were attacking them with the same mindless drive that the Amalites did. It didn't make any sense. Was greed for wealth this powerful? Didn't they know that she was willing to stand and kill everyone that came at her till their bodies littered the ground?

After only a few minutes engaged with the Marching Night Radkin's opponents were ever fewer in number, and not just because she was killing them as fast as she could but because they were starting to run away back into the garrison. And then there it was—an axe head. There was no way she could block it and no way it was going to miss. She would finally be released from her pain. Then the head of the axe fell right off and the man who'd been holding it was dead only slightly after that. She fully expected to turn and see that idiot Kasiria covered in blood and grinning like a ghoul, but when she turned to see who had saved her she saw instead her son Laz. He shook his head.

"Not today, Mother. Not today." Then he took hold of her arm and started pulling her back towards the others and there was Kasiria all catted out following and watching their backs as they retreated.

The fighters of the keep were running, which meant they had a short window in which to beat a hasty retreat. Soon the enemy would realize they were in a keep and run up to their towers and start raining arrows down on them—which was the last thing the Katabull wanted.

"Let's go," Tarius ordered. "Yri!"

Tarius whistled twice and her horse was there before Yri appeared with the rest. In seconds they were mounted and gone.

When they were well out of range of arrows Tarius called a halt. She rode up beside Jestia. "Jestia, is there some way you can block them riding out of the keep after us? Stop them from leaving here at all for at least a few hours?"

"I can hold them for longer than that by casting snares."

"How does that work?" Tarius asked.

"I cast ring of snares all around the keep. If anyone tries to go past it they will be stuck to the ground unable to move at all for as long as a day—maybe longer. It depends on their size really," Jestia answered.

"Jestia how is being stuck to the ground a snare?" Ufalla asked, making a face. "A snare catches something in a rope and entangles it."

"I didn't name the spell, eternal light of my life," Jestia said. Then without further explanation she got up, walked to the middle of the road and spread her arms wide.

Tarius looked at Ufalla curiously.

"It's a really long story," Ufalla said for answer.

Tarius nodded and while Jestia was doing her spell she rode over closer to Jena. Jena looked at her smiled and then they both leaned over to exchange a kiss.

"You look horrible my love," Jena said, and touched the side of her face.

"Jena I..." Tarius's voice caught in her throat and she just couldn't speak.

"Me too," Jena said. Her voice was choked as tears ran down her cheeks. Tarius reached over and dried them away with her thumb, smearing blood across Jena's cheek. Tarius made a face and Jena smiled at her. "You made it worse, didn't you?" Tarius nodded. "I knew. I knew you would come."

Tarius became aware of her son squirming. She looked at him and realized that he was griping the way he had started doing, but that she couldn't hear him. "Who has enchanted my son?" Tarius boomed.

For answer the wizard who had been in the cell with Jena and Radkin rode over. She knew he was a wizard because she could feel his magic. She knew he wasn't a very powerful wizard for any number of reasons not the least being that he was riding a horse. While witches seemed to be able to ride horses no matter what, the more powerful a wizard got the less likely a horse was to let him ride.

"I'm afraid that was me Great Leader. I didn't want him to scream and alert the guards."

"And I thank you. Now give my son his voice back. He is getting pissed off."

"Now that we are all away, let the lad have more to say,"

the wizard said.

Darian griped a little more and then realizing he had his voice back he smiled and looked at her. She tried to wipe the blood off his face with her thumb and much as she had done to Jena only made a bigger mess. "My poor baby once again you are covered in blood."

Jestia walked over to them. "It is done."

The fact that it had taken her longer than a second told Tarius it was a difficult spell. "Thank you, Jestia, for everything." But Jestia wasn't listening; to her she was glaring at the wizard.

"Cousin Eerin, I should have known. How dare you set a storm on me?"

Tarius could tell that the witch was about to fry him.

Apparently Jena could read the witch too because she said quickly. "He did, Jestia, but he also saved Darian. Before you ask, Tarius, he also did the spell on the wine."

Now Tarius wanted the wizard fried as much as Jestia did.

"But he didn't know it was meant for you."

"Because he is now and always has been a huge dumbass," Jestia said. "Because of you Ufalla was almost killed."

"I am deeply sorry for my part in all of this."

Radkin, who had caught her horse, rode up to them. "He did save the baby. Actually, he probably saved all of us because you know neither Jena nor I would have let anything happen to Darian, and Rorik had it in his head to kill the baby last night. It was only the wizard's lie that stopped him."

"He stood up to Rorik—that's why he was thrown into the cell in the first place," Jena said.

"Rorik." Tarius hissed. Never had any name felt so distasteful in her mouth. Jestia was looking at her and Tarius realized—not without a certain amount of surprise—that Jestia was waiting for orders from her. "Let him live, Jestia. If he turns a hand against us later we can always kill him then."

Jestia nodded and started back for her horse. Half way to him she turned, looked at the wizard, pointed two fingers at her own eyes and then turned them at the wizard—obviously not a spell just a warning.

Tarius smiled then she looked at Jena and said, "I really love that girl."

Chapter Fifteen

It was no wonder Hestia couldn't sleep. There were a million things to think about. Her brother wanted to kill her and take over the country in order to rape the territories for gold. At least that's what Tarius told her.

The Great Leader of the Katabull people's infant and mate had been kidnapped from Hestia's' own castle. If anything happened to them Hestia had no idea what Tarius might do, but she didn't have too much trouble seeing her dear friend leading the whole of the Katabull Nation to slaughter every human on the island.

She had no idea what Tarius really had planned, but soon every royal in the kingdom would be attending her castle because she had sent for them. Of course the royal summons she had sent out had to be written in such a way that it didn't sound like it was from her, nor did it explain to them why they were to attend. The best part of that was that she had no idea why Tarius wanted them all here, either, but suspected it might be because if she didn't get her wife and son back unharmed, it would be easier for her to kill the entire royal line.

Yes there were a great many things to keep her from sleeping, and it might have made sense if any of those things were what was keeping her awake. But they weren't. No all she could think about—all she'd been able to think about for days—was what Tarius had said about her. That she couldn't understand what Tarius was going through because she had never known love.

Hestia gave up, got out of the bed, walked to the window and drew the drape back. The sun was barely coming up. She looked down at the garden three stories below her. It no longer gave her any peace because it was from this garden that Jena and her baby had been kidnapped. There was no place on earth that was really safe and no one who couldn't be touched, not if someone would take Tarius's mate and child from within the very walls of Hestia's castle. Not if someone would beach the ship Jestia was on in the territories.

Tarius said I couldn't know what she might do or how she felt because I have never known love, and she is right. My parents never loved me any more than I loved my own children. I wanted love—craved it—just as my children did. Yet just like my mother and father before me I didn't give them what they needed because I was so empty myself.

And why was she so empty? Because she had given up any hope of what she wanted in order to serve the crown. She had completely embraced her responsibilities. Hestia was a good queen who always did what was best for the country, what was right. When her kin wanted permission to go and rape the territories she told them no because it would be wrong, and now all of this pain had been caused because she'd tried to do the right thing.

They'd gone behind her back and raped the land anyway, and she'd been none the wiser. Which meant the conspiracy was much deeper than just Rorik, so that should be all she was concerned with—finding out just how much this disease had spread and who she could and could not trust.

But even sitting there with all those books and scrolls, Tarius near ordering me to find the answers, all I could hear her say is that I have never known love, that I have no depth of feeling because I don't know how to love. I put Dirk out of my bed years ago not because he had no love for me—he did. I put him out because I have never had any love for him. When he started to have other women I was just happy that he was leaving me alone. When he started to drink I didn't care about that either, and when he started to drink yet more after Katan died I still just didn't care. He disgusts me. I'm not sure there was ever really a time when he didn't—at least on some level.

Why didn't she care? Why didn't she care about any of them more than she cared for any man on the street? She would make only the right decisions for total strangers and be completely concerned about the welfare of her people and care nothing about the feelings of her husband or children. What did it all mean? Her brother wanted to kill her, and she hardly cared. Tarius was doubtless going to kill him, and she cared even less about that. He might as well have been the servant who changed her bedding.

It's because she's right. I don't know how to feel because I don't know how to love, and I don't know how to love because no one has ever loved me... But that's not true. My children loved me and I returned little to nothing to them. I haven't even had a lover since I tossed Dirk from my bed and why? Because I don't want to give anyone even the tiniest part of me. I don't want to have even a moment's vulnerability. I don't want to be

*capable of having the pain Tarius has. A ruler can't afford to
have feelings and attachments because then you act rashly
the way Tarius is doing right now. You put everything at risk
just to save your loved ones.*

*If you don't really love anything like that then you just
always do what is right... What a miserable, empty life I've
lived.*

She had given everything to the crown. She hated her
life. Only once had she followed her heart and that was to go
and kill people in a foreign land. She justified her action by
saying she did it to make a name for herself to add to the
glory of the crown. Hestia purposely moved to the window on
the other side of her massive room and drew the drapes back.
The darkness was fading as the sun was slowly rising and
light started to dot the landscape. She looked down at the
capital city and out past it to the forest. She was ruler of all
she could see, of the whole island of the Kartik, but in that
moment she'd trade it all just to feel anything but empty.

Jazel cast a spell on them before they entered the capital
so that they all looked just like ordinary Kartiks: soldiers,
street sweepers, merchants, scullery maids, and grounds
keepers. They crept in and took up places all around the
palace and in it. Jazel herself in the glamour of an old washing
woman told the two members of the Marching Night perched
outside the queen's door who she was. Without questioning
her further they let her in because being Katabull—even in
human form—they could feel the glamour though they
couldn't see through it.

Hestia was standing at her window in her night gown just
staring out.

"Oh, you're ripe for killing," Jazel said, removing the
glamour from herself. The queen didn't turn around. "I could
have been anyone."

"I don't think just anyone could have gotten past the two
Katabull at my bed room door, and I really don't think I care
whether I live or die anymore. I am so tired... so tired of
being Hestia. Let someone else deal with all this; I just don't
care anymore."

"You lost your son, Hestia. That is a hard thing. Being
queen won't protect you from the ravages of grief. It hasn't
even been eight full months since he died."

"I wish I was in grief, Jazel. I wish that was my problem. I
wish Katan's death weighed so heavily on my soul that I just

couldn't think of going on. Instead I am left to wonder what sort of monster is incapable of feeling real pain at the death of their child."

"Odd, you look like you are in pain to me. Has it never dawned on you that this is how you are grieving him, Hestia?" Jazel asked gently.

Finally Hestia turned around. "What?"

"This is how you are grieving Katan. Do you think people grieve for the dead? They do not. They grieve for themselves and what *they* have lost, the dead no longer feel. You, dear friend, are bearing the full weight of his death alone. You are as badly grieved as any person I have ever seen. You wanted to love him more, you wish you did, you didn't and now you never can. You have lost the chance to have the relationship you wanted with him. The depth of your despair is cavernous. Your sorrow is tangible."

Hestia walked over, threw her arms around Jazel's neck, rested her head on her shoulder and started to cry. Jazel held her and patted her back. She let her have a good cry then pushed her to arm's length.

"Tarius has Jena and the baby; they are on their way. The whole of the rest of the Marching Night is situated in and around the castle. The last of your family members are arriving and Tarius has constructed quite a plan..."

Rorik looked around the throne room. They'd been assembled here for nearly an hour and still no sign of Hestia. No word of why they were here, either, and that could mean only one thing. He worked to keep the feeling of rapture off his face. He looked at his cohorts Sedrik and Finias in turn. Finias did not have a good betting face, and Rorik just hoped no one else was reading Finias as easily as Rorik was.

Dirk walked in and Rorik waited to hear the words the "Queen is dead." Then Rorik would announce that the murderer was the Great Leader and show all the proof he'd made ahead of time. Then the Katabull would fall. He had fulfilled all he had been asked to do; now he would be king and all would prosper as he had been promised.

Dirk walked up and stood beside the throne—not in front of it as he would if he was announcing something. Then Hestia entered followed by a man and woman in the armor of the Marching Night who were immediately followed by Princess Jestia.

Rorik had to stifle a gasp. *What is all this then?*

Hestia sat on the throne and looked around the room at them all. "I know you have all been waiting for me to appoint a new heir apparent. There is now no need to do so because Jestia has returned. I renounce my decree allowing her to step away from her duties, and when my days are no more Jestia shall reign as queen of the Kartik."

Rorik took in a deep breath and held it. He looked from his sister to his niece. How could this be? He had the Great Leader's woman, her brat, didn't Tarius know he would kill them both? What was happening to his perfect plan?

"Jestia is a magic user. Let us not forget what happened the last time one of our line who was filled with magic sat on the throne," his cousin Fredrik said. "He nearly destroyed the coasts with his storms. Inland crops were killed by his droughts for decades."

"You mean the way someone destroyed land and killed forests in the territories with a mine I forbade?" Hestia said. She looked right at Rorik then. He did not blink but held her stare. "Someone kidnapped the Great Leader's wife and child. I don't think I have to tell any of you what it would mean to have the whole of the Katabull Nation come down upon us."

"Who would do such a thing?" Fredrick said. He was now outraged for a whole different reason.

"One or more of you," Hestia said, never taking her eyes off Rorik. It was only then that he realized Hestia's sword was strapped to her side as was Jestia's.

Rorik watched as his plans unraveled before him, but he'd have his revenge. He'd kill the Katabull's wife and child and make rugs of them. Hestia would be unable to connect him to the kidnapping or the mine.

Then from the drapes covering the wall at Hestia's back Tarius the Black folded herself into the room, and Rorik felt the cold sweat gather across his skin.

Tarius looked at Jestia who nodded and then Tarius looked at every one of the men and women in the room in turn. She sniffed at the air then turned to look at Rorik, pulled her blade and held it in front of her pointing it at him.

"I smell them on you—my woman and my child," she said. "And what was it you said to my wife? That you'd lay with my woman and feed my baby to your dogs." She smiled at the look of shock and terror on his face. Jena walked from behind the drapes to stand just behind her. Jena looked at Rorik and she actually smiled. "This huge man here, he is our oldest son. Why don't you tell him what you planned to do to his mother and his brother? Better still; tell everyone here the ransom price you asked of me for their return."

"You ordered her to kill me, Rorik!" Hestia stood up then and looked down at her brother. "To kill me, your own sister, so that you could take the throne."

"Surely you wouldn't take the word of the Katabull," Rorik said to Hestia.

"From what land do you come? Of course I would take the word of the Katabull, for it is well known among all our people that the Katabull stand always by their word," Hestia said.

Tarius looked at Rorik then and growled before she spoke. "You know I hid all that I was in the Jethrik for years and yet not one of them forget what I am. I think in my own land that many of you forget." She called on the night. "Any one of them would have known they could *not* take my mate and my baby and live." She started for him and he dropped to his knees on the floor and looked at Hestia.

"Dear Hestia, spare my life! I swear to you I did not do this foul thing. You must believe me."

"What is this disrespect? Why not just call me a fool and have it done with? Jestia is right here; she found your filthy mine. I know what you have done—the raping of the land, the enslaving of people, the murder you have committed just to cover yourself. Jena stands right there, you great idiot! How do you think you can hide that you took her? She was found in your keep, Rorik. Jestia herself was with them. You should have known that the Great Leader was not ignorant enough to kill me. Tarius has dealt with worse bastards than you and she would know that the minute she killed me you would have no reason to keep them alive. I don't know what makes me sicker the fact that you are so deviant or that you are so stupid."

"Forgive me then sister, forgive me," Rorik begged. "I was led astray. I was promised things, I was…"

"There can be no forgiveness for what you have done. You took the mate and child of the kingdom's greatest ally from the very halls of the royal house. You plotted to kill me so that you could lead our army against the Katabull. Your greatest crime was against the Great Leader, so she alone will decide your fate."

Rorik looked at the Katabull. There was a moment when it looked like he was going to plead for mercy, but Tarius didn't give him the chance. "If you think I will not kill you because you are on your knees you are wrong. I have killed men for doing less while they slept. At least have the back bone to die standing and with a sword in your hand."

Rorik got shakily to his feet and slowly drew his sword. He ran at Tarius and she stepped into him, slapping his sword out of his hands with the might of her block. Then she shoved her sword up under his rib cage and twisted it so that when she pulled her blade out his heart fell out on the floor to be shortly followed by his body.

Filled with a rage that wasn't yet quenched, Tarius turned to Jestia. "Who else?"

Jestia pointed. "Sedrik and Finias."

Hestia clicked her tongue as if she hadn't just watched her own brother killed in front of her and said, "And I've always liked you, Finias."

"Jabone and Ufalla, take these men to a cell and question them. Jestia, go with them," Tarius said. She noticed Jabone had catted out, too. He walked over grabbing one man by the collar in one hand and then the other in the other hand, and he started pulling them out of the room. Ufalla and Jestia followed them out. She noticed through the door that Kasiria joined them in the hall.

Hestia stood up and looked at her remaining relatives. "Now that all this unpleasantness has been dealt with let us all go clean ourselves up and prepare for a feast to celebrate the Great Leader's good fortune and Jestia's return."

The Marching Night had already dispatched of all Rorik's people before Rorik was even dead. Then they fell on Sedrik and Finias's people. Within minutes there was nothing to do but carry dead bodies to waiting wagons.

It was a bad day to be aligned with the forces of evil.

Jabone shook the man again violently and Jestia wondered how much more Finias could take before his head just fell off. She also wondered why Jabone didn't think her truth spell was good enough.

"Answer her!" he roared, pointing at Jestia.

"Hestia wouldn't let us mine. Rorik promised us that if he was king we could do what we wanted in the territories. And if we defamed the Katabull…"

"My madra!" Jabone said.

"I asked if your household knows of your treachery," Jestia

said again.

An unwilling *Yes* came from Finias's mouth as he looked at the dead body of Sedrik. Then he sat his jaw and glared at Jestia. "You witch you do not know what you have started. You cannot win. We are just the vanguard of a huge army. The Katabull beast and her whore have won today but an abomination is still an abomination..." Jestia would never know what else he might have told them because Jabone slammed the man's head between his two fists, popping his head like some huge zit and covering all of them in brain slime, skull fragments, and blood.

"Great going, Jabone," Jestia said, wiping some of her cousin's gray matter from her eye.

"Really brother." Ufalla wiped her hands down her face to clear the slime off.

"You heard him. He called my madra a beast and my mother a whore."

"Besides it was pretty clear he wasn't going to tell us anything worth knowing," Kasiria said, defending her husband.

Jestia nodded not as sure as Kasiria was, then she did a spell to clean them all off.

"Thanks honey," Ufalla said

Jestia nodded and started out of the cell. "There is something not right in the things he was spouting."

"How so, Jestia?" Jabone asked.

"I'm not really sure just something off. It was the same sort of thing Rorik was saying. It just didn't sound right." They all nodded like they knew what she meant which was absurd because not even she knew what she meant. She moved to take Ufalla's hand, and Ufalla squeezed it in that slightly-uncomfortable, too-tight way that always made her feel like nothing in the world could ever hurt her. Jestia started pulling Ufalla along in front of Kasiria and Jabone. "Come on, my love, I noticed Mother had new drapes behind the throne and I can make the most wonderful gown from them. Besides I'm starving for real food—not some swill made from fish I make into food, but the real thing."

Kasiria looked at him and made a face and he knew why. "I just meant to kill him. I didn't know I'd actually bust his head all over everyone."

Kasiria laughed. "It was pretty gross. As big a pain in the ass as she can be it's always good to have Jestia around. I mean the gods alone know how many hours we would have spent just getting the goop and bone fragments out of our hair."

Jabone nodded then asked her, "Kasiria if you had been there when my mother went to feed the baby..."

"Jabone I don't know if I would have gone with her or not and what does it matter now? Everyone is fine."

But he knew nothing really was. You went through bad things and you didn't forget what you'd seen or how you felt just because for a moment you felt safe. The older he got the more he realized that "safe" and "sure" were illusions. Certain things happened and you never really felt safe again.

The tub wasn't really big enough for both of them, but the water was nice and hot. There was no part of her that wanted to tell Jena no when she'd showed up in the bathing room naked and crawled in mostly to sit on top of her. Water splashed out of the tub and onto the floor, but the floor was lattice work with a drain under it, so it was made to get wet. Tarius wrapped her arms around Jena and pulled her tightly to her resting her head on her back. Then she pulled her head up again. "Jena, where is the baby?"

"He is asleep with Radkin on her bed."

Tarius sighed with relief. She knew it would be a long time before she'd be able to relax unless she could see them both. She lay her head back down on Jena's back listening to Jena's heartbeat. "I'm so sorry, Jena..."

"Tarius I knew you would do this. It wasn't your fault. If either of us should be sorry it's me. If I hadn't put modesty before safety this wouldn't have happened. We're all okay; let's just be glad we're all alright and not think about it."

"I felt like my soul had been ripped in two. Jena, I wouldn't live a day without you."

Jena stiffened in her arms and then said in a whisper, "Tarius I know what you did."

In that moment with all that had happened Tarius really couldn't imagine what Jena was talking about. "What?"

Jena turned around to face her. It wasn't an easy task, and had Jena's knees straddling Tarius's legs by the time she'd finished. Jena was hanging onto the sides of the tub to keep their heads from banging together. "Don't pretend you don't know what I'm talking about, Tarius. I know what you and Hellibolt did."

"Me and Hellibolt?"

"The spell, the reason I look twenty."

"Oh that," Tarius said.

"Yes that! How dare you do that without even asking me?"

As if it was a defense Tarius said, "Hellibolt wouldn't cast the spell. Jestia did."

Jena was silent for a moment, thinking. When she spoke again she was obviously even madder. "Hellibolt wouldn't cast the spell because he wouldn't do it unless I knew about it." Tarius's silence told Jena she was right. "But Jestia... She would do whatever you told her to because she near worships you. You didn't even ask me what I wanted; you just did it."

"Would you have said yes?"

"No!"

"That's why I didn't ask you," Tarius said with a smile, as if it were a perfect defense. Jena obviously wasn't happy, so Tarius wiped the smile off her face. "Who told you?"

"Yes let us now blame the one who told me instead of you. The wizard. Imagine, he thought it was the sort of thing I would have to know. Can Jestia undo it?"

"No and I wouldn't let her if she could. Why are you being so selfish?"

"Selfish! Tarius I feel as if you've found a way to have me help you kill yourself. I don't feel right that you have given half of your life to me. How is that selfish?"

"Because I have told you over and over that I couldn't live a day without you. Half my years to have you always with me seems a small price to pay."

"That's almost exactly what Radkin said."

Tarius was glad when Jena turned around and sat back down and she could just hold her again.

"What am I going to do about Radkin and her death wish?"

"I'm sure I don't know and... Don't try to change the subject."

"Don't be mad at me, Jena. I can't stand it when you are."

"What about Darian, Tarius?"

"What about him?"

"We're both going to outlive him, Tarius. How do you think that's going to feel? To watch our baby grow old and die."

"I was always going to outlive him and do it without you. Now you will help me and I will help you. That is a hundred years away, so why worry about it now?"

"Humans don't live to be a hundred, Tarius."

"But he will live a good, long life and we will love him and care for him, and he will have children we will love and care for and right now he is safe and we are together. Turn back around, though it is awkward and uncomfortable, and take a good look at my face."

Jena turned and when she did her features softened. She took a hand and put it against Tarius's cheek. "Oh Tarius, you look worse than I do, and I've been in a cell eating swill for three days."

"I was drunk. I went into a Katabull rage and beat myself to pieces on the bars of a cell in Hestia's dungeon. Jena, I literally couldn't draw a breath without pain and not because of my injuries—you know these are minor for me. I can't live without you. I won't apologize for doing something that hurts no one to keep you with me. I won't."

Tarius woke with her arms around Jena to the sound of the gong telling them the feast was ready. All she really wanted to do was sleep. She pulled Jena closer and smelled her hair.

Jena giggled. "Come on get up. I'm starved. I haven't eaten anything that tasted better than horse shit in days," Jena said.

Radkin appeared in their doorway with a screaming infant in her arms. "He's hungry and I've got nothing for him."

Jena got up pulling the cover off the bed with her to cover herself as she walked over to retrieve their son, leaving Tarius naked in the middle of the bed.

"Apparently it's alright for me to see you naked." Radkin grinned.

Tarius shrugged. "Yes, apparently so."

Jena sat on the edge of the bed with her back to Radkin and started to feed Darian. Just for a moment Tarius was reminded of how close she had come to losing them both, and her anger was rekindled.

"I'm hungry. I haven't eaten in days," Radkin announced. She took off.

"It seems I am always to owe Radkin a debt I can never pay," Tarius said. She moved to rub Jena's back.

"She's a good cuddler," Jena said jokingly.

Tarius knew she had nothing to worry about. She had complete faith in both her friend and her mate. She kissed the side of Jena's neck.

"Why don't you get dressed so we will be that much closer

to going because it takes you longer to get all your armor on than it does for me to throw on a dress and there is no way I am going anywhere in this castle ever again without an armed escort or two," Jena said.

Hestia no longer needed to ask why Tarius had all the royals brought. Now it all made perfect sense. Tarius was sure that while Rorik was the instigator he didn't act alone. Jestia had easily found his cohorts simply by judging the fear of the people in the room as Tarius looked at them. If you had any part in taking the Great Leader's mate you weren't likely going to be able to hide your fear when she looked at you.

Mostly having seen how quickly and brutally the coup was put down she didn't imagine any of them would be so quick to plot against her or Tarius in the near future.

Hestia had to admit she was more surprised that Jestia and Ufalla were on time than that Tarius and Jena were late. She knew Tarius wouldn't be insulted if she started the feast without her, so she did. Hestia picked at her food; she didn't have any appetite. She wished she could say it was because she was greatly grieved that her brother had been killed for plotting her death, or that it was because she had just seen her friend in fact cut his heart out of his chest. That wasn't it. He was obviously no brother to her. The fact he'd wanted to kill her proved their lack of closeness.

Radkin and Jazel walked in together a little late and Hestia smiled. She often forgot how huge Radkin was. Since Radkin was usually in the company of Rimmy who was as tall as she was and Tarius who was only a few inches shorter it was easy to forget she was so tall. Seeing her tower over Jazel, who wasn't particularly short, made her height obvious and striking.

Radkin had always been a wild-looking thing. She wore nearly as many rings in her ears as Hestia herself did and had one in her left nostril. When they had fought in the Great War, Radkin had worn her hair—which nearly reached her waist at the time—in hundreds of tiny braids all over her head that she drew back into a single pony tail. She never wore a helmet because her hair protected her head. Hestia smiled at the distant memory; they had all been so young then. She had felt so alive, so present.

Radkin's hair now only reached the middle of her back and she kept it in a single braid yet she didn't look much less wild.

Jestia waved wildly at Jazel and pointed to the seat beside her. Jazel walked over and sat beside Jestia.

Radkin looked around briefly and then walked right over to the queen—no bowing, no scraping, no protocol. Maybe that's why she enjoyed the Katabull so much, they didn't treat her like she was anything special so she could just relax.

"Tarius and Jena will be here in a minute. They lost track of the time."

"I'm sure they did."

Catching Hestia's meaning Radkin shook her head. "They were both very tired; I'm sure they were just sleeping."

"Oh of course." Radkin seemed off. Knowing she'd been with Jena, Hestia asked, "Are you alright, Radkin?"

Radkin gave her a crooked smile. "Unfortunately, yes."

Radkin looked around for a seat. Not only were all the royals—except those who had died that day—in attendance, but the whole of the Marching Night were still at the castle. While most of them were eating in the barracks, all the officers were in the feast hall and nearly every seat was taken. Hestia looked at the empty seat on her left. The two on her right were for Tarius and Jena when they arrived. She looked to where Dirk had found himself a seat across the room next to some young woman who had probably smiled at him. It didn't take much to peak Dirk's interest and if he could rub it in her face all the better. He had never seemed to notice that Hestia really didn't care.

"Sit here, Radkin." Radkin looked unsure. "Dirk has chosen another seat, and I don't bite."

Radkin smiled. "Actually I don't mind a woman that bites." She sat down and started filling her plate with food. Then she was eating the way the Katabull usually did—like it was her first and last meal.

"How are your children?" Hestia asked, making conversation.

Radkin stopped eating abruptly and swallowed the food in her mouth before she spoke. "There's Riglid and Laz, and over there are my blood children Jadon and Rea. I swear the boys make me proud every day and are no problem at all, but that girl." She rolled her eyes.

Hestia laughed. "I know the feeling. And how is your mate?" As she finished the question she knew she shouldn't have asked because all the light seemed to leave Radkin's face.

"Irvana died two years ago of a wasting sickness."

"I'm sorry, Radkin. I didn't know."

"How could you? It's not like she died in battle and became part of a glorious tale." There was bitterness and deep sorrow in her voice. "No, she died in pieces taking the best part of me with her. Now I want to die, too, but every time I turn around someone is saving me. So I must be alive for some reason, but I don't know what it is."

Hestia was at a loss; she had no idea what to say. For a human to die so young and in such a way would be tragic, but for the Katabull who lived so long it was unthinkable. Finally Hestia just told the truth. "I can't even imagine what you are going through. I have never cared so much for anyone as you obviously cared for her."

Radkin nodded and went back to eating though now she was picking at her food and no longer seemed to be enjoying it. Hestia felt like a great ass.

Then Tarius and Jena walked in. She knew it before she saw them because every member of the Marching Night in the room got to their feet as one, cheered and started thumping their chests with their fists. Tarius raised a hand and put it down which obviously meant they should get quiet and sit down because that was what they did.

Tarius sat beside her, the baby in her arms, and Jena sat between Tarius and their grown son. Jabone immediately grabbed Jena, hugged her and started crying on her neck as she held him and whispered things Hestia couldn't hear in his ear. Hestia guessed they probably hadn't really had a chance to talk to one another till that moment.

Jena held her grown son and he held her. It was obvious that they loved each other in a way she had neither loved nor been loved, and she felt a wave of jealousy wash over her. When Jabone at last calmed he released his mother and Jena almost immediately started eating.

Tarius set the baby on the table in front of her and kissed his face over and over again. If the baby was traumatized by his ordeal it didn't show as he laughed at Tarius and tried to grab the braids on either side of her face.

Dustan left where he was sitting and moved to hunker down between Tarius and Jena. The baby held out his arms, pawing the air with his hands, and wordlessly Tarius handed the baby to Dustan. Dustan took the baby and stood up. He hugged him tightly and the baby put his head against Dustan's. Arvon was talking to Kasiria and they were both laughing—over what Hestia could only guess.

When she looked at them together her heart broke a little more. They were a mixed up mess—Jethriks and Katabulls, half breeds and a royal princess thrown in for good measure—but they knew what family was supposed to be. They loved and supported each other. Even when they were at odds they were ever only at odds because they were so connected. She looked to where her own daughter sat talking to her lover. Jestia glowed not from the power she wielded but from the love she gave and received from this common sword woman. Jestia had spoken barely a handful of words to Hestia and mostly about the plan. Jestia didn't feel anything but maybe contempt for Hestia, and she made it clear.

Again Hestia found herself in a room full of people and utterly and completely alone.

"I just feel empty inside," Radkin said beside her.

Hestia sighed. "Now that's something I know only too well."

"He didn't," Arvon laughed.

"He did," Kasiria answered. "He said he just wanted to kill him, that he didn't mean to splatter him all over us. It was the cutest thing."

"I'm sorry that I was so angry with you and with my son but..."

"You had every right to be. We should have gone with them, and he knows that now."

"Dustan wanted to leave me in the compound. If I had stayed Tarius would have taken him with you to go get Jena. He knows it and I know it yet he doesn't say a word."

"You were needed here, Arvon," Kasiria said.

"A trained monkey could have done what I did here. Young Tarius could have done it for sure. She just didn't want me to feel useless, and she didn't want to take me with her."

"There is nothing useless about you, Arvon," Kasiria said.

"You know Dustan is much younger than I am. He deserves someone who doesn't hold him back."

"He loves you," Kasiria said, putting her hand on his shoulder.

Arvon nodded. He looked over not at Dustan but at Tarius. "She has always taken care of me. You know she saved my leg and my life."

"I have heard the stories."

"She taught me how to be the Katabull."

"Jabone told me."

"Together she and I were invincible—a force to be reckoned with. Now I can't keep up, and soon Harris won't be able to, either. If anything had happened to Jena or that stinking baby... Have you taken a good look at Tarius's face, hands and arms?"

Kasiria nodded.

"She is covered in bruises and cuts. Rimmy told me they made wine taste like juice. Tarius drank the wine; she immediately knew what they were up to and she had them lock her in a cell. She flew into a Katabull rage and all of her injuries are self-inflicted. I worry about her. Jena is human, and what met us on the road—that is what will happen to Tarius when Jena is gone. Tarius believes I would have been in the way if I had gone and Dustan couldn't go because Tarius would never separate us. She tries never to separate any couple because she can't stand to be separated from Jena."

"Why dwell on it now? The worst didn't happen. We're all safe."

"Are we? Look at Tarius. It might look like she is completely at ease, but I know her. Her sword hand twitches; she is still raw." He then turned to look at Jabone appearing to want to change the subject. "Look at him. He is beautiful. When I was a young man living in the Jethrik, being what I was, I never thought I'd have a child. Yet there he sits. Tarius gave me a son. I won't lie; I like this baby Tarius has fished from the floor of a cave, but I feel no real bond to him." He lowered his voice still more till if she hadn't been Katabull there was no way she would have heard him over the din in the room.

"When we made Jabone she'd never been with a man, any man. I'd had sex with women before, but it was always awkward and only made me more certain of what I am. I love Jena, but when I'd lain with her to try to make her pregnant it had been very clumsy and uncomfortable for both of us, but... Tarius and I have a strange love for each other. It isn't like you have for your mate but more than you feel for a parent or a sibling. It is hard to explain; it is just different from any other relationship I've ever had. Our coupling was not forced or clumsy it was tender and loving and it brought us close in a way we hadn't been till then. That doesn't mean we ever had any desire for each other, we didn't. But we both wanted Jabone and our love made his conception a moment I look back at fondly."

Reading the look on Kasiria's face he smiled. "I don't tell you this to make you uncomfortable. I tell you this so that you will know that Jabone was not made in some ugly 'let's do this and get it over with' way. It makes him special among the Katabull who come from cross pairings." He paused looking at Jabone again. "Everyone always says he is just like her, no doubt because he looks and moves just like her. You know as well as I do that he is not just like her. He is my son, too. My blood runs through his veins with hers and he is also very like me. Because as much as I owe, love and admire her, I also get very tired of being a minor character in her rather extraordinary life.

"When you rode out to meet us I was so mad at you both because I knew she wanted you to go with her and I knew why he didn't want to go. And it is at least in part my fault because you see I passed my resentment on to him." He looked back at her and smiled. "You Kasiria are more like her than Jabone is."

From the tone of his voice it was hard to tell if he thought that was a good or bad thing.

Seeing her confusion he said, "Jabone told me what you did today. How you followed Radkin to meet the fight. Kasiria, do you not know that Radkin has a death wish?"

Kasiria shrugged.

"Well she does, and I know why her son would go after her but... Tarius wants to leave me behind these days, but who she really needs to pull from active duty is Radkin."

"I don't think that would help with her death wish." Kasiria looked at Radkin where she sat beside the queen. She couldn't imagine that her father would sit beside some common sword sling at a royal feast. She said as much to Arvon and he laughed.

"He did precisely that with Tarius."

Kasiria was a little shocked, but put it out of her mind. She looked at Radkin. "Why is she so unhappy?"

"Well to hear her talk it is because you saved her life," Arvon said. "In reality she lost her mate a couple of years ago and has not been the same since."

"Yet you don't understand why Dustan and Tarius want to protect you."

"Oh I understand it. I just don't like it."

Ufalla's brother Tarius was talking; in fact, he had not shut up or quit drinking. He was in his cups as was his wife Eric.

With all that was going on Jestia hadn't allowed herself more than a few sips. She noticed Ufalla hadn't either, and she thought with a mental gasp *my gods we have fooled around and become responsible.*

She started to pick up the bottle of wine that had just been delivered and down it, but then her attention was drawn to Tarius. Not her mate's scrawny, annoying brother, but Tarius the Black. She was looking at her, and when she caught her eye she moved her head and Jestia nodded her understanding. She leaned over and whispered in Ufalla's ear. "Tarius calls for me." Ufalla started to get up and Jestia put a hand on her shoulder. "Stay and visit with your brother and his new bride."

"Why, what did I do wrong?" Ufalla whispered with a grin.

Jestia kissed her on the cheek, got up and moved to meet Tarius just feet behind Jena's chair. The baby was asleep in Tarius's arms, his head resting on one of her pauldrons. *He certainly is a resilient baby.*

"What?" Jestia asked.

"The things Rorik said..."

"Odd in an almost-familiar, can't-quite-put-a-finger-on-it way," Jestia finished, and Tarius nodded. "The same is true of the two men we interrogated. I might have gotten more out of Finias but your huge son splattered his head all over us because he said rude things about you and Jena." She made a face at the memory of it.

"My son has his mother's quick temper." Tarius grinned.

"That's odd. He looked just like you when he did it."

"How long will the spell hold the men at the keep?"

"Not too much longer now."

"We will have to ride out to attack Rorik's keep soon."

Jena turned around then, no doubt looking for Tarius. When she saw Jestia talking to her she cut Jestia a look that would spoil cheese.

Jestia actually cringed. "So I'm guessing from the go-to-hell look I'm getting from Jena that she knows what we did."

Tarius looked at where Jena was watching them. "Yes, your stupid cousin told her."

"I'm surprised she didn't figure it out sooner. Maybe not what you'd actually done, but that you'd done something. She looks fantastic. I can see why you fell mad in love with her."

Tarius looked at Jena, grinned and Jena quit scowling at them.

"You do know that I was just as crazy about her when she looked twenty-five years older."

"Whatever."

"Jestia, you are now heir apparent."

"Oh no, no, no that was just for show." Jestia shook her head violently. "There is no way…"

"Until we know for sure that we have squelched this plot you have to be heir to the throne. Hestia's safety depends on having an heir, and having one who is known to be a powerful magic user makes us all that much more secure."

"If we are 'secure' now why didn't you so much as touch your dinner?"

"Now you sound like my wife. Last time I drank here I might as well have been poisoned."

"I can check your food for you."

"That would be great but in a minute. Jestia, I need you to embrace your role as heir apparent at least temporarily."

"I will not do any of the things my mother thinks I must do…"

"Nor do I want you to. I need you to be you."

Jestia smiled. "You didn't ask my mother about this did you?" Tarius shrugged. "I didn't think so. Is that all?"

"Not quite. Is there anything you can do about Radkin? You saw her today it is only a matter of time till she gets herself or someone else killed," Tarius said.

"There is no spell that can cancel out another person's sorrow and certainly no tonic could remove her death wish," Jestia said sadly. "I faced only a modicum of what she has lived through, and I could hardly bear it."

"Aye," Tarius agreed. "The problem is if I take her into battle she endangers us all, but if I don't she will have nothing at all left."

"Can you not do like you did to Arvon and give her a job where so much isn't dependent on her?"

"That didn't fool Arvon. He is heartbroken; I can see it on his face. I might as well have betrayed him. It certainly wouldn't fool Radkin."

Chapter Sixteen

Tarius couldn't remember when she had slept any harder. She opened her eyes quickly but relaxed as soon as she saw Jena lying beside her feeding their son.

Jena smiled at her. "I tried not to wake you up."

"I have slept enough. I have much to do today. I must line out a battle plan and we must be leaving for the keep by false dawn tomorrow." She got up on one elbow leaned over and kissed Jena softly on the mouth. "We take too much for granted, Jena." She lay back down on her side and ran her hand over the baby's head of blond curls.

"I know what you mean. Simple things like just being able to reach out and touch each other." Tarius nodded and Jena looked into the depth of her mate's nearly black eyes. "You know I can't go with you, Tarius." From the look on Tarius's face it hadn't occurred to her. Tarius looked at Darian, still petting his head, and then she smiled at Jena.

"So... you finally fell in love with him."

Jena had never told Tarius how she felt—or didn't as the case may be—but she wasn't at all surprised that she had known. "Yes I did, and that's why I can't go, Tarius. We didn't have this dilemma with our other son because he was born in a time of peace. Twice now this baby has been bathed in blood. Twice his life has been as endangered as any of ours." Tears came to her eyes and her throat felt full. "That can't be. We need to protect him. He deserves to be safe the way Jabone was safe, and that means I have to stay behind. But I don't want to be left behind."

Tarius got up on her elbow and leaned over to kiss her again and Jena kissed her back. Tarius leaned back a bit and the baby reached up and grabbed the beaded necklace Tarius wore and had every day since Jena had given it to her the day they had been legally married in the Jethrik. Even though the whole Tarius-being-a-woman had made that marriage null and void and Jena had been forced to marry a man whose life had been violently ended when Jena stabbed him in the heart and twisted, Tarius still wore it.

"You are always with me, Jena, even when we're apart." Tarius lay back down on her side watching her. "I won't tell you I won't miss you by my side. That would be a lie."

"The last time I sent you off to do battle without me seems like a lifetime ago. Remember when you were trying to get rid of me you said you would always be going off to battle and I told you I'd always be waiting for you."

"I do."

"Well I was stupid then. I didn't know the nature of war and now I do. You could leave and I'd never see you again, and now that you have cursed me to live a hundred and twenty more years..."

"I did not curse you." Tarius sighed and rolled onto her back. "I will be fine. I came back to you then, and I will come back to you now. I shouldn't be gone more than a week tops. I'm not Radkin; I have everything to live for. I will not do anything foolish."

"We both know none of that matters."

"Wrong. I don't know that," she said loudly. Then she lowered her voice. "I have only been near death twice and neither time did I have a sword in my hand. I have everything to live for. I tell you I will not die, and I certainly wouldn't have the bad taste to do it without you by my side." One look at her mate's face told her that Tarius fully expected her words to put Jena at ease.

Jena shook her head. "I swear by The Nameless One, Tarius I have lived with you over half my life and yet I still do not know why when you say things like that I'm supposed to find them comforting."

Tarius stood in the "war room" surrounded by the officers of the Marching Night and the Kartik army with the baby on her hip. Arvon smiled. *I can't imagine how this would go over in the Jethrik even today much less all those years ago. If the men who followed her then thinking she was a man could see her now. Just as in charge, commanding as much if not more respect, while she is so obviously female that she carries her child on her hip.*

Tarius was addressing the whole group. "There is no way of knowing how many noncombatants we will encounter or what part of the keep they will stick them in if they even have a siege plan. Once we enter the keep we will have to keep an eye out for those who are unarmed. I do not like the term 'collateral damage' to explain the unnecessary killing of people who were not trying to kill us. Doubtless there will be many children in this place. There is a fine line between keeping ourselves and our fighter's safe and mowing down people who are trying their damndest to get out of our way. And these are not Amalites..." Everyone spit on the floor. "...these are our people."

There were maps and plans of the keep spread before them on the massive table.

"We must only trust that these plans of the keep are close," Tarius said pointing. "They seem to match what little Radkin reported seeing inside the walls and what we saw outside, but since Rorik..." All the Kartiks spit on the floor again, and this time Arvon chuckled. "...was a great traitor we must be aware that he may not have told the kingdom every room or passage in this keep."

Jena moved up to his elbow and he put his arm around her. "What's wrong little sister?" he whispered.

"I'm not going with her."

"You can't, Jena, you have to take care of the baby."

"I know, and my heart tells me she will be safe and she's only going to be gone for a week tops, but I keep remembering the last time she went off to war without me."

"That was a long time ago, Jena."

"Was it? Look at me; do you know what she has done?" she said, turning her face to him. "Do you?"

He shook his head. He had noticed Jena looked considerably younger when she came back than she did when she left. When he'd tried to talk to Tarius about it she had mumbled something about breast feeding and the baby and walked off to check on a goat stuck in a fence, so it was obvious she didn't want to talk about it.

"She had Jestia do some irreversible spell—at least she says it is irreversible we both know she lies as easily as she tells the truth when it comes to what she wants..."

"That's a little harsh, Jena."

"Is it really, Arvon? Because she gave me half of her life."

He looked at her, not really understanding.

"She is a full-blood Katabull. She should have lived nearly three-hundred years, but she split her years between us..."

"Which is why you look twenty again," Arvon said and smiled. "So... my worries that she will someday be alone are unfounded."

"I could be alone, Arvon..."

"Fate would not be that cruel, Jena." He squeezed her shoulder. "Look at her. That's Tarius the Black with your child on her hip giving orders to the whole of the Kartik army. Nothing is going to happen to her." Jestia joined Tarius and a model seemed to appear on the table in front of her. "I don't think Jestia would allow it."

"Do you not think giving me half of Tarius's life is actually killing her? Killing her in the future but it's still killing her. Jestia didn't have any problem doing that."

"First off you don't know that she had no problem doing it. For all you know Jestia thought long and hard about it."

"I'm wondering if you have actually met Jestia," Jena whispered in a hiss.

Arvon chuckled.

"It's not funny, Arvon."

"It sort of is when you're talking to a Katabull man who at fifty-seven is beginning to see that his years are numbered. I'd give nearly anything to have my health and my youth again. She gave you the most amazing gift, Jena—more time with her. Selfishly she kept herself from ever having to live without you. I told you many years ago, but I think that even now you don't understand the depth of Tarius's love for you. She lives for you; she would die for you."

"And see no matter how many times I hear such things it is still not comforting."

Radkin looked at Tarius in disbelief and asked, "What?"

"Jena and the baby have to stay here, and I'm not sure the threat against Hestia is not still very much alive. I want you and Laz to stay here..."

"Babysitting!" Radkin bellowed. "You want me to sit here and babysit?"

Tarius smiled at her friend's anger. "They are very important babies to be sure."

"It's still babysitting. Is this because of what I did the other day?"

"It's because I nearly lost my woman and child, Radkin, and you saved them. I don't trust anyone else but you to watch them—or the queen for that matter. I know that you would die for Jena or my baby. I know you'd die to defend the queen. I trust no one's skill or loyalty except maybe Harris—and he's only a human—as much as I trust yours. If I am going to fight this battle with my head in it I need to know that Jena and Darian are safe."

There was a second when it looked like Radkin was gearing up for a fight but then she took a deep breath, let it out and nodded.

"Good. Please, Radkin, don't drop your guard. Right now

I trust no one but my own people. Please don't treat this like a babysitting duty. To me this is the most important thing any of us will be doing."

Tarius left Radkin, thinking she'd taken care of her last problem before they left, but as she walked out of the room and started down the hall to where they were to eat dinner in the queen's quarters Arvon met her and started to walk with her. She slowed her pace.

"I can keep up you know," he said, agitation in his voice. So she sped up again and tried to ignore him limping along beside her. "I'm coming with you..."

"Arvon..."

"No, Tarius, hear me out. I can still command. There is nothing at all wrong with my voice or my mind and I am the Katabull. There are three hundred of us and three hundred Kartik soldiers moving out at first light. That is the very definition of over kill. I can see why I shouldn't have gone with you to get Jena. I would have been in the way on a mission which was go in get them and get out, but in this battle I will not be in anyone's way." He took hold of her arm and stopped her.

She turned to face him.

"Tarius, I need this. I need this one more battle. I need our son—the son we made together—to see me as I once was, a warrior in command. Not a cripple made old before my years."

Tarius kissed him on the cheek then stepped back from him. "Then that is what you shall have, my brother, and I will be proud to have you with me and our son shall fight by your side."

As she started walking again Arvon followed. Tarius wondered when just going to war had become so difficult. When did it become less about slicing people in two and more about not hurting anyone's feelings?

It was just the queen, Jazel, Harris, Elise, and Tarius and her family in the queen's dining room. Radkin and Laz were standing inside the room on either side of the closed door.

Glorified guard duty, there is no chance I'll get killed doing this unless I just die of boredom, Radkin thought. *Laz doesn't seem to mind at all. He's so like Irvana that he just takes whatever comes his way and is happy.*

"I could go with you," Hestia said.

"No, you really could not," Tarius said sternly.

"But it would be good for the country to see me going to battle against those who would turn their hand against my house and my allies."

"It's too big a risk," Tarius said.

There was a knock at the door behind her. Radkin opened it a crack and saw it was Jestia and Ufalla. She was expecting them, so she let them in.

When Ufalla walked even with her she whispered in Radkin's ear, "Help me."

Radkin chuckled and popped her on the ass with her palm.

"Why must you always be late and wearing pieces of my drapes?" Hestia asked.

"I move in my own time, and you have excellent taste in fabric even if you have lousy taste in clothes." Jestia sat down at the table to her mother's left and Ufalla sat in the empty chair beside her between Jestia and Jabone. "Where is father? Is he out with one of his many whores this evening or just not hungry?"

"Jestia, for pity's sake," Jena scolded in a whisper.

Hestia ignored Jestia and went back to the argument she was having with Tarius. "I don't think it's a risk at all. Three hundred members of the Marching Night, three hundred of the best-trained Kartik soldiers—in the right part of the formation I'd be as safe as I am in my own bed."

"And your bed is very safe since no one but you has been in it for years," Jestia said.

"Why must you try my patience, child?" Hestia demanded.

"Because it would be wrong to make fun of your face," Jestia said. Radkin couldn't quite keep the grin off her face. She noticed Kasiria nearly choked on the food in her mouth. It was odd. When Rea said such things to her or Rimmy they didn't think it was funny at all, but when someone else's kid was doing it to their parents, it was pretty funny. *I'd rather raise my boys three times over as raise their sister again even once. In one weekend she managed to sleep with Jabone, Ufalla, and her brother, and had each of them thinking they were the only one for her until they spoke to each other. Then she cried like a baby for a week because none of them would speak to her—as if she were somehow the injured party.*

Ufalla whispered something in Jestia's ear, and Jestia—realizing what her mother had been talking about—glared at her as if it were her mother saying hateful things to her instead of the other way round.

"No, you will not go to the battle."

"Now see here, Jestia. I will not have you talk to me this way in front of my friends."

"They are my pack," Jestia reminded.

"You are not a Katabull."

"Neither is the Great Leader's wife," Jestia said. "You are not going anywhere where anyone might kill you."

Hestia's features softened, no doubt thinking her child cared for her, but of course Jestia wasn't finished talking because Jestia rarely was—finished talking that is. "Until you once again release me from my responsibilities as heir apparent I don't want you to do anything more dangerous than combing your hair."

"As long as I am queen I will say what I will and will not do," Hestia said.

Radkin smiled. *There she is; there's the Hestia who fought the Great War with us. Well this explains why Jestia is so snippy tonight. She's made no bones at all about not wanting to be queen... which means she'd be perfect.*

"Who do you think you're talking to, old woman?"

"Jestia!" It was Tarius, loud and forceful. "Show your mother some respect, please."

Jestia mumbled and started to actually eat her dinner, showing that she had more respect for the Great Leader than she did her own mother. That had to sting.

Hestia wasn't done. For the moment ignoring Jestia she turned back to the Great Leader. "Tarius, as a friend I ask you..."

"And as your friend I say it would be wrong for you to go. You are a target, Hestia. Us they will stand and fight against because we will be fighting them, but you they want dead. You are a great queen. No one who cares for the Kartik wants to see your bones. You have governed in fairness and with respect for the land and the people—*all* of the people. We know those who want to usurp your rule want to do so only so they can tear the land of the territories up for gold."

"I need you to live a good, long time or at least until you release me," Jestia said. For reasons Radkin could only guess at, Jena glared at Jestia and the witch visibly shrank and tucked into her plate again.

Suddenly Dustan boomed at Arvon, "You're doing what?" He looked embarrassed when all eyes turned to him and pretended to be all about eating.

The baby, who had been sitting on the table in front of

Jabone turned and looked at Dustan with big eyes. Then he turned right around and continued to play with the braids on either side of his big brother's face.

Dustan mumbled things to Arvon. Arvon mumbled things back and then Dustan was just glaring at Tarius.

For a second everyone was sort of silent and brooding, eating or just ignoring each other until Hestia tried to make small talk.

"Jena, you look fantastic. What have you been doing?"

"Jestia did a spell that allowed Tarius to give me half of her life," Jena said sharply.

Well, that explains why Jena is mad at Jestia. It wasn't Hellibolt who did the spell after all, Radkin thought.

"She did what!" Jabone shrieked.

"I have half your madra's life. There, now everyone knows. That's why I look so good. Because Jestia and Tarius decided..."

"Wow! It wasn't my idea, Tarius came to me," Jestia said, trying to shift the blame. It didn't work.

"How did she find out about the spell in the first place?" Jena demanded.

"Jazel told her," Jestia said, pointing at the other witch obviously happy to now have successfully shifted the blame.

Jazel was suddenly very interested in the food on her plate.

"You give Jena half your life and send Arvon into battle," Dustan accused Tarius. "You huge hypocrite!"

Radkin looked at Laz with a grin, and he grinned right back.

"You know how she is! Why would you tell her about that spell, Jazel?" Jena demanded.

"Seriously, Jena, have you not noticed in all these years that Helen ages with me?" Jazel said, giving up on any pretense of eating. "Tarius asked why and I told her. Besides, I didn't do the spell; Jestia did."

"Can you undo it?" Jena asked Jestia.

"I can't."

"I wouldn't let her if she could," Tarius said. "Jena, I talked Jestia into doing the spell."

Radkin nodded. She didn't doubt that for a minute. It would have been easy to do. Jestia had a partner she was crazy about, so all Tarius would have had to do was play to that. Jestia, understanding a love bond, wouldn't have thought of it as killing Tarius a hundred years before her time; she would understand that when Jena died after a normal human life span of at best seventy years, Tarius wouldn't be long behind her. Jestia wouldn't have had any trouble at all believing she was lengthening both women's lives, not shortening one.

"I don't understand," Jabone said to his Madra. "You gave mother half your life. What does that mean?"

"It means..." Dustan told his son as if it were some horrible curse against him personally, "...that she will never have to live a day without your mother, and yet she sends your fadra into battle."

"I am not some old woman; I am the Katabull," Arvon said through gritted teeth. "I will lead again. I will fight again. It is like Hestia said; I will be as safe as if I were in her bed."

"Excuse me!" Hestia hissed in indignation.

"Oh... You know what I mean." He looked at Dustan. "I will leave to do battle tomorrow. You can ride with me or not, and if I die I die."

Dustan got up and stomped towards the door. Radkin and Laz stepped aside and let him out. He slammed the door behind him.

"If I die I die." Jena scolded. "Really, Arvon? You weren't even raised here and yet just like all the Katabull you think the most idiotic things are comforting."

Radkin and Laz looked at each other and shrugged. They thought "If I die I die" was a pretty comforting thing to say really.

Arvon got up wordlessly to go after Dustan. When he got close to Radkin he rolled his eyes and said, "Men." Then he walked out the door and was gone.

Now they were all talking at once. Tarius was the only one who was silent. She looked over at Radkin and shook her head.

Through the din Radkin could hear scattered fragments. Kasiria saying, "It's her life; if she wants to give it away I don't get the big deal." Jena saying to Jazel, "Well someone taught her the spell or she couldn't have done it." Jabone saying his fadra shouldn't be riding with them because he could barely walk much less fight. Hestia whining about wanting to go and fight, and Jestia saying over her dead body because she'd rather be dead than be queen.

It was looking more and more like Jestia would make a really good queen. Radkin noticed the baby just kept playing with his brother's hair and laughing as if they were all acting this way just to entertain him.

"Enough," Tarius said. Then when they didn't stop she said louder, "Enough, I say!" Everyone was quiet except Darian who looked at her and laughed. She smiled at him. "That goes for you too, mister." He just laughed louder.

Tarius looked at the rest of them in turn. "What is all this noise?"

She pointed at Hestia. "You are not going."

She pointed at Jabone. "Your fadra begged me to go. He is going and that is final."

She looked at Jena. "Jena, my dear love we have already talked about this. Blaming anyone but me won't change anything, and Kasiria is right. It's my life; I should be able to give it to who I want."

She pointed to Jestia and Jestia squirmed like a toddler about to get a spanking. "Show your mother some respect, not because she is the queen—you know I don't give a damn about that. Show her some respect because she is your mother." Jestia nodded.

"Ufalla..."

"I didn't do anything," Ufalla said, defending herself.

"Hand me the rolls."

Laz hit Radkin in the ribs hard and whispered in her ear, "See, Mother, what you would have missed if you had died yesterday?"

Chapter Seventeen

As they rode out the next morning the castle was barely out of Tarius's sight when Jestia started to sing. It was a song about those who waited for fighters to come home. Surprisingly, instead of making her feel worse about being separated from Jena it made Tarius feel better. Jestia had a wonderful voice and there was something calmingly familiar about the way she sang. Tarius was lucky to be able to talk, and couldn't sing at all. Because of this few people appreciated singing more than she did. Ufalla had a good voice and so did Jabone, and soon they were all singing songs about battle and warfare and friendships forged in combat.

One of the songs they sang was one her father used to sing, and she found hearing it put her in a mood... to just kill everything in that keep.

My father could sing. I think I remember my mother singing, and my son can sing. If the Amalites hadn't cut my throat maybe I could sing. Instead I'm a killer.

There was only one road into the keep. It had taken all of them most of a day to make a trip that could usually be made in a few hours because most of the Kartik soldiers were on foot. Just out of view of the castle they made camp for the night, but she was sure those in the keep were well aware of their presence.

At first light the next morning Tarius pulled a cold charcoal from the edge of the fire pit and used it to mark her face in the pattern of a skull. Some of the others marked their faces as well. She noticed Ufalla among them, but when Ufalla tried to talk Jestia into it saying having the black under her eyes would block glare Jestia simply looked from her to Tarius and rolled her eyes. She wasn't having any part of it.

They ate quickly and by first light they marched towards the fortress. As they closed in they started to fan out till they completely surrounded the keep. It took them several hours to get in formation. Tarius broke the Marching Night into two groups and put all the Kartiks into two. They were just inside the tree line, well out of range of any archer's arrows.

The Kartiks would run the right and rear flank. She, Harris and Rimmy would run the main campaign centered on the keep's main gates. Arvon, Jabone and Kasiria would run the left flank.

Jestia and Ufalla were with Tarius, Jazel was with Arvon, and the Kartik unit was witchless. Tarius always protected her people first; it wasn't anything personal.

Tarius paced her horse in front of her unit. Perhaps the only element of surprise they had was that there were so many of them. The four towers on the corners and the tops of the walls were covered with archers and crossbow men, so they obviously knew they were up against several hundred Katabull.

"Jestia." Tarius rode up to her. "Is there anything you can do about the archers? Our bow men can take them out, but that will take time."

"There is a spell Jazel taught me, one that keeps the archers from really seeing you but they can still hit you if they aim in your direction, and if you look at them they can see you clearly."

Tarius took in their situation at a glance and said, "I know that spell. I think in this instance that won't serve us well. I can have the ballistae target the archers in the towers at this range, take many of them out that way. But once we attack with anything... Well if I were them I wouldn't wait for us to sit and pick off all their archers. I'd open the gates and send my people out to try to pull us into range of their archers. I would not call a charge; I would make them come to us, but the others probably won't. Even if they did there will always be those who break ranks and run in to meet the fight instead of waiting for it to come to us. I wish to take as few casualties as possible." Tarius was calculating. It was what she did.

"What about that weaving spell, Jestia?" Ufalla said.

"What good would that do?" Jestia asked. "My love, I'm afraid that hit on your head has dulled your wit."

"Those little trees flying around would be distracting and damn hard to fire a bow around with any accuracy."

"True, but it's a mending spell. There has to be something to fix."

"A bow was once a tree then a chunk of wood," Ufalla said with a shrug.

Jestia looked at Ufalla and smiled. "You are the best mate a witch ever had, my great and amazing love."

Ufalla looked at Tarius, rolled her eyes and popped herself in the forehead with her palm.

Tarius rode up beside Ufalla as Jestia got off her horse handing her reins to her mate.

"It must be a big spell if she's getting off the horse," Ufalla said.

"Ufalla, what is with…"

"Jestia gushing at me all the time?"

Tarius nodded,

"Short version, I took a bad hit on the head." She took off her helm and turned to show Tarius the spot, not that Tarius could see it through her thick black hair. "I forgot who I was. Jestia thought I was going to be a ditzy, panty-waisted titty baby for the rest of our lives. Ever since I came back to myself I've had to deal with two unpleasant things: everyone who saw me making fun of the way I acted, and Jestia having the need to express her love for me every time she speaks."

"I suppose there are worse things."

"Are there Tarius, are there?" Ufalla asked. She popped her helm back on her head but she couldn't keep the smile off her face. They were about to do battle, but Ufalla was unafraid.

Tarius wasn't afraid; she never was, but she missed Jena and she guessed there would always be a part of her that wouldn't believe Jena was safe unless she could see her. She certainly hadn't felt good leaving her in the very place she'd been abducted from, but there just didn't seem to be anything else to do. While she'd mostly been trying to keep crazy Radkin out of the fight in an effort to keep her and everyone who would try to save her from herself alive, she hadn't been exaggerating Radkin's devotion to Jena. Radkin would never let anything happen to Tarius's wife or her child even if it meant she had to live to save them.

Jena had said goodbye to Tarius, Jabone and the rest of her family. Then she had stood at this very window and watched till every last rider was out of sight. Except for the fact they weren't all peeing in a corner, the food, the smell and the furnishings, she might as well have still been in the cell in that keep.

As soon as she thought it she wanted to kick her own ass for even thinking such a thing. No one here was threatening her baby. She was actually staying in Jestia's room and Darian was enjoying playing with Jestia's old toys. Radkin was staying in what used to be Katan's room. Jena remembered him as a sweet, somewhat timid boy. Thinking of Katan she felt doubly guilty about feeling sorry for herself. She and her baby were safe, and maybe Radkin was right and you couldn't be too careful.

It was easier to remember that her baby needed her when he wasn't sleeping. Jena thought seriously about waking him up just for that reason, but she didn't. Radkin walked in to check on her and read the look on Jena's face.

"Don't worry, Jena, they will be fine."

Jena nodded. She couldn't very well tell Radkin she didn't know how Jena felt. Three of Radkin's children and her children's fadra had all gone with Tarius. She knew exactly how Jena felt. Her loved ones were away getting ready to do battle if not already engaged, and she was stuck here with nothing to do but think about whether they were alive or not.

The difference being that Radkin was one of the reasons there was so little to do. To keep them all safe she had Jena, the baby, and the queen sequestered in the queen's quarters. The quarter were large and lavish, consisting of two bathing rooms, the small room that held the commode, three bedrooms, the room that held the huge dining table as well as what passed for an informal sitting area, and the queen's office. All the doors to the rest of the castle and the outside were locked, and the only people allowed in were the wait and household staff. Radkin made the wait staff taste all their food and she checked the household staff for weapons when they came in then made them do what they were supposed to do and leave. Radkin only allowed the door into the dining and sitting room to be used, and she'd had a bed and chair moved to the door. She'd stationed Laz there to check the staff as they came in and out. He slept there, and of course Radkin allowed him to sleep because he was Katabull, so if anyone so much as touched that door he would be up.

And all of those things were why Jena had for just a second thought this was really no different from being locked in the cell.

"My heart tells me she'll be fine, that they will all be fine. My head is a lot less sure."

Radkin nodded. "So, the queen is still asleep?"

"Well there isn't much else to do."

"I'm sure her office is filled with unfinished tasks. Things she's used to doing and should be doing—not like you and I who are used to being outside."

"About that, Radkin…"

"No, Jena, I will not let you go outside. It will only be a week—tops. You, the queen and Darian are my responsibility."

Jena decided if Tarius came home safe she might strangle her. She didn't have to do such a good job of making Radkin believe that this was the most important position of all. Radkin was checking for spies in the oatmeal. She wouldn't even let them do their business without standing guard outside the door. She had even suggested that the three-story shoot that went from the commode down to an open composting pit might be used for an attacker to crawl up, and so she checked the hole before she let either Jena or Hestia use it. Hestia seemed to have no problem with it; Jena on the other hand thought it was ridiculous.

When she'd voiced her opinion to Radkin she had said, "You can't be too careful, Jena."

"You seriously think someone would walk through an eight-foot by eight-foot, two-foot deep pit full of human waste and then climb up a crap-covered poop shoot to attack us?" Jena said in disbelief.

Radkin shrugged. "I'd do it if it was the only way in."

And she would, too. If Tarius told her to do it she'd wade right in the shit up to her knees to do whatever Tarius wanted done, which was why Jena didn't bother to argue with Radkin when she said they couldn't go outside. Radkin had been asked by Tarius to protect her and Hestia and the baby, and that was precisely what she was going to do whether they liked it or not. Never mind that she and Hestia could sling steel as well as Radkin could.

"I think you should talk to her," Radkin said.

"Hestia? Why."

"Because she needs someone to talk to, and you're a woman."

Jena laughed and shook her head. "So are you, Radkin."

"Two things, Jena; first, you know what I mean."

Jena did. Followers of The Nameless God believed in three sexes. According to their belief Arvon and Jabone were both male, Jena was female, and Radkin, Tarius and Dustan were all third sex. They rarely talked about it because they thought it was obvious who was what and it really didn't matter. There was no difference in their anatomy; that Jena knew for a fact. She thought she had it all figured out and was sure she knew what they meant till Tarius said she thought Kasiria was third sex. Then it went right back to being something she didn't really understand. However she did know why Radkin thought she would be better equipped to talk to the queen.

Radkin continued. "Second, I'm the last person who

should talk to someone when they are depressed."

"Alright, I might as well. You won't let me do anything else." She looked to where Darian was still sleeping.

"I'll watch him," Radkin said.

"Aren't you going to walk with me down to the queen's bedroom and check inside?" Jena teased.

Radkin just smiled back. "I just came from there so I know it's clear."

Tarius watched as small trees and bushes, their roots still attached, started flying through the air towards the archers. Several of the archers, seeing the rapidly approaching shrubberies, dropped their weapons and ran screaming into the keep.

"Fire!" Tarius ordered.

Three ballistae fired, doing a huge amount of damage to the men in the front tower.

"Fire!" she called out again, and three more fired.

"Fire!" She had nine ballistae total, and as the last ones fired the first ones were ready to fire again.

"Fire!"

The whole time the archers on the walls and the towers were having their bows ruined as trees, twigs and bushes attached themselves to them and started weaving.

When the top of the walls were mostly cleared, Tarius called on the night and then called, "Charge!"

As a whole they moved towards the keep. Their battering ram was in front and the six Katabull carrying it only had to hit the main gates seven times to bring them down. Then the soldiers in the keep were boiling out and Tarius didn't have to tell her people to attack because they just did.

Arvon heard Tarius call the charge and a few minutes later he echoed her order. Dustan and Jazel were on his left, his son and Kasiria were on his right, and he was the Katabull. As he shouted orders to his troop, all pain left him and he felt reborn.

The gate they were to attack was not as big or as well built as the main entrance, so they only had to ram it once to break it into a million pieces. It nearly exploded, and the men who had been standing inside, obviously trying to hold it in place, fell like trees in a gale. Then their enemies were just boiling out of the keep, and they were suddenly everywhere.

Sitting beside him, Jabone said, "I don't like this, Kasiria, it is too much like the hive."

"And we will kill them as easily," Kasiria said. Then she jumped off her mount because the horse was getting in the way of her killing. The girl really was like Tarius. Maybe a little too much like her because she didn't have the skill to match her bravado. Of course what she didn't know her sword did.

Neither he nor Jabone had time to worry about Kasiria because then they were on them and they were trying to pull them off their horses. Arvon wasn't having any of that.

Beside him he became aware of Jazel chanting, and then a blue fog fell over their opponents but not on them. Arvon instantly knew why Jazel had cast such a spell when he saw one of his fighters apologizing to another who had a nasty sword wound on his arm. Their enemy looked too much like their own people. For the first time in battle Arvon, Kasiria, Dustan and Jazel didn't look just like the enemy. It was the rest of them now that looked just like the enemy... well until Jazel cast her spell.

There were so many of them coming from the keep yet none of them were women and none were Katabull. Not all Katabull lived in the compound; they were scattered more or less sparingly all over the island. However all came under Tarius's authority, so they may have simply refused to fight when they saw their leader at the gates.

He couldn't understand why there were so many coming out of what had been nothing more than a small rear entrance, and then he knew why. Tarius had come in the front and they were all trying to run out the back. They were trying to get away, but Arvon wasn't about to let that happen. These people had dared to come after his family.

Tarius and her people killed all those who ran at them and then they barreled through the open gates into the keep, killing everyone who was cloaked in the blue smoke. Harris had taken Elise and a small group on horseback in to clean out the common ground in the middle of the keep.

Having killed everyone who met them outside the walls, most of the Marching Night with her dismounted and went on foot into the keep. She split them into groups and sent them in different directions. The keep would have to be cleaned floor by floor and room by room. She kept Jestia and Ufalla, Rimmy and Riglid with her and they took the right wing of the bottom floor. Radkin had been right; Tarius wasn't seeing a single female fighter. In fact she hadn't seen a single noncombatant yet; she got a bad feeling in the pit of her stomach. The place felt dark, and the energy was bad. She could tell Jestia felt it, too, by how close she was standing to Ufalla. The soldiers they encountered were mostly trying to run from them until they engaged them and then they fought poorly until they were killed. Tarius and her group left the dead behind them and kept moving on.

Rorik's actions made less and less sense by the minute. Who had trained these men to fight? Whoever had done it had done a piss-poor job. Yet they had all stayed, no doubt preparing for battle. But why, for the promise of gold? No amount of money was worth death. If Rorik's plot was to make her kill Hestia and then prove that she had plotted against the queen herself and then take her down, not just the Marching Night but the whole of the Katabull Nation would have fallen on them. They didn't have enough men—even if they were well trained—to consider such a battle.

There was simply no way they could have ever thought they could hope to win, but it appeared they had been completely unaware of that till the Marching Night was cutting them down like wheat in a field. Had Tarius not had the witches with them, had she only brought the Marching Night and left the Kartik soldiers at home, they could have taken this keep easily. The three hundred Kartik troops alone could have done it. Hell, she could have done it with a third of the Marching Night.

Tarius was in front leading when Jestia took hold of her arm. Tarius turned and looked at her.

"That tapestry." Jestia pointed to one on the opposite side of the room they were standing in. "It hides something sinister."

Tarius nodded and readied her sword. "Take it down."

It vanished completely—which was a pretty neat trick—to reveal an open doorway. When they moved forward to check it out they found a narrow staircase going down into the earth. Tarius went in first followed by Jestia and Ufalla. Rimmy and Riglid brought up the rear. Normally she wouldn't have attempted to go down the stairs until they had cleaned everything above them. At the very least she would have left someone guarding the opening at their back, but she had not found a remotely worthy opponent yet and she simply wasn't afraid of them. The staircase bottomed out about twenty feet underground, and they entered a massive hallway the walls of which were dotted every few feet by doors with bars on them. The air was stale and foul smelling.

It was a limestone mine. Obviously the stones had been carved out of here to make the keep above. Clever really, kill two birds with one stone. Build a secret complex underground while getting the stone you needed to build the keep above.

She wanted to check out what were obviously cells, but Jestia was pointing down the hall in the other direction to an open doorway. The staircase and the hallway were all lit with candles, but the light emanating from the room at the end of the hall glowed too brightly to come from mere candles.

Tarius turned, feeling a sudden need to be more cautious. "Riglid, stand guard at the bottom of the stairs."

Riglid nodded and took up a position at the base of the stairs. Later he would tell her how happy he was to have been put there.

"Is it magic light, Jestia?" Tarius asked.

"No, oil lamps maybe," Jestia said. "But the evil I sense emanates from that room."

Tarius walked down the hall towards the door in huge strides. As she got closer she could hear chanting and her blood ran cold. Whoever was chanting wasn't speaking Kartik. When she walked in and saw them praying at their altar she didn't hesitate. She ran over and slew the three unarmed priests without a moment's hesitation. Then she turned to look at Jestia.

"This cannot be!" But of course it was, and it explained every idiotic thing Rorik had done. His plan with holes in it a child could throw a wet cat through made perfect sense now. It explained why he had come after her and her people. He should have known to do so would mean death to himself and all who followed him. He wasn't allowed to think, though; he just did what he was told. They promised him his heart's desire if he did as they told him, and he thought he couldn't lose because his gods had promised him victory.

Jena walked into Hestia's room and found her as Radkin had told her. She was in her bed but she wasn't asleep; she was just lying there. "Hestia, it's after noon and you've eaten nothing. I have nothing to do but take care of my baby, but you have an office full of things I'm sure you could occupy your time with."

"But I don't care about any of it," Hestia said, not bothering to even turn and look at Jena. "What am I?"

"You are the queen. You are fair and just and..."

"I am no one. I don't even remember what it means to want something for myself any more; do you know that, Jena? I have no personal desire left in me. I don't even know how to have a simple conversation. I try to make small talk with Radkin and find out that her mate—who I've just asked about—died years ago and then her despair is so evident she might as well be bleeding on my feast table. I again try by complementing you and wind up starting a huge fight with your whole family."

Jena grinned. "Oh that fight was coming with or without your help."

"I... I hate my life, Jena. It is a joyless pool of the most horrid swill from which I drink daily and never feel full. Tarius said I don't know my people—that I live around but not with them."

"Hestia, I'm sure Tarius said a great many things after I was abducted, and I doubt she really meant half of them."

"But she was right, Jena. I don't know them and they don't know me. Usually I'm never alone. People help me bathe, they help me dress, and they cook my meals and bring them to me. I know their faces but know nothing about them— who they love, who they hate, even how many if any children they have. I smile and I'm pleasant and they return that. I'm never alone except when I'm in here at night. Jestia is also right about me; no one but me has been in this bed since I pushed Dirk away. And the fact that I told him I didn't want him in my bed hurt him, but it didn't hurt me at all."

"He's not a bad fellow, but I never cared for him any more than I do for the girl who helps me dress whose name I'm not even sure I know. I never had any desire for him. Any desire I had in me I had to put away before I put the crown on. Jestia is closer to Tarius than she ever has been to me. She has nothing but contempt for me, and I can't find it in my heart to blame her. My son died..." Her words caught in her throat and she had to clear it. "My son died and I never once looked at him the way you look at your sons. I suddenly want things that it is way too late to have."

"That's not true, Hestia. As long as you breathe you can change your life," Jena said softly. She sat down on the bed beside Hestia and took hold of her shoulder. Hestia finally turned to face her. "If I had given up and let my fear win the day I never would have had the life I've had. I would have stayed in the Jethrik and let a man I hated do anything he wanted to me. I'd have had his children hanging from the rafters until I just couldn't have any more and then I would have died in childbirth and left a room full of motherless children to be raised by that bastard. It's your life, Hestia. It doesn't really belong to the crown or the kingdom, so you can change it whenever you like."

"But I have duties, responsibilities to the kingdom..."

"And all are just excuses not to do what you really want, because what if you follow your heart and you hate that, too? The kingdom is your excuse to stay in a rut of misery because at least the misery you have now you know. You're comfortable in it."

"I don't feel comfortable any more, and I tried to do something different." Hestia defended then added in a pout, "I wanted to go to the battle and Tarius wouldn't let me."

"You wanted to go to the battle so that maybe a stray arrow or blade would kill you and you wouldn't have to live any more." Jena smiled at the look on Hestia's face. "Don't look so shocked, Hestia, while I might look it I am not that young, mostly-naive Jethrikian girl that you first met. Tarius leads a great people and for all the years she has been their leader I have sat beside her. If I didn't gain some wisdom I'd have to be an idiot."

"She gave you half her years. Tell me what that's like."

"It's infuriating..."

Hestia chuckled. "I mean what it's like to be loved like that, to have someone as amazing as Tarius the Black love you so much she would give you half her years. Put her love and desire for you over the welfare of her people. What's it feel like when she looks at you and you know she aches for you and only you? You should have seen her Jena, what she was like. As odd as it may sound it was seeing what the thought of losing you made of her that made me realize all that was lacking in my own life. There was no part of the level-headed war lord, the Great Leader, I have come to know and depend on in this castle. While you were gone and no one knew who had taken you or where, she was torn to shreds. Her pain was etched on every feature of her face and she couldn't think clearly. What's it like to be loved like that?"

Jena sighed lay down beside the queen and looked at the ceiling. "It's like owning the sun and dancing with the moons. When we sleep, when I breathe she breathes, and when we make love I don't know where my body ends and hers begins. She will hold me in this way that is so tight it is almost uncomfortable, and in those moments I just know nothing bad could ever happen to me. Decades after our first kiss her touch still makes me weak in my knees. And we can look at one another and say more than some people could say if they talked a whole lifetime. Mostly her love makes every doubt I ever had about myself vanish."

Hestia moved to look at the ceiling as if Jena were seeing something she, too, wanted to see. "I'd give all I have for one night with your love."

Jena sat straight up and looked down at Hestia. "What!"

Hestia seemed to take a second to go over what she'd said. "No. No I didn't mean with Tarius, I meant the love you share with her. See what I mean? I can't even make normal conversation."

Kasiria was too far away from her own forces, and there were suddenly way more blue smoke-covered fighters around her than she could keep up with. Jabone jumped off his mount and ran towards her. Before Arvon had time to think about it he pulled his horse around and went after his son. In mere minutes they had run out of combatants and had to go chase down some more. The Marching Night was dispatching these men easily. Arvon was reminded more of scything grain than fighting a battle. Soon the ground was littered with the corpses of their foes.

Arvon wiped his fingers down his sword to clear the blood then sheathed it. He wiped his hand on his britches and then wiped his face with his hand knowing he'd probably mostly smeared blood there. He looked to where Jabone was obviously having words with his mate.

"I don't know what's worse, Radkin's death wish or Kasiria's blood lust," Arvon mumbled. His attention was drawn to one of his men running towards him. That was something you never wanted to see. Someone coming for you at a dead run across a field of bodies after a battle meant someone you loved was injured or worse. Arvon's heart suddenly stopped and he looked around him in horror. Dustan was nowhere to be seen. He spurred his horse forward towards the runner. When he saw it was young Tarius, his panic only grew sharper.

"Arvon, it's Dustan..."

"Where?" Tarius pointed towards the tree line and Arvon

spurred his horse on, forcing him to walk around and on bodies. To his astonishment his son ran past him on foot.

Medic stations were set up in the tree line. He saw his son standing over a blanket that was laid out on the ground, dismounted and went to join him. Jabone turned to look at Arvon and said, "Father is fine."

"Fine, fine!" Dustan screamed. Arvon felt like he could finally breathe again. "I'm mortally wounded and near death. The last of my blood is running from my body. I love you, my son."

"It's not that bad a wound, Father."

"My arm has been cut off."

Arvon pushed his son aside. Dustan was lying on the blanket with his eyes closed, not looking at the sword wound he had on his shoulder. It was a bad wound but not a horrid one. Certainly Dustan was nowhere near losing an arm much less death. Arvon was relieved. "It's just a flesh wound," Arvon said.

The medic poured some Montero spring water on the cut and it bubbled.

Dustan yelled out, "It burns! It burns!"

The medic shook his head, smiled at Arvon, and then grabbed an already-threaded needle. Arvon nodded his understanding. Knowing it would take him even longer to get up than it would take him to get down he turned to their son. "Jabone, you will have to hold your father still so he can be stitched."

Dustan opened one eye a crack and looked up at him. "It... it really isn't that bad?"

"No, my heart, it really isn't. I wouldn't lie to you."

"I can be still," Dustan said, seeming to find his courage. Then he looked at the medic with the needle, lost it again and closed his eyes. "On second thought, Jabone you'd better hold my arm still."

Jabone smiled at Arvon then knelt on the ground beside Dustan and held his arm. But he didn't have to do it long because the minute the needle touched Dustan's arm he passed out cold. Jabone still held his arm just because it made it easier for the medic to stitch the wound closed, but Dustan wasn't jerking around making it impossible to stitch him the way a man did sometimes no matter how still he was trying to be if he was awake for it.

Arvon remembered he was still in command, so he walked back over and got on his horse. "We must assemble our troop and send them into the keep to finish what we started. Come as soon as you're done here, Jabone."

Arvon started shouting orders to his troops and they quickly regrouped and then entered the keep. He sighed. Kasiria was nowhere in sight which meant she had run into the keep on her own. "I swear that girl thinks she's Tarius the Black."

Chapter Eighteen

By early the third morning a rider came in with good if incomplete news. Tarius and the army had taken Rorik's keep. There were few casualties on their side and all of their loved ones were safe. However the note written in Tarius's hand ended on an ominous note.

"We have uncovered a horror that I cannot bring myself to write. There is much that must be done here; we will be here two more days and then make our way back. I will tell you what we've found when I return."

Knowing all that Tarius had seen in her life the fact there was something she wasn't comfortable writing did nothing to put Hestia's mind at ease.

Hestia had overheard the argument Jena had lost with Radkin about going to join Tarius and the Marching Night now that the battle was over. It hadn't lasted long. Jena had explained all the reasons they could go then Radkin had told her why it wasn't a good idea ending with, "If Tarius wanted you and the boy brought there or me to abandon my post guarding the queen she would have said so in just that many words."

Now darkness was once again blanketing the land and Hestia just stood at the window looking into the night. It was drizzling, and both moons which would have been full were barely glowing behind a bank of clouds. It was as dark as her mood and she felt chilled to the bone. She wore only a blue silk night gown but it wasn't the sheerness of it that let cold in. Neither the weather nor the room was that cold; she was. Behind her a breeze caused the light in the oil lamp to dance making strange shapes on the wall. She looked at them seeing if they might have some hidden meaning for her, but there were no clear images and no answers there.

"Are you alright my queen?" Radkin asked.

Hestia nearly jumped out of her skin. So quiet were the Katabull that she hadn't heard her come in.

"I'm sorry, I should have knocked but if you were asleep I didn't want to wake you."

"It's alright, Radkin; I should have known someone had entered by the way the flame danced. Jazel is right; I am ripe for killing." She turned slightly so that she could see the

Katabull. "You would have known."

Radkin smiled, nodded and started to go.

Hestia turned the rest of the way around. "What are you doing now?"

"I was going to go to bed. Just making one last check on everyone, Jena and Darian are already asleep."

"Could you stay a minute? I don't wish to be alone with my own thoughts. They torment me."

"Why so, Hestia?" Radkin asked gently. She walked completely in the room and closed the door behind her.

Hestia walked towards her saying. "I... I don't really know why. I don't know what I want or how to get it, and..."

"You just keep doing what's expected of you and nothing really matters to you at all."

Hestia stopped when she was maybe a foot away and said, "Exactly."

"And exactly why I'm the last person you should be talking to. I know how you feel, but I don't have any answers for myself, Hestia. How could I possibly help you?"

Hestia took a deep breath and let it out. "You're right of course. I'm sorry. I should let you go to bed."

Radkin started to turn to leave, but Hestia reached out and took hold of her arm. "Wait."

Radkin spun on her, took her in her arms and moved with her till she shoved her back against a wall. At first Hestia was sure they were under siege, but then Radkin lowered her head and started kissing her on the mouth over and over until Hestia started to respond in kind. Radkin's hands kneaded the flesh of Hestia's waist through her gown.

Radkin stopped kissing her and moved her lips till they were nearly touching Hestia's ear. "You are a beautiful woman, Hestia, and I have been too long alone. Maybe we both need to do something that will make us remember what it means to be alive. If you want me to stop I will." Then her lips were kissing Hestia's throat.

"May the gods help me; there is no part of me that wants you to stop."

Radkin picked Hestia up carried her to the bed and more threw than laid her down. Radkin took off her sword and then she started removing clothing. She looked at Hestia expectantly, and Hestia couldn't remember ever getting out of her clothes so quickly. Radkin stretched herself out on top of her, taking Hestia's hands in hers and holding them and then she was kissing her again and Hestia felt like a storm was going through her whole body.

Radkin was very passionate and obviously experienced and she just didn't stop until Hestia had her sheets balled up in her fists and was biting her own tongue to keep from screaming. Hestia exuberantly returned the favor, and then they did it again, and then they did it again till the lamp was nearly out of oil and they were spent.

Hestia lay more on than beside Radkin whose arms were wrapped around her holding Hestia tightly to her. "What the hell did we just do?" Hestia asked.

Radkin laughed and held her tight. "I feel better. Do you feel better?"

"I'm just happy to actually feel."

Chapter Nineteen

Tarius stared into the fire. The Keep's common area was open to the sky, and they had built a huge fire in the middle of it. She couldn't remove the horror of what she'd seen from her brain or dull the knowledge of what it meant. Worse than all that was that it pushed up memories she'd spent most of her life trying to forget

Beside her Ufalla said, "I'm a little sick."

"I think all of us who went below ground are. How is Jestia?"

"Spent. She's finally sleeping."

"But you can't?"

"No," Ufalla said.

Tarius had yet to allow anyone else to go into the catacombs nor had she told them what they had found there. Let them wallow in their victory and get some rest. The truth could wait till morning.

"Jestia says they are the same as the ones from the hive, but how can that be?" Ufalla asked.

It was a good question, one she'd spent most of the day trying to figure out. "The Amalite's religion didn't allow for any variations. In order for the priests to maintain complete control they alone can say the 'truth.' This splinter group had to hide even from the other Amalites. My guess would be that the priests that started this order must have been unable to break into the priesthood so they just started their own group, hid them in the cave and apparently they sent their missionaries here. Their reasons are clear; imagine if this splinter group had been able to do what the rest of the Amalite cult couldn't. If they could have wiped out the Katabull then they could have taken over the entire religion. Since the Great War killed off all other Amalites who followed the religion, I imagine they already felt like they'd won against their own people. It would have proved to them that they were the only true believers. It would have become their mission to finish what the others had only started."

And why did they think it was the same group as the ones in the cave? Because just like the temple in the hive the walls of the temple in the catacombs had been painted with human blood and there was evidence of cannibalism—

neither were practices of the old Amalite religion. The three priests she had killed had all been ancient and each one of them an Amalite. They found two younger priests who both looked like Kartiks hiding in the keep, and they killed them, too. There was no doubt that Rorik and his people had been followers of the Amalite gods, but that alone wouldn't have had she and Rimmy, Riglid and Ufalla huddled up to the fire looking into its depths and drinking the warmth their bodies didn't really need from it.

The catacombs held many rooms and each one they looked into was littered with dead women and children. They had taken them below no doubt under the pretense of protecting them, and then they had killed them all. From the look of the corpses it happened not long after the Marching Night and the Kartik army had set up camp the night before. Rigor mortis had already set in.

"Why... why did they kill their own people?" Ufalla asked. She sounded as sick as she said she felt.

"Many reasons. First, their religion has no regard for women, less for female children, and only slightly more for male children. I'm sure you noticed there were no female children and no blond-headed children, though every one of the women was Amalite. I'm assuming that like the Amalites in the hive they were sacrificing and eating any children that they didn't find suitable for their breeding program. I have a feeling that nearly every man we fought and killed today was born and raised right here. Many, if not most, were probably Rorik's own children."

"Where did all the women come from?" Rimmy asked.

"The Amalite. We know he had the mine there," Tarius answered. "Rorik probably sent raiding parties out regularly to get new breeders when these were spent. He planned to fill the Kartik with 'believers,' and rot the island from the inside out."

"What would make Rorik—any Kartik for that matter—turn to the Amalite gods and join their religion? It doesn't make any sense," Ufalla said.

Rimmy nodded his head in agreement.

"No religion makes sense. It preys on our need to know things we can't know. We long for answers to questions that have no answers. Religion allows a person to pretend they have those answers. It promises to deliver to people the things they want or need. Priests promise greedy people wealth, hungry people food. The Amalite priests get their power by telling shallow, greedy people like Rorik that praying to their gods will give them the things they most want. They promise them wealth and victory and tell them that the ends always justify the means because after all it's not what they want but what the gods want.

The Amalite priests told him right where to find gold. After he actually found it—a lot of it—he was hooked and followed them blindly. I imagine these things have been here since shortly before the Great War. You were with me, Rimmy. You remember how the Marching Night started. We swept the shores of the Kartik looking for, finding and killing Amalite missionaries. Some of them must have gotten through. Rorik got to sit on the throne for a brief period of time while Hestia went to fight the Great War with us. The power went to his head and he was easy prey for those devils, a weak-minded, woman-hating man with delusions of grandeur and galloping ambition."

"Why did he hate women?" Ufalla asked confused.

"Because he hated his mother—everyone knows a man who hates his mother will despise all women."

"What makes you think he hated his mother?"

"Because he couldn't have done the things he did to these women unless he hated his mother. The religion told him he should be in power not his sister. Filthy Amalite missionaries told him exactly what he wanted to hear; that their gods—which they believe are the only real gods—thought women should be subservient to men. They told him that he should be king and then they devised a plan. The same plan they always have used, make as many believers as you possibly can. Bring up children in the religion and make sure they know there is no choice but to believe the utter bullshit that flows from the priest's mouths. When they have made as many of them as there are of us then they take over the land and make everyone bow to their gods."

"Why would anyone believe something that brings only death?" Rimmy asked. "What we saw today in that hole... what we saw in the hive. I still don't understand why they would kill their own children."

"They've been doing it for a while... not on this scale, but they have been. The priests told them their children and women would be better off dead. That we would do horrible things to them, and mostly that we wouldn't allow them to pray to their gods. They told their 'sheep' that and they believed them. They killed them all because there are more of them hiding. The priests didn't want anyone left alive to tell us about the others. If you were one of those women and had knowledge of more groups like this one, the first thing you'd do is tell us who and where they were."

"Finias and Sedrik," Ufalla said.

"Let's hope it stops there," Tarius answered.

"The Amalite religion hates the Katabull," Rimmy said.

"Which is why they wanted Tarius to kill the queen so that the whole of the army would rise up against us," Ufalla said.

Tarius looked at her goddaughter and nodded. "They hate us because they fear us. They hate us because they know they cannot beat us and that we will never convert to their filthy religion." Tarius took in a deep breath and let it out. "I always thought if our people were attacked by them it would come from the sea. It is only now I realize I have built our wall on the wrong side of the compound."

Harris and Elise were approaching.

"Change the subject. There is no reason for no one to sleep in peace tonight."

Harris limped up to the fire laughing. He looked at Tarius. "Have you talked to your son's father yet?"

Tarius smiled and nodded.

Harris continued. "He is crying like a baby over a minor wound, and when I said something nicer than that to him he told me that first he rode behind Gudgin, then he rode behind you and me, and then he rode behind Arvon. Apparently till now he'd never had much more than a scratch, and he is surprised at the amount of pain he is in and... He's just acting ridiculous."

Ufalla made a face and looked at them all. "Hey cut him some slack, maybe he hit his head."

Eerin had made himself scarce after Rorik's death. Unsure that the Marching Night wouldn't decide he needed killing, too, he had changed out of his robes and into britches and a simple tunic during the many skirmishes that had ridded the castle of all of Rorik, Finias and Sedrik's people.

Then in the hubbub created when most of The Marching Night and a large unit of Kartik soldiers had gone to lay waste to Rorik's keep, he had apparently been completely forgotten. So he just wandered aimlessly around the palace and the grounds sleeping and eating in the servant's quarters until someone put him to work tending the very garden the Great Leader's mate had been abducted from.

He had in fact been ordered to replant one of the beds that had been trampled in her attack. He was digging a hole for a plant when he saw something that caught his eye. A clay medallion of some kind on a torn leather thong. Someone must have lost it in the scuffle and then it got buried in the earth. He picked it up and turned it over. When he did his blood ran cold.

What did it mean? His mind raced. *That Rorik and his people were followers of the Amalite gods. That can't be. He used me, but they hate all forms of magic. If they were followers of the cult how could I not have known? I lived there for years, but I was never allowed to leave the west tower, and why was that? Because they were hiding some huge secret. I knew they were and it makes sense that this is it.* He looked at the medallion in his hands. *It just can't be; it* doesn't *make sense. If this is true then I have not only betrayed the queen but I am a traitor to my own kind. And there will be no way to convince Tarius the Black and Jestia that I didn't know exactly what I was working for and... I am as big a dumbass as they think I am and I'm a dead man.*

The morning light was streaming in the window when Hestia woke from sweet dreams to find herself still wrapped in Radkin's arms.

"Hestia, I must go check in with Laz and check on Jena," Radkin whispered. Hestia realized Radkin's voice was what had woken her. Hestia nodded rolled off of her and stretched. Radkin kissed her gently on the lips. "Thanks for last night."

Radkin got up and started dressing and Hestia watched her. *What's that mean? Thanks for last night. I shouldn't have thought it was anything more, right? And I can't really have an affair with Radkin. Can I? Tarius will be back soon and then she'll have to go with her and...*

"Can you come back, just for a little while?" She couldn't believe the words had spilled from her mouth.

Radkin smiled back at her. "Oh I think it will take more than a little while."

Hestia felt desire creep over her body, "Could you come back anyway?"

"I will." Radkin had just put her sword on her back, but she walked over and kissed Hestia again. This time Hestia kissed her back.

Radkin went to the bathroom first, did her business and washed up. She tried to wipe the grin from her face before she went to check on Jena. The baby and Jena were both still asleep and everything seemed secure.

Laz was awake and sitting in the chair by the door. He stood up as she walked towards him and then he started grinning at her. When she got close he whispered, "I know what you did. I can smell her all over you, and I don't think you were as quiet as I'm sure you thought you were being."

"Hush, boy." Radkin looked around quickly. "No one can know about this."

"Know about what?" he said with a smile and a shrug.

Radkin glared at him through slitted eyes. "You know a nice boy would have just pretended not to know what his mother was doing."

Laz chuckled. "Ah, but I'm my mother's son."

"Do you... Do you think I've made a terrible mistake?"

"When the noise first woke me I thought you were with Jena. I don't think I was ever so releaved in my life when I realized who you were with. I think anything that could put the spring back in your step even for a minute could never be a mistake." He grinned. "And if you die you die."

"Exactly," Radkin said.

She headed back for Hestia's bed chamber like a woman on a mission. She walked in closing and locking the door behind her. Hestia walked in from the bathing room closing her robe around her, but when she saw Radkin she smiled and undid it letting it drop to the floor. She gave Radkin a seductive smile and Radkin took off her sword, threw it on the end of the bed, and then she walked over took Hestia in her arms and half carried half drug her to the bed.

Hestia started undoing the buttons on Radkin's shirt. "I need you," she said against Radkin's lips, then pulled them together so that their flesh met.

Radkin kissed her then followed her own need.

Jena woke up when Darian did. She saw him looking around as he sat up in bed, and she knew who he was looking for. "She'll be back soon now, Darian." Jena kissed his forehead. She looked around and was a little surprised that Radkin wasn't there. The last three mornings it had been Radkin checking on them that had awakened Darian.

She fed the baby then got up and got dressed. She picked him up and put him in the floor to crawl around, and for the moment he seemed happy to play with the toys he found there. He'd been a little cranky. He missed Tarius. He loved

Jena and she noticed that he loved her more now that she was fully-invested in him, but he was and probably always would be closest to Tarius. Done with the toys he crawled around getting into things she had to get him out of till he was tired of it, so she picked him up and headed for the dining room.

Radkin walked out of Hestia's room and announced, "The queen is fine." Jena cut her a look wondering why she thought she had to announce that and Radkin said, "Well she is."

"I have no doubt since only someone willing to climb up the poop shoot could get in here the way you've got us boxed in. And surely you've already checked that this morning," Jena said. "Why don't you admit that you're as bored and claustrophobic as I am, and then we can just leave and go to Tarius..."

"We aren't going anywhere, Jena. Tarius told us to stay here and stay here we shall."

Jena sighed. She supposed after all she'd been through she should be glad to be so safe. Most common girls in the Jethrik would die to be able to stay in a castle, any castle, and surely Hestia's palace was far more beautiful than the Jethrik king's palace. But Jena would rather be home in their own huts or better yet outside. The closest she could get to that was looking out a window. Her baby was fussy; they both wanted the same person and could only be partly content with each other.

The servants came with breakfast and she got to sit and watch as Radkin made them taste and drink every single thing they had brought then made them stand there a few minutes to see if any of them were going to get sick or die. Meanwhile, Hestia walked out of her room and walked up beside Jena.

"Auntie Radkin has gone completely round the bend," Jena whispered to the baby.

To her surprise Hestia reached over and started petting the baby's head. Till that moment she'd showed nearly no interest in Darian at all. Then Darian held out his hands like he wanted to go to her, and before Jena had a chance to wonder why her baby—who had always been very picky about who held him—was suddenly so interested in the queen, Hestia reached right over and took him from her as if she normally just grabbed babies up and held them.

Hestia smiled at him. "Oh you're quite the little charmer aren't you?" she said, and then she was just hugging him.

Jena looked at her like she had a cat coming out of her ear. "What?" Hestia asked.

"Nothing. It's just he doesn't usually go to people he doesn't really know. Tarius said they have to smell right to him." Across the room Laz laughed and Radkin smacked him hard enough to rock him on his feet.

Hestia looked at Jena and smiled. "Perhaps I smell right."

Jena was pretty sure the whole lot of them were going stir crazy.

In the morning Tarius called everyone together and told them what they had found. She ended with, "We need to clean this place up and get back to the palace post haste. We can't give Sedrik or Finias's houses any time to leave and hide elsewhere. The Amalite religion has darkened our shores, and we must eradicate it."

Then she was giving different jobs to different people. She had the Kartik soldiers carry all the dead into the catacombs, and then Jestia did a spell to fill the whole of the empty space with dirt while Jazel did a spell to remove blood from the interior and then the exterior of the keep. They would be leaving a force of one hundred Kartik soldiers to hold the keep and make repairs to it. The keep would now belong to the Kartik throne and house part of the army. Knowing what they sat on top of couldn't help but make the people who served there ever vigilant against the Amalites and their filth.

Tarius sent most of the Marching Knight back to the Katabull compound and told them that until further notice the whole of the Katabull Nation was to be on high alert.

The weaving spell Jestia had done on the bows had an effect none of them had counted on. Some of the dead archers they found had literally been woven to their bows. It was pretty grotesque, but after what they'd seen below the ground it hardly affected them at all.

The spell Jestia was using to fill the catacombs with dirt was building a trench on the west side of the castle. Tarius figured it would fill with water and act as yet another deterrent. When Tarius had asked if Jestia could maybe just go ahead and do a moat around the whole keep, Jestia had cut her a look and simply said no.

The dirt rolled in balls up out of the ground through the keep's gates down the hallway and into the stairwell. When it was full of dirt the spell stopped. Tarius ordered the opening blocked up, and the captain who would be in charge there said he would make sure it was done as soon as possible.

The rest of the Kartik fighters that weren't staying went back as soon as they had thrown in the last of the bodies. The members of the Marching Night she kept with her would stay one more night and leave at daybreak. Tarius longed to hold Jena and their baby. She needed them to wipe out what she'd seen and what seeing it had awakened in her, but she wouldn't be able to stay long before she had to ride out and she'd have to leave them behind again.

She hated this whole thing for any number of reasons but the thing that was nibbling at her brain and wouldn't stop was that it must be her fate to always fight the Amalite menace. Every single thing in her life—good and bad—was there only because of the curse of the Amalite gods. If Jena hadn't been taken they never would have known what was hiding right under their noses and in the royal house. If they hadn't killed her father Tarius never would have hidden as a man in the Jethrikian Sword Masters' Academy and she never would have met Jena in the first place.

Every time she tried to get rid of anything linked to the Amalite blight the whole of her life unraveled like an old rug in the wind. It was unsettling, and gave her yet another reason to despise them.

Jena looked towards the window in disbelief. "Are you kidding me, Radkin? We just finished eating. The sun hasn't even completely set yet."

"You look very tired. Obviously you are still worn out from your ordeal. You should make an early night of it," Radkin said. She'd been acting strangely all day.

"Do I have to remind you that physically I'm about twenty? I'm in great shape, my 'ordeal' was over a week ago, and I'm fine and not at all tired," Jena said. Then she pointed at Darian who was crawling around playing a game of chase with Laz. "And even if I was tired he's not going to go to sleep for hours now that Laz has stirred him all up."

Radkin glared at Laz and Laz smiled and shrugged as he kept running from the infant.

Hestia's office door opened and she popped her head out. "Radkin, can I see you for a minute?"

"Ah, yeah." Radkin turned on her heel and took off for the queen's office at a near run. Jena looked at Laz. He smiled and shrugged and went right on playing with the baby.

"Giant child..." Which described Laz pretty well. "...be

careful not to step on my son," Jena said.

Laz chuffed at her. It was something the Katabull did when they were happy—a sound like nothing else she'd ever heard. "You cut me to the quick, Jena. I'd never step on the Great Leader's magic baby."

"Magic baby?"

"Yes. Have you not noticed his eyes have turned green?"

Jena jumped up, walked over, scooped her son up off the floor and looked into his eyes. He grinned back at her and started to laugh. His eyes were no longer brilliant blue but were now the darkest emerald green. "Jethrik babies eyes can change color the first year. It doesn't mean he's magic."

Laz shrugged and grinned. "If you say so."

Jena looked hard at Darian. "You aren't magic are you?" The baby just laughed and squirmed, wanting down, so she put him back on the floor. "You know Laz he's not Tarius's birth baby; he's mine."

"I know," Laz said as if it were an actual fact. "Your baby is magic."

"Just because his eyes are green?"

"That and he hums a little."

"Hums a little?"

"The whole Everything—it hums. The Katabull and witches hum and we hear the hum The Everything makes. Your baby hums; he's not Katabull, so he must be magic."

Jena ran after the crawling baby again. She grabbed him up and held him against her ear. "I hear nothing."

Laz laughed at her and said, "Can you hear The Everything humming? Have you ever heard Tarius humming?"

"No, and even after all these years I find that I still don't fully understand the nature of The Nameless One."

"No one does. You are very devout," Laz said approvingly. "When the baby's eyes turned green he started to hum."

Darian started to laugh hard. He obviously thought it was a great game. She still couldn't hear any humming. She held him out and looked into his green, green eyes. "My baby." She thought of all the magic users she knew—each one a little crazier than the next. "My poor, poor baby."

Radkin walked into the office and Hestia shut and locked the door behind her then threw her arms around Radkin's neck pulled her head down to her and started kissing her. Radkin kissed her back. She cupped Hestia's ass in in her hands and walked with her till she sat her on the edge of her desk. Then she worked her hand up under Hestia's dress and was only a little surprised to find that Hestia wasn't wearing any under garments.

She pulled her lips away from Hestia's. "I see you were expecting me."

"Wanting you is closer to the truth," Hestia said, huskiness in her voice.

As she touched her with one hand Hestia's back arched against her other. And just for a second Radkin wondered how wise it was to be doing this with Jena awake in the next room. Then when she could feel Hestia's pleasure she just didn't care.

As they rode out the next morning Tarius felt no triumph just a desire to put as much distance between her and what was behind them as she could. She had a burning need to see and hold Jena again, fueled in part by the fact Jena had been held in that place and what he meant for her, and in part by the death Tarius had seen there. She needed Jena to completely wipe all the ugly images from her head—the new ones, but mostly the old ones.

Dustan had assured them that he couldn't ride, so he was in one of the wagons. It all seemed very contrived to her and she wondered what he was really up to. She, Arvon and Kasiria were completely unsympathetic, and Jabone was only slightly better. Dustan had accused them of being the most unsupportive family ever. Telling them that they just didn't understand his pain, that he must feel pain more deeply than the rest of them.

Arvon and especially Jabone tried to humor him, but Tarius and Kasiria were openly disdainful of his whining on and on about what was in their books a minor injury. Ufalla defended him, insisting he must have hit his head, because she was convinced that anyone who got a bad hit on the head just turned into a simpering, whining, whimpering sugar tit. Which of course made her feel better about the constant teasing she was getting over the way she'd acted, after all if it happened to everyone then... Well maybe someday they'd quit ribbing her about what she'd done. Though Tarius doubted that was ever going to happen.

Jestia was too quiet. Too quiet for a normal human, so certainly way too quiet for Jestia. Tarius moved her horse closer to the witches.

"Well?" Tarius asked simply.

"Do you ever sometimes feel responsible for the whole world?"

"Oh aye," Tarius said. "Sometimes I feel like I just can't do even one more thing. I ask too much of you, Jestia, and I'm sorry."

"Because of course you think you should have to do everything yourself. You don't ask too much of me, and as you have seen, if you ask me to do something absurd I have no problem at all saying no. I'm not tired, Tarius; my energy isn't even depleted. It is because you *can* do the things you can do that you *can't* just walk away, and I've just realized that neither can I. I have all this power for a reason. Magic power doesn't really belong to the caster, and I'm just beginning to understand that. The power isn't really mine; I'm just borrowing it. Having the ability to use this power is going to force me to do things I'd rather not do and be places I'd rather not be."

"Don't look so miserable about it, Jestia. In spite of fate I've had an amazing life which in many ways is just beginning. You'll have the life you want, too."

"Will I? Or will I be forced to take the throne? Because it becomes increasingly clear that none of my relatives can be trusted to wear the crown. And would it not be the same to let the crown fall to thugs when I could stop it as it would be to stand here, have a spell that could save us, and not cast it?"

"Your mother will live a good, long life, and while I breathe, Jestia, no one will force you to deny Ufalla. Nor will I allow her to be pushed to some back room in your life."

"I have no desire to lead, Tarius, none at all."

"Neither do I. Look how well that has worked for me." Tarius laughed. "You do understand that the more you say that to me, and the more I know it's true, the better queen I think you'd make. We saw too much back there, and we're all a little heart sick. We will get back to the castle. I will spend the night in my Jena's arms, and you shall spend your night with Ufalla. Come morning neither of us will see so brightly what we leave behind us and slowly the images will fade."

Jestia caught her eyes and held them. "That is a very pretty lie, Tarius, because I can clearly see that what you have seen has opened an old wound. Are you alright?"

"It will go back to sleep and I will be fine."

Chapter Twenty

Eerin looked at the medallion in his hand and then back at the door. He didn't know what was more likely to get him killed: drawing attention to himself by showing them what he had found and reminding everyone that he'd unwittingly helped with the plot, or waiting for them to figure it out on their own decide he was the worst traitor in the history of the island because he had helped them and then wait for them to hunt him down and kill him. He was beginning to think that there was less and less chance that he was going to make it out of this whole thing alive.

He could try running into the countryside and living as a hermit, but the problem was he had no real hermit-type skills. In fact he had no practical skills at all, and if he tried to get work as a wizard they'd find him. If he ran and tried to hide they surely wouldn't believe that he didn't know anything.

Finally he knocked on the door. The young Katabull who opened it seemed to take him in at a glance. Then he yelled into the room, "It's that wizard!"

He couldn't hear the answer, but the next thing he knew a huge hand had grabbed him by the collar and dragged him into the room shutting and locking the door behind him. Then he was being patted down rather roughly by the Katabull as he checked Eerin for weapons.

"He's clean."

Radkin walked up to him and demanded, "What do you want, wizard?"

"I... I have been working as a gardener around the castle. We were replanting in the spot where Jena was kidnapped and I found this buried in the earth. It hasn't been there long." He held it up, cringing a little.

Hestia walked up and yanked it from his hand. She looked at it and then back at him, then she handed it to Radkin who promptly spit on it then threw it to the ground and stomped it, busting it into a billion pieces.

"I hope that wasn't anything we needed," Jena said.

"It was an Amalite blessing, so a Katabull curse," Radkin said.

Hestia looked at Radkin. "What could it mean?"

"That Rorik and his fellows are... were... followers of the Amalite gods. That is the horror that Tarius wouldn't tell us in a letter," Radkin said.

"That can't be," Hestia said.

"But it makes sense," Jena said. "Remember Radkin, you said you didn't see a single female with a sword. And the things Rorik said and that the kids said the others said. They all make sense..."

"If they were followers of the cult," Hestia finished.

And then Radkin was staring at Eerin, and he found himself shrinking. She looked at him through slitted eyes. "You said you lived there with them. How could you not have known?"

He spoke quickly. "I was never allowed to leave the west tower except to go outside, and as you've noticed already I'm not terribly clever."

It looked like Radkin wanted to break his neck or worse yet split him.

"Doesn't the cult... Don't they hate magic?" Hestia asked.

"They do, but it wouldn't be the first time their priests decided it was alright to use a witch or a wizard. Don't forget that's how Tarius first met Jazel," Jena said. "He had no reason to come and tell us this. If he was working for them how could he gain from this? I really think he's just a dumbass."

Eerin never would have thought he'd be so happy to be called stupid.

"Didn't you say he was a weather wizard?" Hestia asked Radkin, and she nodded. Hestia looked thoughtful then turned her attention on him. "Our grandfather was a mighty weather wizard but a very angry man and not a very nice one. He battered our shores with typhoons and created droughts inland on his whims until the people rose up and slew him and my father took the throne. If you wish to show me you are with us and not them, send many storms on Finias's palace and Sedrik's keep. Let them rage until I tell you to lift the storms, and I will forgive the fact you helped Rorik in his plot against me and Tarius."

Eerin not only felt he was getting a reprieve but he thought he was on the verge of actual redemption not just in their eyes but in his own as well. He nodded eagerly. "I can do that. I will do it now." He happily left their company to go outside and find some nice, nasty storm clouds he could seed.

Tarius had only kept fifty of the Marching Night with her. She was sure that whatever they faced at Finias's palace and Sedrik's keep they could easily handle with Kartik soldiers to take up the slack, and she wanted the Katabull Nation secure. The cult was here. Killing Hestia was all really just a way to get rid of the Katabull. Tarius was the Great Leader and the Katabull were her people. She had to make sure they were safe first, and the best way to do that was to send the bulk of the Marching Night home armed with the knowledge that the cult was here. She needed to make sure they stayed on high alert while she dealt with this threat at its source.

Tarius was in the lead riding her horse hard. She could see Jena standing at the queen's entrance with Darian in her arms, and she made her horse go all the faster. She dismounted and quickly ate the distance between them. She hugged them both and kissed Jena on the lips. Jena kissed her back, and Tarius could already feel her pain receding. Then she stepped back and took the baby from Jena. She hugged him, he hugged her, and when she did she could hear him humming. She held him out and looked into his now green eyes and frowned. He just laughed, happy to see her.

Jena looked at her, reading the look in her eyes and sighed. "So you hear him humming, too. It's true. Laz isn't full of it; our baby is magic."

Tarius looked at her and smiled. "On the plus side we aren't going to outlive him."

"No, we'll just wish we did," Jena said, looking with meaning at Jestia. "Radkin almost wouldn't let me come to meet you. She's had us locked in the queen's quarters this whole time."

"I'm surprised to see Hestia has come."

"It was the only way Radkin would let me come. She must be able to see us both at all times don't you know," Jena said.

Tarius grabbed her gear off her horse, handed the horse's reins to the waiting groom, then she said to Hestia, "We have much to discuss."

"I'm sure we do," Hestia said. She looked over Tarius's shoulder at her daughter. "I am glad to see you are well, Jestia." Jestia looked a bit taken aback. She gave her mother a curious look but said nothing—a testament to how upset she still was over what they'd seen.

Hestia looked at Radkin and Radkin looked back at Hestia, though Tarius couldn't imagine why. She took Jena's hand and started walking towards the queen's entrance to the castle. To do so she had to walk between Hestia and Radkin. When she did so, it hit her—the queen's smell was all over Radkin and Radkin's smell was all over the queen. Tarius looked at her old friend, smiled leaned over and whispered in her ear, "So, I see you've been busy."

"You and your nose." Radkin looked at her and frowned. "I took a bath."

"You might have tried taking it alone."

Tarius turned to look at Hestia, giving her an all-knowing smile.

Hestia turned bright red and shot Radkin a look.

Radkin just shrugged.

Tarius laughed and headed straight for the room she normally shared with Jena when they came to visit. It wasn't in Hestia's quarters.

"We will speak at length after I've had time to take a bath and rest," Tarius said over her shoulder.

Hestia was being dismissed, and she should have been pissed as hell. Tarius had obviously already figured them out; at the very least she should be embarrassed, but all she could think was that there was finally no one in her quarters. She looked at Radkin with meaning and nodded her head in the general direction of her rooms. Radkin nodded and after embracing her children and making sure there was no one who was going to stop her, she left.

After a few seconds had passed Hestia started to leave but then Jestia walked up to her. "Mother the cult..."

"I already know. We can talk about it later. For now go and get cleaned up. You look like you can use some rest." Then she just let her heart tell her what she should do. She took Jestia into her arms, gave her a hug, and kissed her cheek. "I am so glad that you are back safe." She released her daughter, looked at Ufalla, and then walked over and hugged her, too. "You too, dear. Thank you for taking such good care of Jestia." It felt good. She smiled at them then said, "I have this... thing I have to do. I will talk to you later."

Jestia watched her mother take off at a near run. She turned to Ufalla. "What the hell just happened?"

Ufalla shrugged.

"That was a real hug filled with affection which makes me very nervous," Jestia said, her eyes narrowing to slits.

"Maybe she loves you and is just happy to see you."

"She wasn't happy to see me a few days ago. It's very suspicious."

"I swear, Jestia, sometimes you'd find a bitter taste in the milk of human kindness."

"I would if the milk came from the underbelly of a snake."

"Your mother isn't a snake." Ufalla laughed and repositioned their saddle bags on her shoulder. "Come on let's go. I could use a bath and some rest so could you."

Jestia nodded and started following Ufalla, casting a half weight spell on the bags Ufalla was carrying. She looked back at Jestia, smiled, then reached back and took her hand with her free one. "Everything is fine."

"Fine Ufalla?" Jestia followed after her. "Have you forgotten the Amalite cult is here and... how could mother know?"

"She has a witch. Perhaps the witch looked for us in that mirrored thingy..."

"Scrying mirror," Jestia said. "I have no idea what a 'mirrored thingy' is."

"Apparently you do, smart ass," Ufalla said. "Anyway maybe she saw us in the temple and put it together."

"That's a long shot. Twilla would have trouble making a toad grow warts, and I haven't yet figured out how to use a scrying mirror myself."

"Don't worry about it, Jestia." She looked back over her shoulder again and said, "Isn't it time we rebuild your power?"

Jestia looked at her and frowned. "Whatever are you going on about, Ufalla? Rebuild my power..." Seeing the look in Ufalla's eyes she smiled realizing what she meant. "I'm pretty sure my mother said I needed rest."

"Are you going to pick today to start listening to your mother?"

"Not when I could be rolling around naked with you."

"Oh for the love of The Nameless One!" Kasiria thundered. "Quit talking about it and just do it." She pushed her way around them and started down the hall dragging Jabone behind her. He looked at them and grinned like a huge idiot as he happily followed.

"She regularly nearly gets him killed," Jestia said. She looked at Ufalla and smiled. "Don't listen to that Katabull slut. Talking about it is half the fun."

Hestia watched Radkin as she sat on the edge of the bed pulling her boots on. Hestia was in no hurry to get dressed. She couldn't remember a time when she'd been this happy to be naked. For years she'd watched as her body sagged and wrinkled and just felt ugly. Now she looked at the same body and felt desirable. Radkin, sensing she was being watched, looked over her shoulder and smiled. "What?"

"Will you go with her?"

"With who?"

"Tarius of course. Will you ride out with her when she leaves?" Hestia didn't like the way the tone of her voice gave away how much she didn't want Radkin to go away.

"I can't pretend to know what Tarius will want me to do."

"What do you want to do?" Hestia didn't want these words to spill out of her mouth. She just didn't seem to be able to stop herself.

For answer Radkin stood up, jumped off the floor and landed with her knees on either side of her. Radkin grabbed Hestia's wrists and held them against the bed over her head in one hand.

"What do you want me to do?"

"Kiss me," Hestia breathed. Radkin released her wrists, bent down and kissed her so gently on her lips that it felt like being touched by the sun. Radkin moved her head away from her and just stared right into her eyes. "I don't want you to go," Hestia said.

Radkin smiled and kissed her again, this time with more passion. When she finally removed her mouth from Hestia's she got off her and off the bed in one movement and Hestia felt immediate frustration.

"I don't want you to go, Radkin," she said as she watched Radkin strap her sword on her back.

Radkin curled a finger towards her and Hestia crawled over to her raised up on her knees and wrapped her arms around Radkin's neck.

Hestia looked her in the eyes and held her gaze and said. "I want you to stay with me."

"Then that's what I'll do. Tarius doesn't really need me. Do you..." Radkin looked away from her for a minute. "Do you need me?"

Hestia picked Radkin's chin up with her finger, moved her head till she was looking at her again and silently nodded her head.

Radkin kissed her again wrapped her arms around Hestia and pulled her tightly to her. "Tarius thinks she owes me a debt she can never repay. If I tell her I think I should stay with you to protect you she will let me stay, but you better be sure that's what you really want."

"It is. It's all I want."

Tarius stepped out of the tub and dried off. She caught a glimpse of herself in the full-length mirror that graced one of the walls. She walked over continuing to dry herself and took a good long look at her reflection. She had only looked at herself for more than a few seconds a handful of times in her whole life. She was not only Katabull but she was third sex, so what she saw in the mirror was only ever really a fraction of what she really was and when she looked at her reflection she never saw herself. Still this was what most people saw most of the time.

She looked long and hard at her face. The spell hadn't aged her—not enough that even Jena could notice, but she could feel it—not a lot but she could. The nature of the spell meant that it treated her body as if she had a one hundred and fifty year life span instead of three hundred, so she had lost some of her youth. She didn't care. If nothing else having Jena kidnapped had completely removed any doubt she had about her decision.

This form bore the scars this life had put on it. Her two most noticeable scars were visible to the world—the one on her throat and the one down her face. A third one in her belly few people saw, but everyone knew about it, and they all knew where it had come from. It was a famous scar.

This scar on my throat led to all the others. Without it what would my life have been like? My fadra and my madra would still be alive. I never would have gone to the Jethrik. How different my life would have been. How different Jena's would have been. Every single thing that this thing I'm looking at has been through has made me what I am. If I'd been born male or even if my soul matched my body my life would have been so different. If I was human instead of the Katabull everything about me would be nothing like what I am.

But this scar on my throat, it's the one that started it all...
What am I?

I am Tarius the Black, I am the Great Leader and why am I those things? Because it is what I need to be to get the job done.

Everything I am is what I need to be in this time. The Nameless One has set me a hard task, but it has filled my life with love and people to help me, and I wouldn't trade any of my scars for a normal life.

I almost lost Jena and Darian. I could have but I didn't. I haven't even really had time to think about all that. I won't let myself think it because I couldn't bear it. Darian is magic and what does that mean? The baby who was supposed to be sacrificed to false gods by people who acted like monsters, I scooped him off the floor and saved him and Jena and I love him as much as the son I bore. Twice covered in blood, the blood of the people of his birth, what path will all those truths lead him down?

A cold chill ran down her spine, and then she saw it as clearly as if she were watching it outside a window. What she knew shook her to the core. She took in a deep, shuddering breath.

Tarius finished drying off, her hands shaking. She took another long look at her own face, turning it to the side and back.

Jena walked in. "Are you alright?"

"I have seen the past and the future."

"In there," Jena said with a smile.

"I'm not making a joke. I have seen the future in my head. I had a vision." Tarius turned to face her. "I was looking at this piece of me that everyone sees that isn't quite me, and I saw things I try to forget and then I saw things I'd rather not know and heard things I didn't want to hear."

"Bad things?" Jena sounded worried now.

"The past yes, the future mostly just frustrating for me. I wanted to utterly destroy them and now I see all I'm doing is knocking them back and keeping them from spreading. It is our son who shall be the scourge of the Amalite gods. He will be more a curse to them than I have ever been."

"Jabone?"

"No Darian," Tarius said. She took in a deep breath and let it out. "It's why his soul was born to the Amalites in the hive and why Jabone went to the territories with Jestia and the others. It's why they found the cave and it's why I was the one who scooped him up—why he always felt like he was mine. Our souls, his and mine, have danced together many times just like yours and mine have. He will finish what I only started."

"He's a baby, Tarius," Jena said, her brow furrowing as

she tried to comprehend what Tarius was saying.

"I was a mere child when the event that shaped me took place. He is an infant, I know and his destiny unsure. But certain things happen to us, Jena, and they shape the course of our lives. Who can know the mysterious ways of The Nameless One? And Darian is not just anyone's son; he is our son, and I am who I am and you are who you are. Among our friends are not one, not two, but *three* of the most powerful magic users our world has ever known, and his brother is married to a princess of the Jethrik. He will be raised among the pack of the Marching Night. Jestia is bound to our goddaughter and our son is magic. Jabone was not bathed in blood ever. When he was a child there was peace and yet when there were Amalites to fight we could not keep him home, because of who we are."

Jena handed her a robe and she slipped it on without thinking only realizing as she pulled it closed that she was cold.

"We can't worry about things that may or may not happen, Tarius."

"Yeah, good luck with that." Tarius smiled and tied the robe closed. "Where is the future magic warlord?"

Jena cut her a hard look.

"If you mean Darian, he is sleeping, which is what you should be doing instead of spouting things I only half understand and that I'm not sure you understand any better."

Jena lay with her back against Tarius and Tarius was holding her. Tarius chuffed and Jena sighed in contentment. "I love it when you do that because I know it means that at least for the moment you are content. I have to admit I still get a little worried when you are too serious for too long."

Tarius chuffed again and pulled her even closer, laying her head on Jena's so that her lips were nearly touching her ear. "How would you like me to be when I came so close to losing you and our baby? And I saw things, Jena, things I'm not ready to talk about, things no one should see, that brought old horrors to the front of my mind."

"In your vision?" Jena asked now more worried.

"No, I told you about that."

"I still don't understand, Tarius... Followers of The Nameless One believe in free will. Doesn't this vision you had, what witches do, even my dream, don't they negate free will?"

"You are very devout," Tarius said.

Jena took in a deep breath and let it out. The less she claimed to understand the more devout they said she was, but it didn't really help her understand anything.

"The question becomes *when* did we have the free will? When certain things happen the choices we make or that other people make in that moment shape our destiny, but ultimately we all have a purpose to fulfill and those choices either help us or hinder us. I survived against all odds not once but twice. Darian survived against all odds and now he will thrive with us and it will shape what he will become and though what I've seen may never come to be it is certainly a possibility all things considered."

"I swear with every word you say I understand even less and if you tell me how devout I am again I'm going to smack you."

Tarius laughed. "So did you enjoy your stay at the castle?"

"Of course not." Jena turned in her arms to look at Tarius. "I wanted to be with you. Our son was cross and Radkin wouldn't let us go anywhere or do anything. We were locked in the queen's rooms the whole time and... Why are you grinning like that?"

"You really don't know?"

"Know what?"

Tarius laughed. "Oh my love, you must have been miserable if you couldn't see what was going on right under your nose."

"What? Could you just tell me? I get so tired of everything being something I must figure out..."

"Radkin is banging the queen."

Jena took in a sharp breath. "Well you didn't have to just blurt it out like that!"

Chapter Twenty-one

Jestia looked at where her mate was sleeping soundly. Perhaps the thing that was most endearing about Ufalla was that she wasn't stupid but she was uncomplicated. All Ufalla needed to be happy was Jestia. She didn't worry all the way up a hill about how to get back down. Ufalla didn't realize it, and she wasn't going to tell her, but some day she would take her father's place at Tarius's side. Ufalla was so much like her father she could have been cut from the same block.

Jestia was like neither of her parents. Her mother had acted very strangely and then disappeared, and when she made a half-assed attempt to find her father he wasn't even at the castle which meant he was off with one whore or the other. She didn't know what bothered her more the fact that her father was a whoremonger or that her mother just didn't care.

Jestia stopped watching her lover sleep and started pacing the length of her room back and forth. Her room in her mother's quarters in the castle. She felt neither comfortable nor at home. The truth—though she doubted she'd ever admit it aloud—was that she felt more at home in a cabin on a boat or in a tent or even one of the earthen and stick hovels the Katabull lived in. Why? Because Ufalla was more comfortable there, and for Jestia home was where Ufalla felt at home.

Jestia was a powerful witch and she knew that was her calling. But she didn't have any idea where fate was taking her; she just knew she didn't want it to be here. She stopped and looked at Ufalla again.

Tarius gave Jena half her life. She asked me to do it and I never even questioned her about it I just did it because I understood. What I don't understand is why Jena is so mad about it. Why Hellibolt and even Jazel wouldn't do it. I mean Jazel really? What a hypocrite! She did it to Helen and let's face it Helen is pretty, a decent cook and she loves Jazel but she's as dumb as a box of rocks and about as exciting. Maybe it's the whole asking first thing. Why? And if someone offered you half their life and you said no well isn't that the ultimate looking a gift horse in the mouth? Isn't that just as much as saying I'd rather die than live a few hundred years with you. That's just rude if you ask me.

Bless The Nameless One I should have asked her first. I have no idea what my life span was supposed to be or what it will be now, and if she's living hundreds of years and doesn't want to she's going to be super mad, and if she should stupidly get herself killed doing some dumbass thing—and let's face it she's always doing some dumbass thing—then I will have just thrown away half of my years for nothing.

If she had stayed an imbecile I would have been stuck with her gods alone knows how long, and I never even really thought about what I'd done till then. I just did it because I couldn't stand the idea of not having her always with me. But we're both very young and what if someday we fall out of love? It happens. I should tell her what I did. I will... No I won't, she'll probably be mad at me just like Jena's mad at Tarius and if it took Jena months to figure it out when she overnight lost twenty years it will be another ten or fifteen before Ufalla even suspects. If I did a glamour on her so it looked like she was aging normally she could be sixty before she figured it out.

That is if she hasn't already figured it out and since it can't be undone just doesn't want to fight about it. That would be just like her. I did something permanent that affected us both and I didn't even ask her about it. If she had done that to me I'd be furious.

Dammit! Now I know why Jena is so mad. I'll have to apologize, and I really hate apologizing. This is why Tarius wins battles and wars because she knows just who to use where. She knew I'd do it without questioning her because I understand her and she me. Though I really don't know why.

Jestia didn't want the burden of the crown. She wanted them to appoint someone else heir apparent. But while only a few weeks ago she would have been happy with anyone holding the position in her stead, with Jena's kidnapping the plot against her mother and all that they now knew to be true about Rorik and the others, she began to understand how important it was that someone trustworthy hold the position.

She just wasn't sure she was trustworthy. After all she tended to do what she wanted to do, what worked out best for her. Didn't the fact she'd given Ufalla half her life without even thinking about how it might really affect either of them more or less prove that she was too impulsive to be the queen?

If she accepted her title what was she going to do about Ufalla? She refused to even consider being separated from her and sneaking around with her was only slightly better.

Even if I hadn't given her half my years I couldn't bear to be parted from her or to hurt her in any way. I don't see why it matters. So much of what I have been taught is "right" for royals isn't actual kingdom law but just crap the royals have laid upon themselves in an effort to somehow separate themselves from the "common" folk. It's just a code of conduct which... They all break. Everyone knows my father is a drunk who beds whichever woman will take him. I'm pretty sure that's not "proper." My great-grandfather trashed the whole of the Kartik with storms and no one said anything... well not until they rose up and killed him anyway. I don't think there is anyone in the Kartik who doesn't know my grandfather had half a dozen lovers of both sexes on the side. Hell my uncle kidnapped the Great Leader's wife, tried to have my mother killed, and was trying to install the Amalite cult as the kingdom religion. If I have to do something like take the throne then I will do it on my own terms. If they won't let me then they can sit a monkey on the throne for all I care and if the Kartik becomes a festering dung heap we'll just go somewhere else. I'm a witch; I'll do what I want.

Hestia had everyone's dinner served to them in their rooms mostly because she didn't want to deal with any of them and just wanted to stay in her room alone with Radkin. Of course she told them that it was to give them all a chance to rest and relax after their battle. None of them had argued at all, no doubt because although they had much different reasons none of them were feeling very social either.

She and Radkin had eaten a quiet dinner alone in her room and then just used the night to their best advantage.

Her brother was dead; he'd tried to kill her. The Amalite cult was here and the gods alone knew what other horror Tarius had to tell her. She should have been thinking about the kingdom and what this meant for her people, but she was tired of thinking only about problems and what other people did or did not need.

Somewhere in her head she knew it was crazy and completely irresponsible to be having an affair with anyone at all much less Radkin, but she just didn't seem to be able to make herself care. She'd given away most of her life for the country. She deserved this... whatever it was. She needed it and more importantly she wanted it.

She looked at Radkin's back where she lay beside her.

Then reached out and stroked her hand across Radkin's shoulder and down her back to rest on her hip. She slid up to Radkin's back, sliding her body against hers and kissed her between her shoulder blades.

"Woman," Radkin said, sleep in her voice. "Are you trying to wear me out?"

"Are you complaining?" Hestia asked.

"Not yet." Radkin turned around, took hold of Hestia's shoulders and slammed her onto her back then jumped straddle her. Hestia received her kisses eagerly and when Radkin started to move her lips down her body she quaked with her need and then...

"I'm a very powerful witch, and if I am to be heir apparent then I will do what I want, and if you don't like it you can appoint a monkey in my place!"

And then there was light because just like the lock on the door hadn't deterred Jestia, darkness wasn't a problem for her, either.

"Gods and spiders!" Jestia yelled out. Then she just started laughing. "No wonder you were in such a good mood." She turned on her heel and started to go. "I think this rather makes my point, Mother. I'll do as I please." The light was gone and Jestia closed and locked the door behind her without using her hands. Hestia was pretty sure she was never going to get used to her daughter's magic.

Radkin looked at her smiled, shrugged, and started to go right back to doing what she'd started doing.

Hestia pushed her gently away. "I... I better go talk to Jestia." She got up, lit the lamp, threw on her robe and started for the door. She stopped and turned to look at Radkin. "Can you wait for me?"

"If I go back to sleep again I'm sure you'll find a way to wake me," Radkin answered with a smile. "Hestia, don't look as if you are going off to meet your executioner. It is only Jestia."

Hestia nodded then hurried out the door. Jestia was already most of the way to her room. Hestia had thought they were all alone in her quarters at last and she had completely forgotten that Jestia's room was here. "Jestia," she whispered. When she got no answer said a little louder, "Jestia."

Jestia turned and came back to her. Then before she even spoke she just started laughing again.

"What? I don't see what's so funny."

"Really, Mother." Jestia just laughed harder. "Radkin? Mother Radkin makes Ufalla look like a refined, pinky-waving lady of the court."

"I... I told you Ufalla's a lovely girl..."

"Just not for me, right?" Jestia was smiling. She shook her head. "What in hell's name are you doing with Radkin?"

"What's wrong with Radkin?" Hestia said quickly.

"Nothing at all. She's loyal, trustworthy, honest, and helpful and the gods know if I wasn't with Ufalla I'd give her a roll in a heartbeat, but you..."

"You know, Jestia, I am not so different from you."

Jestia laughed again. "Apparently not."

"I... I meant I'm a woman. I have needs..."

"Which can apparently be fulfilled only by a huge Katabull sword woman." Jestia laughed even more.

"I'm glad you find this so amusing. I needed something... someone. She was there. One thing lead to another, it happened."

"I'm not judging you. I'm laughing because it's funny. If you were me you'd think it was funny, too." Then in a voice that didn't just *sound* like Hestia's it *was* her voice Jestia said, "You cannot marry that half-Jethrikian girl from those horrid Katabull mud huts who dresses badly. You will marry a man who will make you miserable and squirt out many squalling heirs for the kingdom and have fun no more."

Hestia smiled in spite of herself. "That's not exactly what I said."

"But it's close, and now you're rolling around with Radkin and... Well is it true what they say about the Katabull?"

"What's that?"

"You know that their tongue is rough."

"Of all the cheek." Hestia could feel all the blood running into her face.

"Well is it?"

"It is not."

"I guess that's a good thing if she was getting ready to do what I think she was going to do—and I ought to know since I'm as queer as you are."

Hestia took in a shuddering breath. "I... I am not."

Jestia just nodded her head.

"Just because I'm having sex with a woman doesn't mean I'm queer."

"Seriously?" Jestia laughed. "That's sort of the whole deal. Mother again I have to ask what are you doing with her."

"I'm coupling with her."

Jestia laughed harder. "I guessed that. What are you doing with her?"

"I'm not sure I understand your question."

Jestia lowered her voice. "Radkin was about five seconds from killing herself. That's why Tarius left her here but I'm assuming you know that so... What are you doing with her? She's my friend, and I don't want to see her get hurt."

And that was the moment that Hestia really saw why Tarius put so much store in Jestia. Jestia was a woman, not a willful child but a woman, wise beyond her years, who had an intimate knowledge of things Hestia was only beginning to understand.

"I... I don't think she is the one who will get hurt," Hestia said in a whisper so low she could barely hear it herself.

"What I can't hear... gods you love her."

"I do not!"

"You do, you just don't know it yet. How many times have you made love?"

"What's the point of that?"

"How many times?" Jestia demanded.

"A few."

"How many?"

"I don't know! I lost count. Why does that matter?"

Jestia laughed and shrugged. "I was just curious to know how big a slut you are."

"Jestia this isn't funny. Now I need you to keep this to yourself."

"Because you plan to keep doing it?"

"Well, yes," Hestia said, looking at her feet.

"But you don't love her, oh and you're not queer." Jestia giggled then threw her arms around Hestia's neck and hugged her.

"I swear, Jestia, you are twisted in ways I do not understand and..." She hugged her daughter back and was filled with a deep longing and sense of loss. "I love you, Jestia. I cannot bear to do to you what has been done to me. You may marry Ufalla if you want to and have exactly the life you want."

"Even if you don't find anyone else suitable to be heir apparent?"

"Maybe especially then." Hestia stepped back and pushed Jestia to arm's length. She looked into her daughter's green, green eyes and said, "It's time we care a little less about the way things look and a little more about the way they are."

"But you still don't want anyone to know about you and Radkin."

"That's right. I do not," Hestia said.

"You know I have to tell Ufalla right, and you know Tarius has already told Jena."

"How did you know Tarius knew?"

"I guessed. She has a legendary sense of smell even for a Katabull. Right now I can smell the sex on you, so she wouldn't have had any trouble at all knowing what you were doing and with whom. Well I'll just let you get back to what you were doing, and in the future I'll be sure to knock before I enter." She chuckled. "Good night."

"Good night." Hestia started for her room. She was a little surprised to see Radkin awake and sitting on the edge of the bed waiting for her.

"Was the little witch mad?"

"If by mad you mean crazy, not any more than usual." Hestia walked over and looked down at her lover. "Mostly she was wildly amused."

Radkin undid the tie on Hestia's robe and pulled the front open. She kissed her stomach then took Hestia's hands in hers and kissed the back of each one in turn. Radkin looked up at her. "It could have been worse. Laz once walked in on Irvana and I doing it, ran outside the hut and threw up."

Hestia laughed.

"I was afraid she'd be upset and then you'd be upset and then I wouldn't get to finish what I started."

"You should have known better than that."

When Jestia walked back into her room she hit Ufalla in the head with the door and Ufalla, wearing only pants and her sword, fell across the room and landed across the bed. Jestia ran over to her grabbed her hand and pulled Ufalla into a sitting position. "I'm sorry, are you alright?"

Ufalla rubbed her head looked at her and said, "Who are you? Have you seen my little pink dress?"

"Oh my gods not again..."

Ufalla started laughing and Jestia slugged her in the shoulder hard.

"You big stupid jerk I ought to..."

A pot of tea appeared in the air followed by a cup and the tea poured into the cup. "Great!" Jestia sighed, plucked the cup out of the air and took a drink.

"Oh good the tea is back," Ufalla said, holding out her hand expectantly.

"I shouldn't let you have any just for being such a huge ass." Jestia handed her the cup. "That wasn't funny, Ufalla. I swear if you do that again..."

"I'm sorry, but you have to admit if you were me it would be funny. Where the hell were you? I woke up and you weren't here."

"And you came looking for me. That's very sweet, but you do know... Oh never mind. I'm just so glad you weren't really hurt."

"Oh come on, you still can't even work up a good mad at me. I deserve it. That was a terrible thing to do. You should spank me."

"We both know you'd only enjoy that. If you do that to me again, my love, I'll do worse than just get mad."

"Where were you?"

"Well I could have been going to take a pee, not that I feel I need to tell you my every move."

Ufalla smiled. "So you *can* still get mad at me."

"Well it was a really mean thing to do."

"Oh, baby, I'm sorry." Ufalla drank the rest of the tea and then set the cup back in the air and moved to hug Jestia. "You're right it was mean. Now what were you doing in the middle of the night?"

Jestia pushed back from her a bit. "It's hardly the middle of the night. I went to tell my mother that she could put a monkey on the throne for all I care, that I'm a witch and I'll do what I want."

"And did you?"

"I did, but it sort of got upstaged by the whole mother-was-coupling-with-Radkin thing."

"What!?"

"Sshsh! She wants to keep it a secret. Mother and Radkin are having a tryst."

Ufalla started laughing then she looked at Jestia. "Really? This isn't just to get me back for my bad joke?"

"No really. Come on, I couldn't make crap like this up. When I walked in Radkin's head was about here," Jestia pointed to the spot on Ufalla.

Ufalla laughed more and said, "No wonder your mother was in such a good mood. You know I never once saw Irvana— when she was well—that she didn't have a smile on her face."

"My mother told me she loved me, Ufalla. She told me

she loved me and in that moment not only did she mean it but she felt it. Just for a second I could feel her love, then this wave of grief came over her and I knew how much my brother's death has really touched her." Jestia put her arms around Ufalla's neck and lay her head on her shoulder and started to cry. Ufalla patted her back and she felt comforted even as her teeth rattled from the strength of the blows.

"I told you, didn't I?" Ufalla said softly, her lips almost touching Jestia's ear. "I told you she loved you, that she had to. Anyone who sees you falls in love with you, Jestia. I'm just lucky that most people never really see you."

Finias's son Yorik looked out at the rain coming down in sheets. There was no news from the castle, none at all good or bad, and at this point Yorik wasn't sure he would know the difference. The storm didn't look or feel natural and was bad enough that no rider had been able to leave to go to the capital to see what might be going on.

The priest at his shoulder said, "The gods have told us that the storm keeps the good news from reaching us. Hestia and Tarius the Black are dead, Rorik sets on the throne with your father at his right hand, and even now the Kartik army is killing the last of the Katabull menace."

At his other shoulder another Amalite priest chimed, "How convenient of the Katabull to gather together and make themselves easy to kill."

Idiots, Katabull don't just live in the compound. They're scattered across the whole of the Kartik. Even if they could launch a successful attack against the compound—which I doubt—they'd never get them all. But Yorik said nothing and kept watching the storm.

These two had come to the palace two years ago when Rorik had convinced his father that the path to vast riches was paved by the Amalite gods. To Yorik's disbelief two thirds of the household had gladly converted with his father upon seeing just one bag of gold. In the two years that followed Finias had filled the coffers of his palace and successfully bought if not the conversion then the silence of his household. Anyone who wouldn't at least pretend to go along had been promptly killed.

Yorik's father was a weak and greedy man. Yorik couldn't stand against him because he didn't have the numbers, and there were children to consider. More of the women than men secretly stood with Yorik because they had the most to lose if the Amalite religion took hold in their kingdom. But it was hard to fight when so outnumbered and you had your young ones to worry about. Yorik and his followers plotted in private to get rid of the invaders. Till then they hadn't come up with a single plan that wasn't likely to get them all killed.

Yorik wished he had any idea what was going on. He did not for even a minute think these old charlatans were speaking the truth; he didn't believe in their gods. He was a Kartik man and his woman Shadra a fighter who had been walking around swordless for two years. At the priests' instructions Finias had closed them off from the outside world, letting only those they were sure of leave and return, and even then only for supplies. His father must have known on some level that he was not on board, because neither Yorik nor Shadra had been allowed to leave the palace grounds for two long years.

He had thought of escaping, going to the capital and informing the crown of his father's treachery, but he was always being watched and he couldn't have gotten out with his wife and child. If his "disloyalty" was found out they would have been killed.

He had hoped to fight it from within, to turn more of his kin away from the cult, but it was too late for that now. Whatever had happened he wanted no part of helping these things destroy the country he loved.

Yorik decided the time to act was at hand.

He turned slowly, making eye contact with his man standing at the door into the room. The man nodded his understanding. They were all sick of waiting. Yorik looked at the priests in turn.

"Our day is at hand," One told him reading the look of indecision on his face all wrong.

"Funny, that's just what I was thinking," Yorik said.

"Our gods will deliver…"

"Nothing! They will deliver nothing but the death they always have. I think my father was a fool who followed you and forced his household to debase themselves by worshiping your hateful gods for the promis of gold. And I think he and all those who went with him are now dead. I think Hestia still sits on the throne. I think Tarius the Black had one of her witches build this storm, and I think when she is ready she will sweep in and kill us all. The only way we will any of us be spared is to hand them your heads."

He pulled his sword. The priests turned to run and found

another sword behind them. Yorik killed one and his fellow killed the other.

"We must gather all the others as silently as we can. Take the children to the stables," Yorik said. "We shall attack the members of the cult in their beds as they sleep. The time has come to rise up against the unholy followers of the Amalite gods. If we kill them all and meet the warlord with these men's heads she might just let us live, and if not we shall have died returning the honor of our household.

Chapter Twenty-two

Eerin looked at the empty table where he'd just made tea. He sighed and sat down hard. He was still staying in the servant's quarters and so glad to still have his head that he couldn't have cared less. But he'd like to be able to drink his tea in peace.

As if he'd cast a successful spell his teapot and cup returned. He shook the pot, noticed it was still mostly full, and poured himself a cup. It was late he should find the bed he'd been sleeping in and get some rest. The problem was that he was suddenly aware of just how close to death he'd come. At the time he hadn't had time to think about it, and now that he did he found that he wasn't tired at all. The more he thought about everything that had happened the more he was sure he wasn't supposed to be alive.

Why did none of them kill me? Knowing now how twisted Rorik was I'm shocked he didn't kill me. I was sure Radkin was going to. Tarius and Hestia, well if I was either one of them I would have killed me, and I would have had trouble blaming them for it. Yet here I am alive and that must mean something but I can't for the life of me think of what.

He didn't think it was to make tea for Jestia and her friends. Even the storms he'd put on Finias's palace and Sedrik's keep had been cast already, so what now?

"May I?" the head gardener—whose name he could not for the life of him remember—had come in without him noticing and he pointed at the teapot.

"Be my guest," Eerin said. The old man got a cup and sat down across from him. He poured himself a cup of tea then wrapped his hands around it.

"The heat feels good on my old hands." He took a sip. "Wow, that's really good tea."

"It's a special blend I make myself," Eerin said and sighed.

"What's wrong, boy?"

"I'm hardly a boy," Eerin said with a smile.

"When you're my age everyone's a youngster. Now what's wrong?"

Eerin wasn't about to tell the man he probably wasn't much older than he was. "I sometimes think making tea is all I'm really good at."

The old man chuckled. "Oh child at least you're good at one thing. Some people grow old and die and are never really good at anything."

"I have done some really stupid things, the kind that get you killed, and yet here I sit making tea."

"A Katabull once told me that if you learn from a mistake it wasn't a mistake at all."

Eerin gave him a confused look.

"Do you know what kinds of people never make mistakes?"

Eerin shook his head.

"People who never do anything, who never take chances, never try anything new. You can't fail at something unless you're trying to do it. If you learn from a mistake it wasn't a mistake at all; it was a lesson. You have made bad choices, so don't do that any more. Or you could just make tea all day and never have to worry that you will fail at anything ever again."

Was it really that simple? Eerin looked at the old man; he was just a gardener how could he know so much? "How did you get to be so wise?"

The old man finished his tea in one gulp and stood up. "By not dying and living to fight another day. By owning my mistakes and learning from them. And now I'm off to find my bed." He grinned. "By now my wife should have gotten it nice and warm for me." He got up and left.

Eerin watched him go and sipped at his tea thoughtfully.

One of the younger gardeners walked in. "I passed Hedrin as I was walking in. He said you had made some tea."

Eerin nodded towards the pot. Hedrin... that was his name.

"So, was he telling you wild stories about the Great War?"

"No, I didn't even know he had fought in the Great War."

"Oh aye." He got himself a cup and sat down. "He was a general leading right beside the queen. He fought with Tarius the Black and the Katabull troops, the Marching Night even. He has some wonderful stories to tell."

"What's he... Why is he gardening now?"

"He says it's all he ever wanted to do," the young man said with a shrug.

"But he was a general, a man respected..."

"And he would tell you that he'd rather be respected as the best gardener than as the best general."

"He's content," Eerin said, barely above a whisper.

"I suppose." The man finished his tea. "Good night, Eerin."

"Good night." Eerin nodded back and he couldn't remember this man's name either. Why?

Because I saw them as commoners and myself a royal somehow above them. I didn't learn their names because I had judged them as servants. Hedrin works here on the grounds and among the plants because he loves to, not because he has to. He was a general so most likely a noble, some distant relative. He was once a powerful man and now he works the earth and he is at peace.

All my life I have felt like the odd man out, like a toad among gods. When Rorik said he wanted me to work for him I was so happy to be included that I never even considered or questioned my restrictions in his keep or what he was asking me to do. I was happy just to be wanted. My mother loved me but she died giving my father his sixth son who died shortly after her leaving me the youngest. My brothers despised me because I was magic, and my father encouraged them to hate me because he did. My father loathed magic because his father was magic and he had hated his memory—not because he tried to destroy the kingdom and nearly destroyed the royal line, but because his death put my father's brother on the throne. Then instead of being a prince he was just the king's brother, a duke who the king stuck on the far side of the island away from any policy making because he didn't like or trust him.

Eerin was a constant reminder of all the duke had hoped for and all that he'd never had. He despised magic, so Eerin had never been properly trained. When Eerin had struck out on his own to find a teacher he'd had to deal with the likes of Jadin—an old wizard at the end of his days who had little power or knowledge. Jadin had a kind disposition, a nice place to stay, and a staff that provided three meals a day. All Eerin had to do in return was pretend to love him which since Jadin was the first person who had been nice to him since his mother died wasn't hard to do.

In return for his "love," Jadin had taught Eerin everything he knew. How to use Eerin's natural ability to affect storms. How to shift one thing into something else. How to mix a few healing powders and potions and how to make a really good pot of tea.

So in other words Jadin had taught Eerin everything Eerin knew. Jadin had died of old age and left all he had to the servants, apparently forgetting about Eerin. So Eerin went back to his father's palace where his father and brothers no longer abused him but they still disliked him and only left him alone because they feared his magic. At the time he had been happy with that, but looking back he realized being despised and feared was no better than simply being despised.

Rorik had showed up at his father's palace one day, and his father had made it clear he wasn't welcome. When Rorik sought Eerin out before leaving and told him he'd like to hire his services, Eerin had been more than happy to go. The fact that his father didn't like Rorik just made it all the more appealing.

Now he realized just how big a fool he had been. Looking back knowing what he now knew there were a thousand different things that should have let him know just exactly what Rorik was up to.

Then old Hedrin's words echoed in his head. *If you learn from a mistake it isn't a mistake at all.* What had he learned, really learned? *That things that sound too good to be true are lies you tell yourself because you don't want to investigate the truth. That I know just enough about magic to get myself in trouble and cause others pain and that to wield magic without real knowledge of the world is dangerous and irresponsible.*

Tarius and Jena, Arvon and Dustan, and Ellis and Harris had joined her, Ufalla and her mother at the dining table in the queen's quarters for breakfast. Shortly before breakfast Tarius had told them what they had found at Rorik's keep. It was an undetailed, streamlined version, yet most of them had very little appetite for the breakfast they were served.

Radkin and Laz stood at the door doing guard duty Jestia supposed though she thought it was ridiculous. There wasn't a single person in that room that couldn't hold their own in a fight.

"As soon as Eerin showed us what he had found and I realized my brother had been part of the cult, I had the wizard send storms to both Finias's palace and Sedrik's keep," Hestia said.

"Not telling you what to do, but if I were queen I'd ban all religion from the Kartik," Tarius said.

"All religion?" Her mother was obviously confused. "But you and your people follow The Nameless God."

"That it is not a religion!" Tarius sounded insulted. "It is a way of thinking. Religion says 'Don't think; follow what you are told'. When is the last time you saw a temple to The

Nameless One or ran into a priest of The Nameless One or read from the book of The Nameless One? There are none; none are needed. A belief in The Nameless One is just that. There is a power that runs through All. We are part of it and it is part of us. That is something we all know till some priest comes and tells us something else. Then before you know it people are cutting up animals and letting them bleed on stones and building huge, worthless buildings few people live in and making armies to kill everyone who doesn't believe what they believe while the priests grow fat on the ignorance of the people."

And this was the sort of thing that passed for pleasant breakfast conversation with this group. Jestia was just glad they weren't talking about mothers and their babies being slashed to pieces in the bowels of the earth. *And there goes what was left of my appetite, but Ufalla just keeps right on eating. She saw the same things I did; she can put it out of her head but I can't. When I look at Tarius it's obvious she can't either, and Mother...* She looked at her mother and caught her looking at Radkin. Jestia shook her head and looked at her plate. She needed to eat something, so she started picking at her food. *Mother didn't see it, and Ufalla saw but didn't look. She didn't look long enough for it to imprint on her brain. I didn't want to look but couldn't look away, it just didn't seem real. It did something to Tarius; she doesn't feel right to me.*

Tarius looked at her caught her eye and then nodded her head towards Jestia's plate.

Jestia smiled back at her and nodded her head towards Tarius's own full plate.

Tarius started picking at her food.

So now I have to eat, and I just don't feel like it. I just need to think about something else, anything else.

"Where are Jabone and Kasiria?" Ufalla asked.

"They went into town. Jabone wanted to show Kasiria around the capital," Jena said.

"There are two empty spots." Jestia turned to look at Radkin. "Why don't you and Laz join us? There is really no sense in anyone guarding the door." Then she turned and looked at her mother, and Hestia's face turned red as she glared at Jestia, so Jestia had found the distraction her brain needed so that she could eat.

"Yes, sister, join us," Tarius said. "It's absurd for you to sit guard on the door. Come, Laz, sit in Jabone's place."

Jestia turned just enough to see Radkin's reaction. She

was looking at Hestia and Hestia was looking at her. Jestia had no idea how these two thought they were going to keep their "thing" a secret. Hestia shrugged, this helpless look on her face, and Radkin and Laz walked over and sat down. Laz purposely took the seat farthest from the queen so that Radkin had to sit right next to her. Beside her Ufalla had her face nearly planted in her plate in an effort to keep everyone from seeing her grinning, and Jestia tucked into her breakfast looking at her mother with meaning.

Hestia took in a deep breath and let it out then she looked at Dustan and seeing the sling he was wearing said, "I see you took damage. Is it bad?"

"I was nearly killed," Dustan said hotly. "Not that my family seems to give a diddly damn."

"He was not nearly killed. It's a minor flesh wound," Arvon said, rolling his eyes.

"I had worse before I was six, and didn't cry as much," Tarius added.

"See what I mean?" Dustan said. "I looked death in the face and my whole family—including my son—thinks it is some huge joke."

"We don't think it's a joke. We just think you're overreacting," Tarius said.

"Over reacting! Over reacting? Would it hurt any of you to show a little compassion?"

"We gave you a little compassion. What you want is wailing, the rending of clothes and the gnashing of teeth. You want a ballad written about your agonizing brush with death and an elegy explaining the depth of your pain," Arvon said.

Jena smiled turned to look at her mother and for reasons Jestia could only guess at said, "You really aren't good at this, are you?"

Since Hestia's intention was to take the focus off herself and Radkin she wasn't really upset at all about the argument she had started. She felt Radkin's hand on her knee under the table and flushed for a whole new reason. In spite of herself she looked at Radkin who removed her hand and started to eat the way a Katabull did, and Hestia just smiled at her, for the moment oblivious to the rest of the room. *She is magnificent.*

"You have done nothing but whine since it happened. For the love of The Nameless One let it go," Elise said.

"I have cut myself worse shaving," Harris added.

"He probably hit his head. When you hit your head you get all sissy," Ufalla said.

"Sissy! Really Ufalla!" Dustan yelled. "Did you really just call me a sissy?"

"Hey! I was trying to help you out," her daughter's lover yelled back.

Hestia looked at Jestia who was just eating happily. A few minutes ago she hadn't been eating at all and now there was a huge argument and she was eating as if everything was fine. *This roaring and hollering equals normalcy to her. It calms her. Why? Because it's what she's become used to. I bet if they came to blows she would barely look up from her plate. Why? Because she is one of them and knows it will come to nothing. These people love each other and even when they argue all is forgiven. They don't hold grudges.*

"Even Hestia has taken a worse blow than that," Tarius was saying.

"Well I don't know about that," Hestia said. She had taken a couple of injuries in the Great War, the worst an arrow in the hip during the last battle. She remembered just the night before Radkin running her hand over the scar and felt a little thrill.

"I have seen your wounds and I have seen his," Tarius said. She looked at Dustan. "You want us to support you in your belief that none of us have ever known the pain that you have yet there isn't a person at this table who hasn't had as bad if not worse. Gods and spiders, Ufalla and I cut off our own fingers."

Ufalla held up her hand to prove the point. Until that moment Hestia had no idea that Ufalla's finger was in her sword just like Tarius's. She knew Jabone's was but not Ufalla's. She wasn't sure how she felt about that. She just hoped Jestia wasn't going to cut off one of hers, but she supposed if she did she'd get used to that, too.

"I just don't think it's so much to ask that my own family be a little more thoughtful."

"What you want, my love, is for us to be your mother and none of us are," Arvon said, and that seemed to be the end of it. Hestia took a deep breath and decided she just wasn't going to say anything else for the remainder of the meal. She moved her hand under the table and gave Radkin's' knee an affectionate squeeze. Radkin grinned back and let her eyes roam to Hestia's cleavage and cut her eyes towards Hestia's bedroom.

Hestia leaned over and whispered, "As soon as possible."

Darian had been asleep in the crook of Tarius's arm through the entire argument, but he woke up as soon as it got quiet and immediately wanted down. Tarius sat him on the floor and he crawled right over to Jestia and grunted at her. She looked down at him and couldn't think what he might want. She hadn't really been around him since he was a tiny baby to do more than just look at him. He grunted again and Ufalla said, "He wants you to pick him up."

"Why?"

Ufalla shrugged.

"You pick him up you're the one who knows about babies," Jestia said.

"He doesn't want me; he wants you."

Jestia looked down at him and whispered, "Go to someone else."

He grunted again and sort of glared at her till she *saw* him. She reached down, took him under the arms and lifted him up. Holding him at arm's length she looked into his eyes. "Why you little turd." He laughed at her. She looked from the baby to Tarius and back. What did it mean?

Beside her Ufalla started cooing at the baby, and Jestia looked at her like she was an idiot.

Laz looked at Jena and said around a mouthful of food. "See I told you, your baby was humming."

Jestia felt faint, so she quickly handed Darian to Ufalla which didn't seem to make either of them unhappy.

"Jestia are you alright?" Tarius asked.

"No... not at all," Jestia said. "I need to talk to you right now."

Of course she rarely got to talk to Tarius alone because Jena was always there. She had led them to her room and closed the door. The baby had happily stayed with Ufalla. Jestia kept looking at Jena. Tarius she could just talk to, she was not so sure about Jena.

"What is it Jestia?" Tarius asked.

She spoke her mind. "I'd feel better if it was just you and I."

"If it concerns our son I want to know and don't think I have forgotten what you did the last time you two were alone together."

"You make it sound as if we had a tryst. What we did we did for you, but... Well I am sorry about that. It turns out after I thought about it that we should have asked your permission," Jestia said, glaring at Tarius.

Tarius shrugged and Jena looked shocked but then said, "I accept your apology. Now what's wrong with our baby?"

Jestia talked to Tarius. She wasn't ignoring Jena; she was just one of the few people who knew them who found Tarius easy to talk to and Jena a little intimidating. "There is nothing wrong with him but we all know he's not really your baby and we all know where we found him. You know he's magic because if Laz figured it out I know you did." Tarius nodded. "But his eyes were blue and now they are green."

"Baby's eyes can change color the first year," Jena said. "There isn't anything abnormal about that."

"Yes but his went from blue to green, and not just any blue to green but brilliant blue to brilliant green. That is what all the magic users in the Kartik royal line do. Other magic users are normally born with green eyes. We know that these Amalites follow the same practices as the ones in the hive. Rorik had a breeding program here for at least the last twenty-five years, but what if initially they made a trade." She looked at Tarius. "You said yourself that the Amalites in the hive would have become inbred. What if early on Rorik traded them some of his children for their women..."

"Then Darian would belong to the Kartik royal line," Tarius finished for her.

Jestia nodded.

"But what difference does that really make?" Jena asked.

"You are very devout," Tarius told Jena, and it was pretty obvious Jena was only seconds from smacking one or both of them.

"His magic comes from the same well as mine, and gods help us, Eerin's does." Jestia explained. Jena obviously still didn't get it.

"Jena," Tarius said, "there is no way to prove that he is related to royals, so he is now and always will be our son. But the magic knows where it comes from. He doesn't really know Jestia, and no offense but she isn't the most maternal person on this planet."

"None taken," Jestia said.

"Darian has always been particular in who he goes to and he went straight to her and more or less insisted she pick him up. He *knows* her. He will know and we will not be able to hide from him the fact that he isn't our blood son. We can hide it from the rest of the world, but someday we will have to tell him how he came to be ours."

Darkness fell over Jena's features, and it was clear that she now fully understood the impact of what Jestia was telling them. They had hoped to shelter him from knowing how they had found him, but now they would have to tell him. How would he feel knowing the truth of his birth?

"I handed him to Eerin and he didn't fuss even before the spell. He went straight to Hestia the other day, too." Jena said thoughtfully. She looked at Tarius. "I had thought when you said she was banging Radkin that was why. You know... that she smelled right."

Jestia smiled then and decided to see if she couldn't lighten the mood a bit. "I caught them coupling last night. The look on mother's face was priceless."

"Wicked child." Tarius grinned and shook her head.

"Hey I didn't know, and it occurs to me that you would have known both of their mental states and that if you left them here together there was a good chance that they would wind up... Well just like I found them."

Tarius just shrugged and Jena slapped her. "Seriously Tarius, that's the oddest piece of match making you've done to date."

"I think they look good together," Tarius said. Then she got serious again, and she reached over and took Jena's hand. "This thing with Darian, it will be alright. In fact my vision makes even more sense now."

"You had a vision?" Jestia asked. She didn't like the sound of that. "Warlords shouldn't have visions."

"I did, but it was nothing to worry about."

"Please tell me I wasn't queen in this vision of yours."

"I honestly could not say one way or the other."

When they walked back into the dining room Tarius wasn't too surprised to see Hestia holding her son. What was more surprising was that Hestia actually seemed to be enjoying doing so. *Even now my son starts to weave spells. I never wanted to tell him where he came from as much for us as him. I just wanted him to believe that we are his parents. Now I know I will have to tell him that his birth parents despised him so much they gave him up to be sacrificed and eaten. There will be no gentle way to tell him; it won't be like it was when Jena had to tell Jabone why she couldn't have him and she was able to do so in a way that made him understand that he was way more important to us than he thought. Darian will* *have questions, he will know things and we will have to tell him the truth all of it. How will he feel about himself and how will he feel about us?*

As if she were able to read her mind, Jena walked up behind her, got on her tip toes and whispered in her ear. "We will continue to love him as our own. We will treat him as we always have—as our child. Then when we have to tell him he will know that it never made any difference to us and the way we feel about him. He will be even stronger for knowing. In our lives we've never been able to live with lies."

Tarius nodded. She took Jena's hand and lead her back to the table though she had even less appetite now.

She looked across the table where Radkin was trying to feed Darian a piece of egg and he was trying to eat it. He obviously liked the taste considering the happy noises he made, but it kept slipping out of his mouth and Radkin kept taking her finger catching it on his chin and sticking it back in.

Jena got up walked over and took Darian from Hestia. She said because Radkin's feeding techniques were likely to make Darian sick, but Tarius knew the real reason. Jena just needed to hold him and reconnect, and she didn't want him to be in the arms of someone who was most likely actually connected to him in a way she wasn't connected to either of their children. When Jena sat down next to her, Darian in tow, he immediately wanted to come to her so Tarius took him and held him tight.

She whispered, her lips touching his ear, "You are my son."

He, Kasiria, Tarius and Tarius's wife Eric had just had a wonderful breakfast of fruit and jerked meat that they bought in the open-air market in the heart of the capital city and eaten as they walked around. He was still eating a piece of jerky when Tarius said, "So you could have had breakfast with the big wigs in the queen's quarters and instead you decided to spend the morning with us. I'm honored, brother."

"Well first, I'm sure you were as welcome as we were. The truth is we'd all rather be outside than stuck in there. Second, if I have to hear my own father whine about that scratch on his arm even one more time I think I will die of embarrassment. The only thing worse could be hearing my fadra and madra and yours making fun of him about it. They put me right in the middle and I find it is not a place I enjoy being."

Kasiria and Eric had been stopped by something shiny and Jabone and Tarius were disinterested so they were standing mostly in the street while the ladies were picking up and fondling every item in the booth. Every Kartik man who walked by had to get an eyeful of he and Tarius's mates. While Kasiria was a beauty Eric was sort of plain but she was as blonde-haired, blue-eyed and light-skinned as Kasiria, so she turned just as many dark Kartik heads.

"I can't say I get it," Tarius said, nodding his head towards where their wives were shopping. Jabone sighed as he watched Kasiria pick up a huge broad axe she couldn't have wielded successfully even in her Katabull form. It was a ridiculous weapon one more for show than actual warfare.

"In the Jethrik it has only been a few years that women have even been able to touch swords and weapons, and most still won't. This is all still pretty new to them and Eric more so than Kasiria, because face it Eric was playing a man when she was in the Jethrik and the territories."

"Aye I guess you're right. I'm glad Kasiria has gotten over being mad at Eric."

"Me too, I think it's good for Kasiria to have someone from her own country to talk to. Someone her own age who doesn't hold her a grudge because of who her father is. I can't say I ever really understood it. I mean Eric had basically done exactly what my madra did and Kasiria near worships her."

"I know right," Tarius said. "She is much too reckless your Kasiria, and I never thought I'd say that about anyone because it was all they used to tell me about myself until I was about to scream."

"My fadra says she is too much like my madra but without the skill. It's only one of the reasons we are moving back to the compound..."

"You are moving back home!" Tarius bellowed and then he hugged him. "Oh, my non-blood kin that is the best news ever! I have to say with you and Kasiria off in Montero and my annoying sister and her even more annoying but very beautiful mate gone it's been kind of lonely."

"My arse, you've had Laz and Riglid and Jadon and Rea just to name a few." Jabone hugged him back.

"Laz is infatuated with Eric and can't talk to me for even three seconds without looking at her boobs. Riglid is as he has always been—altogether too serious. Fadra says he's just like Tweed. Jadon is completely moping about the latest in a long line of fellows he claims to be in love with till they break up. Seriously I think he just likes to be unhappy. Rea is busy drinking too much and screwing anything that doesn't move fast enough... you know nothing new there. Every other member of our pack who is our age has cubs."

"Can Eric cook?" Jabone asked.

"Oh aye, I hardly ever get to."

Jabone lowered his voice. "Kasiria cannot cook at all. She ruins food, yet she insists on cooking. I sneak out and eat at inns or I would have starved by now."

"When you move home your mothers and fathers will feed you," Tarius said.

"I thought I wanted to be away from it all and I find that now that we have decided to go back the longer I am away the more homesick I become. If Kasiria is to be like my madra she must learn to fight like her, and I find I cannot teach her..."

"Because everything you try to teach her just seems to piss her off." They said together and then they laughed wildly and Jabone couldn't remember the last time he had laughed so much or so hard. "I have really missed you." Then he saw Kasiria lift the axe over her head.

"Kasiria no!"

Too late. She lost her balance and the axe went backwards breaking a rack holding a dozen swords. The swords went everywhere. Kasiria looked at Jabone, grimaced and cringed.

Jabone walked to the merchant as Kasiria put the axe back where she'd found it. "I'm so very sorry," Kasiria said, starting to pick up the swords.

"It's alright princess," the merchant said.

Kasiria gave him an odd look.

"I will happily pay for the damages," Jabone said.

"That will not be necessary prince," he said.

Kasiria nodded her head, understanding why he had addressed her as princess. Jabone never really considered himself a prince but not only the Katabull but the Kartiks as well often called him prince. Kasiria was a princess of the Jethrik but the Kartiks didn't know that. They called her princess only because she was his mate.

"I'm sorry," Kasiria said to Jabone.

He smiled and nodded. The fact that in all her training she hadn't learned there was a point of no return on such a heavy weapon only strengthened his resolve that she needed to train with his parents.

Jabone helped her clean up the mess, whispering in her ear. "At least buy a dagger to pay the man for his broken stand."

Kasiria nodded and he stood up.

As Kasiria was finishing up making her purchases, Jabone saw Eric looking down the street, a troubled look on her face. He walked up to her, looked in the direction she was looking, and clearly saw what her human eyes could only barely see, yet it showed she was no sleeper. There was a man coming in on horseback fast and he was obviously wounded. Jabone called on the night and took off running towards him. When he got closer he could see the man was barely conscious. Jabone grabbed the horse's reins and drug him to a stop, catching the man as he fell from his mount.

As Yri, Jena and the queen's surgeon worked on the rider, Tarius went through his clothes looking for clues as to who he was and what exactly he was doing here. Tarius was about to give up when she found a piece of wet, crumpled paper in the bottom of the man's pants' pocket. She took it out, but it was stuck together and she didn't know how much good it was going to be.

"Did he say anything?" Tarius asked Jabone.

"No. He was unconscious when he fell from his horse."

"Those are Finias's crests," Hestia said, pointing to the filigreed emblems on the shoulders of the tabard the man had been wearing.

"Jestia, can you do something with this?" Tarius said, holding out the piece of ruined paper. Jestia held out her hand and Tarius dropped it into her palm. Tarius turned back to Jabone and the others.

"Were there others with him?"

"No only this one," Jabone answered.

"Who saw him first?"

"I did," Eric said. "It was a long way off but I could see the rider wasn't in his saddle right."

"Think hard, did you see anyone else close to him, someone who might have been riding with him?"

Eric thought for a minute and answered. "Not that I saw."

"He was alone, Madra, I'm sure of it," Jabone said.

Jena walked out of the room at her back. Tarius turned and Jena shook her head. Tarius looked back at Jestia expectantly. Jestia sighed and closed the wet note in her fist. A few seconds later she pulled a dry piece of paper with writing on it from her hand. She handed it to Tarius who looked at it then handed it to Hestia.

"Jestia find your cousin Eerin. We will need him," Tarius said.

"Do I have to?"

"Yes immediately." Jestia grumbled but took hold of Ufalla and left. Tarius turned to Hestia. "Well?"

"This time I insist on going with you."

Chapter Twenty-three

At first it had seemed like a battle they would easily win.
They had killed a couple of dozen and no one was the wiser
then someone just had to make noise. Someone on their
side had let out a battle cry. No one knew who, no one owned
it, and who knew but that they weren't already among the
dead. Why they did it was also lost on Yorik. Did they just get
caught up in the moment? Did they think it was wrong to kill
them in their sleep so wanted to wake them up to make it a
fair fight as if a hundred and fifty men against fifty fighters—
mostly female with a bunch of children to try to protect was
fair. Did they do it out of fright? It didn't matter. Whatever
the reason, that one person's moment of weakness had gotten
nearly a third of them killed and was likely going to leave
none of them, adult or child, alive to tell the tale of the idiot
who screamed.

They had all retreated to the stables because it was easier
to defend than anything else on the grounds and it kept the
cult from getting to the horses. Yorik had sent two riders out
towards the capital, but both had been shot through with
arrows just out of the gate and he'd given up.

The only reason they were still alive at all was because of
the storm. The lighting strikes were horrible and the rain
cold. The ground was more like soup than earth and when
the cult tried to approach them in the stables the few archers
Yorik had were able to easily pick them off. That didn't keep
them from trying till their bodies littered the ground. They
didn't dare drop their guard because the people they were
fighting were religious morons and nothing was more
dangerous.

Yes the stables had been a good idea; there was only one
real problem. They had nothing to eat except the horses,
and if they had any chance of escape they needed the horses.
Finally he had allowed them to kill and butcher one horse.

Yorik couldn't say whether it had been good or bad for
morale. His wife pressed a piece of cooked meat into his
hands. "You need to eat," she said.

He nodded he knew he needed food, but he'd always
loved horses and a little part of him had died when one of
the fighters drove her sword into the horse's brain by shoving

it in behind his ear as he and three others held the animal still. It had been quick and he assumed painless. Much quicker than many of his people had died, no doubt because they had a need to try to save them even when there was no hope.

He ate the meat not thinking about it. It was tough and mostly tasteless but when it was in his stomach he found that he could think a little clearer.

"I fear I have led our people to their death," Yorik told his wife. He looked back at the stable where the children were huddled in one stall eating.

"I'd rather die a hundred times than live one more day the way we have been living. You have done the right thing, my love, and if I die I die."

His head shot up and he shook his head. "Shadra... They will kill you on sight."

"You know they will have to work to do so. It may be the only way to save any of them. Let us eat well. Get our strength."

"I will go with you always, and for the chance to save our son I'd do nearly anything," Yorik said. "And if I die I die."

He put all that was left of his people on horseback, mounting the children behind them which meant most of them were riding double. It wasn't much of a chance, but it was the only one they had.

He kissed Shadra and she kissed him back. He knocked his arrow and she called on the night. He lept out first and killed the archer waiting in the tower. Shadra, sword in hand, took to the shadows and ran along a wall. A troop of men spotted her and came at her and the Katabull started to make a swath through them. Then she jumped over them and kept running.

The rain stopped and suddenly they were bathed in sunlight. His targets were clear but so was he, so Yorik would aim and fire at one and then move. On his command the whole of his people on horseback ran from the stable and towards the palace gate, swords in hand, doing what damage they could as they rode. Shadra opened the gates and the horses carrying his people ran through. His son turned and looked at him and Yorik smiled at him.

Shadra was mowing fighters down and Yorik seemed to be killing someone every time he let an arrow fly. He began to believe they just might win, but then he felt the blood running down his side. He'd been hit but there was no pain, which told him he wasn't long for this world. He kept firing arrows as fast as he could. Then he saw ten of them attack Shadra at once. She was killing one after the other till a sword ran into her heart.

The strength left Yorik's own body and he fell even as she did. They would never be apart. He didn't want to live without her and he wasn't going to have to. Through the fog in his mind he heard a familiar voice and forced his eyes open. There, to his amazement, stood Hestia, Queen of the Kartik. He became vaguely aware of her holding his head up.

"Yorik, hear me. We have saved your people and the children with them. I will make sure that everyone who lives from this moment on knows your name and that of your wife how you were heros to the crown when we most needed you. Hear me, Yorik, your fight was not in vain. The cult will not win. We have killed Rorik and all who followed him. When we leave here we will ride on to Sedrik's. We will not stop till there is not a single member of the cult alive in the Kartik. We could not have done it without you and your wife."

Then someone laid Shadra's body beside him. He saw her face one last time and he died.

Thirty some people on horseback were riding out even as fifty of the Marching Night and two hundred Kartik troops reached Finias's palace. In fact they had almost attacked the wrong people, but Tarius quickly realized these people weren't charging. They were running and were being chased, and then she saw the children riding behind them. She and Harris moved the Marching Night to the right, letting them ride through and then attacked the men at their backs who were on foot.

She tried to have the riders moved to safety, but upon seeing the Kartik army led by none other than Tarius the Black and their queen they insisted on being part of the fight. They took the children into the woods, dropped them off, then rode back in to join them.

Since the gate was already open, the fight didn't last long, and those who had outnumbered their opponents soon found themselves out numbered and outclassed.

With the help of the resistance fighters they were able to find all the hidden places in the palace the members of the cult were hiding in. In minutes the siege was over and they were mostly just making sure that everyone that should be dead was.

Tarius found Hestia with Radkin standing over a couple of bodies and joined them.

Hestia looked up at her. "It's Yorik and his wife. One of their people told me they sacrificed themselves to save the others. I can't help but think if we'd arrived only a few minutes sooner... "

"My dear friend, I have found in matters of war it is never good to deal in the what ifs. Did they die together?"

"No she died over there," Radkin said. "I moved her to him when he was still alive. She is one of us." There was a confused tone to her voice.

Tarius looked closely at the woman's face; she didn't look familiar. "What was her name?"

"Shadra," Hestia said. Tarius took in a deep breath and held it. "What?"

"That was my madra's name. I have thought of her a lot these last few days. She must have loved him a great deal to be willing to stay in hiding," Tarius said. Hestia nodded and she looked at Radkin briefly. Royals were taught a reverence for the Katabull, but they weren't supposed to intermarry with them. "She must have believed in him more to stay when the cult arrived and took over."

"How can you tell she is one of your people, Tarius?" Hestia asked. It was a good question. Upon death a Katabull normally reverted to their human form.

"A beast can smell its own kind and... well through the cut across her ribs I can see she has two rib cages. Do not dwell on the dead, Hestia. You can't bring them back. They died together. If you must die what better way to go than fighting beside and dying with the one you love?"

Hestia watched the Great Leader walk away slinging mud from her boots and bellowing orders to the troops. Hestia looked at her own sword still in her hand. There was blood on it, and it felt good.

She looked at Yorik and his Katabull wife and the joy left her. "If we'd gotten here only a few minutes earlier..."

"Tarius is right," Radkin said. She took hold of Hestia's elbow and led her away from the bodies. "It is better not to think such things. If you just must deal with ifs, then think of these. If the children hadn't been in the market, if they hadn't seen the rider, if Jestia hadn't been able to fix the note, and if we hadn't ridden out immediately *all* would have died and we never would have known that there were people here who remained loyal to the crown, who did not join the cult and who rose up to try to put them down. It was their day to die."

"They think such things are comforting," Jestia said from behind her making her jump.

"What?" Hestia said, not understanding.

"The Katabull, she is trying to comfort you. They think saying things like 'it was their day to die' is comforting. I can tell you that he heard you, he saw his wife, and he died content. Of course I don't know whether that's any better than 'it was their day to die'." The thickness in Jestia's voice told Hestia there was sorrow attached to such knowledge.

"Thank you," Hestia said. Jestia walked away and Hestia noticed that her daughter wasn't actually walking in the mud but on top of it.

"I think it's very comforting to say it's their day to die," Radkin mumbled beside her.

Hestia turned and smiled up at her. "I find that you want to comfort me is comforting."

Jestia found Eerin puking behind a tree. "Did you not make a big enough mess of things?" she said, waving a hand around at all the mud. "Really, Eerin, how are you ever going to be a proper wizard if you can't stand the sight of a little blood and guts?"

Eerin straightened wiping his mouth on the back of his sleeve. "Seriously, Jestia, I never planned to be a battle wizard."

"What did you plan to do, Eerin? Hold that thought. Here comes the love of my life to find me and make sure I'm safe. Please don't let on that I am more than capable of taking care of myself and don't really need her protection. That would just ruin her day and she's always so happy when she has just killed people."

Ufalla came skidding up to her covered in mud and blood and fit to be tied. "Gods and spiders, Jestia, don't just go running off like that. I had no idea what had happened to you."

"My love, I didn't leave your side till the last of them was dead."

"You can never be sure, Jestia, there could still be some hiding."

"You are so right, dear. I will be more careful in the future."

Ufalla frowned. "No you won't. You're just saying that to shut me up."

"I would never do that, light of my heart."

"You are such a little liar, Jestia."

"Have you met my cousin Eerin? You know, the toad that almost got you killed in that storm but instead just turned you into a sniffling whining sissy for a few days leaving you the brunt of your pack's favorite joke? Even now your brother is writing a story about it."

Ufalla glared at him then took off her sword and handed it to Jestia.

"Prepare yourself." Ufalla hissed at Eerin and took up a wrestling stance.

"What?" Eerin said, not understanding.

Jestia bent over to whisper in his ear. "My mate grew up with the Katabull. When they have a disagreement they can't settle with words they wrestle. I'm not really sure how that solves anything really but it works for them."

"Can't I just tell her she's right and forgo the wrestling?"

Jestia shook her head. "No she needs to wrestle with you and when she beats you to a pulp you tell her you're sorry and she'll forgive you."

"But I don't know how to wrestle."

"Then it should be over quickly but you'd better put up some fight or you're just going to piss her off more."

"But..."

Jestia interrupted slapping him gently on his cheek. "I suggest you do what she said and prepare to defend yourself."

She stepped away as Ufalla ran at the wizard burying her head in his stomach. Thank the gods it was already empty. Jestia watched as the wizard tried to defend himself against the might of Ufalla's anger. Ufalla knocked him down till he couldn't stand on his own any more.

"I'm sorry," Eerin squeaked out, holding his hands up in front of him.

Ufalla stopped mid stride, put down a hand and yanked him to his feet. Then she took his hand, brought their elbows together, and released him.

Ufalla reclaimed her sword then turned on her heel and started back towards the palace. "Come on, Jestia. We have work to do."

Eerin wiped some mud from his eye and looked at Jestia.

Jestia smiled at him and said, "Never, ever jack with me

again. Do you understand me, Eerin?"

Eerin nodded and wiped some more mud off his face. "I really am sorry, Jestia."

"Oh I'm sure you are."

"Jestia come on," Ufalla ordered.

"I'm coming. Don't get your drawers in a knot."

Rimmy had wound up in charge of the children. There were twenty in all, and they were cold, wet and scared. He was glad when Jestia and Ufalla showed up. Jestia did a spell to dry the kids off and clean them up. Ufalla helped him hand out blankets and calm them down. One boy was crying uncontrollably; he was about four. Rimmy wrapped him in a blanket.

"There, there boy. It will all be alright."

"No it won't; both his parents are dead," Jestia whispered in his ear. "They died so the others could get away. He is Yorik's son and he is half Katabull."

"Yorik was married to a Katabull?" Rimmy whispered back.

"It would appear so. I guess Katabull is what all the stylish royals are wearing this year."

Rimmy had given up a long time ago trying to understand Jestia. He looked at the boy then back at Jestia. "The poor little guy." He reached down and picked him up. The boy hugged his neck and Rimmy patted his back. As the boy's teeth started to rattle he seemed to calm down.

"It's alright boy, you'll be fine."

Jestia gave Rimmy a look that near screamed *you're an imbecile* then walked away to do a spell that started gathering sticks for a fire. For the moment the children all seemed mesmerized by the sticks floating through the air to come together in the middle of their group.

Only a witch could start a fire in all this wet. Poor kids in mud up to their ankles. At least they are dry now. I understand why Tarius doesn't want to take them inside till the bodies are cleaned up, but there is nowhere to stand where the mud doesn't swallow your feet. He noticed then that Jestia's feet were clean as were her clothes and armor. *Unless you're a witch.*

Jestia dried the wood and then started the fire and the children moved close to it for warmth. He heard Tarius call for Jestia, and Jestia silently started in the direction of the palace. Ufalla saw her leaving and rushed to catch up complaining about her just running off and Rimmy realized that Ufalla hadn't heard the Great Leader call Jestia. He sometimes forgot Ufalla wasn't Katabull. He never made that mistake with any of her siblings, just her.

Jestia found Tarius standing with her mother and Radkin. Both Tarius and Radkin were still the Katabull, and Jestia was a little surprised to realize that Hestia was as completely comfortable with them in this form as she was their other.

I forget how long she has known them and how much history she has with them. She watched with amusement as Hestia reached back and took Radkin's hand hiding their linked hands behind her own back as if that somehow hide from the world what she was doing. *I wonder if mother has hidden this desire for years or if she was as shocked as I was when I realized that what I'd been missing in my bed was a woman.*

She had reached them so she stopped and Ufalla nearly ran into her, mumbling things Jestia couldn't understand and didn't really try to.

"What?" she asked the Great Leader.

Her mother let go of Radkin's hand as if it were hot. Jestia smiled and shook her head. "Relax I already caught you naked together."

"You know, Jestia, a nice girl would pretend not to know what her mother was doing," Tarius said with a grin.

"Considering how I found them I'd have to be nice and really stupid," Jestia said.

Radkin laughed, so it was clear that Jestia's teasing was only really bothering her mother which was great because Radkin was a huge Katabull easily as big as Jabone, so not someone you wanted to goad.

Jestia turned to Tarius and asked again, "What?"

"Could you find Kasiria, Jabone, Tarius and Eric and go clean the kitchen and start preparing a meal?"

Jestia didn't have to wonder why she was put on this task. These things were known to cannibalize. When Tarius told her to 'clean the kitchen' Tarius meant she wanted her to remove anything humans shouldn't eat... like each other.

"Whatever you do, don't let Kasiria cook," Tarius added.

"We'll let Kasiria cut things up." Ufalla suggested with a smile.

Jestia started to go, but her mother reached out and took hold of her arm. When Jestia turned to look at her she said, "I'm very proud of you."

Jestia looked at her mother and found herself so filled with emotion that she just had to say something really horrid that had nothing to do with how she was feeling at all.

She looked at Radkin and said, "You must be amazing in bed."

Before she could say anything else, Ufalla grabbed her hand and started dragging her away.

"Seriously, Jestia, your mother was nice enough to not only let me keep my head but to even give us permission to get married and she is being so nice to you…"

"I know, I know. I just… I was so touched I couldn't think of anything appropriate to say," Jestia said, feeling miserable.

"Did it ever occur to you that you could just say nothing at all?"

"You know sometimes Ufalla I wonder if you really know me at all."

Rimmy hugged the half breed child close and rocked him trying to comfort him. It had been so long since any of his cubs were this little. They were all grown now and each with their own special problems. The boys never really gave him cause for concern, but that girl.

Hared walked over to him. "The Great Leader has decided that I should join you in babysitting," he said. Like she had Rimmy, Tarius had Hared go back to his human form for this task. These children no doubt had little or no knowledge of what the Katabull were and for someone who had never seen one the Katabull could be a frightening sight. These children were traumatized enough. Rimmy only knew about the little one he held. He had no way of knowing which of these other children had lost one or both parents.

From here he could see bodies being carted out and stacked on wagons, but the children couldn't see it. The resistance fighters would get proper Kartik burials, the members of the cult would be hauled into the woods and dumped to be devoured by animals, rot and feed the earth. Far enough away that they would neither damage the water fields nor be able to be smelled by humans. Rimmy was the Katabull, so he didn't really understand the whole burial thing. The truth was that the same would happen to both. Once dead the body no longer deserved reverence; enemy or friend the dead were all the same.

He thought back to what he'd seen only a few days ago. What these things had done to their own children… and he held the boy tighter. Jestia had assured them none were alive below ground, but Tarius had sent them all up out of the hole and she had checked each of the dead just to make sure they were.

"Are you alright, Rimmy?" Hared asked.

"Riding with the Great Leader, being her runner, has been a privilege I wouldn't trade, but I have seen much that I wish I could unsee."

Hared nodded his understanding.

"Rimmy!" Tarius called.

Rimmy looked at the boy and Hared said, "Give him here." Rimmy handed Hared the child and ran to find Tarius.

He found her standing in front of the stables covered in blood and mud. There had been a lot of fighting here, so the mud was way worse. He ran through it, oblivious to the filth that splashed all over him and anyone near him. Radkin and Hestia were with her, but Jestia and Ufalla were nowhere in sight so he assumed Tarius had sent Jestia to do something specific. When he skidded to a stop in front of them he slipped and probably would have fallen had Radkin not reached out and grabbed his arm. Radkin and Tarius were both still Katabull. So Radkin easily caught and steadied him.

"Rimmy are any of the children in need of medical care?" Tarius asked.

And that was why Tarius was such a good leader; she didn't forget anyone. "All seem to be physically well. They could use a hot meal and a good night's sleep."

"Which they will get when we are finished cleaning the palace. Even now I have people preparing food. At least here there was no cannibalism... yet," Tarius said. "Eventually it would have come to it. They would have started another breeding program here and then started culling."

"Great Leader, Jestia said the baron's son is half Katabull, but how could one of our own stand for the cult?" Rimmy asked in confusion.

"She couldn't. That is why she and her man lie dead. Why did she do nothing before now? She was in hiding here. She had a child and a man she loved and she couldn't have gotten them both safely away. When you have small children your first thought always is for their safety. That is how these things creep in. Their filthy missionaries and soldiers come into people's homes where they live with their families, not into barracks filled with fighters." Tarius spit on the ground. "They corrupt from within. Greed is a powerful weapon and some people will believe anything if it promises them wealth and power. By the time they ordered everyone to convert they were so outnumbered it was do or die. The Amalite religion grows like a disease in people's bellies. They often take over without ever drawing a sword, without letting an arrow fly, until the people of the land they have swarmed to inhabit turn on their own kin and kill them because they refuse to bow to the Amalite gods. "

Rimmy nodded. "It makes my heart sick."

"Rimmy, do you and Hared mind watching the children until things are settled here?"

"Not at all."

"When you return to them you may tell them that of the people they rode out of the palace with all are alive and well. We know the baron's child is orphaned, but I have no way of knowing whether there will be other parentless children among them. If there are, they already knew that beforehand."

"If you don't mind me asking, what is to become of the boy? Does he belong with us or them?" he said, nodding at Hestia.

Tarius looked at Hestia for an answer.

"I will take your council in this matter, Tarius, for you more than I know best were a half breed child would be happiest," Hestia said.

But Rimmy heard, *It is a great embarrassment to the crown to have a half Katabull royal.*

"I will not pretend to know what is best for him. In this moment I, like Rimmy, am heart sick and frustrated beyond belief. For decades I have taken troops and searched our shores and killed whatever Amalites we found. We raised children and felt safe, we thought we had gotten rid of the Amalite religion, but it was growing in the ground in the territories and all the while Rorik and his allies, like worms were chewing on us from the inside and we were none the wiser. Let me sleep on it and we will talk in the morning."

Hestia nodded.

"In the meantime, Rimmy, will you and Hared care for the child?"

Rimmy nodded and started back the way he had come. In short order he found Radkin by his side. "I know that look, Rimmy. What are you so mad about?"

Rimmy looked back to make sure he was far enough away from the queen not to be heard. After all he was the Great Leader's runner; he couldn't afford to be heard saying disparaging things about the queen. "You heard Hestia. She doesn't want to accept responsibility for the child because his parentage makes him an embarrassment."

"No, she doesn't want to take responsibility for him because she's a crappy mother and he would be raised by servants. She'd rather he were with people who would love him in a way she doesn't feel she can, who would be able to help him embrace what he is in a way she cannot."

"Oh."

"Don't assume things. Isn't that what *you* always say, Rimmy?"

He chuckled and punched her hard on the shoulder. "Yes it is. Radkin... what are you doing with her?" He hadn't been a hundred percent sure he was reading the signs right until Radkin found the need to defend Hestia which had been the final piece of the puzzle.

Radkin started walking so that he was going in the direction he was supposed to be moving in, no doubt so that they didn't draw attention to themselves. "I don't really know, Rimmy. I needed something, she needed something, and it just sort of happened. All I know for sure is that when I'm with her—and I don't just mean in the sack—when I'm with her I don't feel all dead and empty in here."

She pointed at her chest and Rimmy nodded. He knew exactly what she meant because it was the same thing that had happened to him when he'd found Hared. Suddenly the pain and emptiness was just gone.

He stopped and grabbed her arm so that she had to stop as well and then he hugged her tight and said, his lips nearly touching her ear, "My dear sister, if she takes away your desire to leave me and our children for even a minute then that's all I need to know. Our children are grown. It is your life, and if she brings you any happiness then I will stop thinking any of the evil thoughts I was having about her." He released her.

"Thanks brother."

She started back towards Hestia and Tarius and he continued his trek towards the woods and the children. He could see that Hared was still holding the boy and the other children were huddled close to the fire. When he got near all the kids started questioning him at once: Were their parents alright, could they go home, they were hungry, they were tired, and a dozen other things.

Rimmy laughed. "Calm down children. All the adults who

rode out with you are well, food is even now being prepared, and when the palace has been cleaned they will come get us for dinner."

Not long after that relatives started showing up to huddle around the fire with the children and wait. It was almost dark when Riglid ran over to tell them Tarius had given the all clear and dinner was ready. He noticed that every child seemed to have someone who came to get them except of course for the one Hared was holding.

Rimmy walked over to Hared to walk with him to the palace. The child was asleep. "You want me to take him?"

"He's not heavy; I've got him. Do you know what they are going to do with him? I mean does he belong with the Katabull or with the royals?"

"I asked the same thing. Hestia left it up to Tarius and Tarius said for us to watch him tonight and she will make a decision in the morning."

"Poor little guy," Hared said. "He told me his name is Petrid but that they call him Pete."

Rimmy made a face. "That's an odd name for a Katabull. Did he say anything else?"

"He asked for his mother. I said nothing, like a big coward, and he just cried till he fell asleep."

"My children lost two parents but had two others and yet their other parents' deaths have shaped them in ways Radkin and I living have not. I can't imagine what it must be like to so young lose all your parents," Rimmy said.

"I lost three parents in the Great War," Hared reminded him, "both of my birth parents and my father. I have three sisters—all younger than me. I was maybe ten. The Great Leader would come and bring us meat she had hunted herself and she would sit and tell us stories about our parents and when she did I didn't miss them as much."

Rimmy smiled at a fond memory. "She did the same with our children. Always stories of Tweed."

Hared nodded. "Tarius will make a story about his parents and when he hears it he will know they are always with him."

Jena found herself left behind again, but this time even Hestia and Radkin had gone which left her with Darian and Laz. Dustan had stayed but he was in the infirmary mending from his wound and she had no desire to hear any more of his whining.

Laz was now her appointed body guard, and while she would have liked to have told Tarius she didn't need one, recent events proved that she did. Laz at least let her get out and walk around. Still she really hated being left behind.

They had gone to the very garden from which she'd been abducted just because it was pretty and mostly because she needed to confront her fears. She found on returning that knowing those who had perpetrated the crime were all quite dead and that a huge Katabull man was watching over them she felt no fear at all. Darian loved it here, and if he remembered the abduction at all he showed no signs of it. Jena was mostly glad to be able to see the sky again.

In this place the worst could have happened, but it didn't so as twisted as it might seem instead of having bad memories of this place I have only good ones. I handled myself well and neither my son nor I were harmed, and who is to say that it wasn't the natural magic of this place that saved us.

Laz picked a flower and brought it to her; she took it and smiled. He was a kind boy she'd known all of his life, only a few years older than her own son. Of course now she looked like she was his age which must be only slightly less confusing for Laz than it was for her.

"Thank you, Laz."

"Well I know I'm no longer a child but it seemed appropriate." It was customary for Katabull children to pick a flower and give it to the mate of the Great Leader if they were walking alone. If they had no flower they would run up take her hand and kiss it. If Tarius was with her walking through the compound and they saw them they would just wave. If Tarius was walking alone the children would often follow her around staying several feet behind her, but not because it was an ancient custom. No they followed Tarius around because if she wasn't too busy she would turn around and tell them a story.

So far from home and so far from Tarius, when Jena realized the reason Laz had given it to her it made it that much sweeter.

"Laz, have you found a special girl yet?"

"Aye, but you are already taken, Jena," Laz said.

Jena laughed at him. "You young cad. Seriously?"

"Not yet. In truth I stopped looking for a while. My fadra died when I was really too young to remember him or even know what his being dead meant. My father never showed us his grief; he hid it. It was easy because we were only

children. I know he must have suffered but I never saw it."
Laz shrugged. "Watching my madra die the way she did left
me deeply grieved and feeling raw, but seeing my mother
turn into someone I didn't know... so lost she went out of her
way to die... left me feeling sort of cynical about love. It never
really lasts. Even if nothing else goes wrong eventually death
will take one from the other."

She started to get up and run after Darian but Laz put up
his hand then ran over and caught the baby as he was about
to go into the water. Laz brought him back to Jena. She took
him and for the moment he was happy to sit on her lap and
look around.

"My madra on her death bed said to me, 'Nothing is ever
really over. I will always be with you.' At the time it brought
me some comfort but when she was actually dead I saw her
words as nothing but very pretty bullshit. You see I waited to
feel or see my madra's spirit. I didn't and it just made me so
mad. But I'm young, life goes on and I got over it... but my
mother didn't. Every time I saw her grief etching itself onto
her face I thought, *That isn't for me* and I didn't let myself
even start to get serious with any girl.

Then the other day I saw my mother smile a real smile,
her smile, and in it I remembered clearly my madra because
my madra made her smile like that. Since then I feel my
madra's spirit all the time and see her clearly because I can
now think of her and not instantly remember how she died.
She was right. She is still with me, and now my memories of
her warm me. If the right woman catches my eye my heart is
open."

"Your madra was a wonderful woman," Jena said, a catch
in her voice. "My own life has been so filled with life and
death. I never knew my mother, and my father died in my
arms during the Great War. Tarius has twice put babies in
my arms. I think we sometimes forget how closely life and
death are related. You can't live as long as you fear death."

Laz looked at her and smiled. "Jena you sound more like
the Katabull every day."

Chapter Twenty-four

Tarius had slept... or had tried to sleep in a bed in one of the rooms of the palace with Arvon. He was huge, he snored, and he lay on more of the bed than he should. She couldn't remember why either of them had thought it was a good idea to share except that neither of them was used to sleeping alone. There was a knocking on her door. "Who is it?"

"Rimmy."

She sat up and moved so that her feet rested on the floor. "Come in, Rimmy."

He looked at Arvon still sleeping, snoring and drooling and said, making a face, "I remember when I thought he was so cute."

Tarius nodded and motioned towards the door. Rimmy walked back out and she stood up and followed him. "Maybe it's best to let him sleep. He tossed and turned most of the night." She closed the door to the room quietly. "He's not well, just riding nearly kills him. Dustan stayed at the castle—in the infirmary no less—over a nick on his arm, but Arvon insisted on coming again and he is in bad shape. Jestia gave him a potion for the swelling and then he took more powder than he is supposed to. I really think the powders make him worse; at best all they do is make him sleep through his pain. He wants our son to see him as he once was, but I'm afraid if he keeps pushing himself to do the things he should no longer be doing he will not live long. And if he keeps taking so many powders no one is going to care because they change his spirit and make him act a huge ass."

Rimmy nodded. "I know you have your own problems, Great Leader, and I'm sorry if I have woken you."

She grinned. "I would have had to be asleep for you to wake me. I know you would not even risk waking me unless it was important."

"It's about the boy, Tarius..."

"I'm sorry, Rimmy. I completely forgot. I'm afraid I haven't had time to think about it. Is the boy well?"

"He is. I know this may sound mad, so please hear me out Tarius. The boy should be with our people, he is above all else Katabull. As you know Hared is younger than I am and has no cubs. Radkin should not bear more cubs, and I don't think she would if I asked her to because her quiver like mine is full." Meaning they had the number of children they were supposed to have. Most people who believed in the Nameless God had only enough children to replace themselves. "Hared and I were up most of the night talking, and we would like to foster the boy and raise him as our own. Just he and I. We would not need Radkin's help. My other children are grown and on their own."

Tarius thought of what this would mean, not so much for the child or for Rimmy and Hared but for her. Arvon was in bad shape. He shouldn't be with her at all; riding near killed him and walking was right out. Jena had to take care of Darian. Radkin—at least for the near future—was attached to the queen in more ways than one. If Rimmy and Hared fostered this child she would have to send them back to the compound to raise him. This boy had lost both his parents, and he needed to be in a home where neither was in danger. Rimmy couldn't be her runner anymore, and he knew it as well as she did. Everything was changing, but change wasn't necessarily bad. She ran her hands across her face and through her hair. She noticed Rimmy was holding his breath.

"I think that is a fine plan. I will talk to Hestia about it. When we return to the capital we will have Yri make a thorough examination of the boy, and when you have all rested you and Hared can take him back to the compound."

"When he is old enough..."

"Riglid will hold your place till... What's the boy's name?"

"Petrid."

"What a horrible name for a Katabull."

"They call him Pete."

"That's not much better... Riglid will hold your place till Pete is old enough."

"Thank you, Tarius." He hugged her and then took off no doubt to go tell Hared.

I owe Rimmy a debt I can never pay. How could I not let him have his heart's desire? The child deserves parents who will love him. I am not alone, things are just shifting. This is the way of fighters; some leave and others take their place. But I thought I was done, I thought this part of my life was over, and I find that as much as I thought I missed the fight when there was peace is how much I miss the peace now that there is fighting. And how was this peace broken? First my son and my god children were nearly killed in the territories and then they took Jena and Darian from under my nose. In my youth I knew, but peace made me forget how insidious is this religious plague.

She just wanted to go home; home to the compound with Jena and their baby. She just wanted to enjoy them and sit in peace by their campfire.

She stood there looking at nothing feeling tired and more than a little beaten.

It wasn't supposed to be like this, not with them here. We are beating them easily yet I still feel defeated. I cannot even protect my own family in my home land. The kingdom war lord let a tumor grow in the heart of the country.

"Madra," a soft voice said at her shoulder. "Are you alright?"

"No Jabone. No, I'm not alright." She didn't turn to face him. She started to tell him all that she was feeling and thinking, but she the great and powerful warlord turned out to be too cowardly to show her belly to her own son. In fact she still had trouble looking him in the eye after she had cried all over him in the middle of the road. "I shared a bed with your fadra last night. He snores, he takes the whole bed, and he moves all night. I got next to no sleep. He is a poor replacement for your mother."

"I'm confused. Do you want yet another baby?"

Tarius shook her head. "Gods and spiders, son, once was quite enough for me. We were just *sleeping* in the same bed... well he was sleeping anyway. Have you any idea where Riglid is?"

"Not really." He walked around in front of her so that she had to look at him, and the look on his face said he knew she was thinking more than she was saying. But just as she wouldn't tell him what was really on her mind he wasn't about to ask her, which spoke more about the complexity of their relationship than words could ever tell. Then he said something that was perhaps the one thing he could have told her that could have lifted her even an inch from the hole she was digging for herself. "Kasiria and I have decided to move back to the compound. Kasiria is far too reckless and she needs more training than I can give her."

Tarius didn't say anything she just hugged him tightly and kissed his cheek.

"Your mother will be so happy."

Jabone smiled an all-knowing smile, and she kissed him again and then released him. She took his hand and started walking, sniffing the air as she did so. "Come help me find Riglid."

"Why do you need him?" Jabone asked.

"Rimmy and Hared are going to foster Yorik and Shadra's son. I need a new runner."

"Tarius is..."

"The fastest human I know but not Katabull. My runner is an extra nose, eyes and ears for me, and he must be able to take my words where they need to go. No human is as fast as a Katabull. Besides, the whole his name is the same as mine would just be confusing for everyone,"

"It already sort of is," Jabone said with a smile, gripping her hand tighter. "My fadra..."

"Should not be with us at all I know, but you cannot tell him. You must only tell him how magnificent he is and you hope that someday you shall be as good. When we get back to the castle before we regroup to attack Sedrik's keep I will tell him he can't go with us. He will be furious with me."

"Can you believe how father..."

"No I can't, and I don't. Between you and me I think it's an act. My good friend Gudgin died and I inherited Dustan, so Harris and I watched out for him, then your fadra did and he was surrounded by the Marching Night. This may very well be his first nasty wound, but I doubt it. Dustan has always been a very brave, even at times reckless, fighter with much skill. If you want to know what I really think, I think he is playing it up because he wants your fadra to quit fighting and knows the only way he might succeed is if he quits himself. I think he hung back now thinking your fadra would not leave him behind. I imagine no one was more surprised than Dustan when he realized Arvon had done just that."

"I certainly prefer that explanation to my father is a whining mama's baby," Jabone said, pulling a face.

"When will you move back?"

"As soon as possible. When we get done with this I guess we will have to sell our house in Montero. I really kind of feel bad about closing the school..."

"Jabone, you are a genius!"

"I am?" he asked in confusion.

"Yes you are, but we will talk about it later. Have you told your fadra yet that you are moving?"

"No."

"Well don't." Tarius released his hand, stopped and knocked on a door in front of them.

"You found Riglid."

"No, but I found Jestia." Tarius grinned up at her son.

"Jestia can find him much quicker than I can."

Tarius had left a troop of fifty solders at what had been Finias's palace to help put the place back in order for those who had fought against the cult. They would be staying indefinitely to make sure the cult couldn't overtake it again.

They had questioned the survivors at length, and Tarius was sure Sedrik's keep was every bit as corrupted as Rorik's had been. Right up to and including being full of fighters from their breeding program. She wanted time to rethink, regroup and rest, so she searched Eerin up before they had even reached the castle.

"You wizard," she said, riding up beside him. She smiled when she realized he was riding an ass—so not quite a horse—and it was still giving him trouble.

"Yes, Great Leader."

"I want you to send one storm after another on Sedrik's keep. Can you do that?"

He seemed to think about it for a minute. "I don't know that one wouldn't cancel out the other." He seemed to think some more. "I might be able to word a spell in such a way... I'm afraid my training has been lacking. Perhaps with Jestia's help."

Tarius smiled. "You don't sound too pleased about the prospect."

"I don't mind making storms for you. It's the least I can do but... Jestia doesn't like me. Her woman beat me up pretty badly, and if I make her mad..."

"You will be fine, wizard. Jestia's bark is far worse than her bite."

Eerin watched her ride away and muttered, "Apparently she missed the part where Jestia had her woman beat me up." It was all he could do to control the mule under him and... *I never wanted to be a battle wizard.* He looked at his cousin. She was beautiful in her black Marching Night armor and helm, her blue, green and yellow gambeson showing underneath it, her black cloak blowing in the breeze, a long sword strapped to her hip; she was more like a character from a story than anything real. She was as confident on horseback as she was walking. *Now that's a battle witch. She rarely utters her spells, and I believe she only moves her hands or arms for show. The power of the universe flows through her every fiber. She is magnificent and terrifying. I have no desire to do what she does to be so attached to the Katabull of Katabulls, Tarius the Black, who is even more terrifying than*

Jestia. I don't want to ride into battles with swords all around me barely being missed as I cast spells I don't really understand. And what the She Beast asked me to do just now—that is the sort of thing she asks of Jestia constantly. "I have this problem. Please pull the impossible right out of your arse." Except of course that nothing seems to be impossible for Jestia. She can fight as well as any human in the Marching Night and wield magic at the same time while I have trouble drinking while I'm walking.

As they dismounted at the castle and the grooms grabbed their horses Tarius began to get the odd feeling that she had just done this. Jena greeted her even as Jestia was complaining loudly in her ear.

"But he annoys me," Jestia said.

"Can you make a cloud become a storm?" Tarius asked.

"Given time…"

"You might learn something from him, Jestia. He will definately learn from you, and if you combine your power…"

"Alright, fine. Can I at least change and bathe first?" Jestia looked with meaning at Ufalla and Tarius chuckled.

"Oh at least that, Jestia."

Jena hugged her. Darian wanted her to take him so she shifted her gear and did so. She kissed the top of his head.

"So this feels strangely familiar," Jena said.

"I was just thinking that." Tarius lowered her voice as they started inside. "This isn't something I want to get used to."

"Nor I," Jena said. She put her arm around Tarius's waist then noticed something. She looked around quickly then asked in a panicked whisper, "Tarius, where is Rimmy?"

"He is fine."

Jena sighed with relief.

"He and Hared are closer to the middle of the group."

"But."

Tarius dipped her head towards where Riglid was getting his gear off his horse. "Riglid has taken his father's place."

"Why? What happened?"

"Rimmy and Hared have decided to foster a child orphaned in the battle. For this reason Rimmy cannot be my runner at this time. I will explain more later." She leaned down and whispered in Jena's ear. "I have had no sleep and this whole undertaking has saddened me in ways I cannot deal with on little food and no sleep. I feel like I have failed us all."

"You have failed no one. It is not your duty to know things that no one knew. No one was more diligent than you were to try to keep them out."

"But I know what they are and how they work. I didn't look at our own people because I didn't believe it could happen here. I didn't want to believe that Kartiks would be stupid or blind enough... but all people are the same. I know that."

"We will have you a warm bath made and I'll rub your back and get you something to eat. You will get some sleep and when you wake up we will not talk about how anything that happened is your fault. We will talk only about what we do next and when we can go home."

Tarius smiled at her then, a real smile, and said, "Some good news, our son and his mate are moving back to the compound, and before you ask... no, I did not order them to do so."

"That is great news. This horror is almost over and then we can all go home together."

"We will still have to deal with this thing, Jena. They are here. We will have to question every soldier, every beer serving wench..."

"You can talk about all of that with Hestia in the morning. You are all I care about right now Tarius... what this is doing to you. I am going to take care of you."

Tarius smiled at her. "You always make everything better Jena."

They really had no idea what the storms were doing, but with Jestia's help Eerin had set six on the keep. While helping him Jestia of course had learned in a matter of minutes everything it had taken him a lifetime to learn about seeding clouds. Then improved on his spells and then... Well then it was clear he was no longer of use to anyone.

And meanwhile what had he learned from her besides that he was no longer needed by anyone? Nothing. Not one blasted thing. He left her company and went back to work in the garden.

They had been back at the castle two days, but in spite of Jena's help Tarius was still unable to sleep and far from feeling like her old self again. She couldn't unsee what she had seen or get her mind to stop reliving the past. And there were things she had put off that she now had to deal with.

She was having the "conversation" she'd been dreading,

the one that no one else wanted to even be present for let alone have. They were alone in the room she and Jena were using at the palace and she was sitting on her throne which probably wasn't her brightest move all things considered, because it near screamed *I am ruler; do what I say.*

Arvon sat down in a chair across from her. He was walking with a crutch and since they normally couldn't beg him to use one, it spoke to how bad he was really hurting. He leaned the crutch against the wall beside him. "What do you want, Tarius, or am I wasting my time asking?"

"My brother, you said one more battle, just one, and then you insisted on coming to Finias's palace and now you can hardly walk and your pain shines through your eyes. There is no crime in growing old or in saying I can no longer live a fighter's life."

"That's easy for you to say, Tarius. Look at you, you gave half your life to Jena and yet you still look like you did on the day I met you. My body decays rapidly. It's not just because I'm aging like a human, and it's not just my old wound; it's the poison the infection sent through my whole body..."

"All is a small price to pay. You should have died and you didn't. We have a son and he has seen how amazing you are in battle and you have trained him. You have a mate who loves you so much he'd take a blade for you. He'd cry the whole time, but he would. If you don't stupidly throw your life away you will have many more years to enjoy the sun. I will no longer help you to put yourself in harm's way. I'll not stand by and watch as my son sees you die by a blow that never would have hit you even ten years ago."

"Don't try all your pretty talk on me, Tarius. I know how you use words to twist things."

Tarius stood up and thundered. "Do you think it pleases me to tell you these things? If the tables were turned, Arvon, if I were you and you were me, look me in the eye and tell me now what you would do were I near crippled and eating powder like candy. Look me in the eye and tell me that it wouldn't near kill you to have to tell me—or tell the truth and say you would let me die because you'd rather I died than have to tell me I can't fight anymore."

He looked her in the eye, started to speak and then looked away. "If I had the strength to utter the words I would not let you go into battle. I would send you home, and I am happy in this moment that I do not have to be the one to do what you must do. Any of the detestable things you must do." He fought his tears, looked at her again and nodded. "I will take Dustan and we will go home."

She walked over to him helped him to stand and they embraced. Then Tarius pushed away from him holding him by the shoulders.

"Actually, I don't want you to go home just yet. I want you to go to Montero. Jabone and Kasiria have started a fighting school there and while I drag them with me their students go untaught and they fear they are losing business. The springs will do you good and you and Dustan can keep our son's business going for him. They have a house you could stay in."

Arvon nodded. "Even now you find a way to keep from putting me in the pasture."

Tarius stood in the doorway and watched him walk away. Even with the crutch he was having trouble. He was physically and spiritually broken, and she felt like her head was about to crack.

"You have done the right thing," Jestia said at her shoulder.

"I know that. Let me tell you something, Jestia. Knowing you have done the right thing sometimes brings no comfort at all," Tarius said, not turning to look at her continuing to watch Arvon walk away. "Was there something you needed?" She turned to look at the witch.

"When I first started casting without being aware and was petrified, you said many things that calmed me, but I have suddenly realized that one of the things you told me is not true," Jestia said.

"Only one?" Tarius grinned at her fondly and started walking towards the war room. Jestia followed her.

"You said you never knew a witch or wizard to cast a wicked spell."

"I have not."

"My great grandfather made storms trash the whole of the island."

"I didn't know him though I did know his storms."

"You said, and I have read in books, and Jazel confirmed that casting evil spells makes the caster something less than human. Yet my great grandfather cast spells against his own kingdom and Eerin sent a storm for me and..."

"Eerin didn't know the wine was meant for me, and he didn't mean you evil he just wanted to confound you. Witches and wizards are not beyond mistakes. Often the best of us will do something that turns out to be evil without knowing it. Your great-grandfather seeded clouds with storms and sent them on his own people they say because he was unhappy and crazy."

"You don't think him leveling the island with typhoons was evil?" Jestia asked.

"I don't know why he did it, Jestia, nor will I, all these decades later, pretend to know. I was only a small child. My parents were still alive when the people rose up and killed him and your grandfather took the throne. This is what I do know... sometimes doing the right thing brings no comfort."

Jestia grabbed her arm and Tarius stopped and looked down at her. "I am afraid of what I might do without knowing."

"I am not afraid at all of anything you will ever do. Jestia, as long as the storms were on the island the Amalites didn't even try to attack us. It was only when the storms stopped raging that they fell on us. Your great grandfather... How do you know he didn't make the storms for good? Only because the people rose up and killed him because only the victor gets to write stories. Perhaps the only wrong thing he did was that he didn't know how to explain what he was doing or why he was doing it."

"I... I don't understand why you trust me so much when I don't fully trust myself."

"Don't you? We are two parts of the same story, Jestia. I don't fully understand why but I know you like I know my own hand. My own hand would never turn against me nor would it willingly do evil. Your magic is not some strange thing; it is part of you as my sword is part of me. My sword does not work without me and your magic doesn't work without you. You said the magic doesn't belong to you, but it works through you—not the other way round."

Jestia nodded and removed her hand from Tarius's arm. Tarius started walking again and Jestia followed her.

"So what did you do this time that has you so worried?"

"Did you ever get in a position while coupling and wish you had another hand?" Jestia asked, pulling a face.

Tarius laughed out loud put an arm across Jestia's shoulders and pulled her against her tight. "Oh, Jestia, if the worst thing you do is diddle your lover with an extra hand I think the kingdom is safe."

"I suppose." Jestia finally cracked a grin. "And it wasn't like I grew another hand or anything it was more that I could hit the spot I wanted to hit without having to give up anything I was already doing. At first Ufalla found it a little off putting but... well she's Ufalla and unless something has blown up right beside us she will get off."

"Seriously," Jabone asked, "Another hand?"

"Well it wasn't really but it felt like it," Ufalla said, grinning like an idiot.

"So she had to go talk to Madra..."

"Yes because it worries her when she casts something without trying. But I have to tell you... great tea and better sex... I'm not hating it," Ufalla said.

After breakfast he'd gone to check on his horse in the stables and was only some surprised to find Ufalla there doing the same thing. They'd wound up leaning against the gate on his horse's stall talking.

"My madra went to talk to my fadra to tell him he can't go into battle with us anymore. She told me I shouldn't tell him but... I never could have. No I would just go to Madra and tell her to do it."

"What's wrong?"

"I'm afraid I must say that I am like everyone else. I want to be as great and as celebrated as she is but I don't want to do even the smallest of the unpleasant things she has to do. I don't want to make decisions in seconds from the back of my horse that affect people's lives forever. I don't want to fill my head with things like what you saw in those tunnels under the keep. I have envied her fame without realizing all that it has and still costs her." He turned around to look at his horse, not able to look at Ufalla as he continued. "You remember what Jestia told me on the road that day, and she was right. I resent Madra because I know I will never outshine her.

"She ran to me that day, grabbed me and held me and it was familiar but then she started to sob and the look on her face was no one I knew. Then I could feel her ripped apart on the inside. In that moment I knew her better than I ever did before and she was just my madra. Then in the wink of an eye the warlord was back. She pulled it together and got the job done. But when I look at her now I can still see the edges of that pain; it has dulled but it isn't gone. I didn't know how to help her then and don't know how to make it better now."

"No one could have helped her then," Ufalla said, turning around to lean with her elbows resting on the gate. She turned her head to look at him. "You comforted her in a moment when no one else could have come close."

"That's not true. She calmed down as soon as she saw Jestia. This is going to make me sound terrible; I've had to work at not being jealous of the baby, but I think I'm more jealous of Jestia because I know my madra would listen to her before she did to my own mother."

"Between you and me, Tarius and Jestia's relationship sometimes makes me uncomfortable, but then I remember that Jestia loves me and that no one has ever loved anyone the way Tarius loves Jena."

"My madra gave half her life to my mother." Jabone frowned. "I don't know how to feel about that. I love Kasiria but I don't think I could do that."

Ufalla was silent.

"What?"

"Can you keep a secret?"

Jabone nodded.

"Jestia did the same thing to me that your madra did to your mother, exactly the same thing because she did it without asking me. I have half Jestia's life."

"How can you be sure? I mean Mother got young again, but you look the same."

"I knew the minute your mother said what Jestia and Tarius had done to her because I know Jestia and... Well, during that storm at sea I had hold of her and for the first time I could feel her magic going through me. Ever since then I feel her magic every time she uses it. I feel it because I have half her life. I just know it."

"Have you confronted her?"

"Why? What would that do? I'm sure she'd be as clueless as Tarius is about Jena as to why I would be pissed off, and knowing Jestia... Well she'd likely as not find a way to be mad at me about what she alone did. There is nothing I can do about it because the spell can't be undone. She did it because she loves me. What good is being mad about it going to do? Neither Jena nor I have anything to fear; you don't give half your life to someone you don't have a huge love for. Jestia and Tarius are connected in a way that I think only they are, and that even they don't fully understand."

"I wish there was some way to see what the storms are doing to Sedrik's keep," Tarius said, thinking she had sent Jazel home too quickly because Jazel would have been able to see. But Tarius couldn't afford to leave the belly of her people open not when the cult was in the Kartik. She needed Jazel in Montero, close enough she could be in the compound in only a few hours if there should be an attack on the Katabull Nation.

"Scrying isn't some easy trick. It may seem like it but it isn't, mess it up and they can see you as easily as you can see them. It takes time to learn to do it correctly," Jestia explained.

"It is less than a day and a half's ride away. We could send scouts." Radkin suggested.

Tarius nodded and looked thoughtfully at the charts and building plans before her. She looked again at the purchase order. Sixteen Jethrik floor-mounted ballistae and four hundred missiles had been delivered to Sedrik's keep only a few months ago, which told her two things. First, they had been planning their revolt for a while, and second, they were armed against a Katabull attack. But why were they more prepared than Rorik had been? Certainly Rorik's keep was closer to the Katabull Nation. *Rorik's keep is too far inland and there is no road from any port to his keep that doesn't go right through the capital. For Rorik to have procured weapons like these would have drawn suspicion. But Sedrik's keep is a stone's throw from Port Charesh, and since it's so close to the coast anyone noticing he was installing such massive weapons would have thought he was just fortifying against attacks from pirates.*

To work properly the ballistae would have to be mounted on top of the battlements. The ballistae were metal and wood in construction. If the storm was bad enough to tear tarps some if not all of them could be damaged just by rain which would cause the wood to swell and make them near useless. If the wind or lighting was really severe they might have totally destroyed them.

"We will send scouts and do a thorough recon. When they return we will have a better idea..."

"Couldn't she," Kasiria said pointing at Jestia, "just pop over there and see what's going on?" Everyone was glaring at Kasiria. She looked sort of confused then realizing what she had done, cringed. "I didn't mean to interrupt, but Hellibolt could do it."

Jestia clicked her tongue. "Don't worry, Kasiria, everyone will forgive your horrid, out-country royal manners because you're pretty."

Tarius shook her head. She wasn't sure Kasiria meant to goad Jestia at all, but Jestia certainly knew right where to poke Kasiria. "Can you do it, Jestia?"

"No. To astral project I'd have to know how to scry first. Frankly I blame Mother. If I had been able to study with Jazel all these months instead of casting one fishing spell after another I have no doubt I could just pop around wherever I wanted," Jestia said.

"We will send scouts then," Hestia said, mostly ignoring Jestia's little dig and obviously bored to tears by the whole the-country-has-been-overrun-by-the-cult thing. From the looks she kept giving Radkin, Hestia had but one thing on her mind and couldn't care less about planning a battle. She proved it with the next words that left her mouth, "Well there is really nothing we can do till the scouts get back. Why don't we take a break for today?"

"We could figure out the best entrances and exits through which to route an attack on the keep," Radkin said, smiling at the queen and getting the stink eye from her in return.

"There is apparently a village surrounding two thirds of the keep," Harris said, pointing with his finger to the marks on the map. "If we could get our people in here—if the storms haven't flooded them out—we might be able to find out a great deal about the keep and the people holed up there. At the very least we could find out if the villagers would stand with us or against us."

"Very good, Harris," Tarius said nodding.

"We could do it, Jabone and me," Kasiria volunteered.

Tarius laughed and shook her head. "How quickly these girls forget their Jethrik ways and start to order men around. My son is not even here to say yes or no, and him I would send to do such a task, but you I would not."

"Why not?" Kasiria asked sounding hurt.

"Because all you care about is killing things which isn't good for a scout or a spy, and your big blond head sticks out like a sore thumb," Jestia answered.

"My head's not big," Kasiria mumbled.

Tarius took a deep breath and let it out she couldn't lie; her head was no more in this than the queen's was even if her lack of focus was for completely different reasons. "I will assign scouts to check out the keep and spies to infiltrate the village surrounding it. Let's adjourn for today; we are all battle weary."

It was a lie. She wasn't battle weary; she was life weary.

Chapter Twenty-five

Jena had been mostly asleep on the Katabull throne with Darian sleeping beside her when Tarius came to get them to leave the war room. Jena hadn't slept much the night before and she couldn't blame the baby because he had started sleeping through the night while Tarius had been gone this last time.

No she couldn't sleep because Tarius was exhausted but she wasn't sleeping—or if she was she was having nightmares because she was tossing and turning all night, every night. And Tarius was still hardly eating.

Jena rose as Tarius approached. Tarius picked up the sleeping baby then turned to the two Katabull as they lifted her throne. "Take it to our room. I believe Jena and the baby and I will go out to the market." To Jena she said, "Maybe a walk outside will help me sleep."

"Or at least give you some appetite," Jena whispered. She smiled as Riglid fell in beside them. As they were about to walk out of the castle Laz came running up to join them. He was some out of breath, and Tarius nodded at him wordlessly.

As they walked down the steps Tarius turned to her. "I think I forget sometimes just how much I detest being inside always." She took a deep breath and let it out.

They hadn't gotten more than few feet from the castle when a beggar woman approached them. Before the woman could get close Riglid and Laz both stepped between them and the beggar. Tarius pushed the boys aside, threw some coins into the beggar's cup and walked on.

The baby was still asleep cradled in the crook of Tarius's left arm. Darian was no light weight anymore and there was no way a human could have held him like that for any length of time. Jena reached over and took Tarius's hand, and it was only then that she realized Tarius had become the Katabull. She looked up at Tarius, a little shocked. Tarius just shrugged and gave Jena no answer as to why she had changed form.

We are going to the market and Riglid and Laz are with us. We are all armed and she is the Katabull, yet I know she wouldn't have left the castle if she really thought this wasn't safe. Something is terribly wrong with her.

They went to the market for only a few minutes. Darian woke up and he wanted down but of course they couldn't put him down in the middle of the busy market. Tarius used it as an excuse to go back to the castle. Darian wasn't afraid at all of Tarius all catted out, after all this was the form Tarius had when she had saved him from the cave and when she'd carried him from Rorik's keep. In fact as they were walking back Darian started to pull at one of Tarius's protruding canine teeth, then he started playing with the hair on her cheek.

Jena realized with a sudden jolt, *He knows there is something wrong with her, and he is trying to comfort her.*

"Great Leader," Riglid said. He pointed towards the gate to the royal stables—the queen's cousin Joran had just arrived.

Tarius nodded then her mouth turned into a grin that actually made the hair stand on the back of Jena's neck, and Jena was not now and never had been afraid of Tarius.

"Riglid, have Joran taken to the queen's office. Do not give him time to bathe or eat and don't let any of his fellows go with him. I will get Hestia and meet you there."

Riglid took off in the direction of the gate and she and Laz followed Tarius through the queen's entrance into the castle. When the guards closed the door at their backs Tarius stared at each of them in turn. When they didn't flinch she nodded as if satisfied then handed Darian to Jena.

"Laz take Jena and Darian back to our room." She started to walk away without even saying goodbye to her which was beyond abnormal.

"Tarius," Jena called, running to catch up with her. Positioning Darian on her hip she took hold of the collar of her mate's shirt and pulled her big Katabull head down to her. "My love, you are not yourself and I don't mean because you wear this form. You need sleep, real sleep; you aren't thinking right."

Tarius growled a low, throaty growl—not an *I'm going to rip your head off* growl, more a *shut up woman* growl—which just confirmed what Jena already knew. There was something seriously wrong with her mate.

"You know I'm right. Don't do anything you will regret later." She kissed Tarius on the lips then released her. "I mean it"

Tarius nodded and then she took off.

Jena watched her go, and when she was well out of hearing range turned to Laz. "Help me find Jestia."

Laz smiled. "She's easy to find because she smells so good."

Joran didn't know what he had expected, but it wasn't this. Summoned to the queen's castle and now to her office and none other than Tarius the Black all catted out and looking huge and menacing was sitting on the corner of the queen's desk as the queen sat behind it.

The queen indicated he should sit and he did. There were two other members of the Marching Night in full armor in the room, and he was pretty sure they were Katabull as well. What did it mean? What was he to be accused of and was his fate to be the same as Rorik, Sedrik and Finias? News from the castle had been sketchy at best, but he knew those three and much of their retinue had been killed for treason.

"May I ask why I have been summoned?"

"Because you are a human and a royal, and that means you are suspect," Tarius hissed at him.

Hestia sighed, apparently not in any more hurry than he was to tell the beast that Hestia was also human and royal. "You petitioned to mine for gold in the territories."

"I did, but you denied my petition..."

"Did Rorik come to you? Did you know he planned to kill the queen and destroy my people?" Tarius demanded.

"I have heard only in the last few days that there was a plot against you and the queen. I did not know... You must believe me..."

"But I do not!" Tarius thundered and stood to her full height. "I do *not* believe that you didn't know. Are you a member of the cult?"

"The cult? What cult?"

"The Amalite cult."

"I would sooner die," Joran said, standing up himself. Tarius started to circle him, sniffing him, looking deep into his eyes.

"I fought *with* the queen and *for* the queen in the Great War. Many times I followed orders directly from your mouth."

Tarius stopped right in front of him and moved till they were almost nose to nose. He knew to show any sign of fear would likely as not mean death.

"Did Rorik ask you to make the petition?"

"He did not. I admit I wanted to mine for gold in the territories, but I would not be any part of a plot against Hestia, and certainly I would never follow the Amalite gods." He spat on the ground.

"He tells the truth, Tarius," Jestia said. He had not seen her come in; she had suddenly appeared at the Great Leader's shoulder. "Think about it, he fought in the Great War. Rorik would not have tried to recruit anyone so patriotic." Jestia pushed something into the Great Leader's palm. "Come with me and Riglid. Mother and Radkin can handle this."

There was a moment when it looked like Tarius was going to refuse, but then she stood to her full Katabull height and followed the girl out.

Hestia looked at him, then at the Katabull who had stayed. He knew her... Captain Radkin... great stories were told of her. He remembered her from the Great War.

"The Great Leader has been under a tremendous amount of strain lately. Rorik, Finias and Sedrik have brought the cult into our country."

"The cult... I don't understand," Joran said. He didn't either. "Why have I been summoned? Why am I being questioned?"

"Rorik was mining the territories. The gold of the territories is what he was using to buy converts to the religion here. Sedrik petitioned to mine for gold, and so did Finias. Since you were the only other person who petitioned to mine the territories, that makes you suspect."

"Well that and being human and royal," Radkin said with a broad smile.

"I swear on the lives of my children that I would never betray you, Hestia, and certainly I would never do anything that would further the cause of the Amalites." He spat on the floor again.

"I know that now, Joran. If Jestia thought for a minute you were lying she would have told Tarius and delighted in watching her rip your head from your shoulders. Surely you can see why I had to question you. My own brother wanted me dead."

Hestia told him all that had happened, and when she had finished he knew exactly why the Great Leader was all catted out and fit to be tied.

"Do you... Do you think there are more of them? I mean besides the ones in Sedrik's keep."

"I'm afraid I don't know."

"My queen." He bowed before her, and the Katabull turned her head in disgust. "Let me I pray of you show my loyalty to the crown and our country. Let me and my house infiltrate every royal house in the land, and if we find even a hint of the Amalite curse we will bring the curs to justice."

He sat back down in his seat. Hestia seemed to study him a good long time. "What is it you want in return?"

"Nothing just to serve. This cause is not just yours, but that of any person who cares for the Kartik and their freedom. Of course if you were to accept my petition to mine the territories I would consider it a great favor, but one does not and should not hinge on the other."

"I cannot tolerate nor will I allow the destruction of the land and the enslavement of the people."

"We would mine with a minimum of damage to the land. Shaft mining is only slightly more dangerous to workers than pit mining and does far less damage to the land. We would use no foul minerals to extract the ore and would repair damage we did to the land when we close the mine as we do here. We would pay our workers a wage and use mostly Kartiks—who I understand could use the work there."

Hestia looked at Radkin—he couldn't pretend to know why—and Radkin said, "You could send people to inspect his operation every few months to make sure he does what he says. The greater question is whether you can trust him to truly search for the members of the cult..."

"It would be a pleasure."

"I wasn't finished." Radkin smiled at him, and even in human form she looked wild. "Can we trust that you won't use this to hunt out old enemies and lie about their involvement in the cult just to be rid of them?"

"You cut me to the quick! Has my honor not taken enough of a beating this day? I swear to you that I would not do that."

"If you should," Hestia said coolly, "if I should have even an inkling that you have lied about anyone, I would have you publicly executed."

He looked at her in shock and she answered the look. "This is to be a true cleansing. I don't want a single person who prays to Amalite gods left alive, but I don't want more bloodshed than there has to be and certainly I am not as trusting as I was before my friend and her child were kidnapped from my house and my brother plotted to kill me. As much as I would like to argue with my Katabull friend, there is some truth in what she says; the fact that you are human and royal makes you suspect."

Tarius looked at the vial of blood Jestia had handed her and then at Riglid. Riglid looked away, but Jestia held her gaze. "Tarius, you are not yourself. That being the case, you should not be the Katabull. Please drink it and change."

It was the second time in only a few weeks that someone was telling her to change back to human form. What none of them knew was that she hadn't changed on purpose this time, either. She hadn't had this happen to her since she was a youth.

The beggar had approached, Laz and Riglid had reacted, and something inside her had been so scared that she had just changed.

"Drink it Tarius, please."

Tarius growled at Jestia and was only a little surprised when Ufalla—who had been waiting in the hall—jumped in her face and growled right back. The ridiculous aspect of it made her remember herself a bit more, and she drank the blood. It was old and cold and left a bad copper taste in her mouth, and the part of her that didn't want to shift back fought for control a minute before she was able to force herself to be human again. She guessed the fact she didn't want to be human said more about how right Jestia was than anything else.

"Come on, let's get you to your room. Jena is worried sick," Jestia said.

Tarius had no problem believing it. Jena would have to be worried if she'd hunt Jestia up. She followed them. "Riglid."

"Yes, Great Leader."

"Go watch over the queen."

"Aye." He took off.

Jestia walked up beside her. "No one can go this long without sleep, Tarius, not even the Katabull. I'm going to give you some tea, you're going to drink it, and then you're going to sleep"

"No one understands," Tarius said. "I see it when I'm awake, but when I'm asleep I feel it as well."

"What Tarius?"

"Bodies. Bodies on top of me, under me, all around me, the dead pressing down on me, and I can't cry out for help because my throat has been cut." Tarius stopped walking.

"I told you they were all dead," Jestia said, a catch in her throat, "but I knew why you had to check even though you—

of all the people on the planet—you should have been the last one to stay in the ground with the dead." She took Tarius's hand and held it. "Come on." She started gently pulling her along beside her.

Jena was waiting for her in their room. She helped her get her clothes off and put her in bed as Jestia brewed some concoction that smelled like cat piss. Laz was keeping Darian busy and Ufalla was guarding the door, so they could all pretend like it hadn't touched them at all—but they were all full of crap. They were all as worried as Jena was.

Tarius didn't want to drink the crap, she didn't want to sleep that soundly, but she knew Jena and Jestia were right. She needed to sleep, and she knew she wasn't going to be able to go to sleep without help. Jena told her to lie on her belly, she did and Jena rubbed her back.

They were all trying to help, yet they were driving her crazy. She was reliving things they could never really understand. She had failed Jena and Darian and the country and her people. How was making her comfortable and rubbing her back going to make her forget that good people had died because she had laid napping while the cult grew? Make her forget that women and children and babies were buried under Rorik's keep with the very people who had tormented them in life. That they had slit the throats of their children the same way they had slit hers.

How was she ever supposed to sleep when everyone was suspect? She couldn't think straight because her mind wouldn't stop second guessing her. Nothing was sure. There was a battle to plan and all she wanted to do was go back to the compound with her family and friends and build another wall.

Jena coached and helped her to sit on the edge of the bed. When she had Jestia pressed the cup into her hand, and nothing looked or felt real.

"Drink this."

Tarius looked at the tea in the cup.

"It smells worse than it tastes just drink it."

And she did because *Jestia* she trusted.

She didn't know how long she slept, but when she woke she could hear the humming of The Everything. Odd she hadn't even been aware she hadn't been hearing it until she was hearing it again.

She felt someone sitting on the edge of the bed and

opened her eyes slowly. She expected to see Jena or maybe Jestia, but there sat Harris. She smiled stretched and yawned. "It's good to see you."

"My sister tells me she thinks you are trying to go mad," Harris said. "I'm sorry."

"For what?" Tarius asked.

"I wasn't here when they took Jena; that couldn't be helped. But I haven't taken the time to talk to you about anything. I know it must have near killed you, and then what you found in the earth under the keep, knowing what he meant for Jena and the baby. I don't want to think about it, so I didn't want to talk to you about it. It has dawned on me—well actually Jestia told me—that you don't want to think about it either, but you can't stop."

"I saw the dead in those cells in the ground—all those children with their throats cut—and I was five again in a stack of dead bodies. And that, Harris, is why I love Jena so much."

He gave her a look that said he thought she was as crazy as Jena was afraid she was.

"Until Jena that was always in my head. It was the first thing I saw every morning the last thing I saw every night. Then it invaded my dreams. That and all the other trauma in my life was always right there in the front of my mind. Something would happen—I could usually not remember exactly what—and I'd see it, I'd shift without trying, and when I came back into this body some poor animal would be ripped to shreds in my hands and I often had no idea where I'd been or what I'd done. Jena healed me. She filled my heart and mind and changed the images there. Until now." Tarius sat up. She wiped a tear quickly out of her eye. "What good am I if I can't protect her, and how can I protect her in a world full of humans?"

"My dear friend, Jena is human, I am human, my wife, my children, the queen, Jestia…"

"Jestia is not a human; she is a witch," Tarius said. "I trust you, but… I really thought humans were no different from us. Only now I realize I don't understand how human minds work at all. Why would a man kill his own sister for gold and power only to give it over to priests to serve gods that don't exist? Why would a Kartik man turn to a religion that forces conversion or death where the people toil and work to amass great wealth for worthless priests who spit nothing but lies and make promises they cannot keep? Why would any Kartik woman stand for—much less join—a religion that subjugates women? They want to kill my people, Harris, and this is the Kartik where my people have always been celebrated. They want to kill all the Katabull, the witches and the wizards, every person who is different from them, every contrary person, every person who paints or sculpts or tells a story. They want to build a world without magic, without love, without beauty because then they can easily control the people. That is hard enough to understand, but why do the people follow?

"Greed? Is it all about the gold? We found barrels of it in Rorik's keep and now they fill the kingdom vault—towards what end? What's worse, blindly following some stupid priest because you really believe in his gods or following because he has told you he will make you rich? What good are riches if there is no magic, no beauty and no love? I don't understand. Tell me, can we trust any humans, or are we alone in the world?"

Harris took in a breath and let it out then looked deep into her eyes. "Humans are stupid, short-lived creatures. We barely get things figured out when our bodies start to die, but most of us you can trust. You have never really trusted royals, and as has been proven over and over you are right not to do so. But the privileged are not like the common folk, Tarius. These priests promised the royals the subjugation—not of them—but of all those they saw as beneath them. Amalite priests give power to get power; they always have. You are seeing combatants behind every tree and in every kiosk in the market, yet those are just people. This is different for you—killing people who look like you— but this is what I did in all the other wars in which we have fought, and in the cave, and in countless other battles. Till now I have *always* been killing people who looked just like me."

"They took Jena. I let them take Jena."

"You didn't *let* them do anything. They had a good plan and they had magic help. They took her and the boy, and you were far more traumatized than she ever was," Harris said.

Tarius cut him a look.

"That's right, they weren't nearly as destroyed as you were, and do you know why?"

Tarius shook her head.

"Because they knew *you* were going to come save them. Because *you* trained Jena to take care of herself, and because *you* trained Radkin to track. You *did* protect her, Tarius. You protected them by giving them the tools to protect themselves. And then *you* saved them. The worst didn't happen—except for you—because you just keep playing in your head what *might* have happened over and over again.

"You are Tarius the Black. You have never had a crown, yet the weight of it has always pushed your brow low because you are asked to do more than anyone should have to do. This was too much for you, Tarius, yet no one will just let you stop and breathe and deal with what almost happened to you. No, you have to deal with this horror, this horror which you know so much more personally than the rest of us do. When we heard those people back at Finias's palace tell their story, how one of their own people screamed, do you know what I remembered?"

Tarius shook her head, drew her knees up and hugged them to her.

"That day you told the line to attack the Amalites at their back as they were running away and the men wouldn't do it. You explained to us all that day the error of our ways. Many of us died and we almost lost the war because we didn't listen. And we didn't listen because we didn't yet understand what you have always known—that when these things come to power they kill all the magic, all the love, and all the beauty in the land. That they start breeding programs and spit out kids and kill the ones they don't want and eat them. For every one of them that is happy hundreds must suffer. We have stopped them before, and we will stop them again."

"But it was supposed to be over and certainly it was never supposed to be here."

"Yes, and I'm sure that is all your fault because you haven't been working to make sure they couldn't come here and you have made no fortifications to protect the compound or the country and... The whole world is not your responsibility alone to bear, my friend."

Tarius nodded. "How's Jena?"

"How are you? You should know that Jena is only ever as good as you are. Jena needs to make you better." Harris laughed. "She needs to be the one to pull you out of your dark place and into the sun. She doesn't like having to get Jestia—or me for that matter—because she has run out of ideas. We are in the royal palace. Look around you; we are encased completely in luxury. Why don't you let Elise and I take your little one for a couple of hours and let Jena try to make your pain go away?"

"But... that's part of the problem, Harris," Tarius said in a whisper. "When I don't see her I'm afraid and when I do see her then I feel ashamed."

"Well don't do that," Harris said.

"What?"

"Don't do that. Don't worry when you don't see her, and don't feel ashamed when you do. Just don't do it; it doesn't serve either of you."

Jena didn't really know what to expect when she walked in. Tarius was sitting on the Katabull throne wearing a blue robe. Her elbow was resting on the chair's massive arm and her chin was resting in her palm. When she saw Jena she smiled, and Jena felt a little calmer. She closed the door behind her.

"Are you alright?" Tarius asked, moving her hand and sitting up straight.

"Yes... no. No I'm not. I can handle anything, anything at all except the thought that I might lose any part of you. I'm worried about you." She was trying not to cry, but she wasn't having very good luck. She wiped the tear off her cheek, walked over climbed up in Tarius's lap and wrapped her arms around her neck. She rested her head on Tarius shoulder.

Tarius held her tightly and kissed the top of her head. "I'm sorry I just... I'm going to be alright; I just need to get some more rest. To... not see anything horrible for just a few days. To not have to think."

"Are you really going to be alright, Tarius?"

"I will be because I must." She kissed the top of Jena's head again then smelled her, and Jena felt her anxiety start to leave her. "Sometimes, Jena, I wish I was just any woman, not the Great Leader, not Tarius the Black, just a woman who had a beautiful Jethrik wife and two amazing sons. I wish that I fished all day and in the evening we would sit on our porch and look at the ocean, sew nets and not know what it feels like to be stacked with the dead, to not know that the cult has infiltrated the land, and to not remember the sound a man's head makes when it rolls off your blade and hits the ground."

"And I never want you to be anyone but who you are." Jena caught Tarius's eyes and held them. "All those things make you who you are. I do wish that sometimes everyone would just give you time to catch your breath; that they would take away some of your problems instead of adding to them. I'm just as bad as everyone else because I expect you always to be able to make the impossible possible. I knew something was wrong when you came back from Rorik's keep but I said and did nothing because I really thought you'd fix yourself because you always have and I don't know how." She started to cry and buried her face in Tarius's shoulder.

"Yes you do. You've always been the only one who knows how." Tarius held her tighter and started rocking her and then she started humming. It was a strange sound that Jena found infinitely calming.

"I'm supposed to be helping you," Jena said with a sniffle.

"You are." Tarius kept humming. It wasn't a tune just a sound.

"What are you doing?"

"It's the sound The Everything makes. I took it for granted that everyone hears it. It's the sound Darian makes, that I make to a lesser extent, and that you make but can't hear."

"It's very soothing," Jena said.

"Yes, I had forgotten how much." She moved her hand finding a fold in the wrap-around dress Jena wore and running her hand into it so that she could rub Jena's bare stomach. "I have been so afraid of losing you, Jena, that I forgot that I didn't."

"Oh Tarius... I'm sure someday I will figure out just what that means and it will be beautiful."

Chapter Twenty-six

Jestia watched with interest as her father stumbled in the queen's entrance of the castle. It was early morning, and Ufalla was still asleep. As Jestia woke she'd felt him coming and she'd dressed quickly and come to meet him. There was something not right about his coming and going. She got the impression he was purposely avoiding her and though they'd never been close, he'd never worked so hard at not being in the same space she was in.

I have always found him to be so innately boring and now I realize the only things of the least interest about him are that he loves whores and drink—both things I despise about him. He is who they chose for her and who the kingdom chose to father me. When I look at him now I realize that Mother was the best mother to us that she knew how to be; she knows better now, so she is trying to do better, but him...

She stood in the shadows and could smell the liquor on him even though he was still twenty feet away. He spoke briefly to the guards on the door then stumbled down the hallway. She fell in behind him; guilt came off him in a wave. It had nothing to do with his whoring but explained the increase in his drinking. Jestia silently followed. He was still half tipsy from a night of drunkenness and hard to read. She glided up to him and whispered in his ear.

"What is it you have done?"

Dirk jumped, spun around and almost fell. He looked at her and then looked quickly away, unable to hold her gaze.

Jestia demanded, "What is it you have done?"

"Will you put a spell on your own father girl?" Dirk hissed. "Make me talk?"

"Is that why you have avoided me?" Jestia asked. "Do you fear my magic?"

"I fear you?" he said, looking at her and then quickly looked away again. "I fear you alright! I fear what you have become."

Jestia heard his words and felt their sting, but she didn't let it stop her. "What have you done?"

"Is there not some spell that tells you?" Dirk spat back at her. "I am your father. Do you owe me not one ounce of respect?"

"That rather depends on what it is you have done," Jestia hissed back. "Were I showing you no respect I would have already put a truth spell on you. I would call Tarius to me and we would question you in front of Mother. This is the respect I am showing you. Now tell me, what have you done?"

"I stole from your mother to give crown jewels as trinkets to whores," he said as if the words were torn from him, but she'd cast no spell.

"That alone would not cause what I am seeing. What is it you have done?" she demanded.

"I killed your brother, alright? I killed my son." He started to cry and moved to lean against a wall. "It was an accident, Jestia. I swear to you on all that is holy I never meant to harm him. Katan caught me pilfering her jewels, and being Katan he ran as fast as he could to tell her. I tripped him. I just wanted to stop him getting to Hestia but... He was always so clumsy! He managed to tumble down the length of the hall and then right down the stairs. I killed my own son. I caused all of this. I brought all this on our heads." Dirk buried his face in his hands.

"You have a huge allowance. Why would you steal mother's jewels?"

He was silent.

"Why?" she demanded.

"Because she put me out of her bed and out of her life and it made me feel good to see her jewels on a whore's throat or her wrist." He looked at her then and said, "Do you have any idea what it means to be the queen's consort? I was always invisible in the kingdom's eyes and in hers. Do you know there was a time when I actually cared for her? But she never cared for me more than one would a pet. She liked me; that was as good as I ever got from her. She would occasionally couple with me, but she never even pretended to have passion for me. Then one day she just told me she could no longer bear my company in her bed. For years I would nearly parade my women in front of her, but she just didn't care as long as I left her alone.

"The first time I stole from her it was an accident. There was a feast. She took off a diamond bracelet she was wearing and left it on the feast table. I picked it up intending to return it to her. But when I went to her room to give it to her she dismissed me like a common servant. Obviously she thought I wanted something from her and she just couldn't be bothered. Every time I took a piece of her jewelry and gave it to some woman that tart treated me better than your mother ever had."

"I find that I am sickened less by the fact that your larceny led to my brother's death than I am your total disregard for my mother's feelings. Katan's death was an accident, but you went out of your way to hurt Mother and why? Yours was a contract marriage that you willing agreed to for the privilege of being the consort which you now say you despise. You were given a life of privilege and in return what do you do? Openly disgrace her with your whoring, steal from her and ultimately kill her son all to feed your needs. So now what do you do? You drink because you feel the sting of guilt, and she grieves for Katan alone."

"I bought back all her jewels and returned them. I have not stolen from her again..."

"Only to cover your own ass. Do you expect I will forgive what you've done—all that you have done—because you returned a bunch of worthless rocks and gold to their rightful owner? Do you not think she would trade every jewel in even her crown to have my brother back? Your carelessness took something that can't be replaced and now I am heir to a throne that I do not want. And what do I do with what I know now? I believe you when you say it was an accident, and I believe you are sorry. I will not tell her what you have done any of the things you have done. I would never make what is already horrible for her even worse. I will keep what I know to myself because bringing your crimes into the light will not bring Katan back."

"Can you forgive me, Jestia?" Dirk asked.

"In time and for myself, but I never want to see you again. I want you to leave the castle and move far away from the capital immediately. You will go to Mother and tell her you know she loves another...

"Your mother has a lover?"

"That is not important in what you must do. Tell her you know she loves another and you wish to be released as her consort. She will deal fairly with you and you will still get a decent allowance and live out your days far better than you deserve."

"I don't suppose you will give me a choice."

"If you don't do as I have told you I will tell Tarius what you have done—all that you have done—and let her decide if you own any part of Jena's kidnapping or not," Jestia said with meaning. "That is your choice." Without another word

278 The Burden of the Crown

she turned on her heel and started back for her room. *Tarius is right. Knowing I have done the right thing isn't bringing me any comfort at all.*

The guards moved aside to allow her access into the queen's quarters, and she walked through the door closing it quickly behind her because it was obvious that her mother didn't understand that her room wasn't sound proof. *I wish the bastard would come to talk to her right now and catch her with Radkin. Of course she never wanted him because she's queer. Where do I put what I know about my father?*

She walked into her room glad to see Ufalla was still asleep. She was hardly in the mood for the daily "Where were you what were you doing?" lecture. She took off her clothes and slid under the covers. She wrapped herself around Ufalla's back and Ufalla stiffened. She didn't have to wonder why— Ufalla was warm and she was cold. As Ufalla relaxed into her, Jestia held her tight and in spite of herself started to cry. Ufalla woke up and spun around. She looked at her in the dim light coming in the curtains and took a thumb and rubbed away her tears.

"What's wrong?" Ufalla asked. So Jestia told her everything, and Ufalla held her and told her it would be alright. She believed Ufalla, and that was comforting.

Hestia looked at him over the stack of papers and scrolls Tarius had her going through. Most were purchase orders. Tarius wanted to know everything that had been delivered to the keep not just weapons but food, clothes anything that might be an asset to their enemy. Radkin stood at her shoulder, and it was sort of cute the way the Katabull was snarling at him.

"What do you want, Dirk? I'm rather busy," Hestia said, indicating the paper everywhere.

"Hestia, I know you love another..."

He now had her full attention. Her head popped up to look at him in spite of her best efforts.

"You and I have never really been a couple in any more than the most rudimentary way."

"What are you getting at, Dirk?"

"I wish to be released from our marriage contract."

Hestia looked at him then she looked over her shoulder at Radkin. Silently Hestia took a piece of paper from a drawer in her desk, inked a quill and started writing. "I think you'll find the settlement more than fair."

"And it's that easy for you, Hestia," Dirk said. "We had two children together. We fought side by side in the Great War and..."

"We have been done with each other a long time, Dirk. Why pretend at feelings we do not have?" Hestia signed the paper and handed it to him. He looked at it and nodded and she handed him the quill for his signature and said, "I divorce you, I divorce you, I divorce you."

He looked at the paper and the quill in his hand then back at her. He was obviously mad. "That simple, Hestia?"

"You came to me; it was your desire to dissolve our contract. That I share your desire to dissolve our farce of a marriage should make it all the more sweet a victory. I am queen. I said I divorce you three times in front of a witness. I don't need your signature; it's just a formality," Hestia said.

He signed the paper and handed it back. "I will pack my things and be gone at first light."

He obviously wanted her to show some emotion but since the one she was feeling included singing and dancing she doubted he would find that appropriate. It happened so quickly and yet she felt as if a twenty-five year curse had been lifted from her. Her country was falling to pieces, her marriage had just abruptly ended, she felt like singing, and he wanted her to do... what?

He wants me to deny that I love another and fall to my knees and beg him not to go so that he can be the one to make me feel bad. Well that isn't going to happen.

He stopped at the door, turned and yelled, "Ice woman, do you feel nothing at my going?"

Before she could stop herself she smiled and said, "Happy. I feel very happy."

He opened the door and walked through, slamming it behind him.

"Radkin, could you please make sure he leaves and tell the guards outside my quarters that Dirk is no longer allowed entry?"

Radkin left and Hestia looked at the paper in front of her and started to laugh. She felt absolutely giddy.

Radkin walked back in, closed the door, looked at her and smiled. "So, I wonder if it will be as good now that neither of us is cheating."

Hestia stood up and untied her dress looking at Radkin and licking her lips. "No time like the present to find out."

Radkin took off her sword and propped it against the door.

"None at all."

"Gods and spiders," Jestia said as she and Ufalla walked out of her room. "They are at it again," she said, cocking a thumb at the office door from which the noise was coming.

Ufalla was just grinning.

"What?"

"Well I guess now we know where you get it from."

Jestia grinned. "And you know I was just thinking I was nothing like either of my parents. The scouts and spies should be returning midday tomorrow. I just hope Tarius is over her funk and Mother lets some of the blood return to her brain before they get here. I am ready for this thing to be over so that we can finally go home to our spring in Montero and I can study with Jazel properly."

They walked into the hall and the guards closed the door behind them. Ufalla bent down and with her lips nearly touching Jestia's ear whispered, "What about you my love are you over your funk?"

"I will be."

"It's a lot to eat, Jestia."

"Aye, but you always help me clear my plate. I admit it's yet more things I know that I wish I didn't, but it's a small price to pay. The Secret of Everything lies balanced on my tongue. If that's not enough, I have you; so the things I know and wish I didn't—they bring balance. Without them I wouldn't understand that there are consequences to all actions, and that would be a very dangerous thing for someone as powerful as I am who still knows so little."

One of the spies they had sent out was talking. "They are sogged under and their spirits are as damp as the weather, but the worst of the storms are right over the keep. The villagers are under Duke Sedrik's rule, but they clearly despise him. They have no idea what goes on inside the keep. No one is allowed inside and few leave it and when they do they don't interact with the villagers. They get their supplies and then go back into the keep. Sedrik has been taking so much of their crops and livestock as taxes that they scarcely have enough left for themselves, and when we told them he had been killed they rejoiced. When we told them he was a traitor to the crown they were not surprised at all."

Tarius nodded and contemplated what she had heard. "If we could get the villagers to attack any who tried to leave the keep we could pull the storms off for a few days and stop us from being bogged down in the mud ourselves when we go to attack," she said. "Could you see the ballistae?"

"Barely, the rain is intense, but two of the four towers have been destroyed by lightning strikes. We think we counted what could be eight tarped ballistae, but we can't be sure."

Tarius was thoughtful. She walked around the table adding what she was being told to what she already knew.

"I wish there was some way to drive them out of the keep the way we drove them out of the hive. I'd rather fight them in the open land on all sides of the keep. I don't want to fight them inside," Tarius said thoughtfully. "Jestia, do you think that weaving spell of yours would work on those ballistae?"

"I don't see why not." Jestia was looking at her nails. It was pretended indifference; Tarius knew Jestia was listening to every word spoken. Hestia was a completely different story. She was standing way too close to Radkin if she really wanted to keep her affair a secret, and she was pretty sure Hestia was holding Radkin's hand under the table.

She liked it better when Hestia at least made a pretence of making some of the decisions. One of the Kartik generals, a woman, pointed to a spot on the map the scouts had just drawn. "What is this?"

"It is a huge stone ruin, some old fort from antiquity," one of the scouts said. "It's about two stones' throw from the back of the keep and directly across from the keep's back gates."

"A good place from which to launch archery attacks. A good place to fall back to if we must," Tarius said thoughtfully.

"That is what I thought as well. From there an arrow from a Katabull cross bow or ballista could safely and easily take out any archer on the battlements on the back of the keep," the scout said. "It would be out of range of everything but their ballistae and if they're out of the picture nothing they'd have could reach us."

"Is there any way to stop them killing their women and children?" Ufalla asked.

Tarius shook her head no. "I'm sure they have already done that. Days of storms and no word from their sire—the priests wouldn't have waited to kill them. I have a feeling they killed them in part as a sacrifice to appease their gods. It is their sin and lies on their heads not ours little sister."

Ufalla nodded.

"If there is nothing worth saving in the keep it makes our

task easier," Harris said.

Tarius caught Jena's eyes where she sat on her throne with their son. Tarius smiled at her just to let her know she was alright, and Jena smiled back.

"Queen Hestia, will you ride into battle with us?" one of the male Kartik generals asked.

Hestia looked startled because as Tarius already knew she wasn't really listening. "What?" she asked, letting go of and stepping away from Radkin quickly.

"Will you ride into battle with us?" he asked again.

Hestia looked at Tarius for answer.

"No she is not going." It was Jestia who announced it. "Her recent divorce leaves her distraught."

"Divorce?" one of the generals asked. Obviously he was not happy, which meant he was most likely related to Dirk. After all most high-ranking Kartik officers were in some way related to the royals. Which was why Tarius didn't really trust their judgment and why she made a mental note to keep an eye on that one.

Hestia took in a deep breath let it out then said, "I was waiting to formally announce it, but you might as well all know. Dirk and I have severed our marriage contract and he is no longer my consort. It was a mutual agreement between two people who no longer wish to live together on any level. I am not distraught and am fit for battle if Tarius thinks it's appropriate."

The general started to speak again but before he could Jestia insisted, "It is too dangerous. As long as I am heir apparent I don't want you to do anything more dangerous than knitting and even then only with very short needles. I was sure I had made myself clear on that point."

"Though annoying and more than a little disrespectful, Jestia is right. It was one thing when we went to try to save your noble kin against a small force. There is no one to save here, and it is too dangerous. Further until such time as we are sure we have at last and for truth killed every cult member in the Kartik you shall be kept under guard."

"Oh great," Jena said. "Radkin won't let us leave the rooms and she'll be checking down the poop shoot before we relieve ourselves..." She seemed to realize she was complaining in the middle of a war meeting. "Sorry."

Tarius just smiled at her then turned to look at Radkin. "Did you really check the poop shoot?"

"Yes," Radkin said, obviously not understanding why this

was either a cause for concern on Jena's part or amusement on Tarius's.

"Why?"

"Because it is an opening that goes up the height of the castle wall that is open to the outside," Radkin defended. At Tarius's shoulder Riglid laughed. Radkin cut him a look and he was silent.

Laz laughed out loud, not nearly as respectful as his brother. "Mother, who would wade through a pit of shit then climb up a chimney covered in crap?"

"I would to get the job done," Radkin said, as if being willing to wade through a trench of knee-deep crap and climb a shit-covered chimney to assassinate someone should be considered praiseworthy. Everyone including Hestia was laughing now. Radkin obviously was not amused.

Sudden Tarius actually heard what Laz had said. "A chimney covered in crap." Tarius repeated slowly, "A chimney covered in crap."

Everyone was silent.

Jestia looked at her and then together they said, "They are *chimneys*."

Tarius turned to Radkin. "You, my friend, are a genius."

"See?" Radkin said, feeling vindicated, though Tarius was sure Radkin didn't understand why.

"How many shit holes are in the keep?" Tarius started going through the pile of papers digging for the plans. "It is three stories. There are two on each story. That's six chimneys." She looked at Jestia. "We can smoke them out."

"Just like we did in the hive," Jestia said.

As they continued to strategize, Hestia became aware that she was being scrutinized by one of the generals. She didn't recognize him and couldn't remember his name, but the crest on his shoulder told her he was a member of Dirk's family. Most likely he was angry because the divorce disgraced his whole family and lowered their status. She could have cared less, but she would have had to work at it.

If she wasn't going to be allowed to go she didn't see why she needed to be there. She found a moment when Tarius was neither talking nor being spoken to and pulled her aside. "Is there any reason you need me here? I have a bit of a headache."

Tarius gave her an all-knowing smile. "And would you need my captain to help you with this headache?"

Hestia felt herself blush. "I really do have a headache, Tarius."

"Then Laz could go with you?"

"I'd rather have Radkin," Hestia said, lowering her voice still more.

"Radkin!" Tarius hollered in an authoritative voice. "The queen has a headache; please escort her back to her rooms."

Radkin nodded silently, joined her, and in minutes they were out of the room and walking down the hall.

"Do you really have a headache?" Radkin asked.

Hestia smiled at her. "Have one, going to get one, what's the real difference?" She was about to take Radkin's hand when a voice rang out.

"My queen!"

She turned and there was the general whose name she didn't know who kept glaring at her. He was running towards them which was his first mistake. Radkin drew steel and jumped between Hestia and the man. He stopped midstride and threw up his bare hands. Hestia noticed Riglid wasn't far behind him and knew this meant Tarius had the man followed. She saw Radkin nod at Riglid. He nodded back and went back towards the war room.

"I need to speak with you," the general continued.

"Then do so from there," Hestia said.

He looked at Radkin but spoke anyway. "My queen, I believe you give the Katabull too much power."

"Which Katabull?" Hestia asked, in the moment confused.

"Tarius the Black. Twice already we have attacked our own people on the word of the Katabull. And now we move to attack a third and..."

"First, a Katabull's word is enough. Second, I have seen with my own eyes that the royal family has been infiltrated by the cult of the Amalites. Third, I was there when my brother admitted to his plot to kill me."

"And Dirk is he also a part of the cult?"

"He is not."

"Then why have you divorced him?"

"He wished to be free and I released him. It is that simple and frankly none of your business."

"A divorce in the middle of all this, people will think..."

Hestia glared at him. "How dare you speak to me this way? I don't care what people will think of him or of you because you are related to him. He was no longer an asset to the crown, wanted out of our contract, and is not my problem anymore."

"You won't be happy till you give our country to the Katabull."

Hestia patted Radkin's shoulder and looking at the general said, "Go ahead and kill him. I know you want to."

"Draw your weapon," Radkin said, her voice dripping with venom.

The man pulled his sword and slung his blade... once. Radkin jumped up, landed on the blade of his sword and pulled it from his hand. Then in almost the same motion she spun, hitting him in the neck so hard it almost took his head off. Radkin jumped back from him out of the spray of blood. She ran her fingers down the flat of her blade clearing it, and then sheathed it as the body fell to the floor. She walked over leaned down and wiped the blood from her fingers onto the man's shirt then stood up.

Hestia looked at her and smiled lustfully. "You are magnificent. Now where were we?"

Radkin walked over reached out and took her hand.

Hestia gave her hand an affectionate squeeze. "Exactly right."

Having heard swords engage, two guards came running around the corner. Hestia was glad to see they were so diligent. She pointed at the corpse on the floor. "Please clean up this mess. This man insulted me and I had him killed. I can do that; I'm the queen. I think too many people have forgotten that."

Chapter Twenty-seven

"The Katabull Pete," Tarius said to Hestia and Hestia grimaced. Tarius was right; it didn't sound right. "Tell me that doesn't sound absurd. What were his parents thinking?"

"What did you say his given name was?" Hestia asked.

"Petrid," Tarius said.

"The Katabull Petrid," Hestia said and then making a face added, "that's worse."

"Exactly," Tarius said and picked at the food on the plate in front of her. Hestia couldn't remember the last time she'd seen Tarius really eat. It was troublesome because it meant she still wasn't back to her old self, and tomorrow Tarius would lead her people into battle against Sedrik's keep.

"I see no problem with either Petrid or Pete," Jena said, shrugging.

"Maybe for a human but not a Katabull," Rimmy said in a whisper.

"Even for a human Petrid's a horrible name; it sounds too much like Putrid," Jestia said.

"Why not just change his name?" Radkin suggested.

"We had talked about it, Radkin, but so much of his life has already and will already be changed," Hared said.

"Then one more thing won't matter," Tarius said as she looked at where the child was on the floor playing with her son. Hestia had noticed that the boy seemed to be delighted with the baby and vice versa. When Tarius spoke again it was in her very best *I am the Great Leader* voice. "I'm going to call the boy Tweed."

Beside her she heard Radkin take in a deep breath. Hestia watched as Rimmy and Radkin looked at each other and nodded. Then Rimmy looked at Hared. Hared smiled and nodded his head as well.

Hestia looked briefly at the boy. *Have I done the right thing? They will change even his name—not that I can blame them—his life will be so different. He is Yorik's son, but he is first and foremost the Katabull and only the Katabull know how to raise him to his full potential.* Hestia looked over at Jestia and saw her watching the boy and Jena and Tarius's son, and the look on her face said she was seeing things the rest of them could not. *My poor child; her power is both a blessing and a curse. And she would know exactly what I should do regarding the boy and his future.*

She stood up. "Jestia, could I talk to you alone a moment?"

Jestia had been more than a little startled but followed her mother into her office. She had no idea what her mother wanted, but she hoped she wasn't going to ask her if she had anything to do with her father's decision to divorce. Jestia was a good liar, but she didn't know if she could cover up her disgust where her father was concerned. "What?"

"Sit down for a minute please."

"My dinner is getting cold."

"I'm sure you can fix that when we return," Hestia said with a smile, and Jestia relaxed. "It occurs to me that you know exactly what my duties should be concerning Yorik's son."

"You were right to send him with the Katabull. Rimmy and Hared will treat him no different than they would their own. They have already fallen in love with him."

"But are we to have no part in him, Jestia? No responsibility to him?"

With a sudden jolt Jestia realized her mother was asking her council. Her mother the queen was asking her what she, Jestia, thought the queen should do. Better than that Jestia actually knew what to tell her.

"What do you suppose that was about?" Jena asked her looking at the closed office door.

Tarius shrugged. "I'm sure I don't know." She looked at her food. She knew she should eat. Down the table Arvon and Dustan had been mostly silent for the whole meal. In the morning as they rode towards the keep Arvon, Dustan, Rimmy, Hared, and the boy would ride out towards Montero. The next day Rimmy and Hared would take their new son and head for the compound.

Her son and Kasiria, Harris and Elise and young Tarius and his wife had all gone into the capital—they said because there was a special place they wanted to eat, but she knew it was mostly because they didn't want to have to face Arvon's brooding. His misery was tangible and the main reason she couldn't bring herself to really eat. Dustan wasn't much better, and it was obvious to anyone with a soul that they had been fighting.

Tarius gave up any pretense of eating got up and walked

over to sit on the floor where the children were playing. Darian crawled over to her and then pulled up on her knee to stand. She laughed and called out, "Look our baby is standing!"

Jena looked over at them and smiled. The boy walked over with a ball which Darian had been throwing away and that he'd been running and getting and bringing back to him. He now handed the ball to Tarius who took it and set it on the floor. She took the boy firmly in her right hand and sat him on the knee not occupied by her son. The baby laughed and slapped his new friend on the leg.

"Do you know who I am?" Tarius asked the boy.

"The Great Leader," he said. Tarius cut Rimmy a look, and he just grinned and shrugged.

"I am Tarius, and you are part of my pack the Marching Night. I would like to call you Tweed. Do you like that name?" He nodded. "Do you like stories?" He nodded again. She told him an old fable about a turtle who tricked a goat into eating mud. It had been Jabone's favorite when he was a boy. Half way through the story Darian stopped fidgeting and started listening as intently as the other child. Since he was magic she couldn't be sure whether he just liked hearing the sound of her voice or if he really understood what she was saying. What she was sure of was that Darian knew as well as she did that he was attached by blood to this orphaned boy.

By the time Jestia and the Queen returned Tarius had gotten out of the floor and come back to the table to eat. Except now she had a child on one side of her lap and an infant on the other, and she was feeding them more than she was feeding herself. Jena wondered if she was ever really going to eat again.

Tarius was losing weight, and Jena was worried about that and a whole list of other things—most to do with Tarius. Tarius seemed to be herself again but then little things like the not eating kept nagging at the corners of Jena's mind.

Jena couldn't even look at Arvon because his brooding about not fighting was pissing her off no end. Tarius was struggling, and all he could think of was himself. He knew he wasn't fit to fight; he shouldn't have forced Tarius to tell him he couldn't. He should have just bowed out gracefully. He needed to quit sucking powders down and actually work at taking care of himself. The truth was Arvon's obvious sulking probably wouldn't be making her so mad if she didn't have to pretend like it didn't bother her at all to be left behind.

"Tarius, give me at least one of those babies and you eat," Jena whispered in her ear. Tarius nodded and handed her Darian—or she tried to. He immediately made it really obvious that he didn't want to leave his new friend. Tarius moved the boy to her other leg so that Darian could still talk to him—and he was, too, not in words that could be understood, but he was talking. "See, Tarius, he's taken an instant shine to the boy. Maybe Darian has just gotten over being wary of strangers."

It was a nice thought that she didn't get to keep because Hestia then said, "The boy will be raised by Hared and Rimmy as their own, but he shall retain his title and inherit his father's lands when he comes of age. He will be accepted as both a royal and the Katabull to honor both his parents."

Jena looked at Darian then whispered in his ear. "So you like him so much because he is some distant cousin." Darian laughed and gave her a sloppy baby kiss. "That's right don't you forget it. You're my baby."

Tarius set Pete on the floor and he ran off to go play with the toys Jestia had brought from her room for both he and Darian to play with, and then of course Darian wanted down so Jena put him on the floor and he crawled away to go play with his new friend.

Tarius continued to pick at the food on her plate. Most of it she had fed to the children any way.

Jena grabbed a plate of sausages from the center of the table and put three on Tarius's plate. Tarius looked at her and Jena said, "Eat."

When they prepared to ride out for the keep at day break the next morning Hestia and Radkin showed up armored and with their gear in hand. Jena didn't know when they had talked Tarius into it or when she had changed her mind, but it was obvious Tarius had expected them. Jena was glad Radkin was going with Tarius, and not just because Laz by himself was so much more agreeable about where Jena could go and what she could do. Tarius was used to having Radkin with her. Radkin was someone Tarius trusted to run a troop or to go into the heart of a battle beside her. Radkin going eased Jena's mind some.

Jena wasn't really surprised that they wanted to go. Radkin was a fighter, and so was Hestia. She was more surprised the whole kingdom hadn't been awakened when

Jestia learned her mother was going. After all she had made it clear she didn't want her to go. But as Hestia and Radkin showed up Jestia did nothing more than look at Hestia, grumble something incoherent, and get on her horse.

Laz stood at her shoulder holding Darian. Jena looked from Tarius to Jabone and tried to find some suitable words. None came, so finally she just said, "Both of you please come back whole."

"Always Mother." Jabone embraced her and she held him. Then he released her walked over and got on his horse. He took the horse's reins from Kasiria's hands and then they rode off to meet the rest of the company.

Jena looked at Tarius, and if Jena had spoken at all her resolve not to cry would have evaporated.

"Our son rides off so you will not see his soft heart," Tarius said. Then she grabbed Jena and held her so tightly she felt her bones were on the verge of snapping. "I am fine," Tarius whispered, her lips touching Jena's ear in a way so familiar she almost immediately felt comforted. "I know you are worried about me, and I'm sorry I gave you cause to be, but I am fine now. I will be even better when this is done and we can go home. I love you."

"I love you," Jena managed to get out.

Tarius released her and pushed her away. She kissed Darian on the top of the head and smiled just for him. Then she walked over, got on her horse and took off, and all the others followed.

Jena watched them till they were out of sight. She wiped her tears away on the back of her hand and started into the castle. Laz followed and once they were in the guards closed and bolted the doors behind them and resumed their posts.

"I wonder why Jestia is suddenly alright with the queen going into battle," Jena said.

Laz looked to see if they were far enough away from the guards then he whispered, "Jestia knows my mother no longer has a death wish."

Jena gave him a curious look, and he answered with what he no doubt thought was obvious. "My mother would never let a blow touch Hestia as long as there was breath in her body."

Jena nodded knowing it was true.

"And you're wrong, Jena."

Jena turned to look at him in total confusion. "My brother will serve the Great Leader every bit as well if not better than my father has."

"Laz… How did you get so wise so young?"

"By not dying and living to fight another day."

They had ridden half the day when those who weren't used to it started to do a dance in their saddles. Tarius hadn't let her cast speed on their horses, comfort for the riders or anything else really. Tarius said she wanted Jestia to be at full power when they got to Sedrik's keep.

What Jestia didn't understand was why Tarius expected worse from Sedrik's people than she had from Rorik's. It was true that she'd had all of the Marching Night with her then—nearly three hundred Katabull—and now she only had fifty of the Marching Night and not all Katabull. She'd also had Jazel, too, and now she only had Jestia. But they had two hundred Kartik soldiers with them and had sent for a troop of three hundred to come in from the west and two hundred from the Port of Charesh which was south. It should be a simple in and out.

Jestia rode up next to Tarius. "Why are you worried?"

"Excuse me?"

"You don't want me to cast speed on the horses…"

"It wouldn't be good for us to arrive before the others."

"Yes but you said you wanted me to save my energy. What are you expecting?"

"In the purchase orders I saw where they had booked passage for two very well-known Jethrik mercenaries several months ago."

"So?" Jestia didn't understand. "Two Jethrik mercenaries couldn't stand toe to toe with even the greenest of Kartik soldiers."

"First, that isn't true. Second, they didn't bring them as fighters; I believe they brought them to train the children of the breeding program. The language barrier wouldn't have stopped them from teaching them to fight, but it would have kept the Jethrikians from knowing just who they were teaching and why."

Jestia hit herself in the forehead with her palm and didn't have to wonder why Tarius smiled at her; it was a Katabull thing that she'd learned from Ufalla, and Tarius was amused to see Jestia do it. "Of course."

"And Jestia, just like any person who grows up in any belief, these people will be wholly invested in their religion. Like the ones at the keep and the ones in the hive they will just continue to swarm till they realize they can't win. Then they will try to run away, and we can't let a single one get away, not one. The storms will have battered them. I'm pretty sure they have been out of real food for days, and the priests will have spent all these days getting them to butcher their women and children for the cause. Now that they have done that they *must* believe in their gods or the only excuse for the evil they have done is that they are weak-willed and stupid. Religion builds a strong wall against truth."

"Then... Why didn't you call for the rest of the Marching Night, and why on earth did you convince me that it was safe for mother to come?"

"I am Great Leader, Jestia. It is not a duty I take lightly. My first concern always has to be the welfare of my people. I think we will kill these people and the land will be cleansed, but I can't be sure. The Katabull compound has to be secure and the Marching Night will make it so. You and I are here and fifty of the Marching Night; that should be enough. Then we will also have seven hundred Kartik solders as well, and I have estimated that there are no more than five hundred soldiers in the keep going by the amount of food they normally eat. We should be able to put this dog down easily, but in battle I always like the deck stacked in my favor and... This is why I want you to save your energy. As for your mother, as long as Radkin has no death wish your mother is safe."

Jestia smiled and nodded knowing what she meant.

"There is something else though that is causing me concern."

"What is that?"

"Our strategy relies strongly on using the old ruins."

"Yes."

"Why would they leave them there? Why were the stones not pilfered to build the keep? Why would they leave something that could so easily be used by an attacker?"

"Oh that's easy," Jestia said

"It is filled with traps?" Tarius guessed.

"No it is filled with ghosts."

"I think I prefer traps."

Chapter Twenty-eight

It was the middle of the next day when they arrived, and a few days of sun still hadn't dried out the earth. The ground was still mushy even as the keep came into view. Every villager they passed cheered and held up weapons to show they stood with them. Tarius and her troop made their way to the ruins behind the keep. Jestia had assured her that the ghosts were no danger to them.

"They aren't disembodied spirits of the dead. They are just energy that has imprinted on this spot because it is a place where The Everything is strong," Jestia had explained. "Jazel once went there to gather energy from the well— whatever that means. She told me all about it, but of course I was only half listening. All I remember for sure is that the locals all think the place is haunted by the spirits of the people who used to live in the ancient city, but it's not really ghosts, just energy."

Of course the problem was convincing all her people that anything they might hear or see was first benign and second not real. But as they got closer she could hear the humming louder and she could feel the energy of the place, and when she looked at Jestia, the witch was encased in white light.

Jestia smiled at Tarius and said, "Yep it's an energy well, and no, I have no idea what if any effect it will have on the Katabull, but it won't be anything bad."

They gathered wood and started to make fires as her people took up positions in and around the stones. "These don't look like the ruins of any civilization," Tarius said to Jestia.

Jestia nodded. "You know I think Jazel said it isn't; that it was some sort of stone circle to mark where the well was." Tarius frowned at her and she grinned. "In the future I will pay attention. At the time I really didn't understand the importance... of well anything. I'm sorry."

"I can feel the power of this place flowing through, over and around me. I'd like to know more." Tarius smiled at the girl fondly. "I was young once and while I don't speak of it much I was not always the best student. When my father was training me my mind often wondered nearly as badly as my eye, which seemed to always be able to find some beautiful woman. I wish I had some idea what if any impact this 'energy well' was going to have on the battle."

"I can tell you this; there was never any need to worry about my power. If I had run dozens of spells all the way here and gone for weeks without sleep, I wouldn't have been able to tell it here."

Which was no doubt why the girl was glowing so brightly Tarius had to shield her eyes to see her clearly.

Their Kartik brothers and sisters from the west and south had joined them and fallen into their formations around the keep less than an hour behind them. It appeared that all was going according to schedule.

Tarius pulled the spy glass from her pocket, put it to her eye, and checked out the battlements. They were covered with archers, but only five of the ballistae were in firing condition. The rest along with the two towers on the front of the keep had been destroyed by what she could only guess were lightning strikes.

"Riglid, go to the Kartik generals and tell them to start two fires each on their sides of the keep. Stay out of range of the archers and the ballistae," Tarius said. Then she took his arm and stopped him. "On second thought I am getting ahead of myself." She looked around and not seeing her called out, "Jestia!"

The witch appeared in front of her, so while Jestia might not be able to astral project she could apparently move her whole body from one spot to another with little or no problem. Tarius realize that this was what she'd been doing for a while now, and not just something she could do in this place.

"Yes," Jestia said.

"Could you do your weaving spell on the bows and ballistae, please?"

"I could or I could just cover the top of the wall with ball lighting."

Tarius laughed at the gleam in the young witch's eyes. "Just the weaving spell will do."

Twigs, small trees and bushes started flying through the air towards the weapons in the hands of the men on the battlements and on the rear two towers.

Tarius suspected that Jestia casting her first spell awakened the place because that was when they saw their first "ghost." An old man made of yellow light seemed to dance right in front of her making a ghastly noise. Her stout, courageous fighters started to run away yelling and she shouted, "Stand your ground! It is not real; it can't hurt you!" To prove her point she walked through it then back to Riglid, whose eyes were as big as saucers.

"Now go."

He took off, happy to leave the spot.

Tarius looked up at the battlements and said to Jestia, "How convenient it is for the cult to gather in one place so we can kill them all so easily."

"And so close to a giant energy well," Jestia added with a rueful smile. "I'm going to finish armoring up."

Tarius nodded and Jestia walked away.

Tarius had ten Katabull archers hiding behind large stones in the "ruins." They were already catted out and had their cross bows cocked and ready to fire. Five would fire on her command and then they would reload as the other five fired.

"Archers, ready and on my word... fire!"

The archers atop the battlement, already running and screaming from what they thought was an attack of magic twigs, started to drop under the rain of Katabull cross bow fire. She saw a few of their combatants' arrows fall uselessly many feet away from even the closest Katabull bowmen. As the last of the archers upon the battlement on their side fell, Tarius called on the night as did all of the other Katabull. The change usually caused a surge of power to run through her, but this was different. When she looked at her hands they were glowing. The power of The Everything always ran through the Katabull, but this was greatly magnified.

She looked at her hands and said at the top of her lungs, "These things picked a bad place to build a keep."

Behind her the Katabull all let out battle roars. When she looked at the Marching Night, every Katabull was suddenly enveloped in blue light. The biggest problem was going to be holding her own people back till their plan could be put into action. When Riglid ran back to them, the minute he ran into the ring of power he started to glow. He looked startled but didn't stop running towards her.

"Shield wall, form up!" Tarius ordered. She took the metal-shanked spear Harris handed her from where he sat on horseback. "Hold the line and wait." She got into position.

Jestia walked up beside her in full armor, Ufalla on her heels. Tarius looked down the line to her right where Jabone and Kasiria would lead their troop's right flank. Her son and Kasiria, both still on horseback, were behind the shield wall and the spears. Jabone looked at her and nodded; he was ready. *Nameless One please watch over my son and all my loved ones this day, but mostly watch over Kasiria because if she is feeling what we are all feeling she will be even more reckless than ever.*

Tarius looked down her ranks to the left to where Radkin and Hestia would command her left flank. They were also in place.

She looked down at Jestia. "Are you ready?"

"I am."

Jestia put her hand over Tarius's on her spear shaft and said in Tarius's head without speaking, *Do you suppose we will ever know what this means?*

And it was only then that Tarius noticed that she glowed white like Jestia not blue like the rest of her people. Tarius shook her head no.

"Jestia, move the fires."

The fires they had built on this side of the castle nearly exploded as they hit the walls over the dung pits and dropped in, and Jestia was gone, no doubt moving to do the same thing on all sides of the keep.

Ufalla looked at Tarius in panic.

"Calm down, little sister. In this place Jestia is the very Sword of The Nameless One." She noticed something and smiled. "Ufalla, look at your hands." The girl was glowing as blue as any of the Katabull. The other humans weren't glowing just Ufalla. Ufalla's entire demeanor changed. "I told you, Ufalla, you have a Katabull soul."

Tarius didn't have time to wonder what nature of soul she had since she glowed the same color as the witch. In seconds Jestia was back and soon after smoke started to billow out of every window in the keep. Only moments later they were swarmed by walls of fighters, and as she expected these were better trained. but on this day nothing could touch the Katabull. They had drunk their fill from the well of energy; the Nameless One flowed through them, and the members of the cult dropped in twos and threes at the hands of the Marching Night. Tarius ran through the enemy, killing everything her sword touched.

In seconds nothing that had run from the fortress out the back gate was moving, and the Marching Night ran off to help their Kartik brothers and sisters on all sides of the keep. The Kartiks behind the Marching Night found themselves looking at clean swords as they ran after the Katabull war lord.

The villagers surely didn't get even a chance at revenge. In less than an hour the bodies of all four-hundred eighty-nine members of the cult—including three Amalite priests—littered the earth around Sedrik's keep. Tarius found her son and hugged him, and then Harris and Elise found her. Then she ran off to find Jestia and saw her with Ufalla, Hestia and Radkin. As she started towards them she realized that not only was Riglid keeping perfect step with her now, but he had through the whole battle. She stopped mid stride, turned and embraced him, kissing him on the cheek.

"You are as good at this as your father ever was."

He blushed a little at her praise.

"Go and greet your mother after our victory then quickly go and get all the officers for me. I wish the Marching Night to leave this place tonight." Riglid gave her a puzzled look. "Can you not feel that a little bit of this power is good but too much might not be?"

He nodded, and they walked over together. She hugged them all in turn and then was aware she hadn't seen Kasiria. She looked over at Jabone who was talking to young Tarius and his wife. He either already knew Kasiria was fine, or he'd gotten so used to her taking off on her own and being quite alright that he just didn't think to worry. Tarius was worried enough for the both of them, so she made her way around the battle field looking. Kasiria wouldn't be hard to find.

Tarius found her on the far side of the keep her sword still in her hand looking around the field of bodies. She looked to be uninjured yet the look on her face denied that. Tarius ran up to her. "Are you hurt, Kasiria?"

"No."

"Have you lost someone then?" Because this was what you did after a battle if you didn't see a friend standing, you went looking for them among the dead.

"No." Then seeming to temporarily forget what she was worried about said, "You know I don't think a single one of ours is dead or even badly injured."

"What's wrong then?"

"I've lost something." She was near tears as she held up her wrist.

Tarius knew what it was—it was the cuff Jena had made for her that she'd given to their son and that he had in turn given to his wife when they bound themselves to each other.

"Calm child." Tarius grabbed her firmly by the shoulder. "It is only a thing."

Kasiria nodded silently but kept looking, and Tarius helped her. Tarius found it on the ground in a pool of blood, chopped in two. She looked at it then called to Kasiria. "I found it a little worse for wear."

Kasiria walked over, took it from her hand and sobbed. "What does this mean? It must mean something. It is the symbol of his love for me and it is cut in two."

"It means it is a strong piece of leather that kept you from getting your hand chopped off. You don't by any chance think that in all the years Jena and I have been together and all the many battles I have fought that this string of glass beads she gave me has never popped and beads gone everywhere. Child, Jena has restrung this thing for me a dozen times and even had to replace beads that were lost more than once. Besides, Jestia can easily fix this."

"I hate to ask Jestia for anything."

"Then give it to me. I don't mind at all. Come on, I'm sure Jabone will be glad to see you, and I want all of the Marching Night to leave this place tonight." She started walking and Kasiria followed.

"Because the power is too good," Kasiria said.

"Precisely."

Tarius and Hestia met with the Kartik officers outside the main gates of the keep. No one was surprised when Jestia found a hidden entrance to underground rooms. What was a little surprising was that they had flooded from all the recent storms. There had been a moment when Jestia had been upset thinking the storms she'd helped make might have drowned the women and children. Tarius had assured her that wasn't the case, but the warlord didn't go into what the soldiers said they found in the kitchen because she didn't want to think about it.

The Kartik soldiers would stay behind to dispose of the dead. Then they would clean up and repair the keep to be used as a military post. They would also help the villagers rebuild from any storm damage they had suffered. Hestia would have food sent to the village in an effort to restore the villagers' faith that the crown cared for all of its people.

Yet more gold was packed into wagons to be taken back to the capital to fill the kingdom vaults. Hestia said she would use it in part to strengthen the kingdom's interior security. She planned to use her cousin Joran to help her develop a network of spies that would work to make sure the cult had truly been eradicated and hopefully keep them from ever again being able to get a foothold in the Kartik. Tarius wasn't sure the plan would do any good, but she was glad Hestia seemed to once again be interested in something besides Radkin's hand up her skirt.

As soon as Tarius and Hestia had lined out exactly what they wanted done at Sedrik's keep, Tarius gathered the Marching Night and with Hestia and the wagons full of gold they started back towards the castle.

Just before it got too dark to do so she had them stop and make camp. They had all stopped glowing, and most of the Katabull had gone back to their human form—herself included.

The cooks started to make dinner, and as the smell of cooking herbs started to fill the air they all went to the stream they had camped beside to clean themselves and their armor. Though the water was some cold, they were all in pretty high spirits.

Kasiria sat on a rock and didn't watch as they all bathed together. No sense telling Jabone she didn't like it when he was naked in the water with the likes of Ufalla and Jestia not to mention his own mother. Nudity was no problem for most Kartiks and certainly it was no problem at all for the Katabull. They didn't run around naked all the time, but in a case like this when they all wanted a bath and there was a creek they didn't let something like modesty get in the way. Even their queen was stripped down to near nothing and knee deep in the water laughing and splashing like the rest of them. Kasiria had washed the blood from her face and hands. When it was dark she'd sneak down to the water and bathe.

It was supposed to be the end of winter here—not that she could tell—and they were all saying how cold the water was, but she was pretty sure it really wasn't. Except for those of them that had been to the Jethrik or the Amalite, she doubted they'd ever seen anything even approaching snow. The truth was a Kartik winter was a whole lot like a Jethrik spring, so her excuse not to bathe with the rest of them because it was too cold most likely sounded like the bullcrap it was.

If Jena was here she'd understand. Of course Harris is as naked as the day he was born and he's of our country, so maybe someday I'll just wade right in with the rest of them. At least we have stopped glowing.

Jabone walked up to her a towel around his waist and shook his long hair at her covering her in Katabull rain. She smiled at him then looked at the fixed cuff on her wrist. It looked the same, but she knew it had been hacked in two.

Jabone sat down on the rock next to her. "Kasiria, don't worry about it. I'm glad you still have both your hands. It's just a thing, and Jestia fixed it so you can't even tell."

"Couldn't Jestia have just put my hand back on?" Kasiria said with a growl.

Jabone laughed. "You know she couldn't because she can't do healing spells."

Kasiria laughed, getting her sense of humor back. "I was just sitting here realizing that I'm still so different than the rest of the Katabull."

"No you're not, Kasiria. You don't want to get naked in front of the rest of us, but when we glowed blue today, so did you." Jabone looked into the distance but didn't explain what he meant, which was just as well because after he explained things to her she often didn't understand any better than she had before. Which rather proved that she was very different from the rest of the Katabull, after all they always seemed to know exactly what they meant.

Tarius found herself alone in the dark looking through the trees at the moons. She took in a deep breath and let it out. She looked at her hands; she had two new nicks, one on each hand, both small.

She could still feel the effects of the power she had drawn from the well. She had been glad when they all stopped glowing because it meant fewer of them were likely to notice that she wasn't glowing the same color as the other Katabull. She didn't understand what if anything it meant that she and the witch were the only ones that glowed white, but guessed considering that Ufalla glowed blue that it had more to do with what they had once been than what they now were.

She smiled at the moons. *For a while we could feel the power of All. We were one with each other, the earth, the water, the sky, a part of the moons. We were drawn to that place for a reason. I killed a great many people today, and yet I feel healed—as if so many open wounds are now closed.*

She felt her presence before her hand closed over her shoulder. "I feel better. Do you feel better?"

Tarius smiled and put her hand over Radkin's. "Yes, in part because you feel better."

"The power of that place was an odd sensation to be sure. Very like how you feel at the end of a really good climax."

Tarius laughed and patted her hand. "You know, you're exactly right."

"I want to stay with her, Tarius."

"I know." Tarius turned to face her. "More importantly she wants you to stay with her. I think she loves you."

"I must confess that I have a passion for her I have never felt before and care for her in a way I thought I could never care for anyone again. I won't say I love her, nor would I be bold enough to accuse her of loving me, but I need her as much as she needs me, and that is enough for now. Being with her sets me on a path I never would have taken, and I think the change is just what I need."

"And you're just what she needs." Tarius grinned wildly. "You will make so much better a consort than Dirk."

Radkin laughed. "That is what Jestia said, and then she called me Dad."

Chapter Twenty-nine

On the night of their return a great feast was prepared in honor of their victory over Sedrik's keep. Hestia smiled when she saw that Tarius was eating like a Katabull again.

She looked at where Radkin sat on the other side of her and her mirth left her. The Marching Night would be going home in only a few days, and she and Radkin had yet to talk about whether Radkin was going with them or not this time. Of course any time they were alone they didn't seem to do much talking. She put her hand on Radkin's knee under the table, and it was only then that she realized her hand was shaking.

Radkin looked at her. "What's wrong?"

Hestia looked down, unable to hold her gaze. "Are you going back to the Katabull compound with them?"

Radkin smiled and lifted Hestia's chin with her finger. "Didn't we have this conversation already?"

"Did we?"

"I was not talking about the short term when I said I would stay if you wanted me to. That is why I said you'd better be sure it was what you wanted. Are you ready for me to go?"

"No," she said quickly. "I *never* want you to go." She seemed to suddenly remember that she was in a feast hall full of people. She pulled away from Radkin's touch and looked down at the table. "I don't know if I have the right to ask you to give up everything you know to be with me in secret."

Radkin moved so that her lips were nearly touching Hestia's ear, and Hestia suddenly didn't give a damn if there were a room full of people watching or not. Radkin whispered, "The life I knew made me pray for death. I tried to die in battle not once, but twice. If I had, what good would I have been to the life I know?"

Hestia looked at Radkin and smiled. "What's that mean exactly?"

To her surprise Tarius leaned over getting nearly as close to her other ear and whispered, "It means because of you she no longer wants to kill herself, so being kept a secret is no big deal." Then Tarius went right back to eating.

"And besides there are things we hide and then there are things we just don't talk about with people who would rather not know," Radkin said.

Hestia smiled and nodded. She looked around the feast hall; they were all mostly busy eating, and they were mostly Marching Night anyway. In that moment she just didn't care. She leaned over and kissed Radkin's cheek.

"Oh yes, I can see now that it will be hard for anyone to see through this thick facade," Tarius mumbled and continued eating.

Jabone looked at where Hestia was kissing Radkin and then looked at Kasiria. "You know I think auntie Radkin may be banging the queen."

"No way," Kasiria said.

"Oh please, that's old news," Jestia said, looking around Ufalla at Jabone. "But don't let on. She thinks she's being discreet and that she can keep it a secret. I'm not sure whether she thinks the staff is all deaf or that they think the awful wailing and moaning that comes from her bedchambers will be blamed on a castle spirit or ghost. And I realize it's just us but she sat her right next to her during feast and half the time not Radkin's but Mother's hands are under the table."

"I think it's sweet," Ufalla said, putting her face right in Jestia's, "and I think you should quit teasing her about it."

"Like that's ever going to happen." Jestia chuckled and kissed Ufalla on the nose.

"The queen and Radkin, really?" Kasiria asked, no doubt thinking they were having her on because after all they often were.

"Yes really," Ufalla said, and it was pretty obvious that she was at the very least tipsy. "It's soon to be the worst-kept secret in the kingdom because after all Jestia knows it."

Rea picked that moment to walk by. She winked first at Jabone, then at Ufalla, and finally at young Tarius. Jestia jumped to her feet and glared daggers at the much bigger Katabull girl.

"Keep moving!"

Rea did because she might be a slut, but she wasn't stupid enough to do more than goad the witch.

"What was all that?" Eric asked.

"Just one of the many slutty trollops Ufalla slept with," Jestia said hotly.

"I have to say, Jestia, it warms me all over to see that you can be jealous of me," Ufalla said. Then she just got all handsy with Jestia because as Jabone had already noticed she was a little drunk and she had trouble keeping her hands off Jestia when she was sober.

"Ufalla you are drunk and I am not some common whore to be woman handled by you in front of the gods and everyone." Jestia pushed Ufalla off her with an effort.

Kasiria laughed no doubt because she thought it was funny, and when Jestia turned to confront her Jabone knew he was in for it. "I don't know what the hell you're laughing about, the slut bedded your husband as well."

Kasiria turned quickly and gave him a look that would crush glass.

"I didn't even know you then," Jabone defended.

"And I wasn't with you, Jestia, and I bet if we were to make a list of the people we slept with before we were together yours would be far longer than mine," Ufalla said.

"Are you calling me a slut?" Jestia said, slugging Ufalla in the shoulder hard.

Ufalla grinned and kissed Jestia on the lips. "So, are you finally mad at me?"

"I swear, Ufalla, you are completely twisted." Then Jestia was just grinning at Ufalla and she kissed her on the cheek so he guessed the answer to Ufalla's question was no.

"How many Jabone?" Kasiria demanded.

Jabone glared at Jestia because he and Kasiria had never had this talk before.

"A few not many," Jabone said.

"She's Jethrik; she thinks one is too many," Jestia taunted.

Eric laughed and Jestia looked at her, grinned and said, "And the slut slept with your mate, too."

Eric quit laughing and glared at Tarius.

He shrugged and said with a grin, "Well everyone else was doing it."

The drums started to play and a singer started singing even as Eric and Kasiria were just asking a whole list of questions that Tarius and Jabone couldn't answer without getting in even more trouble. Jestia grabbed Ufalla's hand and drug her onto the floor to dance with her.

Tarius looked from his sister and her mate—who obviously weren't fighting—to their red-faced, angry wives and then back at Jabone. "It's the curse of the Jethrik wives," he whispered.

"How many is a *few*, Jabone?" Kasiria demanded in an angry whisper.

"It doesn't matter, Kasiria, I only love you," he said. He watched as his madra took his mother's hand and led her to the floor to dance with her. "Do you think my mother ever thinks for a minute about the hundreds of women my madra had before her? She does not because she knows she is the only one that was ever in my madra's heart. I don't remember who much less how many because my whole heart belongs to only you." He took her hand and led her onto the dance floor.

Eric looked at him expectantly and Tarius drank the rest of his wine looked at her and said, "I'm tired and mostly drunk. Can't you pretend I said what Jabone said only prettier because I'm a much better bard than he will ever be?" Eric half smiled then punched him in the shoulder hard. He rubbed his arm. "Ouch."

Radkin stood up. She looked down at Hestia and offered her hand. Hestia looked from Radkin's offered hand to the dance floor and then back up at her. Hestia hesitated only a moment then she took a deep breath, took Radkin's hand, and let her help her to stand. Hestia followed Radkin to the dance floor. Her every nerve was on edge till they started to dance and then she just relaxed. She had never felt so comfortable dancing with anyone before yet she knew they were being watched and knew people would jump to all the right conclusions. In that moment she just didn't care what other people thought.

Jestia and Ufalla moved close to them, and Hestia dreaded what would come from her child's acid mouth. Jestia leaned in to her and whispered, "I have heard all the stories. Now I have seen you in battle, and you were amazing. But Mother, this is by far your bravest moment."

After resting at the castle for two days they had all packed and prepared to leave. The Marching Night would be going home. Ufalla and Jestia would be staying in Montero where they planned to run their spring and Jestia was going to continue her training with Jazel. Jabone and Kasiria would stay long enough to put their affairs in Montero in order and then they would join them at the compound.

They had all just said their good byes to Radkin and the queen and started moving their horses down the road when Eerin came riding out on his mule to meet them.

He rode around in front of Jestia and stopped, causing her and most of the company to rein their horses in hard.

"Princess, hear me please," he started.

Jestia sighed looked at Tarius and rolled her eyes. "What is it you want now?"

"I have a favor."

"We let you live. When is it ever going to be enough with you?" Jestia said, but she was smiling now.

"Jestia I want to train. I want to learn more so that I am not a danger to myself or others. You have a spring in Montero; you will need help to run it. I would work for you and you could take any wages I might earn and just keep them," Eerin pleaded. "You could train me."

"I couldn't possibly," Jestia said. "I need to study myself and I have a huge elaborate wedding to plan. I simply don't have the time to train a moron."

"But... You could give my wages to Jazel and she could train me."

"Ah come on, Jestia, take the boy with you. What he says is true; he is a danger to himself and others," Tarius said.

"He could make tea for our guests," Ufalla suggested.

"Oh alright, but I'm sure he will be more trouble than he's worth."

When they started to ride again Eerin pulled his mule up beside Jestia and she glared at him and said, "Already you are annoying me. Move to the back. You've not earned a place at the head of the Marching Night."

Eerin quietly moved to the back of the group.

Jestia looked over at Tarius. "If he gives us any trouble at all I'm sending him to live with you."

Tarius just nodded and adjusted Darian on the saddle. On the way there she had carried him in a sling which he was now too big for. Darian grabbed onto the saddle's pommel and hung on then he turned his head looked up and laughed at her. She smiled back. "You better look where we're going mister or you'll steer us into a tree."

Tarius rode up close to Jestia. "What about the big man?" She nodded her head towards the baby. "When the time comes will you train him, Jestia?"

Jestia looked at Darian and smiled. "Of course I will. By then I will be fully trained and will have already had the big, elaborate wedding, so I'll have no excuse not to."

"I have yet another favor to ask." Tarius lowered her voice. "I am hoping that Arvon and Dustan will stay in Montero. Arvon is a fine sword teacher, and I think teaching would give him a sense of purpose he isn't getting at home. I also think bathing frequently in the springs would help his condition. Since you have a spring..."

"I will of course tell him he is to use it as often as he likes. In fact, maybe I will trade him lessons for baths," Jestia said. Suddenly she sat up bolt straight in her saddle.

"What is it?" Tarius looked around, shifting the baby her other hand half way to her sword.

"I just realized... I am still heir apparent. With everything that was going on it completely slipped my mind. We never even discussed it. Well of course we didn't because mother was way too busy with her hands in Radkin's pants. Mother forgot to choose another heir. Ufalla, we will have to go back."

Ufalla sighed. "Jestia, I think you are the only one who forgot."

"What?" Jestia looked at Tarius.

"Do not turn your horse around, Jestia. Your mother will not choose another heir. You know and I know it is as much your fate to lead as it is mine. Your mother will live a good, long life, and by the time you take the throne you will have convinced the world that it was all you ever wanted."

End

About the Author

I started writing at twelve as an escape. The situations I have lived through are the stuff of which my fiction is born. My relationships with the many and varied people I have come into contact with over the years is a catalogue of characters from which I pull.

I am Jewish but consider myself spiritual not religious. I have studied every form of spirituality and try to live a spiritual life. I don't always succeed, but I do try.

My wife of nearly twenty-four years and I own a small farm where I raise milk goats, rabbits, chickens and a garden. I raise—depending on the weather and bugs—between forty and sixty percent of our food mostly organically. By "mostly" I mean if it looks like I will lose an animal I will do what I think is necessary. We make no trash; we use or recycle everything.

I lived for fourteen years of my life without electricity or running water. I had my only son naturally with no drugs. Though I was married off at sixteen (in an attempt to keep me from being gay) to a thirty-four-year-old man who immediately took me to New York and stuck me in a drug den for a month, I have smoked a total of five joints in my life. I have never done any other drugs.

My son was a prescription drug addict for nine years.

I have worked every shit job you can imagine from pulling car parts in a junk yard and cleaning rich people's houses to home health care. I ran an industrial plane and have logged timber using a team of mules. I have worked at saw mills, framed houses, and poured slabs. I am a carpenter and a rock mason. I can run (install) electricity, and I can plumb (I hate plumbing). I have also built more than one house using only hand tools and a chain saw. I like to hike and cave, and I love the ocean.

I fought heavy weapons (and trained other fighters) with the SCA (The Society for Creative Anachronism) for about twelve years. During that time I broke several bones (mosty mine), and I have a seven-inch plate and eight screws in my left arm as a result of a bastard sword blow. Elizabeth Moon talked me into fencing many years ago and I still do that, but I sold all my armor and heavy weapons last year. Erin Grey talked me into trying Tai Chi to help with my CFS, so I have now been doing a mixture of Tai Chi and Chi Gung every day for the last five years.

Mercedes Lackey helped me get my first short story sale in Marion Zimmer Bradley's magazine. That sale opened the door for other sales to MZB, one of which was included in a German-language anthology, and the royalties came in steadily for many years.

CJ Cherryh line edited the first two chapters of *Chains of Freedom* and taught me more about writing doing that than I had learned to that point.

I'm not just name-dropping here; I'm giving credit to people who helped me who certainly didn't have to. Over the years I've come to know many very famous people, and here's what I know for sure—we are ALL the same.

In the writing community the person who is the most famous and makes the most money is often the least talented or deserving—not always, but often. In our business who makes it and who doesn't is often determined by nothing in the world but dumb-ass luck. That being the case, the near worship we see of the "famous" is something I just don't get at all.

The truth is I always think bios are sort of a waste. Anyone who reads my work knows more about the real me than I could ever put in a bio. If you want to talk to me, find me on Facebook. If you see me somewhere, come right up and talk to me. I am just like you. Luckily, I have a job I love, and the reason I have this great job is that people like you let me.

Friend me on Facebook, or if you prefer you can contact me through my personal website www.selinarosen.com, or Email me at selinarosen@cox.net.

About the Cover Artist

John Kaufmann has over twenty years of experience in the commercial field where he enjoys creating art for the education and advertising markets. He is an avid reader and loves creating Astronomical, Sci/Fi, and Fantasy art for art shows and publishing. John's work appears on numerous fiction book covers and has received top honors at art shows and conventions in the US and Canada.

NOTE FROM THE EDITOR: John's Yard Dog Press covers include *Leopard's Daughter* (by Lee Killough), *Gods and Other Children* (by Bill Allen), *The Guardians* (by Lynn Abbey), and this cover. He has also created covers for Dragon Moon Publishing in Canada, including the covers for *Sword Masters* and *Jabone's Sword*, fantasy novels by Selina Rosen.

Yard Dog Press Titles As Of This Print Date

A Bubba in Time Saves None, Edited by Selina Rosen

A Man, A Plan, (yet lacking) A Canal, Panama, Linda Donahue

Adventures of the Irish Ninja, Selina Rosen

The Alamo and Zombies, Jean Stuntz

All the Marbles, Dusty Rainbolt

Almost Human, Gary Moreau

Ancient Enemy, Lee Killouth

The Anthology From Hell: Humorous Tales From WAY Down Under, Edited by Julia S. Mandala

Ard Magister, Laura J. Underwood

Assassins Inc., Phillip Drayer Duncan

Bad City, Selina Rosen & Laura J. Underwood

Bad Lands, Selina Rosen & Laura J. Underwood

Black Rage, Selina Rosen

Blackrose Avenue, Mark Shepherd

The Boat Man, Selina Rosen

Bobby's Troll, John Lance

Bride of Tranquility, Tracy S. Morris

Bruce and Roxanne from Start to Finnish, Rie Sheridan Rose

Bubba Fables, Sue P. Sinor

The Bubba Chronicles, Selina Rosen

Bubbas Of the Apocalypse, Edited by Selina Rosen

The Burden of the Crown, Selina Rosen

Chains of Redemption, Selina Rosen

Checking On Culture, Lee Killough

Chronicles of the Last War, Laura J. Underwood

Dadgum Martians Invade the Lucky Nickel Saloon, Ken Rand

Deja Doo, Edited by Selina Rosen

Dracula's Lawyer, Julia S. Mandala

The Essence of Stone, Beverly A. Hale

Fairy BrewHaHa at the Lucky Nickel Saloon, Ken Rand

The Fantastikon: Tales of Wonder, Robin Wayne Bailey

Fire & Ice, Selina Rosen

Flush Fiction, Volume I: Stories To Be Read In One Sitting, Edited by Selina Rosen

The Four Bubbas of the Apocalypse: Flatulence, Halitosis, Incest, and... Ned, Edited by Selina Rosen

The Four Redheads: Apocalypse Now!, Linda L. Donahue, Rhonda Eudaly, Julia S. Mandala, & Dusty Rainbolt

The Four Redheads of the Apocalypse, Linda L. Donahue, Rhonda Eudaly, Julia S. Mandala, & Dusty Rainbolt

The Garden In Bloom, Jeffrey Turner

The Geometries of Love: Poetry by Robin Wayne Bailey

Tarbox Station, Rhonda Eudaly
Texistani: Indo-Pak Food From A Texas Kitchen, Beverly A. Hale
That's All Folks, J. F. Gonzalez
Through Wyoming Eyes, Ken Rand
Turn Left to Tomorrow, Robin Wayne Bailey
Wandering Lark, Laura J. Underwood
Wings of Morning, Katharine Eliska Kimbriel
Zombies In Oz and Other Undead Musings, Robin Wayne Bailey

Double Dog (A YDP Imprint):

#1:
Of Stars & Shadows, Mark W. Tiedemann
This Instance Of Me, Jeffrey Turner

#2:
Gods and Other Children, Bill D. Allen
Tranquility, Tracy Morris

#3:
Home Is the Hunter, James K. Burk
Farstep Station, Lazette Gifford

#4:
Sabre Dance, Melanie Fletcher
The Lunari Mask, Laura J. Underwood

#5:
House of Doors, Julia Mandala
Jaguar Moon, Linda A. Donahue

Just Cause (A YDP Imprint):

Death Under the Crescent Moon
Dusty Rainbolt

The Ghost Writer
Selina Rosen

It's Not Rocket Science: Spirituality for the Working-Class Soul
Selina Rosen

Not My Life
Selina Rosen

The Pit
Selina Rosen

Plots and Protagonists: A Reference Guide for Writers
Mel. White

Vanishing Fame
Selina Rosen

Non-YDP titles we distribute:

Chains of Freedom
Chains of Destruction
Jabone's Sword
Queen of Denial
Recycled
Strange Robby
Sword Masters
Selina Rosen

Three Ways to Order:

1. Write us a letter telling us what you want, then send it along with your check or money order (made payable to Yard Dog Press) to: Yard Dog Press, 710 W. Redbud Lane, Alma, AR 72921-7247

2. Use selinarosen@cox.net or lynnstran@cox.net to contact us and place your order. Then send your check or money order to the address above. *This has the advantage of allowing you to check on the availability of short-stock items such as T-shirts and back-issues of Yard Dog Comics.*

3. Contact us as in #1 or #2 above and pay with a credit card or by debit from your checking account. Either give us the credit card information in your letter/Email/phone call, or go to our website and use our shopping carts. If you send us your information, please include your name as it appears on the card, your credit card number, the expiration date, and the 3 or 4-digit security code after your signature on the back (CVV). Please remember that we will include media rate (minimum $3.00) S/H for mailing in the lower 48 states.

Watch our website at
www.yarddogpress.com
for news of upcoming projects
and new titles!!

A Note to Our Readers

We at Yard Dog Press understand that many people buy used books because they simply can't afford new ones. That said, and understanding that not everyone is made of money, we'd like you to know something that you may not have realized. Writers only make money on new books that sell. At the big houses a writer's entire future can hinge on the number of books they sell. While this isn't the case at Yard Dog Press, the honest truth is that when you sell or trade your book or let many people read it, the writer and the publishing house aren't making any money.

As much as we'd all like to believe that we can exist on love and sweet potato pie, the truth is we all need money to buy the things essential to our daily lives. Writers and publishers are no different.

We realize that these "freebies" and cheap books often turn people on to new writers and books that they wouldn't otherwise read. However we hope that you will reconsider selling your copy, and that if you trade it or let your friends borrow it, you also pass on the information that if they really like the author's work they should consider buying one of their books at full price sometime so that the writer can afford to continue to write work that entertains you.

We appreciate all our readers and *depend* upon their support.

Thanks,
The Editorial Staff
Yard Dog Press

PS – Please note that "used" books without covers have, in most cases, been stolen. Neither the author nor the publisher has made any money on these books because they were supposed to be pulped for lack of sales.

Please do not purchase books without covers.

64312362R00192

Made in the USA
Lexington, KY
04 June 2017